A WIND IN THE NIGHT

By Barb and J. C. Hendee

The Noble Dead Saga—Series One

Dhampir

Thief of Lives

Sister of the Dead

Traitor to the Blood

Rebel Fay

Child of a Dead God

The Noble Dead Saga—Series Two

In Shade and Shadow

Through Stone and Sea

Of Truth and Beasts

The Noble Dead Saga—Series Three

Between Their Worlds

The Dog in the Dark

A Wind in the Night

Also by Barb Hendee

The Vampire Memories Series

Blood Memories

Hunting Memories

Memories of Envy

In Memories We Fear

Ghost of Memories

The Mist-Torn Witches Series

The Mist-Torn Witches

A WIND IN THE NIGHT

A Novel of the Noble Dead

Barb & J. C. Hendee

A ROC BOOK

ROC
Published by the Penguin Group
Penguin Group (USA) LLC, 375 Hudson Street,
New York, New York 10014

USA | Canada | UK | Ireland | Australia | New Zealand | India | South Africa | China
penguin.com
A Penguin Random House Company

First published by Roc, an imprint of New American Library,
a division of Penguin Group (USA) LLC

First Printing, January 2014

LIBRARY OF CONGRESS CATALOGING-IN-PUBLICATION DATA:

Hendee, Barb.
A wind in the night: a novel of the noble dead/Barb and J. C. Hendee.
pages cm
ISBN 978-0-451-46567-2 (hardback)
I. Hendee, J. C. II. Title.
PS3608.E525W56 2014
813'.6—dc23 2013021838

Printed in the United States of America
1 3 5 7 9 10 8 6 4 2

Set in Adobe Garamond

PUBLISHER'S NOTE
This is a work of fiction. Names, characters, places, and incidents either are the product of the authors' imaginations or are used fictitiously, and any resemblance to actual persons, living or dead, business establishments, events, or locales is entirely coincidental.

A WIND
IN THE NIGHT

PROLOGUE

Wynn Hygeorht was hiding out in the library of the Guild of Sagecraft in Calm Seatt. The night she'd endured so far had been grueling.

Only a few days before, she had found herself thrown into the midst of a group of nine—two dogs and seven people, counting herself—that had included her companions of old Magiere, Leesil, and Chap. They'd worked in a common cause to begin locating the last two "orbs," ancient devices they believed to have once been wielded by the Ancient Enemy in waging war on the world. Undead minions of that enemy were now surfacing to seek the orbs themselves.

The orbs could not fall into the wrong hands.

With little choice, the nine of them had split up. And tonight . . . the majority had left Calm Seatt to sail off for the Isle of Wrêdelyd, where they might catch a ship heading south to the Suman Empire. And there they would search for the hiding place of the orb of Air. Wynn had chosen to remain behind in order to search the guild's vast archives for any clue to the location of the last and fifth orb, the one for the element of Spirit.

She kept telling herself the same truth over and over. . . . *I made the choice to remain behind.*

Upon returning to the guild grounds tonight, she had needed a few moments of solitude with only Shade, her dog, for company, so she'd headed for the library in the castle's main keep. She herself might soon be forced to embark upon a journey of her own, so she tried to research possible overland routes to the south, and Shade sat quietly nearby with little to do. But it wasn't long before Wynn was forced to face the obvious.

Her thoughts were meandering too much in other directions as she stared blankly at the pile of scattered maps. She could not maintain her focus.

"Oh, dead deities!" she whispered. "This isn't going to work tonight. Come on, Shade."

They left the library through its north doorway and passed the opposing archways into the kitchens and the common hall. In the latter, the great hearth at the rear still burned with low flames though the hall was empty. Even that inviting sight didn't appeal to Wynn with so many things on her mind, most of which she didn't want to face. As if guessing, or not giving Wynn a choice, Shade trotted ahead along the passage. Wynn followed the dog around the far corner as they headed down the corridor along the keep's front to its main doors.

Shade arrived first and sat waiting until Wynn caught up and pushed the left door open. The dog slipped out, but when Wynn did so, she found Shade halted just outside. Shade's tall ears were up and rigid, and Wynn stopped instantly as she followed the dog's stare.

The courtyard wasn't empty.

Two tall figures stood a good distance apart as they glared at each other. The closer of the pair, with his back to Wynn, was Chane Andraso, a companion who had chosen to remain in Calm Seatt with her . . . regardless that the others had wanted him gone and far from her company.

Chane was an undead—a vampire, specifically—and of a more-than-questionable background, though to Wynn he had proven himself capable of change. Over time she had accepted both his friendship and his protection in her search for the orbs.

She couldn't see his face, only his jaggedly cut red-brown hair, which reached just past the collar of his shirt and cloak. And then his hand closed tightly on the hilt of the longer of his two swords. Chane's attention was fully fixed on the other tall occupant in the courtyard.

In the shadows of the gatehouse tunnel's inner opening stood a cloaked and hooded figure with a strangely curved bow slung over one shoulder and a quiver of black-feathered arrows protruding above the other. Next to that quiver, the end of a long and narrow canvas-wrapped bundle stuck up as well, and it was strapped to his back with twine.

Wynn would have known him anywhere, though her mind went numb at the sight of him.

Osha brushed back his hood. The flames of the gatehouse's great iron braziers made his white-blond hair shimmer with fiery orange. Large and slightly slanted amber eyes in his long, dark-toned face returned the same intense glare that Chane fixed upon him.

What was Osha doing here?

Osha, Brot'an, and Leanâlhâm had been the final three members of the strange group that had been thrown together in this search for the orbs. All three were an'Cróan, meaning "[Those] of the Blood"—elves from the eastern continent. All three were supposed to have sailed tonight with Magiere, Leesil, and Chap.

And yet . . . here was Osha in a standoff with Chane.

Osha suddenly sloped his left shoulder. His bow slid off and dropped, and he snatched its wrapped handle without even looking and raised it slightly as he eyed Chane. He didn't reach for an arrow, not until . . .

Chane drew his longer sword of mottled dwarven steel.

Osha's free hand instantly reached over his shoulder for his quiver.

Wynn inhaled sharply as her mind woke up.

"No!" she cried.

Both men froze in surprise, as neither seemed to have spotted her in the entrance's shadows. Wynn rushed out past Shade.

Osha could easily put an arrow in Chane's chest or throat, perhaps both, but that might not even slow Chane down. And although Chane was a skilled swordsman, it would be difficult even for him to land a blow on Osha, but if he did . . .

Wynn grabbed the wrist of Chane's sword arm and tried to pull him back. "No!" she repeated, though her gaze remained on Osha. At the sight of her clutching Chane's arm, Osha's long, somewhat horselike face twisted with an emotion she couldn't quite read.

"What are you doing here?" she called, and her fear came out with anger in her voice.

Osha's eyes narrowed as they shifted to Chane, though two fingers of his raised hand still touched the black feathers of an arrow. When those large amber eyes turned back on Wynn, his hand lowered a little, though he still held his bow at the ready. His brow smoothed, and his eyes widened in wonder . . . or relief, as if he'd found something dear that he'd lost.

Wynn swallowed hard. This was a mess she didn't need. Chane's feelings for her were . . . complicated. Her past with Osha was . . . more complicated.

She glanced up, and Chane now looked down at her hand gripping his sword wrist, but he didn't try to pull away. His handsome face was always deathly pale, and since he'd risen from death, there was little brown that remained in his eyes.

Those eyes now had no color at all. They were like glittering crystals, especially when he—or Wynn—was threatened.

"No," she repeated quietly.

Chane's jaw muscles bulged in a clench, though with his mouth shut tightly, she couldn't be certain of any change in his teeth. Suddenly it occurred to her that Osha might have a reason for not having joined the others on the ship. Her anxiety over a possible clash between the two men gave way to more fear.

"Where's Magiere?" she called, looking to Osha. "What's wrong? What happened?"

That lost, relieved look vanished from Osha's face. He finally lowered his empty hand, and the bow as well, as he stepped toward her. Beneath Wynn's grip, the tendons in Chane's wrist tightened even before Osha stopped a few paces off.

"All is well, I believe," he answered in the an'Cróan's older dialect of Elvish. "Magiere and the others reached their ship and are gone."

Wynn shook her head. When she spoke, she kept to Belaskian for Chane's sake.

"Then why aren't you with them?"

"I stayed to help in your task," he answered ardently, and then he, too, switched to Belaskian. He didn't look at Chane as he added, "I not leave. I stay . . . with you."

Wynn took one quick upward glance. Chane's upper lip curled back, and his irises still had no color.

Osha's declaration sank in. Magiere and the others had sailed away, and Osha was stuck here by his own choice. She couldn't send him away, even if she wished to, and she couldn't abandon him—not him—in a world he knew too little about. And worse . . .

Some part of Wynn began to ache at the sight of Osha, as if she had stumbled upon something unwillingly lost nearly two years ago.

CHAPTER ONE

More than a half moon later and many leagues south from Calm Seatt, two days out from the port of Soráno, Magiere stood on the deck of the *Cloud Queen* and stared out over the ocean as wind pulled at her dark hair. Behind her, she heard a too-familiar squabble begin again.

"Paolo!" a female voice squeaked. "Look at what you're doing. You're wasting half that fish."

"If you can do better," someone answered, "I'll take Alberto and go play rings . . . and you can gut these all by yourself!"

Magiere shook her head and turned from the rail. A trio of young people sat on the edge of the large central cargo hatch, where they were attempting to clean and slice up a pile of fish for the ship's cook. What had the cook been thinking in giving that task to these three?

Nearest to Magiere was a small boy named Alberto, and sitting beside him was a boy of about thirteen called Paolo. Both were now part of the ship's crew. But the final member of the trio was the female scolder, who wasn't part of the crew.

Wayfarer, once called Leanâlhâm, was only a passenger, like Magiere.

Even dressed in her faded maroon pullover and threadbare pants, Wayfarer was a beautiful girl, about sixteen years old. Beautiful even for her own kind, though perhaps more so to some humans' eyes . . . especially the boys'.

Wayfarer's eyes had the unearthly largeness and slight slant of her mother's people, the an'Cróan, but where the an'Cróans' larger irises were amber, hers were the color of the dark, damp leaves and needles of the forest. Likewise, her hair was nearly brown rather than the white blond of elves. The reason for both oddities was that she was a quarter human.

Magiere's eyes lingered with the usual mix of affection and worry on the girl, for in all that had happened before now on this voyage, Wayfarer was now her charge and Leesil's.

The girl looked up to find Magiere watching her.

"Magiere," Wayfarer implored, "would you come show Paolo what to do? Since he will not listen to me . . . and is ruining perfectly good fish."

In a way, such a firm request, tainted with a little ire, was a miracle unto itself. Not long ago, it had been a challenge to get the girl to speak at all. However, Magiere did not particularly relish the thought of jumping in the middle of this argument.

"I've got it," a familiar voice called from the stern.

A slender figure jogged out of the aftcastle door to below, and a different affection flooded Magiere. Even after their years together, she still sometimes just stopped to take in the sight of Leesil.

With oblong ears less peaked than a full-blooded elf's, he shared other traits with his mother's—and Wayfarer's—people of the eastern continent. Beneath a ratty green scarf wrapped around his head, strands of silky white-blond hair hung around his narrow, tan face. Beardless like full-blooded male elves, he was average height for a human, though short by an'Cróan standards, unlike Magiere, who was nearly as tall as he was. Even on the ship, he wore his old scarred-up hauberk with its iron rings.

While Magiere wore a hand-and-a-half, long-bladed falchion sheathed on her hip, and a white metal battle dagger at her back in a sheath, a pair of strange-looking winged punching blades hung in their odd sheaths from Leesil's belt, strapped down against his thighs.

In the spring breeze, Magiere's shirt clung to her beneath her studded leather hauberk. Pushing back her black hair, she knew its bloodred tint probably showed under the bright sun. Everyone here was now accustomed to that, just as she had grown used to her overly pale skin sometimes stinging under the bright sun's glare.

Leesil's amber-irised eyes, so subtly slanted, looked down at the trio. "What is . . . problem?"

His grasp of Numanese, the more common language of this continent, was still questionable, but it was the only language Paolo and Alberto spoke.

"She says he's ruining that fish," Alberto answered in his small voice, jutting his short chin at Wayfarer.

"Am not!" Paolo added.

Magiere agreed with Wayfarer: there wasn't much left of the fish that Paulo held.

Leesil knelt between the boys and eyed Paolo. "Give me knife. I show . . . take out bones."

With a sigh, Paolo surrendered his knife, and the argument ended.

Magiere raised her eyes and spotted the final two members of her group coming out of the aftcastle door. The one in the lead was nearly a head taller than anyone on board.

Coarse white-blond hair with streaks of gray among the strands marked him as old for an an'Cróan. He was deeply tan, with lines crinkling the corners of his mouth and his large amber-irised eyes, which at times never appeared to blink as he watched everything. But the feature that stood out most was the four pale scars—as if from claws—that ran at an angle down his forehead and through one high and slanted feathery eyebrow to skip over his right eye and reach his cheekbone.

Neither Magiere nor Leesil could pronounce his full an'Cróan name, so they'd shortened it to simply Brot'an.

Among the Anmaglâhk, that caste of assassins who viewed themselves as guardians of the an'Cróan, he was one of a few remaining "shadow-grippers," the masters of the caste's skills and ways. But Brot'an no longer wore his caste's garb of forest gray hooded cloak, vestment, pants, and felt boots. Instead he wore simple breeches and a weatherworn jerkin—more scavenged human garb, like Wayfarer's. Unlike the girl, who was merely trying to blend in among human cultures, the old assassin had an additional reason for his change of attire.

Brot'an was at war with his own caste, but to Magiere he was still an anmaglâhk. If she forgot that for even an instant, there were always those scars on his face to remind her.

"Another disagreement?" he asked, frowning slightly as he observed Leesil and the young ones.

"A squabble," she answered.

"My people's children do not . . . 'squabble.' " His eyes narrowed a little, as if Paolo and Alberto were a bad influence on Wayfarer.

"She'll miss them when we have to leave," Magiere countered.

"Perhaps."

A deep growl pulled Magiere's attention. Behind the tall shadow-gripper stood a large silver-gray wolf, almost bluish in the bright day.

Chap was taller than any wolf, for he wasn't one. His body was that of a majay-hì, but he was different from even them and his mate, Lily, as was his daughter, Shade, though in a different way. He *was* a Fay spirit born years ago by his own choice into a majay-hì pup—a new Fay-born in the body of a Fay-descended being. And his daughter, Shade, shared half of that strangely mixed heritage.

Chap was also Magiere and Leesil's guardian and guide—and an overbearing know-it-all. He also hated Brot'an, and he had a long list of reasons for this, which resulted in his penchant for watching the old assassin nearly all the time.

The dog rounded the old assassin and came closer to Magiere.

—Paolo is . . . good . . . for Wayfarer— . . . —He . . . lets her . . . be a girl—

Those words rose in Magiere's mind as Chap called them up in pieces from various memories he had seen in her over time. This was his new method of "speaking" to her, Leesil, or Wayfarer, though he never did so with Brot'an, as far as Magiere knew. Chap found he could never get inside the old assassin's thoughts.

"I know," she answered. "But once we reach Soráno, we'll have to find a new ship."

Brot'an was accustomed to her speaking aloud to Chap and to hearing only her half of the conversation. He looked ahead, out over the waves, and added in Belaskian, "How long to Soráno?"

"About two days. That's what one of the sailors told me."

"Is there no way to change Captain Bassett's mind? We were fortunate to have found this ship traveling all the way to il'Dha'ab Najuum. It may be difficult to find another in a smaller port."

Magiere agreed with the latter part, and it worried her, but she shook her head. "Bassett won't change his mind."

Brot'an had to know this, so asking was pointless and not at all like him. Magiere had learned well that Brot'an rarely did anything without a purpose.

They all had to reach il'Dha'ab Najuum, the westernmost kingdom of the Suman Empire, as quickly as they could. That was the first place where they might begin trying to locate the orb of Air. Magiere, along with Leesil and Chap, had already secured two of the five orbs—Water and Fire—while Wynn had secured a third, that of Earth. Chap had hidden the first two, and no one else knew where. Wynn had sent the orb of Earth to a place of safety in the dwarven underworld.

Only Air and Spirit remained to be found, but it wasn't even that simple.

Most Aged Father, the insane leader of Brot'an's forsaken caste, had learned of the existence of the orb of Water. The decrepit patriarch had sent a team of anmaglâhk after Magiere to take the orb or learn its location. Back in the small port town of Drist, the team had caught up and murdered half the crew of the *Cloud Queen*. Even after the ship and remaining crew had been freed, the captain "requested" that Magiere and her companions disembark at the next port.

She couldn't blame him. Death seemed to follow her, Leesil, and Chap wherever they went. However, at that thought, she eyed Brot'an again. Then

Leesil rose from his crouch and came striding over, leaving the young trio hard at work.

Magiere half smiled at her husband. "Crisis averted?"

He shrugged. "I don't know how much of that fish will be usable. The cook must have been drinking again last night. Can't see how else he would let those three clean and fillet the catch for him."

She looked into his amber eyes and knew what he was thinking. For the first time, Wayfarer was gaining some sense of comfort . . . of belonging. In two days' time, at the most, they would rip her away from people—humans—she'd come to know without fear, and she would again be forced among unknown humans.

"It'll be all right," Leesil said quietly.

Magiere doubted that, though their mission would continue just the same. They had to keep any orbs from falling into the wrong hands. She watched Leesil for a moment, as he was ever her anchor, and then she glanced over at Wayfarer.

Poor girl . . . only two more days.

As evening fell, Wynn Hygeorht knew it was time to leave the solitude of her little room at the Calm Seatt branch of the Guild of Sagecraft. She had an errand she could no longer put off.

Glancing down, she grimaced slightly at the sight of the still-unfamiliar robe of midnight blue that she now wore in place of her gray one. Her wispy, light brown hair hung loose, but she decided not to bother braiding it back.

"Come, Shade," she said, and opened the door to step out.

A long-legged, charcoal-colored dog resembling an oversized wolf hopped off her narrow bed and padded out after her, and in the passage's dim light, Shade's fur turned pure black. It only made her glittering, crystalline blue eyes stand out even more as she twitched her long, pointed ears. Wynn reached down to stroke her companion's large head.

The past half-moon had felt very, very long.

Though the guild had been Wynn's home all of her life, events of recent days—and nights—had left her feeling trapped here as she struggled to find buried answers when too often she wasn't even sure of the questions.

Leaving the old castle's barracks, now a dormitory housing apprentice and journeyor sages, she trudged across the cobbled central courtyard with Shade as they headed for the large building on the northwest side. This entire four-towered castle had once housed the royals of the nation of Malourné, but many, many years ago it had become the residence for the founding branch of the Guild of Sagecraft.

Wynn stopped in the middle of the courtyard as she tried to find any reason to put off the errand a little longer.

"Do you need to . . . do your evening business?" she asked, looking down at Shade. "Should we take a little side trip into the trees in the inner bailey?"

Shade understood, for she was no ordinary dog—or wolf. She was one of the majay-hì. Her kind was descended from wolves of ancient times inhabited by the Fay during the war at the end of the world's Forgotten History. The descendants of those first Fay-born became the guardians of the an'Cróan elves, barring all but their people from the vast Elven Territories on the eastern continent.

Due to a plan hatched by Chap, Shade's father, she had traveled across the sea to the central continent to protect Wynn. She rarely left Wynn's side . . . willingly.

Shade huffed twice for *no* in answering.

Wynn sighed heavily. "All right, then."

Her steps were much slower and shorter as they moved on, and all of the problems Wynn had been avoiding too long came boiling up in her head.

Just over a half-moon ago, several of her closest companions had sailed south in search of the orb of Air. Wynn had opted to remain behind in order to search the guild's vast archives for any clue to the location of the last and fifth orb, the one for the element of Spirit.

So here she was, by her own choice, and so far making pathetically little progress.

To complicate matters, her superiors, with one exception, were bitterly opposed to her taking any action at all. Only Premin Hawes, the head of Metaology, had offered willing assistance. As a result Wynn had been forced to leave the order of Cathology, whose members wore gray robes, and put on a robe of midnight blue in pretending to have joined the order of Metaology.

It was all wearying, and, worse, she hadn't remained behind entirely alone.

Two members of the original group, aside from Shade, had remained as well. One she'd planned for and one she hadn't, and both were now guests of the guild.

Wynn shuffled another step and then another across the courtyard until she stood before the side door of the large northwest storage building, which housed laboratory chambers below it and guests' quarters upstairs.

Shade huffed and let out a grumbling whine.

"All right, I'm going!" Wynn whispered sharply. "Stop pestering me."

With no more reason to delay, she opened the door and, letting Shade slip past her, stepped inside. As they reached the passage's far end and the switchback stairs up to the guest quarters, Wynn slowed to a stop on the midpoint landing in the turn up the next short flight of steps.

She could not stop thinking of the two men—housed in separate quarters above—who had both been waiting to hear from her for the past several nights. She wasn't sure she felt up to talking to either of them, not when she was so aware of the hostility that always crackled between them. Wynn found she couldn't take another step, and, unbidden, her thoughts stretched back to the overwhelming night when Osha had appeared in the courtyard—and Chane had tried to stop him from entering.

After that tense, tangled moment, too many things had happened that were all a fuzzy blur in her head. She'd managed to arrange a room for Osha, which had not been too difficult. The sages of her branch had strong connections to the elves of this continent, the Lhoin'na, for there was another guild branch among them. Some of Wynn's peers, having never met any an'Cróan from the far eastern continent, found Osha an alluring curiosity.

Chane made no secret of his feelings: Osha's presence had not been part of the plan and was not desirable. The following days and nights hadn't been easy.

Neither Chane nor Osha had much to occupy him, and both had too much time to dwell on the other's close, unwanted presence. It hadn't helped that both had to be lodged in the same building, on the same floor, almost right across the passage from each other.

Wynn was desperate to discover the slightest hint to the location of the orb of Spirit. In part, throwing herself fully into that task, spending days in research or working with Premin Hawes to decipher very few clues, was an excuse to avoid facing either Chane or Osha.

Something pushed the back of Wynn's leg, and she spun to look down at Shade.

"Don't start again!" she whispered. "This is hard enough without you butting in."

So far she had learned nothing for all her efforts. At first, every dusk she'd quickly checked on both Chane and Osha to give them some report of what she'd been doing. Mostly that was to make them think she was too busy for anything more. Those visits had become less frequent, for she had nothing to tell them . . . and the less she had to tell them, the more they might start raising other, more personal matters.

This could not go on.

With a labored sigh, Wynn took the last steps to the upper passage lined with narrow doors, three on each side. She looked to the first on the right and then to the second on the left a little farther down. When Shade whined, Wynn looked down, but the dog wasn't beside her. She found that Shade was still standing on the stairs behind her.

Shade glanced left and right, likely at those same doors, and then looked up at Wynn.

—Maybe . . . not . . . talk . . . Chane . . . Osha . . . tonight—

In addition to other unique abilities, Shade could call up words out of Wynn's memories to communicate with only her. Wynn nearly choked in frustration, for only a moment ago the dog had been pushing her onward.

"Will you make up your mind?" she whispered. "It is hard enough for me to do so."

—Wynn come . . . have dinner . . . instead—

Reaching down, Wynn stroked Shade's head. "Not yet," she answered, but she stood there at a loss about whom to see first. At the rattle of a door's lever, she turned her head.

The first door—Chane's door—pulled sharply inward, banging against the chamber's inner wall, but it wasn't Chane who stepped out.

A girl in tan robes, a mere initiate, stormed out with a loud, exasperated exhale and an overloaded pile of books in her arms.

She was only about twelve years old, and her little nose and ivory cheeks were smattered with faint freckles. Two equal braids held back her dark blond hair and framed a too-haggard, grumpy pout for such a young one. She wrestled with keeping the books balanced while pulling the door closed with a petulant slam.

"Kyne?" Wynn said. "What are you doing so late in Ch . . . Master Andraso's quarters?"

Kyne peered over her stack of books. Brief surprise at the sight of Wynn quickly returned to her irritable pout at the mention of Chane. But all of that irritation suddenly vanished again in a wide-eyed smile.

"Shade!" the girl cried out gleefully.

Wynn heard what sounded like a groan from the dog.

Kyne looked up at Wynn, and her little frown returned. "I'm supposed to be teaching him . . . or at least that's what he asked."

Wynn's mouth tightened. "Yes, I am aware of that."

Some time ago Chane had asked Kyne of all people for help in learning to read the Begaine Syllabary, the complex symbols used by sages for recording anything in any language. At first Wynn had been stunned by this, though she knew Chane had a growing interest in all things related to guild methods. Full command of the syllabary was first on his list, and Kyne had learned it more swiftly than any initiate Wynn had ever encountered. Obviously Chane had deduced something similar.

Wynn had helped in the arrangements, as initiates weren't allowed to do such things, especially for an outsider. Plus the girl had the time to tutor him, since often her own lessons seemed too simple for her. The guild had some public schools, though those weren't for adults and had nothing to do with the workings of the guild. And Wynn had also been able to offer a special enticement that had quickly gained Kyne's agreement.

Wynn cringed slightly, not daring to glance back at Shade.

This wasn't the appointed time for Chane's lessons. Kyne had agreed to rise well before dawn and teach "Master Andraso" before her own day began.

"He wanted extra time," Kyne grumbled, rolling her bright brown eyes. "He says we are going too slow, but all the questions . . . and questions! He should be quiet, listen, and practice like I tell him. Begaine is not so hard. . . . I can read it!"

"I see," Wynn said, but she wondered why Chane was in such a hurry.

Kyne's expression suddenly changed again as she scurried right past Wynn—right at Shade—with that wide smile breaking free once more.

"Could I take her outside now?" she called, and leaned so close that Shade began shifting away. "Does she need to . . . do her business?"

This was the enticement Wynn had used to get Kyne to help Chane.

It had seemed the safest way at the time, rather than involving an actual apprentice, let alone a full sage, in one of the orders. From almost the first time the girl had seen a real majay-hì, right here on the guild grounds, she had been utterly smitten with Shade.

Shade had been somewhat unwilling to participate at first. Kyne would bring her water in the large common hall or take her outside to . . . do her business. Eventually Shade had relented—to a point.

If nothing else, Kyne was the only other person Shade tolerated for long at close proximity or as something that took her from Wynn's side. The dog didn't like interacting with anyone but Wynn—or Chane as necessary. And as much as Kyne knew that majay-hì were far more intelligent than mere animals, she was only a girl a bit too caught up with glee in tending a supposedly magical "pet."

Kyne was barely as tall as the peaks of the dog's high ears.

"Do you need to out go now?" Kyne asked Shade this time.

Shade let out a rumble that almost worried Wynn, and then the majay-hì spun to lope off down the stairs. Kyne rushed to follow, pausing once on the landing.

"Wait for me!" she called after Shade, and quickly looked up at Wynn. "And tell *him* not to ask so many questions. He needs to *listen*!" The girl rushed around the corner out of sight. "Shade! Please!"

Wynn groaned in knowing she'd probably hear about this later from Shade. Then she found herself alone, staring at Chane's door. Any amusing images of the poor child trying to tutor him vanished. Once again she was back to her original dilemma about whom to go see first.

No doubt Chane had heard everything that had just happened outside his room. That made the choice for Wynn.

Chane Andraso watched the door of his quarters and grew impatient until a knock came. He had heard Kyne complaining in the corridor, and, at the girl's gleeful squeal concerning Shade, he knew there could be only one other person outside.

Striding over, he opened the door, and Wynn stood on the other side . . . but there was no sign of Shade. He glanced down the passage toward the stairs.

"Kyne took her out," Wynn said.

Though Kyne's tutoring him in the syllabary had been Chane's idea, he was still uncertain about the "compensation" Wynn had offered the young sage-to-be. Foremost, Shade was a fully sentient being, useful in her ability to protect Wynn . . . and other things. She was not a child's playtime companion.

And, second, on several occasions he'd gone out into the courtyard and noticed that when Shade was alone with Kyne, the dog lost all semblance of good sense or manners and ran as she pleased and ignored any instructions. The child was forced to run after her, calling out her name.

It was all very . . . undignified.

In addition, he had wanted Shade present tonight to help him press Wynn on several matters. But as he backed up to let Wynn follow him inside, all thoughts but her fled from his mind. He still hadn't become accustomed to the sight of her in that midnight blue robe, but the dark color suited her well. She hadn't bothered braiding her wispy light brown hair tonight, and it hung loose around her pretty olive-toned face to hang past her shoulders. Her eyes were bright and warm and intelligent all at the same time.

She was so short that she could stand under his chin.

Chane had never thought himself capable of anything resembling contentment. The closest he had ever come was in her company, especially when he was alone with her.

"Did you uncover anything today?" he asked, forestalling other concerns.

The near-soundless rasp of his own voice suddenly bothered him more than usual. Some years past, Magiere had severed his head; he had become whole again only through someone else's arcane means. But his voice had never healed and likely never would.

Still silent, Wynn shook her head and glanced around at his sparsely furnished room. He required little besides a bed, a desk, ink, quills, paper, and the books he was studying.

"No," she finally said, "and I spent all day in the archives."

She sounded strained—and uncomfortable—as if she did not want to be here.

Chane clenched his jaw for an instant. "As I told you . . . I think the archives are a waste of your time. You and Hawes should focus on the scroll."

Wynn looked up at him and nearly snapped, "Premin Hawes has other duties. She can't spend all of her time playing nursemaid and tutoring me in using my mantic sight."

"I do not want you using your mantic sight," he shot back.

He quickly regretted that, considering that her mantic sight was required to read the scroll. They both fell silent for a long moment.

"The scroll is still the more likely option," he said quietly.

He knew he was right, just as she did. He also knew there were issues with his perspective on this matter. Several years ago he had by happenstance stumbled upon that scroll containing a hidden and possibly prophetic poem written by one of the first thirteen vampires to walk upon the world. The verses contained metaphoric clues to the locations of the five orbs, or at least as somehow known long, long ago by the author.

And the poem had been written in the fluids of an undead and then covered with dark ink.

Wynn was the only one who could read those obscured verses.

She had once faltered in an unschooled use of a thaumaturgical ritual, and the taint of that failure had left her afflicted with mantic sight—the ability to see traces of the Elements, or at least Spirit, in all things. Once she invoked her sight, she could also see the absence of Spirit, such as in the fluids of a physical undead used for the poem hidden beneath the ink. But the aftermath was dangerous.

Wynn became dizzy and nauseated, sometimes even disoriented, and she could maintain her sight for only a short time without becoming more intensely ill. Worse, even when she wished to end her mantic sight, she could not. Someone like Premin Hawes was required to step in and help her. Strangely enough, Shade as well could sometimes help Wynn with this, but only if Wynn did not push such a session too far or too long.

So far Wynn had managed to recover and translate some useful phases, including one sentence that might bear on their current task.

The Wind was banished to the waters within the sands where we were born.

Premin Hawes reasoned that the "we" was a reference to "the Children," those first thirteen undead—vampires—who had once served the Ancient Enemy itself. It was reasonable to assume that "Wind" corresponded to the orb of Air, for the other elemental metaphors in the poem, five in all, equally hinted at the other orbs. As to "sands," this might refer to the great desert that spanned the continent between the northern Numan and Lhoin'na lands and the Suman Empire to the south. Hawes asserted that the climate there had changed in a thousand years and what was now a desert might have once been water, at least partly.

It was shortly thereafter when Magiere and those with her escaped from

Calm Seatt to head toward il'Dha'ab Najuum. One of their first tasks upon arrival was to contact a ranking sage of the guild's third branch, the Suman branch: Domin Ghassan il'Sänke, a domin of Metaology.

No one knew whether he would help or not, but il'Sänke favored Wynn, and he was quite possibly the only one who could help find the lost resting place of the orb of Air. Wynn, Shade, and Chane had remained behind in the hopes of launching their own search for the orb of Spirit.

And so far Wynn had uncovered nothing new of use.

The only clues she'd ever found had come from the scroll.

"We need something soon," Chane said. "Perhaps you could ask Hawes to . . . let you try the scroll again."

Premin Hawes was cautious about Wynn using her ability too often. In truth, Premin Hawes was not as cautious as was Chane—or Shade—but he was desperate for something—anything.

Wynn took a slow breath. "I'll ask her." Then she turned away. "I should go and . . . check on Osha."

Chane almost grabbed Wynn's arm.

That elf—an'Cróan, onetime assassin, interloper—should have left with Magiere. And yet Wynn insisted on being solicitous, checking on him.

It was intolerable.

"If something had changed for him, you would have heard of it," he began, trying to find anything to dissuade her. "So why bother if *you* have nothing new to tell him . . . or me?"

Chane only half regretted those words, as Wynn halted halfway to the door. When she did not turn to look at him, he no longer regretted them at all. Then he heard her tired sigh.

"He is all alone here," she said, still not looking at him. "He doesn't have anyone here besides . . ."

She did not finish, so he did so for her.

"Besides you?" he nearly hissed. "And that is likely as he wishes it, planned it."

Wynn started to turn. "Chane, we have more important matters to—"

Suddenly, he did not want to hear any more and pushed past her, opening the door to step out. "I will go check on Kyne and Shade. Someone needs to watch over them, so the girl is not run ragged."

"What's that supposed to mean?"

Chane reached the stairs, never answering Wynn, and he did not hear any footfalls coming after him.

Osha—"a Sudden Breeze"—heard words, out in the passage, between Wynn and the little human girl who came before dawn each day to that undead's chamber. He had almost stepped out of his room but then changed his mind, waiting to see whether Wynn came to him or . . .

She went to that monster instead.

How she could, or why she let that little girl do so, was unbelievable. All he could do was wait in silence for her to come to him last. She would, eventually, now that she had finally returned again.

Osha spent much time in this room. His tall body, white-blond hair, long features, and slanted amber eyes brought too many curious stares from the sages here. And then the questions began, as if the sages were prodding and poking him with their words, some of which he did not understand. In another life so recently lost, he had hidden himself away inside the forest gray cowl of an anmaglâhk. Now he dressed like a human traveler, in a human world he did not understand.

Over the past half-moon, he had begun to question his choice to remain here, to protect Wynn in her efforts as she had once protected him . . . from that same creature now lodged in the room across the passage.

Nothing had transpired as he had envisioned at the moment in which he found her again.

Nothing was like it had been once before.

More than two years ago Osha had accompanied Wynn, as well as her companions and his jeóin and teacher, Sgäilsheilleache, into the ever-frozen heights of the Pock Peaks of the eastern continent. He had helped the best that he could in their search for what he now knew as the orb of Water. At the time he had been an anmaglâhk in training, and his mentor, Sgäilsheilleache, had sworn guardianship to Magiere, Leesil, and Wynn.

Osha had stood true to the promise of guardianship . . . perhaps most especially for Wynn.

That had grown into something more, though his own kind might have found this loathsome.

While on a ship near the beginning of that journey, Wynn had asked him about himself, about his dreams, and, in all his life no one else had ever done so. It had been almost startling. Once they returned to land and began the climb into the snow-covered peaks, the journey became grueling and so long that customs soon broke for the sake of survival.

In the freezing nights with nothing but a thin tent for shelter, Wynn had slept on his chest, wrapped inside his cloak, allowing him to keep her warm. He had scavenged food for her and melted down water for them to drink, and, when threatened by enemies, she had run to him, seeking protection beneath his arm.

It meant something to him—more than he could put into words.

She was nothing like the humans that he—his people—hated and feared. Later she had tried to teach him how to dance at Magiere and Leesil's wedding. No one had ever paid him so much notice.

When he had finally been forced to leave, to catch one of his people's ships waiting nearby in hiding, she had walked to the docks of the noisy and smelly city of Bela with him. And even when they had said farewell, and he had reluctantly turned away through the crowd . . .

Wynn had run after him, thrown herself at him, and kissed him.

Even now Osha could still feel the soft press of her small mouth.

Then Wynn was gone, running off along the docks. He had no choice but to leave for the ship that would take him home, along with the journal she had given to him to deliver to Brot'ân'duivé.

Too much had happened since then—too much blood spilled, too much forced upon him . . . too much taken from him.

For one foolish moment more than a half-moon ago, he had been reunited briefly with Wynn. He had thought if he could only remain with her, all his pain would cease and the world might make sense once again.

Nothing had come about as he had envisioned.

Wynn had changed. He had changed. And, worse, he was now forced to accept that dead-pale *thing* waking each night across the passage.

How could Wynn expect this of him?

Osha heard a door open and then voices, though he missed what was said. At the rasping of that thing in the passage, heavy footfalls rushed away down the stairs. Still he waited, knowing that he would hear . . .

A knock sounded on his door.

He hesitated, glancing at an object lying at the foot of his bed. Slender and long, wrapped in canvas and left on the floor, as if to be hidden even as a known burden—it was unwanted. His longbow leaned against the wall by the door, ever ready along with a quiver of black-feathered arrows. He had few other personal possessions.

And the soft knock came again.

Osha stepped quickly this time and opened the door.

Wynn, wearing the strange night-blue robe instead of her proper gray one of the past, stood outside in the passage. Though she looked at him, this lasted only an instant before she dropped her gaze and asked him something in his own tongue.

"Are you going to the common hall for dinner?"

Though she spoke his language surprisingly well, she still had a strange way with some words. She always asked about his eating habits, and it had taken time for him to understand that this was her way to avoid saying anything that meant something . . . to him.

Obviously that thing across the hall had upset her again—as the vampire had a habit of making her life difficult. Why did she tolerate *his* presence?

Osha wanted to speak only of the past—their past together. He wanted to ask her what it had meant to her, what it still might mean. But it was now clear that this was the last thing she wanted.

Instead she wanted to know what had happened to him after she had left him on the docks.

Why had he left the Anmaglâhk?

How had he gotten the burn scars on his wrists?

Why was Brot'ân'duivé at war with his own caste?

What was happening among the an'Cróan?

Why had Osha left his home again and traveled halfway across the world to this continent, and why had Brot'ân'duivé brought Leanâlhâm as well?

And then, worst of all . . .

What was wrapped inside that canvas lying at the end of his bed?

All that she wanted to speak of were the things he no longer wanted to think upon. So they talked about little else but meals.

"Yes, I will go," he answered. "Will you come?"

Sometimes, if she did not have duties with the strange one of cold eyes, Premin Hawes, she would go to the common hall and eat with him. He should cherish even that little . . . He should have.

She did not answer, and, as so often happened, her eyes strayed to the long, wrapped object on the floor. He tried not to tense, hoping she did not ask about it again. He had not even looked upon what was hidden in there since he had landed on the far side of this continent in following Brot'ân'duivé.

Wynn's gaze shifted to his bow and quiver. She smiled slightly.

"You've become a good archer since . . . since before. How did that happen?"

An innocent question, but it was another way to press him to talk about the few years between their journey to the Pock Peaks and now.

"Many things have changed since . . . before," he said, echoing her own slip, her reference to a past that he wished she would acknowledge. "You once tried to teach me to dance," he countered against her evasion. "I still do not know how."

He spotted the slight wince of Wynn's left eye before she turned away.

"I need to see Premin Hawes, as we have more work to do," she said, this time in her own tongue. Her pace quickened, as if she could not bear him to say anything else. "I wanted to see if you'd eaten, so you'd best go down to dinner."

Osha stared down the passage long after Wynn had vanished. Much as he wanted to, he did not follow her.

CHAPTER TWO

Wynn left the guest quarters floor and headed back down to the old storage building's main passage.

After facing Osha, she hoped not to run into Chane again. Shade would be fine a little while longer with Kyne, especially if Chane had caught up to the pair. Wynn continued along the passage, but as she neared the door out into the courtyard, she turned right into a workshop. Then she cut along its near wall to the back corner and then down another staircase.

She stepped out into a narrow stone corridor on the first sublevel below the storage building's main floor; the hallway was lit by two wall-mounted cold lamps with bulging metal bases. Alchemical fluids provided mild heat that charged the lamps' special crystals, which, in place of a burning wick, produced light. She counted three wide iron doors on both sides of the passage, and behind those were the lower laboratories of the guild . . . except for the last one on the right. Wynn headed for that door, which was as tightly shut as the others, and she knocked softly.

"Premin, are you in?"

She barely heard footsteps on the other side, and then the door opened with a tiny squeal from its iron hinges.

Wynn faced a mature, slight woman in a midnight blue robe: Premin Frideswida Hawes, head of the branch's order of Metaology. With the premin's cowl down around her shoulders, her ash gray, short-cropped hair bristled about her head. Any lines of age were faint in her even, small features, down to her narrow mouth and chin—the latter similar to an elf's. Though severe looking, she was not unattractive until one fixed on her piercing and pale hazel eyes that made one think of ice.

Premin Hawes held a folded piece of paper in one hand. Her eyes widened for less than a blink at the sight of Wynn; that was the limit of surprise that anyone ever saw on this premin's face.

"Ah, Wynn . . . I wasn't expecting . . ." Hawes trailed off.

It was Wynn's turn to be surprised, for the premin looked almost distracted. That never happened, as far as Wynn knew, even when Hawes *appeared* to be lost in thought.

"May I speak with you?" Wynn asked hesitantly. She glanced down the short three-step passage beyond the premin that emptied into the left side of a small chamber. Somewhere to the right and out of sight, a dimming cold lamp lit the space.

"Certainly," Hawes said, though she hesitated again, which made Wynn nervous. "Come in."

The premin turned away, and Wynn followed after closing the heavy door.

All she could see from the hallway were shelves pegged in the chamber's left wall. These were filled with books, bound sheaves, and a few narrow upright cylinders of wood, brass, or unglazed ceramic. But as she stepped into the little chamber, she found stout, shallow tables and squat casements stuffed with more texts along the back wall as well. There were also odd little contrivances and unrecognizable devices of metal, crystal and glass, and wood and leather set erratically on the shallow tables and atop the casements.

Pushed up against the room's right wall was an age-darkened desk of abundant small drawers below a top covered in stacks of papers, parchments, and sheaves. And there sat a cold lamp, with its dimming crystal inside its glass cover, on the desk's corner.

Wynn's gaze roamed over the stacks on the desk, as well as a few mortars and small bowls filled with granules and powders of varied colors. An array of articulated brass arms was anchored to the desk's far front corner, each arm bearing a framed magnifying lens. All the arms were mounted so that any one or more of the lenses could twist in or out of alignment with the others. The chamber was clearly a workspace whose contents had piled up over many years. Premin Hawes did not go to her rickety and plain desk chair or simply turn to face Wynn.

Instead she settled slowly in the old armchair, of tattered blue fabric, which barely fit into the little room's right corner beyond the desk. She leaned back, as if lost in a fleeting thought . . . still with that folding paper pinched in two long narrow fingers.

"What can I do for you?" Hawes asked absently.

She didn't even look at Wynn, though she curled her fingers to grip the paper with her thumb as well . . . tightly.

Wynn had hoped to convince the premin to let her use mantic sight, and together they might extract and translate another few lines from the scroll's poem. Chane had already consented to the scroll's being locked away in Hawes's office, so at the moment it was within easy reach.

But Wynn hesitated, for the premin seemed so unlike herself tonight.

"Are you . . . ?" Wynn began. "Is everything all right?"

"Hmmmm?"

Only then did Hawes's cold hazel eyes fully focus, and the elder woman's mouth pursed.

As one of the five members of the branch's premin council, she was the only person in authority here willing to give Wynn any assistance. Of late, by default, the two of them had begun to trust each other—to a point—in searching out the remaining orbs.

With a soft sigh through her narrow nose, Hawes pointed to the desk chair.

Wynn settled there, now a little more alarmed. "What is it?"

"I received a letter from a master sage in Witeny . . . a Jausiff Columsarn."

"Columsarn?" Wynn repeated. "A relative of Nikolas Columsarn?"

Nikolas was an apprentice sage here in Wynn's own order of Cathology, and one of the few she could call a friend.

Hawes nodded once. "His adopted father. Master Columsarn has been the prime counselor for a southern duchy on the coast of Witeny for many years. I once knew him . . . briefly, though he left the guild for private work shortly after achieving master's status in Cathology."

The premin paused so long that Wynn was about to ask for more.

"Nikolas has been called home for a visit," Hawes added. "Master Columsarn sent him a letter, which included a sealed one addressed to me."

Wynn's gaze shifted briefly to the paper clutched in the premin's hand.

"It is for my eyes only," Hawes continued, "but he requested that I send him certain texts to study."

Wynn blinked. She knew Nikolas was adopted and came from Witeny, but she hadn't known his father was the counselor to a duke, let alone that he was a sage. Then again, she'd never asked Nikolas anything about his past and knew only what little he'd mentioned in passing.

"That isn't so strange," Wynn said. "If this Master Columsarn is in such a remote place, likely he has few resources. But why not send such a request to the annex in Chathburh? It is much closer and right in Witeny."

Hawes pursed her mouth again. "The texts are specific in nature and wouldn't be part of an annex's holdings. He has requested that I seal—package—them. Nikolas is not to know what they are . . . only deliver them."

Wynn fell silent. She wanted to ask about the texts in question but feared that if she pushed too hard, Hawes might say nothing about this strange private matter.

Instead she asked, "Why is Nikolas being called home?"

Hawes shook her head slightly once. "I do not know. He sent a young initiate to bring me this." She rolled her hand upward, displaying the folded paper. "I've not spoken to him myself, though I have asked among the initiates and apprentices on duty at the gate. Apparently a package for Nikolas was delivered last night, given to an attendant at the gate, and from what

Master Columsarn tells me here, inside the package was a letter for Nikolas and this sealed letter for me."

"So you don't know anything about what Nikolas's letter contained or why he's being called home?"

Hawes didn't answer, and her cold eyes locked on Wynn. "You are his friend?"

That wasn't an easy question to answer. Given Nikolas's withdrawn nature—earning him the nickname "Nervous Nikolas"—he didn't have any close friends, except two who had died less than a year ago. But he'd shown her kindness and even loyalty on a few occasions when she'd desperately needed both.

"I know him . . . a little," Wynn answered, though she heard the hesitation in her own voice.

And again Hawes was silent for too long a moment.

"Were I to question Nikolas, he might interpret it as an interrogation," the premin continued. "If you told him that you learned he'd been called home and expressed friendly concern, he might be more open."

Wynn straightened up in her chair. Was Hawes asking her to use her friendship with Nikolas to gain information?

"I am concerned," the premin added, "and possibly more than concerned about the nature of the texts requested . . . as you might be."

That hint of implied collusion on Wynn's part, before she'd even agreed, was very unsettling. "Why?"

"Several are related to folklore and elemental mysticism," Hawes answered, "including extracts from findings dating back to just after the Forgotten History . . . by guild estimations."

Wynn, too, found that strange for an old cathologer handling the affairs of a duchy.

"One text requested cannot even be borrowed without permission from the premin of Metaology—likely why he wrote directly to me."

Wynn stared into those gray hazel eyes when the premin asked again, "Will you speak to Nikolas?"

A cold knot formed in the pit of Wynn's stomach.

This was all a distraction from the work she was supposed be doing . . . finding the location of an orb. But she owed the premin quite a bit in that, and this was about Nikolas. There was also the question of how oddly Hawes acted now. It was the closest thing to uncertainty or worry that Wynn had ever glimpsed in the dark-robed premin.

Wynn finally nodded and rose. "I'll go now. By this time, all the initiates and apprentices should be in the common hall for supper."

Still sitting and gripping the letter, Hawes nodded once with a slow blink. "Come report what he tells you as soon as possible."

"Yes . . . yes, of course."

As Wynn left, she never heard the premin move. After she shut the iron door and scurried away, it wasn't until she reached the courtyard that she took a deep breath. The night air was already growing chilly, and so were her thoughts. She was caught by one mention by the premin concerning texts sought by a remote master sage. . . .

. . . including extracts from findings dating back to just after the Forgotten History . . .

What would a private sage working in a far-off duchy want with such?

Perhaps it was nothing, and Nikolas's adopted father was a bored old man, away from the guild, who'd developed eclectic interests. Here and now, though, with all that she was trying to accomplish, it seemed like something more, though she didn't know what.

Her task for the moment was to learn anything she could from Nikolas, and so she started for the main keep doors. But she'd made it only halfway when a young voice echoed into the courtyard.

"Shade! Come back here . . . right now!"

Wynn turned in time to see the sparks of blue eyes in the gatehouse tunnel . . . just before Shade bolted out into the courtyard. The dog ran straight up to her, and then Shade plopped down on her haunches. Kyne came running out of the tunnel; her cowl had fallen back off her head, and her tan robe's skirt was flopping around her little legs.

"That wasn't nice!" Wynn whispered sharply.

Shade curled a jowl and looked away.

The girl must have taken the dog out into the bailey and only now returned. Wynn was appalled at the way Shade was completely ignoring Kyne's shouts. Before Wynn said anything more to the dog or Kyne could even catch up, Chane strode out of the gatehouse tunnel with Kyne's earlier stack of books under one arm.

"Shade!" he rasped so loudly that Kyne flinched where she stood while trying to catch her breath. Wynn frowned as the girl came trotting closer, still panting.

"It's all right, Journeyor Hygeorht," Kyne got out. "Master Andraso took us out to the bailey's southern grove, and Shade just got excited in coming back."

Wynn's frown deepened. Perhaps Chane had been right about the dog running the girl ragged. Wynn would have more to say to Shade on that later.

"You should go have your supper," she told Kyne, and she looked up as Chane approached. "I'll take Shade inside in a moment. And Master Andraso will hold on to your books until you see him in the morning before breakfast. You won't need them before then."

The girl looked longingly at Shade. "I could take her into supper with me. I don't mind."

"No," Wynn said firmly. "You go on."

Clearly disappointed, Kyne headed off toward the keep's main doors.

Chane stopped a few paces off and looked around. "Going to supper . . . alone?"

Wynn clenched her jaw at such an obvious snipe about Osha.

"No," she returned. "I have an errand for Premin Hawes."

Chane raised one eyebrow.

Fearing he'd want to come along, she quickly added, "I'll tell you about it when I'm done."

He glanced away, as if she was shutting him out, but she couldn't take him along even if she'd wanted to. Nikolas would never speak of anything personal in front of someone he didn't know. Yet Wynn had to do something to pacify Chane.

"It shouldn't take long," she said, though it might. "I'll find you later, at your room."

Chane turned away toward the northwest building.

Suppressing a sigh, Wynn glanced down at Shade. "And *you* . . ."

Shade raised her tall ears and looked up with eyes narrowed, an expression Wynn had learned to interpret as, *"Yes . . . what now?"*

Wynn got the feeling this query had nothing to do with Shade's behavior toward Kyne. She groaned and looked away. Was it not enough that she felt caught in some tawdry triangle out of a romance ballad? Did she now have to put up with a four-footed, fur-faced adolescent nagging her to do something about it? And she already knew what Shade expected.

Though the majay-hì and the undead were natural enemies, Shade and Chane had at least worked around that in serving a common cause for Wynn's sake. Wynn would have never expected Shade to side with Chane on anything else, but they both viewed Osha as an unwanted outsider . . . though for differing reasons.

"Come on," Wynn said tiredly and walked off toward the main doors; the braziers above them had recently been replaced with two mounted cold lamps.

Wynn pulled one door, and Shade pushed past before she stepped into the entryway. Inside, a passage led straight ahead to the main library's central entrance, but Shade had already turned left down the wider front corridor. Wynn followed to the main archway on the right, which opened into the common hall. She stood there looking about as Shade snuffled, nose in the air.

Supper was well under way. The large hall was filled with sages of all the orders' colors and even some initiates who lodged on the grounds. Numerous long tables, benches, and stools were haphazardly placed all about, but for the most part meals were an organized affair. Sages—from initiates to masters—took shifts in the kitchens cooking or washing up or serving the meals. The scent of mutton stew was strong tonight.

Shade whined, and a drop of drool fell from her smacking jowls.

—Supper—

Wynn ignored this and looked about for Nikolas, though she didn't spot him at any of the tables. Her gaze came to a chair near the enormous hearth: there he was, though he wasn't eating. He sat staring into the flames.

A young, high-pitched voice rose over the buzz. "Shade! I can get your supper!"

Kyne stood on a bench among a small bunch of gobbling, gossiping initiates, all in tan robes like hers. Wynn heard Shade's low, grumbling growl, and she stumbled slightly when the dog backed up and hit her leg.

"Oh, stop it!" she whispered.

—Wynn . . . Shade . . . sisters . . . pack— . . . —Wynn . . . not . . . my . . . parent—

Wynn looked down, and, on spotting Shade's ears flattening in silence, she called out, "Oh, thank you, Kyne. That would be most helpful."

As Kyne tried to bound over one companion, she nearly stepped in another's plate.

Shade's head whipped up, and her wide crystal-blue eyes locked on Wynn. Before the dog could even wrinkle a jowl, Kyne barreled into her. Wynn stumbled again as the bulk of the two backed farther into her legs.

"Come on, Shade," Kyne nearly shouted, her arms wrapped around the dog's neck. "And afterward, time for a good brushing."

Shade's eyes narrowed, this time to barely glittering slits, up at Wynn.

All Wynn did was mouth, *Mind your manners,* as she lifted her head and broke eye contact.

Shade stalked off, her head low, with a rumble and the girl now gripping the scruff of her neck. But Wynn already had her eyes on Nikolas again. When she headed across the hall and was only halfway to the hearth, Nikolas looked up and saw her. His eyes followed her the rest of the way as if she were some startling sight that had shaken him from a deep thought.

He wore the gray robes of a cathologer, just as she had until recently. She guessed him to be about nineteen years of age. When standing, he was of medium height with a slender build, but his shoulders often slumped, causing him to look shorter. His straight brown hair always seemed to be half hiding his face. Worse, his hair was no longer fully brown.

The previous year, Nikolas had survived an attack by a wraith named Sau'ilahk and, as a result, his locks were shot with white streaks.

Wynn wondered what in his past had rooted his perpetual state of anxiety. Picking up a stool at the last table she passed, she tried to smile at him.

"May I sit?"

He nodded but still appeared surprised. They had shown each other kindness or assistance in the past, but she had rarely sought him out—and certainly never to socialize. His gaze dropped briefly to her new midnight blue robe, but, like Hawes, he appeared distracted.

Wynn decided to go straight to the point. "Premin Hawes told me you've been called home."

Nikolas winced and looked away toward the fire. She simply waited rather than startle him again, and, when he looked back, barely turning his head enough to do so, his eyes struck her as bleak and pained. If he wanted to talk, he might do so with her, as he didn't have anyone else anymore.

"My father is ill," Nikolas said quietly.

"Nothing serious, I hope."

"No . . . I don't know. He's getting old . . . and he needs my help."

Nikolas's voice was so low that Wynn had to lean in to hear him.

"I don't want to go," he continued, looking away again. "Father says things at home are not good. The young duke was my friend in our childhood, and . . . and I owe him . . . much."

There was something more missing in this last statement.

"Father says the duke is behaving strangely, that he is not well, either, and I must come and stay for a while."

Confused, Wynn wasn't certain what to ask next. She shouldn't mention anything Premin Hawes had said about the second letter's contents; perhaps she shouldn't mention the second letter at all. Nikolas's aging father said he was not well, yet he had asked for strange texts, at least one of which only Hawes could provide. He had asked his son to come home, but the request wasn't just about an ailment of his own.

There were too many hinted, incomplete pieces, but more in Nikolas's own words struck Wynn as odd.

"You don't wish to go?" she asked. "Even for just the visit?"

"No," he answered, his voice as hollow as his eyes. "When I came here, it was to stay. Father got me accepted, though I was a bit old for a start. And he promised that I could stay forever, if I wished. Now he's broken his word by calling me home . . . but I can't refuse."

For as little as Wynn understood, she had many more questions, including why Nikolas apparently never wanted to go home again. She was also afraid he might close off even more if she pressed the wrong way in ignorance.

"When will you leave?"

Nikolas shook his head at first, as if he didn't know. "Not for several days at least. I need Domin High-Tower's formal permission to take leave of the guild, and he will first have to make High Premin Sykion aware—though that is a formality. Then there's funding and transportation and . . ."

He trailed off with a shaky sigh. It was obvious to Wynn that the journey's logistics weren't his true worry.

"I don't want to go," he whispered. "I . . . just can't."

Wynn didn't know what to say except, "I'm so sorry." She knew he wouldn't tell her what it was about his home that made him so agitated. He couldn't have had a happy childhood if he dreaded a return this much.

"I need to think," Nikolas said, still staring into the flames. "Would you mind?"

"Of course not." She stood up. "Come find me anytime. You've been a friend to me when others wouldn't, and I am *your* friend."

Those words made his expression twist briefly, but Wynn couldn't place any emotion she saw there.

"I know," he whispered.

That ended that, and Wynn headed back for the archway. "Shade," she called out. "Come."

Startling a couple of initiates, the dog wormed out from between the tables in a hurry. Kyne rose instantly up on her bench with wide, blinking eyes of sudden shock.

Wynn was in no mood to lecture Shade again about her behavior or to try to make an excuse to the girl. There were too many questions fighting for the forefront of her thoughts.

Nikolas's aging father had called him home for murky reasons involving a young duke. The package Master Columsarn sent included a sealed letter for Premin Hawes with a request for guild texts. Some of those texts were of no worth to a master of Cathology who likely spent his days managing the documents necessary for running a duchy.

Another question struck Wynn as she left the common hall with Shade.

Who had Master Columsarn trusted to carry such nested and hidden communications all the way to the main guild branch in Calm Seatt? Premin Hawes had simply said that "a messenger" had left the package with the attendant at the gate.

Who had been tending the gate yesterday?

Hurrying down the passage to the entry alcove and the main front doors, Wynn stepped back out with Shade into the courtyard's chilly air.

"We need to see Premin Hawes again," she said.

Shade huffed in resignation.

Wynn wanted to know more about the texts that Master Columsarn had requested. But the question of the messenger, trusted to travel so far with such a package, wouldn't leave her thoughts.

"We make one other stop first," she added.

Shade simply huffed again.

Chane was back in his room struggling through a basic history text written in the Begaine Syllabary. He had not encountered Osha nor heard that other door across the passage open. He could only guess that Wynn's past "acquaintance" was sitting in there brooding . . . hoping to gain Wynn's pity, should she notice that Osha had not come out to eat this night.

It was insufferable.

Trying to focus, Chane turned a page . . . and a rapid, firm knock sounded at the door. He would have known it anywhere at any time.

For this was how Wynn knocked whenever she had her teeth into something of urgency.

"I am here," he rasped.

The door opened enough for her to lean in.

"I need a favor," she blurted. "Can you find something out for me?"

In truth he was desperate for anything to do, but her brusque manner irritated him, as if she knew he would say yes. Not yet getting up, he raised one eyebrow casually.

"What is it you want to know?"

After sending Chane off, though he'd been annoyingly difficult, Wynn hurried back to Premin Hawes's study and arrived nearly breathless. The premin quickly drew her and Shade inside, and none of them bothered sitting. Shade sniffed about, seemingly ignoring both women.

"And?" Hawes asked.

"Not much," Wynn admitted. "Only that Nikolas was called home because his aging father is not well, and that the young duke, Nikolas's friend from childhood, is also not well. . . ." Wynn quickly recounted all else that she could, including a mention of the duke's behaving strangely. "But Nikolas is desperate not to go. There is something wrong about all this, and . . ."

She hesitated, uncertain whether she should go further in another direction, but she did not have to ask the next question.

Hawes's stare almost made her fidget. The premin turned away to her desk, picked up the same folded piece of paper she'd held earlier, scanned it, and then pinched its edge at one place. She held the written side out before Wynn's eyes.

Wynn scanned one line near the tip of the premin's finger.

The Processes and Essence of Transmogrification.

Her gaze snapped up to meet the premin's icy gaze. "Transmogrification?"

Hawes let out a slow breath through her narrow nose, but those eyes of hers never blinked. She stared so long that Wynn wondered whether Hawes was calculating how much to say.

"Master Columsarn expressed more than I told you earlier," the premin finally said. "He says in the letter that there have been unexplained changes in the land, people, and even wildlife and livestock of the duchy's territory. I assume he felt the need to give me a reason for requesting such texts."

As Wynn opened her mouth, Hawes shook her head once. "He does not go into more detail than that."

Again the premin appeared to grow distracted, and Wynn began to think it had to do with more than this situation regarding Nikolas and his father.

"What are you going to do?" she asked.

"Do?" Hawes turned away. "I'm going to gather and prepare the material he requested. He is a master sage, and—for now—I have no reason to refuse him. Perhaps he has true need of these texts."

Chane crossed the courtyard toward the gatehouse tunnel, or rather the door to the right in one inner tower that framed it. And what was he to say when he got there?

Wynn had given him a cursory explanation for why she wanted a description of a messenger who had dropped off a small package for Nikolas Columsarn the previous night. She had told him the package contained an inner, sealed letter for Premin Hawes as well, and all this had to do with the "errand" Wynn had been executing for Hawes.

Chane hoped this had something—anything—to do with getting them a direction to the last orb, but logically he did not see how. There were two offices, one on each side, in the small inner towers of the gatehouse. In the evenings, after the outer portcullis was lowered, two apprentices usually stood watch, but only one would be down the tunnel.

He knocked first and then opened the door. "Hello?"

Stepping inside, he found two surprised apprentices in the cerulean blue robes of the order of Sentiology: a young man and a girl who looked to be shy of twenty. Both sat at a small table with a glowing cold lamp atop it. The girl was attractive, with long red hair, and the pair appeared engaged in some game using draughts on a circular board. One of them should have been watching the tunnel's far end at the portcullis until at least the quarter-night bell.

Few sages had ever spoken to Chane, but many knew him on sight; he had been Wynn's guest here more than once.

"Can I help you?" the young man asked, rising to his feet.

Both stared up at Chane's height and his pale face where he stood in the open doorway. He was not armed, as it was improper to bear arms inside the guild grounds. Still somewhat at a loss, he assumed a settled air of authority.

"Forgive the intrusion," he said. "Premin Hawes has sent me with a few questions."

"Premin Hawes?" the girl repeated.

Chane was well aware that the premin of Metaology was widely viewed with a bit of nervous awe by many of this branch's lower ranks. Even the assertive young man stalled with a glance at his companion.

"Who was attending here last night?" Chane asked flatly.

"I was," the male answered.

That made this easier, and Chane nodded once. "A message was delivered for Nikolas Columsarn. Did *you* take it?" He watched the young man, who might have winced slightly in sudden tension.

"Yes . . . sir," he answered. "Is there a problem? Should I not have?"

"Premin Hawes wanted to know who delivered it. Can you remember?"

"Remember?" The young man sat back down. "Of course."

Chane stepped inside, closing the door quietly, and stood watching the young man while waiting. When further elaboration did not come immediately, he raised an eyebrow without blinking.

The girl reached across the table to touch her partner's hand. "It's all right. If Premin Hawes sent him, you should tell him."

Finally the young man nodded. "I heard knocking out at the bailey gate, though maybe it was repeated more than once. I was reading a bit while standing attendance. When I heard it for certain, I was about to go open the gate, and . . . he or she stood right outside the raised portcullis, holding out a package that probably contained documents, by its size and shape. It was windy out, so perhaps I didn't hear the gate open."

"A man or woman?" Chane repeated. "Could you not tell the difference?"

The young sage shook his head. "Either a tall woman or a very slender man, wearing gloves, a black cloak with the hood up, and . . . a mask. All I could see was dark eyes."

One detail fixed in Chane's mind.

He had a mask, which had been made along with other accoutrements. As an undead, he needed these things should he ever have to move briefly in daylight while protecting Wynn. He also wore special glasses with near-black lenses, like the ones she carried for a different purpose, but the messenger's eyes had been exposed.

"A mask?" Chane echoed sharply, and the rasp of his voice caused a flinch in both young sages. "Why . . . What did it look like?"

"Leather, by its color, but it looked carved or etched with swirling lines. Maybe some other markings, but I couldn't see it clearly inside the hood. The hand holding the package was gloved . . . and something like leather armor was on the forearm. Hardened leather, also patterned, though I only got a brief look before the messenger dropped that arm inside the long cloak."

Chane was at a loss for what all of this meant. "What did this person say?"

"Nothing. She—he—handed me the package and stared at me. When I took it and looked at it, the outside was addressed in ink to Nikolas Columsarn, care of the guild at Calm Seatt, Malourné. But when I looked up again . . ."

Chane waited less than a breath at the hesitation. "And?"

"The messenger was gone."

Chane was the one who hesitated this time. "Did you hear the gate this time?"

At that, the young man paused, perhaps not having thought of this before. He shook his head.

"Thank you," Chane said, turning for the door before any reply was uttered as he hurried off to find Wynn.

CHAPTER THREE

It was well past dusk when the *Cloud Queen* made port in Soráno. Leesil was up on deck, while the others remained below.

Captain Bassett descended the aftcastle the moment the ramp was lowered to the pier. He was a thin, wiry man with gray stubble on his jaw and dressed in worn boots, an oiled hide jacket, and a battered brown hat. The captain kept his eyes averted when Leesil or any of his companions were on deck, as if he couldn't bring himself to even look at them anymore.

Leesil, like Magiere, could hardly blame the captain.

"Call the rest of your group and get off," Bassett said without preamble. "There's plenty of time for you to find an inn tonight."

Leesil suspected arguing was futile but still asked in his broken Numanese, "Stay tonight? Leave morning?"

"Off," Bassett repeated.

Leesil headed for the aftcastle door to the passengers' quarters below. When he reached the cabin he shared with Magiere and Chap, he found Magiere already packing. No surprise in that. She was dressed in her studded hauberk and cloak, with her falchion on her hip. She must have expected to be thrown off the moment they docked. Well, they all had.

"I take it Brot'an and Wayfarer are packing up, too?" he asked.

Magiere nodded without stopping, and her black hair fell forward over one shoulder, for she hadn't tied it back. In the dim light of a single-candle lantern, Leesil could barely see the bloodred tints in her tresses. Her beautiful, pale features tightened with worry, always about everything from their journey's success to the littlest tasks at hand . . . or the not-so-little things.

"Wayfarer will be fine," Leesil assured her, and hoped he sounded more certain than he felt.

Magiere didn't respond and continued stuffing their meager belongings into two packs and their small travel chest.

Leesil glanced at Chap, who was resting on one bunk and watching Magiere.

—The girl will . . . have . . . to be—

The dog's words, drawn from Leesil's own memories, rose in his mind: a new little trick learned from Wynn . . . and Shade, Chap's daughter.

—We have . . . no choice . . . but to continue—

This time Leesil didn't snap at Chap to stay out of his head.

Chap was right: they had no choice but to reach il'Dha'ab Najuum, the westernmost nation of the Suman Empire. There they hoped to find a first clue or lead to locating the orb of Air. Privately Leesil longed to forget everything about the orbs and go home to their little tavern, the Sea Lion, nearly halfway across the world. That wish was pointless.

Magiere would never give up the search, and wherever she went, he stayed at her side. When this was over—all over—he knew she would gladly go home with him, and they could finally have some peace together.

"That's all of it," she said, taking one pack and handing him the other before she hefted the small travel chest over her shoulder.

There was little else to say. If they stayed much longer, the captain would throw them off, one way or another.

Leesil shouldered his pack and picked up his weapons. As they headed into the passage, with Chap in the lead, Brot'an, followed by Wayfarer, stepped out of the next cabin. Both were ready as well, but fear was back in Wayfarer's green eyes.

"Léshil," she said, pronouncing his name in an'Cróan Elvish. "Must we?"

There was only one answer, one she didn't want to hear—one he didn't want to say. For all his resignation, he knew this wasn't going to be easy. Magiere said nothing, either, and jutted her chin down the passage.

Chap nosed Wayfarer out ahead as the rest of them followed. Leesil was the last to come up on deck and find Alberto and Paolo standing under a glowing lantern. Behind them was a muscular dark-haired man; Dirken always seemed to wear that ever-serious expression.

Leesil and Magiere had rescued these three from a slave ship back in a cesspool of a port called Drist. Dirken had taken responsibility for both boys and managed to find all of them a place among the ship's crew. His eyes fixed on Leesil.

"We have to stay," he said.

"Of course," Magiere answered. "It's best for all of you."

The last thing Leesil needed was two boys to watch over; keeping Wayfarer safe when none of them would ever truly be safe was hard enough. Still, he felt strange at saying farewell.

"Captain . . . is good man," he said. "You have good life here."

Dirken nodded once, but both boys stared at Wayfarer. Alberto's lower lip trembled, and Paolo was pale with a tight expression. And, to make matters worse, as Wayfarer looked at each of them, none of them said anything.

The young often had no idea how to say good-bye or why it had to hurt.

Leesil had no false comfort to offer, such as *You might see each other again*. That would be a lie, as it would never happen, and he didn't have the strength to sell a lie right now. Instead he took hold of Wayfarer's hand.

"Don't let go," he told her in Belaskian.

She gripped down on his palm, and as the captain watched from the aftcastle, Leesil led everyone down the ramp and onto the pier. They left the *Cloud Queen* for the last time and walked into the port city of Soráno. This time Brot'an brought up the rear.

Leesil glanced back more than once to see the old assassin watching all around, perhaps even more than Chap did out ahead. Leesil never let down his own guard, though he knew there was little chance that any of the anmaglâhk team trailing them could have beaten them to this port. For tonight they were likely safe. As to the port itself, he had no idea what to expect.

This far south, the night air was warm, and the small city appeared orderly and well maintained. But as he strolled along with Wayfarer clinging to his hand, one startling thing about the people on the well-lit street sank in suddenly. Magiere beat him to the first words.

"They all look like Wynn," she half whispered with shock.

She wasn't wrong.

Fine boned but round and oval faced, these people weren't as tall as the Numans of Malourné or as dark skinned as the few Sumans they had met. Nearly everyone walking past wore strange pantaloons, cotton vestment wraps, or long shifts of either white or soft colors to their ankles. But every one of them had olive-toned skin, and light brown hair and eyes, just like Wynn.

Even Chap, with ears pricked up, slowed a little ahead in watching the passersby. Wayfarer was staring a bit too much. Anyone walking by who noticed merely smiled with a slight nod.

"Did she come from here?" Leesil asked.

Chap looked back once, for he needed a sight line to answer. *—I don't know— . . . —She was . . . left . . . at the guild . . . as an infant—*

Oddly Chap knew more about Wynn than anyone else did. Leesil recalled some mention of the troublesome little sage "growing up" at the guild. It suddenly bothered him that he'd never asked her more, perhaps because he didn't like talking about his own childhood . . . as a slave and then a spy and assassin to a warlord.

Sorámo's streets were made of clean, cobbled, sandy-tan stone. Smaller open-air markets, rather than the big central ones of Leesil's land or even those back in Malourné, popped up everywhere. Many stalls were still open for business, and everyone not on the move appeared to be some kind of merchant of dry goods or a farmer with a small harvest from a spring crop. The number of offerings for sale was overwhelming.

Arrays of olives, dried dates, fish, and herb-laced cooking oils were abundant. The scents on the air were spicy and unfamiliar. He slowed briefly as they passed stacked bolts of fabrics with wild, earthy patterns.

At the sight of glass bottles filled with oil and black olives, Leesil considered pausing for a purchase or two. Then he took a glance at Wayfarer.

Any surprise or puzzlement over so many people like Wynn was gone from the girl's triangular face of tan elven features. The old fear of being among too many humans was clear to see there.

Leesil looked behind at Magiere and found her watching the girl as well.

"We should find an inn," she said quietly, and he nodded.

So far Brot'an had been completely silent, and that left Leesil suspicious. The old anmaglâhk master continued his vigil.

Like Chap, Leesil still struggled for a way to be rid of Brot'an's company. As yet, no opportunity had presented itself. As they headed down the strange street lit by glass lanterns that bulged like perfectly made pumpkins of pale yellows, oranges, cyans, and violets . . .

Brot'an quick-stepped past Leesil and even Chap to get ahead. He stopped one of the locals with a nod and raised hand.

"Can you direct us to an inn?" he asked in Numanese.

The fine-boned man in a long shift of saffron cotton over matching pantaloons looked up—and up—at the tall an'Cróan. After an instant of shock, he smiled and pointed down the way at a two-story tan building. Leesil couldn't be sure, but the whole place looked as though it was all made of dried brown clay.

"Our thanks," Brot'an said.

As the man shrugged with a smile and walked on, Brot'an didn't move. Instead he glanced back, his amber eyes moving over Chap, Magiere, Leesil, and finally Wayfarer. He exhaled audibly.

"One more time we take rooms at an inn," he said flatly, and the notion didn't appear to please him. "Tomorrow we try to find another ship."

In spite of Leesil's disgust at ever agreeing with Brot'an, his thoughts echoed *one more time.* He wondered how many more times there would be until all of this was over, and they could finally go home.

Two evenings after Chane had given Wynn the scant description of the messenger, he once again sat in his room at the guild with little to do. After her cursory visit at dusk, she had taken that brooding elf to the main hall for supper.

Chane had no desire to join them, to sit at a crowded table, pretending to eat, while Wynn slathered pity all over Osha, who would pick at his food and speak to her in Elvish. Chane had already suffered through that once the night after Osha's arrival. He would not repeat it again.

Instead he paged through a history text not intended for public use and fought to read the complex and compact Begaine symbols. If he could master these, he would be more help to Wynn in her research—unlike Osha. In fairness to Kyne, the girl was an adequate teacher, and her natural talent with texts and languages was enviable; he was progressing quickly enough.

Chane turned another page.

Later he was uncertain what pulled his attention.

Something made him look up to his room's outer door . . . as the wall beside it appeared to shift. He grabbed the hilt of his longsword leaning against the desk and stripped off its sheath as he rose, his legs shoving his chair back with a scrape across the floor.

Gray wall stones bulged inward as something pushed through them. The color of stone flowed away as a cloak's hood overshadowing a broad face surfaced out of the wall.

Chane relaxed—and frowned irritably—as he set his sword's mottled dwarven steel blade on the desktop's side.

Thudding footfalls landed upon floor stones. A cloaked and stout hulk, easily twice as wide as Wynn but no taller, stood within the room. One overly broad hand pulled back the hood, and a stocky dwarf looked Chane up and down after a glance at the sword.

"Could you not use the door for once?" Chane rasped.

"I did not wish to be heard knocking," Ore-Locks replied. "Especially after our last outing in this keep."

Chane had no response for that, considering what his . . . friend . . . ally . . . or something less definable had done in helping to free Wynn from confinement here not long ago.

Beardless, something uncommon for male dwarves, Ore-Locks's red hair flowed to the shoulders of an iron-colored wool cloak. Though he looked young, perhaps thirty by human standards—so likely sixty or more for a dwarf—Chane knew better.

Ore-Locks was older than that, because of his life among the Hassäg'kreigi—the "Stonewalkers"—of Dhredze Seatt, the caretakers for their people's honored dead. He no longer wore a stonewalker's armor of steel-tipped black leather scales, though he still bore their twin battle daggers upon his belt. But the stout dwarven sword sheathed on his belt, and the long iron staff in his large hand, were both a bad sign.

Why would he feel the need to travel fully armed?

He was dressed plainly in brown breeches and a natural canvas shirt, and Chane saw the burnt-orange wool tabard through the split of the dwarf's cloak. Again, not a good sign.

Ore-Locks had donned his past travel disguise as a holy shirvêsh of Bedzâ'kenge—"Feather-Tongue"—the Eternal, or dwarven saint, of history, tradition, and wisdom.

Chane had once been enemies with this dwarf, but by the end of their journey to Bäalâle Seatt—a fallen civilization of the dwarves—they had forged something between them that led to an unexplainable trust. Even Wynn had entrusted the dwarf with the safety of the orb of Earth.

However, Ore-Locks did not make social calls.

"What has happened?" Chane asked.

Ore-Locks leaned his iron staff against the wall and stepped closer. "Someone breached the underworld . . . managed to get through the portal below the market in Chemarré."

"That is not possible."

Frowning, Ore-Locks glanced away. "We think the would-be thief must have slipped through unseen when the portal was opened to bring down supplies."

"Would-be thief?"

"Whoever it was headed straight for the . . . the spot through which Wynn was first taken to the hidden pocket in the earth where we store the ancient texts for the guild. The same place, with no physical entrance, where I had the orb hidden."

Chane went silent, more than alarmed now.

Wynn had removed a small wealth of ancient texts—written by the first vampires to walk the world—from the library of the six-towered castle in the Pock Peaks of the eastern continent. This was the same place where Chane had stumbled upon the scroll that he brought to her later. Upon Wynn's return to her own guild branch, her superiors had confiscated all the texts and given them to the Stonewalkers for safekeeping. One or two stonewalkers were occasionally given the task of bringing certain texts to the guild for the ongoing translation work.

This was done with great secrecy, and only guild superiors had access to the material.

At present Chane was far more worried about the orb.

"You have to move it," he said.

Ore-Locks shook his head. "The orb is safe where it is. Only a member of my caste could walk through stone to it, let alone know where it is . . . though . . . that wall in line with the deeper cave pocket was where the interloper was spotted. All clan leaders and constabularies have been alerted with a description of the thief."

"You do not have him in custody?"

Stonewalkers could move through any earth and stone, and nothing could elude them. They had once even pinned down the wraith Sau'ilahk.

Ore-Locks drew himself to full height with a long exhale. "No, she—or he—vanished."

Chane's whole body tightened: he had heard a similar uncertain description too recently.

"What do you mean, 'she or he'?"

Ore-Locks settled in the chair before the desk as if weary, which was not like him. "I only caught the barest glimpse of the intruder. My brethren were closing in when the interloper simply disappeared. I had barely arrived at that particular cave and . . . was hit in the face by a strange wind. The others shared what they saw, claiming it was either a tall woman or a slender man, human by build and wearing a black cloak, gloves, and a mask. Master Cinder-Shard ordered a full search that uncovered nothing."

Suddenly Chane needed to sit as well. Cinder-Shard was the leader of the Stonewalkers, the most skilled among them.

"When did this happen?"

"The night before last. I came as soon as I could after the search and preparations. When I did not find Wynn in her room, I came looking for you, as you should both be informed."

Chane locked eyes with Ore-Locks. At a guess, Stonewalkers could make the journey here in less than a day by quickly passing through stone and earth. But there was something more disturbing about the timing of certain events.

"Three nights ago someone matching that description brought a message here for a young apprentice sage . . . from the young man's homeland."

Ore-Locks straightened up in his chair, his mouth partly open but silent as he stared at Chane.

Chane stood up, heading for the door. "We need to find Wynn. She must be told."

Ore-Locks rose instantly. "I cannot be seen here. You know this."

Chane looked back, seeing the torn expression on the dwarf's face.

Ore-Locks might be an ally, but if his brethren learned that he had come here . . .

The Stonewalkers guarded their secrets with a vengeance. Should word get back to Cinder-Shard that Ore-Locks had been seen on guild grounds—with Chane or Wynn—then Ore-Locks could suffer serious consequences.

"I will tell her," Chane said. "Go back before you are spotted. We will investigate from here and try to learn about this intruder . . . messenger . . . and the young sage who received the letters. There may be something more to that. I will let you know, if I can."

Still appearing troubled, Ore-Locks retrieved his staff. "Do not fear for the orb. No one can reach it."

"It was good to see you," Chane said without thinking—and then felt uncomfortable about this, as it was so uncommon for him. Chane was thankful that Ore-Locks did not respond in kind and only nodded once before sinking into the room's stone wall.

In the keep's common hall, Wynn finished her supper of lentil stew and grain bread while attempting safe conversation with Osha—and that was becoming more difficult. Worse, Shade didn't care for lentils, and, after a couple of halfhearted laps from her bowl on the floor, a broken barrage of memory-words kept popping into Wynn's head.

—Meat?—

"No, this is all there is."

—Fish?—

"Eat and just be quiet."

—Cheese!—

Wynn sighed.

"Here," Osha said, and he tossed a large piece of bread spread with thick butter at the dog.

He hadn't needed any memory-words from Shade to understand, and she snapped the bread in midflight. It was gone in three chomps.

With a frown at Shade, Wynn rose from the bench. "Shall we take her outside?"

All around them, other sages glanced or outright stared at Osha. He had tried not to attract attention, but that was pointless.

As far as the company Wynn had kept here at the guild, Chane had been a curiosity and Shade more so. But Osha's height, eyes, and more deeply tan skin and whiter blond hair than a typical Lhoin'na—the elves of this continent—drew far more attention than he or Wynn would have desired. And more so if any gawker knew from where he had truly come.

Still, Wynn felt it was best to drag him out of his room for supper. If nothing else, he was less likely to start prodding her about their past, although she still had many questions about what had happened to him, about his changes, since she'd left him nearly two years ago.

A walk in the courtyard would do him good as well. Together the three of them left the hall and made their way down the passage to the entry alcove. Just as they reached it, one of the huge main doors swung open.

Chane walked in, appearing openly relieved at the sight of her. Then he glowered briefly at Osha.

Wynn didn't have time for the "boys" and their mutual distaste.

"Something happened?" she asked in alarm.

Chane looked both ways, and his gaze settled on the door of a nearby seminar room. "In there," he rasped before walking over.

"Chane, no!" she whispered loudly. The room would be empty at this time, but Wynn did not like the idea of a premin or domin coming along and catching them talking.

"Hurry," he insisted.

With her mouth pursed, she followed him in, and perhaps if Shade hadn't been the last one to enter, Chane might have shut the door in Osha's face.

Wynn pulled out her small cold-lamp crystal, swiped it hard down her robe for the heat of friction, and the crystal ignited with dull light. The small room was empty but for rows of wooden benches all facing two chairs and a single lectern at the back wall.

"What is wrong?" she whispered.

Chane glanced sidelong, just once, at Osha—who glared back—before he said, "Ore-Locks visited me only moments ago."

At that Wynn fell silent and let Chane speak. Ore-Locks wouldn't come here unless it was important. But as Chane recounted the story he'd heard from the dwarf, Wynn's stomach began growing tighter and tighter.

That someone . . . someone else . . . had breached the dwarven underworld seemed impossible. That this someone had gone straight for the wall through which Wynn had been dragged to the ancient texts a season ago was even worse. When Chane assured her that the orb Ore-Locks held in custody was safe, that wasn't quite enough to quell her fear.

Someone had somehow still known where to look for that orb and gone straight to that wall, even though only a stonewalker could reach the tiny pocket in the mountain that held the texts and the orb of Earth.

"The invader was briefly seen," Chane added.

Panic took hold of Wynn again when Chane described the would-be thief.

"Ore-Locks is certain?" she managed to ask. "That's what he saw?"

Osha and Shade were both quiet through this exchange, but Shade was watching Chane, and Osha was watching Wynn.

"Yes," Chane answered, "though he only caught a glimpse of the invader with his own eyes. Others of his caste described someone attired too much like the messenger who brought letters for Nikolas and Premin Hawes."

Wynn stood there trying to breathe.

"How far Dhredze Seatt?" Osha asked in Belaskian. "Enough time?"

That was exactly what was on Wynn's mind. If the messenger and the would-be thief were the same person, then even if a ship had been prearranged and waiting . . .

"I do not think so," Chane said. "There was not enough time to make the journey to the seatt, let alone breach the underworld, from when the letters were delivered."

Perhaps the thief and messenger were not connected at all, and their similar appearances were a coincidence. After the past two years, and all that had happened surrounding the orbs, Wynn did not believe in coincidences.

A greater fear flooded her.

Only Sau'ilahk, the wraith, knew that the dwarven underworld was involved with the texts. Only he might guess at where an orb could be hidden, considering that Ore-Locks had been seen with her and Chane when they'd gone to Bäalâle Seatt. Sau'ilahk had even invaded the dwarven underworld in following Wynn there before she'd learned of that lost dwarven city.

The Stonewalkers had cast out Sau'ilahk, or at least they first thought he had been finished off. But what if it wasn't the wraith but some other new minion? Sau'ilahk had been—was—a conjuror whose skills and power had grown over a thousand years.

Or . . .

Was another faction who served the Ancient Enemy now on the move, somehow having gained clues in trying to seek out orbs on this continent?

Either way, someone had brought Nikolas a message from his father, who in turn had requested texts on folklore going back as far as possible to the Forgotten History.

"I have to speak to Premin Hawes," she said quietly. "Now."

Down in Premin Hawes's study, Wynn rambled out the entire story, the interloper and messenger descriptions, and all of her hypotheses while barely taking a breath. Shade stood listening at her side and for once wasn't causing trouble or sniffing in corners where she shouldn't.

Hawes sat in the corner armchair and listened with her typical cold expression, which could unnerve anyone. But when Wynn finished and finally sucked a breath, she was already too frantic to be affected by the premin's chilling stare.

"What do you think?" she asked. "What should we do?"

Premin Hawes didn't answer. Her gray-hazel eyes shifted, looking here and there but not at anything specific, at least as far as Wynn could tell.

"Domin High-Tower approved Nikolas's leave of absence, along with funding," she finally said. "Nikolas sails the day after tomorrow for the small port of Oléron on the southern end of Witeny's coast. From there he can arrange transport by land to the duchy."

The premin's eyes came back to Wynn's face.

"I cannot accompany him," the premin added. "I have too much . . . There are preparations to finish for the pending expedition."

Wynn started slightly. She knew exactly what "expedition," as Hawes had told her of this guild secret in confidence. Some factions of the guild's upper ranks were planning to launch a journey to the eastern continent, back to the Pock Peaks to the library of the six-towered castle, where Wynn had found the ancient texts. She'd brought back only a small fraction of what existed there.

This was beyond foolhardy for a pack of defenseless sages!

Magiere and Leesil had locked away a thousand-year-old Noble Dead—one of the first thirteen called the Children—in a cavern beneath that castle. Wynn had no certainty that the undead called Li'kän had not escaped, or would not.

Hawes had mentioned that the documented reason for the expedition would simply be to help expand and stock the small but growing guild annex in Bela, on the west coast of the eastern continent. However, Wynn suspected that Premin Hawes was working in quiet ways to ensure that the expedition never took place.

Wynn noticed that Shade had slipped around to her other side and now sat staring in the corner between Hawes's old armchair and the back wall's closest bookcase.

"Shade," she whispered, patting her leg.

The dog looked up, glanced once more into that hidden corner, and finally sidled over next to Wynn.

"You will go with Nikolas," Hawes said suddenly. "If there is a connection between the messenger and the other who breached the Stonewalkers' realm . . ."

The premin never finished, but Wynn knew what was expected of her, what she had wanted in the first place: to go with Nikolas and find any trail to anyone after the orbs. She was then caught off guard by a strange sight.

Premin Hawes's eyes wandered again, and her smooth brow wrinkled so slightly. It was the closest thing to worry that Wynn had ever seen on the face of the premin of Metaology.

"Of course I'll go," Wynn said, "with my companions. I'll need them."

Hawes actually flinched, which made Wynn do so as well, as the premin came out of whatever deep thought had distracted her.

Premin Hawes was definitely not her usual self this night, and she pointed to a bulky oiled canvas satchel on her desk.

"There are the requested texts for Master Columsarn's eyes only," she said, "though you should familiarize yourself with them. You will have to watch over Nikolas in whatever lies ahead."

Wynn nodded as she picked up the satchel, but before she could turn to leave, the premin continued.

"Domin High-Tower and Premin Sykion are worried about Nikolas's state. He has physically recovered from the assault by the wraith, but there are concerns. I should have minimal trouble gaining permission for your leave of absence, since you are now under my charge and will be on an errand for me, traveling to the same destination as Nikolas. High Premin Sykion will likely be glad to have you off someplace else." She rose, stepped to the desk, opened a drawer, and took out a pouch. "I will arrange passage on Nikolas's ship for the three of—"

"Four of us," Wynn corrected. Whether she wanted Osha along or not, she couldn't see how she could leave him behind.

"As you wish." Hawes returned and handed over the pouch. "There is enough for your travel expenses when you land."

Wynn looked inside the pouch. There were far more coins than any stipend she had ever received—would have received—from the guild.

"Premin . . . this is your own money. I cannot—"

"Take it," Hawes ordered. "I have no need of it, and this is too important a matter."

The premin gestured toward the short three-step passage to the door. Wynn nodded and turned to leave as Shade stepped out ahead of her. They had barely walked out into the courtyard when Wynn halted and turned to Shade.

"Anything?" she asked.

Shade shook her head, a too-humanlike response.

Wynn sighed, though she hadn't truly expected Shade to succeed. The dog couldn't catch actual conscious thoughts. But like her father, Chap, if Shade focused on someone, she could pick up fleeting memories rising in anyone's mind, so long as she wasn't distracted in nosing about.

There were very few people Wynn had ever encountered who could hide surfacing memories from Shade. Chane was one, but only because of the brass "ring of nothing," stolen from Welstiel Massing, Magiere's undead half brother, that he wore.

Premin Frideswida Hawes was another.

Much as such subterfuge was ungrateful, considering all that Hawes had done, Wynn needed to know as much as she could about what was going on inside her guild branch . . . and anything the premin of Metaology might be hiding.

—Satchel . . . more . . . books—

Wynn started slightly at Shade's memory-words. "I have it, and . . . what other books?"

Shade slipped in close and tucked her nose under Wynn's palm. At that touch a memory rose in Wynn's mind, and it wasn't her own. This was something unique that Shade could do only with Wynn.

Wynn—Shade—sat off to one side and peeked behind Premin Hawes's armchair, as she had moments before in the study. In that hidden space between the chair and the bookcase's end was a large drawstring sack rather than an actual satchel. The way it bulged with square edges suggested there were possibly books inside of it. Many such.

Shade pulled her nose away and sat staring up. The image vanished instantly.

—Other . . . satchel— . . . —Other . . . books—

Wynn was lost as to what this meant. The only books needing packaging were the ones she held, so what were the others for? Then she thought of the expedition.

—Many spaces in . . . shelves— . . . —Missing . . . books—

Wynn wasn't certain what Shade meant. Among supplies to be taken to the little guild branch in Bela, situated in a decommissioned city guard barracks, there would be many newly copied texts to increase its holdings. Those would be packaged in crates for the long journey across this continent and the eastern ocean. Such books wouldn't come from any private library of . . .

Wynn turned, staring at the door that led back into the storage building . . . and to the stairs leading down to the laboratories and Premin Hawes's private study.

"Oh, no," she whispered.

Premin Hawes had packed books from her own library. There was only one reason for that: she was going with the expedition. That meant that she had failed to stop the other sages from launching the journey.

Wynn grew frantic, trying to think of a way to warn everyone off of this foolishness. But even if she did, that would reveal she knew something she wasn't supposed to know. And there was the messenger, the invader into the dwarves' underworld, and Nikolas, and all of whatever was now rising around her search for an orb.

Why was it that no matter what she did, there would always be a price?

After Wynn had gone off to speak with this Premin Hawes, Osha returned to the solitude of his room to get away from Chane. Though he had said little during the exchange between Wynn and Chane, he had understood the magnitude of what that undead had recounted.

Something was about to happen. Osha simply did not know what. So he waited, sitting cross-legged on the floor of his room. His mind had just achieved a state of stillness when he heard light footsteps in the passage outside.

Someone knocked on his door.

Osha rose fluidly and reached the door in one long step. It would be Wynn, as only she ever came to see him.

So it was when he opened the door. She slipped inside along with the black majay-hì, and Osha took in the sight of Wynn's pretty oval face and olive-toned skin. There was worry, maybe even fright, there, though he did not know where it came from.

Had Chane done something?

"We're leaving the day after tomorrow," she blurted out in Elvish. "Premin Hawes is sending us with the young sage I mentioned, Nikolas. There is not much time to prepare, but his passage has already been arranged. The premin thinks she can get us on the same ship."

"I could leave tonight if you asked," he said, motioning around the room. "I have little to pack."

Although Osha was uncertain this journey would lead to anything of use, his relief at the prospect of traveling outside this guild was profound. But even with Wynn's excitement, there was still that strange concern on her face.

To his surprise, she appeared relieved by his reply.

"You do not mind?" she asked. "You will come with us to protect Nikolas and help me with what might be a wild-goose chase?"

He did not understand what geese had to do with any of this, but her words made him almost angry. Why did she think he had come here if not to help her?

Perhaps his own expression betrayed him.

She stepped closer, and it seemed that her concern, her worry, was suddenly focused on him. Then she glanced away at the long, canvas-wrapped bundle at the end of his bed.

"Before we leave," she began, "could you tell me something of what happened to you since we parted on the docks of Bela? This might prove a dangerous journey, and I feel . . . I feel like I do not know you anymore. You have changed."

"And so have you," he returned. It sounded bitter to his own ears, and he swallowed hard.

What if he was wrong? What if the chasm between them *was* due to how much he had changed and not her?

"What caused this change in you?" she asked, barely above a whisper, and she glanced at the wrapped bundle at the bed's end.

The black majay-hì called Shade never blinked as she watched him. And Wynn looked back to him as well. Now there was as much expectation in her small, brown human eyes as there was frantic worry on her face.

Though she asked *what* had changed him, perhaps *when* would have been the better question.

Well over a year ago, he had still been an anmaglâhk in his homeland on the eastern continent, as he had tried to find some purpose to his life while in the main enclave of the Coilehkrotall clan and the dwelling of Leanâlhâm and the old healer Gleannéohkân'thva. He had come to bring them tragic tidings: the death of their loved one, the great Sgäilsheilleache, who had also been Osha's jeóin, or mentor, for his final training.

Osha had been determined to stay and help them heal, if he could. In this way he could atone for having brought them such news. But also he needed to do so, for he could not face his own losses in all that had happened.

Only a few days after his arrival, the greimasg'äh—Brot'ân'duivé—had uprooted him by showing him a small, smooth stone sent by the Chein'âs—the Burning Ones. Brot'ân'duivé told him what was etched upon the stone in claw marks—"a sudden breeze."

It was the meaning of the name "Osha" had taken when he had gone to the ancestors' burial ground as a youth for his name-taking.

He was being summoned for a second time to the Chein'âs.

They lived in the lava-heated depths of the mountains bordering the an'Cróan's southern territories. Once young initiates completed basic training and received approval by the caste's elders to stand among the caste, word was sent to the Chein'âs via the Séyilf—the Windblown, winged people. When new weapons and tools were ready, the Chein'âs sent a stone—a summons—to a caste elder among the Anmaglâhk. One elder then guided the initiate on a journey to the fiery cavern to receive those precious gifts.

Like all newly approved Anmaglâhk, Osha had received his weapons and thereby was allowed to seek out an experienced member of the caste as a jeóin to finish his training. He had known even before then that he wanted no one but the great Sgäilsheilleache for his mentor.

But young anmaglâhk were never summoned a second time.

Something was very wrong, yet he dared not refuse . . . even if he had known then what waited for him at the end of that second journey.

"Tell me," Wynn pressed, inching closer. "Please . . . What happened to you?"

Even at the sight of her eager, worried eyes, he could not answer, though he wanted to. To do so would only widen the chasm between them, and he needed to cross that before he could take such a risk. And he needed to know why she had changed so much in so many ways: another wayward majay-hì at her side, the strange robe she now wore, and . . . that undead thing who went everywhere with her.

Osha turned away. "I will be ready to leave when you are."

At her sudden intake of breath, he could not bear to look back at any disappointment on her face, though he almost did. Instead, in that quick flinch, he found the black majay-hì still watching him.

After delivering the news to Osha and then Chane concerning their impending departure, Wynn retreated to her room with Shade and sank onto her bed. She knew she had preparations to make, especially informing Nikolas of the change in plan. But somehow she didn't think he would object to having her company foisted upon him on this journey. Even if he did, he certainly wouldn't argue with Premin Hawes.

Wynn had what she needed: the freedom to seek out this messenger and the invader into the Stonewalkers' realm. Though they were described in the same way, she doubted they could be the same person, due to the distance between their two closely timed appearances.

She tried not to think too much more on that . . . or on all the implications connected to Nikolas's father in the attempt to reach one of the orbs. No, in this moment, she couldn't help the rising sadness when Osha had seemed on the brink of finally telling her about things that mattered.

She'd watched him close himself off before her eyes. She shouldn't have asked so much of him in the middle of everything else.

Now that she, Chane, and Shade—and Osha—would embark on a journey where they had to depend on one another, she had no idea what scars or damage Osha was hiding. They could not afford any complications.

Shade whined and pressed herself against Wynn's leg.

"What is it?" she asked, reaching out to stroke the dog's head.

An image flashed in her mind.

She was inside a great tree dwelling, like those of the an'Cróan homes, and in the bottom of her view were knees—her knees in that moment—covered in forest gray pants of worn cloth. This wasn't Shade's memory, though Wynn recognized the home of Gleannéohkân'thva and Leanâlhâm.

Directly in front of her, Leanâlhâm was weeping. For an instant Wynn fought the strange memory passed to her by Shade.

—From . . . Osha—

Shade was passing on something she'd seen in Osha, which meant Wynn was seeing through Osha's eyes. Hoping to see more, she gripped the fur on Shade's back.

The scene changed.

Wynn—Osha—stood before Brot'an, and the elder anmaglâhk's face was visibly tense as he held out a small black polished stone.

Wynn—Osha—said to him, "I already made my journey to them years past to receive my weapons and tools. Why do you show me that?"

"Now they have called you back."

"No!" Osha cried. "They call us once, when the elders of our caste approve an initiate to seek out a jeóin. That stone is a mistake!"

"There are no such mistakes," lashed a soft voice.

Outside the memory, Wynn gasped. Within the memory, Osha turned his head to see Leesil's beautiful mother, Cuirin'nên'a, standing in an archway while holding its curtain aside.

"You are summoned," she said. "This is our caste's way, and the way of our people's elders, based on covenants with the Burning Ones, whom we protect along with the Windblown. This is part of our people's ways as well. And in keeping them, this is part of what your jeóin died to uphold!"

Within the memory, Wynn felt Osha's rush of pain as if it were hers. He was being torn from this place, from Gleannéohkân'thva and Leanâlhâm, and he did not want to go.

The image vanished.

Wynn saw only the stone walls and door of her little room.

"Shade!" she cried, gripping the dog's face. "More! Did you see more?"

With a whine, Shade huffed twice for *no*, and Wynn sagged.

What did it all mean? Somehow, after returning to the an'Cróan territories, Osha had gone to the enclave of the Coilehkrotall. He had probably just delivered news of Sgäile's death, for Leanâlhâm had been crying. And then, in some other moment, Brot'an had shown him the small polished stone from the Chein'âs. And Leesil's mother had insisted that Osha obey Brot'an.

"Oh, Shade," Wynn whispered, looking at the dog.

At least she had a place to start that she might subtly use to get Osha to tell her more. As to what Osha wanted from her, she didn't dare think of that now.

CHAPTER FOUR

Two evenings later, Wynn walked with Shade down a pier in Calm Seatt's port. Nikolas, Chane, and then Osha followed behind her. Though it had taken some doing, Premin Hawes's arrangements had put off the sailing of a cargo vessel until after sunset—for Chane's benefit. Wynn had suggested her old excuse of Chane suffering from a skin malady that made him painfully susceptible to sunlight. Sometimes a partial truth was the best lie.

Preparations had been both rushed and trying. Chane resented Osha's inclusion and made no secret of his feelings. Osha, still stoic and silent, expressed his revulsion for Chane in all ways but words. But at times Wynn had caught flashes of either pain or anger in Osha's eyes.

Nikolas was perhaps the most and least of Wynn's complications among her companions. He had accepted their company on this journey without argument; in fact, he'd barely reacted at all. What weighed upon him was a deep dread of returning home.

Wynn worried about this entire state of affairs, but all she could do was press onward.

Their supplies were minimal, and Chane carried the sealed stack of texts for Master Columsarn. Chane wore a heavy hooded cloak and both his swords: a long dwarven blade given to him by Ore-Locks, and a shorter one that had been broken and reground to a new point. Osha's cloak was lighter, and once again he bore his bow, a quiver of black-feathered arrows, and the strangely narrow canvas-wrapped, twine-strapped object across his back. The only new thing Wynn had learned about that was that whatever was in it had some weight, by the way he'd picked it up and wrestled to strap it on before they left the guild grounds.

Wynn used her only weapon as a walking stick: the sun-crystal staff made for her by Ghassan il'Sänke, the domin of the guild's Suman branch, to whom she had sent Magiere, Leesil, and Chap. The staff itself was taller than her head, and a leather sheath now covered the hand's-length clear crystal at its top. With it she could emulate sunlight. Before leaving the guild, she'd also retrieved Chane's scroll from Premin Hawes's office and stowed it in her pack.

Nikolas carried nothing but his travel bag, and, as Wynn glanced back, his eyes were down, as if he followed her steps without looking where he was going.

Wynn finally stopped at a three-masted vessel with the label *The Thorn* painted on its bow's side. She found that an odd name for a ship. Glancing down at her travel papers in hand, she headed for the boarding ramp without a word to the others. Shade fell behind her and started whining softly. The dog never enjoyed tight quarters or even being on an open deck with too many sailors . . . strangers.

The impending sea voyage was not going to be pleasant for anyone.

Followed by the others, Wynn stepped on deck. All around, sailors were fiddling with this or that, though it was obvious the ship was ready and the crew was waiting for the last of their passengers.

A silver-haired and slender man in a long, heavy coat called out orders from the aftcastle to the crew as a younger man with a shaved head came trotting across the deck.

"You're the passengers from the guild?" he asked without a greeting.

Wynn nodded, but he rushed on before she could speak.

"I'm First Mate Shearborn." He looked over the small group, ending on

Shade. "The request to take on three more passengers arrived only yesterday, but I managed to arrange an extra cabin. You'll have two between the lot of you—and two bunks per cabin."

Wynn frowned; of course Shade could stay with her and sleep on the floor with an extra blanket, but all three men couldn't sleep in a cabin with only two bunks. And that wasn't the only problem.

Nikolas had no idea what Chane was . . . and could not be exposed to the sight of Chane lying dormant—as if dead—all day. Osha was a stranger to Nikolas, who was already under enough stress. And frankly Wynn wasn't certain she wanted to share space with either Osha or Chane, with neither wanting the other anywhere near her.

"It is of no matter," Chane rasped as he stepped forward to look down at her. "You and I will share, as we have done before."

Wynn was more than acquainted with the tones of his damaged voice. He was not trying to be arrogant or overbearing, though he could be both at the same time. He simply stated the least complicated option. They had shared confined spaces in inns, elven tree dwellings, and excavated stone rooms in the bowels of a dwarven seatt, always living by night until Chane fell dormant at dawn.

Yes, his assumption was the best of poor options, but when Wynn looked back and up over Nikolas's hanging head, Osha was watching her sternly. His large amber eyes shifted once toward Chane, and narrowed before looking to her again.

Wynn turned back to First Mate Shearborn. "Thank you for your efforts on such short notice. We'll manage fine with two cabins."

The first mate stepped off with a gesture toward the aftcastle door, and, without looking back at anyone, Wynn followed.

The next morning, far down the coast in Soráno, Magiere began to worry. Though her small group had adequate lodgings at a clean inn, they'd had no luck in finding passage south toward il'Dha'ab Najuum in the Suman Empire.

Part of the problem was Brot'an's insistence that no one risk being seen in the open on the docks. Magiere hadn't disagreed with him as yet. Leesil even thought it was "a fair bet" that they'd arrived ahead of any anmaglâhk still trailing them. But each passing day made it more likely that those assassins might have caught up and would be watching the entire port.

Magiere finally grew fed up with sitting, partly because Leesil had already had enough. It had taken hard arguments with both him and Brot'an to get them to see that she was the most normal-looking of all of them, if she covered herself up well enough. For the past few mornings she'd made furtive trips to the harbormaster's office to ask about any possible ships headed south.

She'd had no better luck than Brot'an.

This morning, barely past dawn, she slipped back into their room at the inn and found both Leesil and Chap expectant and eager. Chap was stretched out across a bed—his silver-gray body long enough to cover its width—and Leesil sat beside him.

Wayfarer was there and hurried over to take Magiere's cloak. Brot'an, possibly checking to see if she had been followed, stood peering between the closed curtains and out the window.

"Well?" Leesil asked too loudly.

Much as Magiere knew he hated sea travel, it was obvious he was starting to hate the four walls around them even more. It was a nice enough room, large and airy with two double beds. Brot'an always slept on the floor, which left the second bed to Chap and Wayfarer. All in all, the situation could have been worse.

But for as long as Magiere remained silent, though Leesil was desperate to press on, the answer to his question was obvious.

He flopped backward on the bed beside Chap and, with a groan, ran his fingers through his long, unbound hair. Chap dropped his head on his paws with a threatening rumble as a stream of memory-words rose in Magiere's mind.

—This isn't working— . . . —We need . . . to walk the piers . . . and . . . talk to captains . . . directly—

Magiere winced. "Don't growl at me! I'm no happier about this than any of you."

Leesil lifted his head and looked first at the dog and then at her. "What did he say?"

"He wants to start talking to ship captains."

"Then I should do so," Brot'an put in, still peeking out the window.

Magiere clenched her jaw. "You'd be spotted quicker than anyone. We've all tried disguises, and I'm sure they've learned to look closer at anything suspicious. You're a head and a half taller than any of the natives . . . even taller than most travelers and sailors in the port."

Glowering in all directions, Leesil sat up slowly on the bed's edge and began tying the old green head scarf over his bright, white-blond hair. Wayfarer glanced at Chap, but she didn't speak and remained standing, clutching Magiere's cloak in both hands.

"They've got to be spread thin by now," Leesil muttered, looking to Brot'an, though normally he didn't speak to the shadow-gripper unless he had to. "Can you guess how many are left?"

"I know exactly how many," Brot'an answered, "and exactly who they are. Three women and one man, and one of the women is crippled." He finally turned to look only at Magiere. "Fréthfâre is with them, for Dänvârfij would not have made some of their rasher choices."

Chap snarled as his head snapped up, and Leesil's mouth fell open for an instant. Even Magiere felt anger rising and had to push it down before she could speak. She had run Fréthfâre through with her own falchion, though that vicious advisor to Most Aged Father, leader of the Anmaglâhk, had survived. Magiere didn't mind Brot'an's guarded secrets, but only so long as he remained useful.

"You've known this since Drist?" she asked him. "Didn't you think that was something you should've shared?"

Brot'an raised his right eyebrow, which made the scars skipping around it spread. "You never asked," he replied passively.

Again not trusting herself to speak, Magiere closed her eyes. They should have attempted this conversation before, but both Leesil and Chap were dead set against sharing anything with Brot'an unless necessary. And the old assassin had a habit of only trading information.

"Én'nish is one of the women," Leesil put in. "I caught her across the stomach with a blade in Drist. She couldn't be fully healed yet."

Brot'an nodded once.

Magiere's anger began to fade. "That leaves two in good health, and two can't cover the entire port."

"The two are highly skilled," Brot'an countered. "They can cover more area than you realize. You are correct that they might spot me, or even Léshil in disguise, more easily among the local inhabitants. You two are also taller than the people here."

"Then what are we supposed to do?" Leesil asked in frustration.

"I could go," Wayfarer said quietly.

To make it all worse, Magiere had already seen Brot'an look the girl's way.

"With Chap," Wayfarer added. "I speak enough Numanese, and I saw other dogs on piers with the people here."

"No!" Magiere snapped.

"I saw a number of black dogs down there," Wayfarer continued without flinching, and her beautiful green eyes were so calm that she almost didn't seem herself. "It seems a common color in this place. We could try the trick Leesil used before."

At that, Chap growled.

Wayfarer actually frowned at the dog, something no one would have expected for how much she, like her people, revered the majay-hì.

"At least the people of Calm Seatt thought you only a wolf," she said to him, "instead of . . . what you are."

Chap silently watched the girl, and one of his ears twitched as he looked over at Leesil.

Leesil stiffened upright to his feet and whirled on the dog. "No, it *isn't* a good idea!"

Magiere could guess what Chap had said.

"I am smaller than any of you," Wayfarer went on. "Covered in a plain brown cloak and leading a black dog, no one would notice me."

Magiere wasn't about to let the girl fall into the hands of the anmaglâhk, and grasped Wayfarer by the shoulders. "You can't walk around the port, not even with Chap. What if you *were* spotted? Have you thought of that?"

—I can protect her—

Magiere ignored Chap, but Wayfarer frowned as she looked to Brot'an. "Greimasg'äh?"

Brot'an had grown too quiet, and that worried Magiere when he looked at her.

"The girl and the majay-hì need only look for the larger ships," he said. "Find one with a captain willing to take passengers, and then arrange for payment."

"No!" Leesil insisted.

"I agree, they cannot go alone," Brot'an added. "I agree that I cannot be seen walking openly around on the docks . . . and neither can you. Wayfarer may be the only one who can blend well enough. I will trail her and Chap to the port but hide off the open waterfront, exposing my presence only should a threat occur." He looked to Magiere. "If you had a better option than what you have already tried, you would have said so. We must find passage and leave this port."

Magiere's thoughts were blank; she didn't have a better option.

Brot'an turned to Wayfarer. "I will teach you how to walk in a way that will support a guise."

Magiere took a step back in defeat and then studied Chap. "We'll need a bucket of coal."

Leesil didn't look fully convinced, either, but he didn't argue. "We'll have to do something with his ears, too."

Chap hopped off the bed.

—No one . . . is touching . . . my ears—

Magiere crossed her arms. "You think not?"

Midmorning of the same day, Dänvârfij—Fated Music—stood at the prow of a small Numan trading vessel called the *Falcon* as it maneuvered into dock at Soráno. Leaning on the rail, she looked out across the port and strained for a glimpse of a large cargo ship bearing the name *Cloud Queen*.

No such ship or any of its size was in sight.

A few of the sailors glanced her way, as she and her small team had remained below deck for most of the short voyage. As she did now, she had often worn a cloak with its hood pulled over her head when she left her cabin, so some of the men still tried for a curious glimpse.

To them she would appear overly tall and slender, with strands of long white-blond hair escaping the hood if the wind was too strong. She pushed such back inside her hood, exposing one pointed ear for an instant.

Any human aboard would have paused at the sight of her slanted, oversized eyes with large amber irises in a darkly tanned face too narrow to be human. And from that they would think her one of the Lhoin'na, the elves she had heard about of this continent. But her homeland was half a world away in a place that humans near there called the Elven Territories.

Ignoring the sailors, Dänvârfij continued studying the harbor.

The sailors soon began throwing lines to men on the pier. None of them hurried, and she did not know whether she wished them to or not. Such complacency was unworthy, but the task she had been given had begun to feel endless.

"You should not carry anything," said a deep voice behind her. "At least not yet. Let me do it."

"The wound is not as bad as it seems," a female voice answered. "I can carry my own pack while you assist the Covârleasa."

Dänvârfij turned her head to see her three remaining companions, a man and two women, coming out of the aftcastle door in preparation for disembarking. Like herself, all three of them were an'Cróan and Anmaglâhk.

Though Én'nish's complexion was tan, and her hair white blond like nearly all an'Cróans', she was smaller and slighter of build than most. Her size was a deception she used in combat to an advantage. She was also reckless, as well as poisoned by their people's grief madness after she had lost her mate-to-be to Léshil's blade.

From the start Dänvârfij had opposed Én'nish's inclusion in their purpose, but at least the young one had proven to be a survivor when others had not. Én'nish had taken a blade wound across her stomach in the last battle with their quarry, back in that degenerate human port called Drist. And again it had been Léshil who had done this.

Rhysís stood towering over Én'nish. His hair was even a lighter shade than hers. He always wore it loose, and it whipped in the wind. None of them now wore the forest gray cloaks and clothing of the Anmaglâhk; they traveled disguised in human clothing. For some reason that Dänvârfij could not fathom, Rhysís had developed an apparent liking for the color blue, even to the dark cloak he wore. His outer arm supported the final surviving member of their team, which had been eleven in count when they had left their homeland.

Rhysís released his hold on Fréthfâre—Watcher of the Woods—once she took her hand from his arm. She leaned heavily on a walking rod as she slid one foot after the other, stepping forward under her own power with great effort.

These were all that Dänvârfij had left with which to hunt the monster Magiere; her mate, Léshil; the deviant one they called Chap; and the traitor greimasg'äh . . . Brot'ân'duivé.

"How soon can we disembark?" Fréthfâre demanded, though her voice was strained with weariness.

Dänvârfij did not answer at first. In Fréthfâre's eyes, even the leisure of the crew in docking the ship would be seen as Dänvârfij's fault.

Fréthfâre held status as shared leader of the team, but she was fit in neither body nor mind. Perhaps not even in spirit. Her wheat-gold hair, uncommon for an an'Cróan, hung in waves instead of lying silky and straight. In youth she had been viewed as supple and graceful, but now she was unseasonably brittle as she approached a mere fifty years . . . barely half or less of the number most would see in a lifetime. The human red dress and light but limp cloak she wore made her appear all the more fragile.

Once Covârleasa—"Trusted Advisor"—to Most Aged Father, Fréthfâre was nearly useless now. More than two years ago, the monster Magiere had run a sword through Fréthfâre's abdomen. The wound should have killed her, but a great an'Cróan healer had tended her. Even so she had barely survived, and the damage would never be wholly undone.

Dänvârfij was ever vigilant in showing respect for the ex-Covârleasa. "Soon," she finally answered. "Once the ramp is set, and then . . ."

She trailed off, for she was still calculating their next step.

A year and a half ago, when Most Aged Father had asked her to prepare a team and sail to this foreign continent, she had not hesitated. Their purpose then had been direct and clear. They were to locate Magiere; her half-blood consort, Léshil; and the tainted majay-hì who ran with the pair. Magiere and Léshil were to be captured, tortured if necessary concerning the "artifact" they had carried off from the Pock Peaks, and then eliminated—along with the majay-hì if possible. The last of that had not sat well with Dänvârfij's team, even Én'nish, though Fréthfâre had not blinked.

Never before had so many jointly taken up the same purpose. Their task had been of dire importance in the eyes of Most Aged Father, who feared any device of the Ancient Enemy remaining in human hands. Eleven anmaglâhk had left together, but one more had shadowed them across the world. After the first and second deaths among them, before they knew for certain, Dänvârfij could not bring herself to believe who that one had to be.

Only on the night when she had glimpsed his unmistakable shadow had she acknowledged the truth.

Brot'ân'duivé, that traitor, had been stealing their lives, one by one, ever since.

Yet they could not stop or turn back. They could not fail Most Aged Father.

"Pull up your hoods," Dänvârfij ordered.

The ramp was soon lowered to the pier, and, without asking, Rhysís took both packs from Én'nish. She did not argue. Dänvârfij stepped in to assist Fréthfâre, and all four departed the ship and headed up the pier into this city called Soráno. It would have been preferable to make port in the night: Dänvârfij did not doubt that the traitor would be watching the dock if he was here. However, as yet, she did not know whether her quarry had stopped here, let alone remained.

"Our first task is to confirm their arrival or continued presence," Fréthfâre whispered, leaning heavily upon Dänvârfij's arm. "Or if they have simply come and gone. I do not see the *Cloud Queen* anywhere in the harbor."

"Nor do I," Dänvârfij said.

The four of them left the waterfront and made their way through a surprisingly clean and organized city—a relief after the filth and chaos of their previous stop. Olive-skinned people in colorful clothing glanced curiously at them, but not with any surprise, as if the locals were used to the sight of what they called "elves." That puzzled Dänvârfij as passersby smiled and nodded. She replied in kind to blend in, and kept moving, helping Fréthfâre down the street.

Though she would never admit it, she was faintly repulsed by the closeness of the crippled woman hanging on her. As they passed a shadowed cutway between two buildings, she glanced back at Én'nish and Rhysís, and nodded. All four of them stepped into the shadows.

"I will make inquiries more easily on my own," she said. "Rhysís, take Én'nish and Fréthfâre to find an inn, and meet me here when finished. We will plan from there once we have viable information." As a mere afterthought, she looked to Fréthfâre. "If this seems wise to you as well."

She knew the ex-Covârleasa was already beyond the limit of her fading strength, but Fréthfâre merely nodded instead of uttering one of her typical accusatory barbs. Such words no longer stung Dänvârfij, and Rhysís took her place in aiding the cripple among them.

Dänvârfij left her companions behind and slipped up the cutway to the connecting alley behind the buildings. She gathered herself in a rare moment of solitude before stepping out of the alley's far end to head back toward the waterfront. In a port of this size, there had to be at least some small place that served as a harbormaster's office.

All such thoughts fled her mind as she turned onto the waterfront's main walkway.

Two tall men walking toward her fixed their amber irises—in lightly tan triangular faces—on her.

Dänvârfij took in their strange wheat-colored hair, pulled back and up in identical fashion in high tails held by single silver rings. The narrow tips of the men's elongated ears were plain to see. They were garbed in tawny leather vestments with swirling steel garnishes to match sparkling armor on their shoulders. Each bore a sash the color of pale gold running diagonally over his chest. Long and narrow sword hilts, slightly curved, protruded over their right shoulders.

Dänvârfij lost her composure for an instant and stared. They were an'Cróan . . . and not an'Cróan.

Her people did not carry swords, and the anmaglâhk kept their weapons hidden. Her people did not dress in accoutrements that sparkled and drew such attention. As the men, walking proudly, strode closer toward her, one slowed while staring at her with equal surprise. His skin was not as dark as hers or any of her people's, though she was tall enough to look him in the eyes.

This continent possessed its own people, somehow akin to hers, called the Lhoin'na, but she had never encountered any of them in her travels. Perhaps this port was closer to their territory than that of other humans. And this pair's matching garb hinted at some kind of military.

A sliver of anxiety crept in as both men closed the distance, walking right up to her . . . studying her as if they were uncertain whether she was one of them.

Dänvârfij knew that by her own people's standards she was not a beauty. Her nose was a bit too long and her cheekbones a bit too wide, and then there were her scars. All anmaglâhk had scars. Worse, she was dressed like some vagabond human in faded breeches, a shirt and vest, and a worn cloak over the top.

It was not a wonder that these two stared at her.

The one on the left, slightly taller and more angular of face than his companion, bowed his head slightly.

"May we be of service?" he asked. "Are you searching for something?"

It took Dänvârfij a moment to understand him. His accent was thick and strange. Some of his words were disordered and incorrectly constructed, but his voice held a tone of authority. His expression was openly concerned, like some guardian meeting one of his own alone in a human settlement.

When she did not immediately answer him, his expression grew even more concerned, then uncomfortable, followed by a hint of embarrassment. He bowed his head again quickly and put his hand to his chest.

"Forgive me. I am Arálan of the a'Ghràihlôn'na Shé'ith," he said, and then gestured to his companion. "Gän'wer."

Dänvârfij was on uncertain ground. Did Arálan feel he had breached some code of manners by not introducing himself? She merely nodded to each of them, and the first appeared confused and more than a little curious about her. She had no intention of telling him where she was from, but one word he had said clung in her thoughts.

Shé'ith.

It was halfway familiar, for in her tongue—the true tongue of her people—the root word *séthiv* meant the state and nature of "tranquility" or perhaps "serenity." If it meant the same in their dialect, then that word for these Lhoin'na might place them in their culture as a guardian caste similar to the Anmaglâhk . . . a term that meant "thief—or thieves—of lives." The mandate of the Anmaglâhk was to take back the people's way of life from any who would steal it from them.

She had to say something, and she glanced up and down the waterfront as if she was lost.

"Harbormaster?" she asked, hoping the one word was close enough to how they would say it and that her accent did not sound too strange to them.

Both men frowned slightly. The second lifted his head with furrowed eyebrows, but the first turned and pointed down the way to a narrow building jutting out slightly between a warehouse and what might be either a tavern or place of prepared foods.

"There," he said, and then he took a quick breath. "Where are you from?"

Dänvârfij had to disengage immediately.

"My thanks," she said with a nod, and moved on, walking past them. She felt their eyes on her but heard no hurried steps trying to catch her. And there were enough people crowded around the spot she sought that she quickly blocked herself from sight. Only when she neared the harbormaster's office and stepped in beside its door did she glance back.

The two Lhoin'na—Shé'ith—were moving onward again. Stranger still, most of the little humans of the place showed them deference or even smiled and greeted them warmly. For one moment the pair paused to speak with a young woman with two children clinging to her skirt. And the first one, who had spoken to Dänvârfij, bowed his head with a hand over his heart.

These Shé'ith were respected here and even welcomed.

An idea came to Dänvârfij.

She turned back through the crowd to follow the pair. A visit to the harbormaster could wait briefly until she finished one new task.

CHAPTER FIVE

With a stab of guilt, Wynn sighed with a welcome sense of renewed freedom. Gripping the railing of *The Thorn*, she looked out across the waves at midmorning. She loved to journey, whether by land or sea, but, given the reason for this voyage, taking pleasure in the wind in her face still felt wrong.

"It is good to see you happy," someone said in Elvish from behind her.

Wynn turned to find Osha, his hair loose and waving in the breeze, standing a few paces off. Dressed in breeches and a dark brown vestment, he hardly looked like the young anmaglâhk she'd once traveled beside. Unfortunately she liked the look of him better this way.

Chane was dormant below in his bunk, and Shade had stayed in the cabin as well, possibly in case Nikolas came knocking. And since Osha had come up by himself, Nikolas was probably still in their cabin.

Wynn couldn't help feeling too *alone* with Osha, even though the sailors were going about their duties. Suddenly she didn't feel so happy anymore.

"I'm sorry," she said without thinking, "considering what we are investigating. I just felt so . . . confined at the guild."

Osha stepped up beside her. "Do not be sorry. I felt the same. There is no shame in happiness when it becomes rare."

At least he appeared less angry now—less intent on trying to dredge up the past. Although, at the moment, she was not so inclined to completely avoid all elements of the past. The memories Shade had shown her rose in her thoughts: of Osha's being shown a smooth stone and forced to leave Leanâlhâm and Gleann.

Wynn was careful not to betray any of this in her expression as Osha pointed behind her. When she looked, two barrels rested against the thick center mast, but there was a space between them.

"Do you remember our voyage down the eastern coastline of my continent?" he asked, his voice even softer now. "And how we sat in little spaces on the ship of my people and played at Dreug'an . . . or talked?"

Wynn swallowed hard. She remembered all too clearly passing the time with him and listening to him tell her things he'd never told anyone. She also knew exactly what he was doing now.

He had questions of his own for her—about her—and topics that *he* wanted to discuss. Perhaps in his current mood that would not be such a bad thing. Without a word, Wynn turned toward the mast, sank down between the barrels, and only then looked up at Osha.

Osha froze as Wynn turned away, and then grew confused as she simply settled between the barrels and looked up at him.

He had been angry the previous evening when that undead thing had forced his way into sharing her cabin. Instinct screamed at him to intervene, but, as Wynn had not openly objected, there had been nothing he could do.

In the night he had realized that an open conflict with that monster would not serve him where she was concerned. Such behavior would only push her further away.

Upon waking this morning, while the young sage, Nikolas, still slept fitfully, Osha realized he had one new advantage: Wynn would no longer spend her days in study or hiding away with Premin Hawes. And Chane would lie *dead* for the day and unable to get in the way.

Osha might have Wynn to himself under the sun.

She'd told him that, once they landed, they would travel by night, but for now they traveled by sea. With a little time he might regain some of what they had lost when last together. No one had ever spoken—or listened—to him in the way she once had.

But now Osha looked at her almost with suspicion. He had not expected her to respond so quickly. Was she inviting him to sit with her and share as they once had?

Slowly he walked over and settled beside her.

"Not all of that journey was so pleasant," she said, pushing a mass of her wispy light brown hair from her face. "The Pock Peaks were difficult."

He had not even had to prod her in this, and he nodded carefully, saying nothing.

"Afterward was even worse." She whispered this time. "The journey through the Everfen and . . . Sgäile's death . . ."

Osha did not want to speak of Sgäilsheilleache's death and looked away.

"But then Magiere and Leesil's wedding . . . and that was a good day," Wynn went on.

Osha turned his head back to find her looking up; even sitting on the deck she was still much shorter than he was. And, yes, that day—and that evening with her—was one of his best memories, no matter the sorrows he had carried then.

". . . And then you and I said good-bye on the docks of Bela."

There—she finally spoke of it, admitted that it had happened. But now that those words were out in the open, he grew lost for what to say.

Wynn shifted a little, turning more toward him with her eyes still on his.

"What happened then?" she asked almost fiercely. "I know you had to go home and tell Leanâlhâm and Gleann about Sgäile, as well as deliver the journal I prepared to Brot'an. Something happened after that, and you were pulled away from them. What happened to you?"

Every muscle in Osha's body tightened as he stared at her. How did she know he had been pulled away? Had Leanâlhâm spoken of things she should not have?

"Tell me," Wynn whispered.

Was that what it would take? He wanted to close the gap between them, one that had begun in their short time together in Miiska and had seemingly widened to a chasm now that he had found her again. Part of him longed to tell her everything, but he feared how she might react to certain things.

Some secrets should never be told to others. There were torments—falls and failures—to be borne in silence, especially with those who mattered most. Least of those secrets, but most of all to others, was her journal.

Wynn still expectantly watched him, and Osha lowered his eyes.

So little within the journal had mattered much to those who did not know her as he did. But the mentions in those pages of an "artifact"—an orb, to those who knew better—had been used by Most Aged Father and Brot'ân'duivé to start an open war among the people. If Osha had known then what he knew now, he might have burned that journal before he ever reached home.

Even so, he could not have done that. The journal—and its too-simple account of their journey together—was all that he had had of her.

Osha studied Wynn's oval face: she was a human he had come to know as so different from all he had been taught in his youth. And she was even more than just different. She was unique to him.

"It began with another journey," he whispered, and . . .

After Osha was forced away from the Coilehkrotall's main enclave, he had followed Brot'ân'duivé through their people's forests for three days. He could not stop thinking of how he had left Gleannéohkân'thva and Leanâlhâm in mourning and was not there to share their grief or to comfort them.

This was also a way to avoid thinking on the reason for this sudden, rushed journey.

The smooth stone that bore his name etched by small claws.

Three days into the forest, as the sun glimmered through the canopy overhead, Brot'ân'duivé halted suddenly and looked back along their path.

"Continue on," he whispered. "I will catch up."

With a puzzled glance back the way they had come, Osha obeyed and jogged onward, wondering what had given the greimasg'äh such pause. He did not have long to wait.

Soon after, Brot'ân'duivé came dashing from the forest, not bothering to be silent. Without stopping, he signaled to Osha to run.

Osha did, but Brot'ân'duivé caught up and took the lead, changing directions many times. The greimasg'äh finally stopped and crouched down beneath the bright leaves of a squat maple. Osha, utterly confused, dropped beside him.

"We are followed," Brot'ân'duivé whispered. "I can no longer come with you, and we must act quickly now."

Osha rocked backward on his haunches and braced against the maple to keep from toppling. Who would follow them? More important, it was impossible for him to continue alone.

"But, Greimasg'äh . . ." he whispered, "only caste elders know the exact way to the Burning Ones."

Young initiates were blindfolded for part of their journey. Even those given assent by their jeóin did not learn those last steps until many years—if ever—into their lives of service. Osha would require a guide.

Brot'ân'duivé snatched Osha by the front of his forest gray vestment.

"Listen," he hissed. "You will travel like the wind to the coastline where the Branch Mountains, what the humans call the Crown Range, meet the eastern coast at the far corner of our territory. . . ."

"Greimasg'äh!" Osha whispered loudly. "Do not break the covenant!"

Telling Osha these things would breach a most sacred oath between the Chein'âs and the Anmaglâhk.

"Quiet!" Brot'ân'duivé ordered.

The greimasg'äh poured out secrets into the forest air, and Osha was powerless to stop him.

Brot'ân'duivé told him how to reach the cave of the Burning Ones on his own. No one should know these things until proven fit to do so. By the time the greimasg'äh finished, Osha had gone numb in disbelief that any of this was happening.

It was not over, for there was worse to come.

Rising, Brot'ân'duivé looked all around, and then walked off toward a patch of bright light in a break among the trees.

"What are you doing?" Osha asked, barely trusting himself to speak.

"Be silent and follow. Do not speak again until instructed to do so."

When the greimasg'äh reached the clearing's edge, he halted and gestured for Osha to stay back. Only then did the master anmaglâhk step to the clearing's center and close his eyes.

Cold grew in the pit of Osha's stomach, though he was lost as to what was happening. Moments slipped by . . . until a heavy footfall made his gaze shift instantly.

Out among the trees beyond the clearing's far side, two branches among a cluster of cedars moved. Then the limbs separated from the others and drifted out around the tree into view. Below them came a long equine head with two crystalline blue eyes larger than those of a majay-hì.

Any deer would be small next to this great sacred being, as large as an elk or any human's horse. Its long silver-gray coat ran shaggily over its shoulders and across its wide chest. What had at first appeared to be branches were the horns rising high over its head in two smooth curves without tines.

Osha's voice choked in his throat until he whispered one word. "Clhuassas!"

The "listeners" were among the oldest sacred beings, like the majay-hì, who guarded the an'Cróan lands from all interlopers. He had seen one of them only three times in his life, and always from afar. That it stood so close to the greimasg'äh was somehow disturbing.

"My thanks," Brot'ân'duivé whispered.

Osha realized what the greimasg'äh had done. Brot'ân'duivé had somehow called a clhuassas, but how . . . and why?

The sacred one stalked slowly into the clearing, and sunlight made its coat shimmer like threads made from the metal of Anmaglâhk blades. Its eyes appeared almost too bright to look upon, and Osha shied away from doing so. More shocking was when it stepped up to the aging greimasg'äh and lowered its great head.

Brot'ân'duivé put his forehead against the bridge of the sacred one's nose.

It snorted and then stamped a forehoof once that made the ground shudder under Osha's feet. But the sacred one did no more than that and became still.

"Osha," the greimasg'äh said. "Come . . . now."

Hesitantly, Osha inched into the clearing. "What are you doing?"

"Climb onto its back," Brot'ân'duivé ordered.

Osha froze as the cold in his belly raced through his bones. "No! I will not ride one of our sacred creatures like some beast of burden!"

"It has already been too long since I received the stone!" Brot'ân'duivé answered angrily. "And this one will carry you far more swiftly than you can run. It has agreed to do this. . . . Now mount."

And then Brot'ân'duivé took out the smooth message stone and thrust it out.

Osha stared in horror between the stone and the listener. Worse, the sacred one swung its head toward him. It watched him as if those large unblinking eyes could see every flaw or failing within him. It took a step.

"This is its choice," Brot'ân'duivé said. "Climb on."

Still caught in disbelief at what was being asked of him, Osha fixated on the words *its choice*. Swallowing hard, he took the stone. Averting his eyes, he stepped in carefully at the sacred one's side and reached up.

When his fingers closed on the mane down the back of the listener's broad neck, he grew sick inside and faltered.

This was sacrilege.

Somehow Osha pulled himself up and swung his leg over; he snatched his hands away from touching the clhuassas.

Brot'ân'duivé stepped closer. "In silence and in shadow."

Osha would neither look at the greimasg'äh nor repeat the oath of his caste. The clhuassas lunged without warning, and Osha was forced to grab its neck. It raced off through the trees too quickly, and Brot'ân'duivé was gone from his sight.

The few days and nights that followed became a blur.

By what Osha could estimate, from where he left the greimasg'äh, the listener had to carry him roughly seventy-five or eighty leagues. He did not know how far it could travel in one day or night, especially in the densest parts of the forest. His mind and heart were both so shaken and sickened on the first day that he did not even pay attention to the distance covered. He barely noticed tree branches rushing past his head as he held on and allowed himself to be carried eastward.

By evening, hunger and thirst and exhaustion began to take their toll, and those awakened the part of him that had curled up inside. He did not know how he could—should—properly address the one who carried him.

Finally desperation drove him to whisper, "Stop . . . please."

The sacred one slowed to a halt and remained motionless.

Osha slid to the ground, and his legs gave way beneath him. He had never ridden any animal, let alone another true being. As he crumpled on the ground, the silver-gray clhuassas stepped farther into the brush and swung its head from one side to the other . . . until its great head came fully around, and those huge crystal-blue eyes pierced him.

The sacred one exhaled slowly, snorted at him, and stomped one hoof.

Osha struggled to his feet, but his legs still shook as he stumbled closer.

There beyond the clhuassas was a vine low to the ground and filled with ripe bisselberries, purple and plump. He dropped to his knees and began to eat, taking advantage of both the food and its moisture. He ate them, bitter skins and all, but, halfway through gorging himself, he froze and stared at the berries in his stained hands.

Osha heard the clhuassas breathing behind him. When he slowly looked up, he then shriveled inside under the sacred one's gaze. It had carried him—*him*, not even a full anmaglâhk now that he had lost his teacher, his jeóin. And here he was stuffing himself in front of it.

How shameful!

Osha averted his gaze as he slowly raised his cupped hands. When he felt its muzzle, as large as either of his hands, touch his fingertips, he shuddered. And then he felt its tongue drag over his hands and the berries. When he dared to look up, all he could do was stare.

It would be one moment he could never forget, for when the clhuassas halted and lifted its head to look at him, he lowered his hands to find he still held three bisselberries. And the listener snorted at him again.

How long had it taken him to understand?

Even when he ate those berries, somewhat slick with saliva, he was still uncertain. Each time he gathered more and offered them up, the sacred one left three behind for him. Finally it turned away and stood silent for a moment, and when it looked his way, it closed its eyes and hung its head in stillness.

Osha did not know what to do at first. He merely settled where he was. Later, not realizing he had fallen asleep, he woke with a start at hearing—feeling—thunder in the ground beneath him.

The sacred one stood waiting.

This was how the following days and nights passed, with Osha clinging to the back of the clhuassas, their journey broken only by intermittent stops for rest in which the sacred one found them food or a stream from which to drink. At some time over one following night, when dawn came, Osha could feel that his guardian was growing weary.

Nothing he did or said convinced it to slow or halt for longer rests. Even when he grew bold enough to plead and beg, it pressed onward. As they drew nearer to the coast, and the trees and brush grew sparser, water became more difficult to find.

One morning, after sleeping only part of a night, Osha woke up so thirsty that his mouth was too dry to speak. The clhuassas stood waiting and watching him. When he climbed onto its back, to his surprise, it turned north and bolted. Osha knew they needed to be heading southeast.

"Stop!" he tried to say through cracked lips, but it did not listen.

Not longer after, it halted. When Osha looked down, his gaze met the sight of a trickling creek. In relief he dropped to the ground and drank his fill. This time he did not flinch at thunder in the ground when the clhuassas stepped in beside him to do the same.

No water had ever tasted so good, and no moment of his life had ever been so serene. Though it did not relieve his grief in losing his teacher, his shame for abandoning Leanâlhâm and Gleannéohkân'thva, or his suspicions concerning the greimasg'äh . . .

That moment of silence beside a sacred one, with only the soft sound of trickling water, would be remembered. This was the way the world should have been and was not.

When they resumed their journey, the sacred one turned southeast again. After a hard and long run, it stopped past nightfall. Osha slid off, knowing now that food and water would be close by. He found a patch of odd wild berries, all red as blood and covered in tiny seeds, he had never seen before. These were far sweeter than the skins of bisselberries.

They shared another meal, and Osha curled up beneath the bare trunk of a tall and spindling pine. He never got to close his eyes, let alone sleep, before the clhuassas walked over and lowered its head, and he could feel its breath on his face.

Osha did not know what to do this time. He had never asked for this journey, but a being sacred to his people had seen him safely this far, never leaving him to struggle onward on his own.

"My thanks," he whispered.

Osha froze stiff as the sacred one pressed its soft, gray nose against his forehead. A feeling of peace swept through him, like that moment by the creek, and he fell asleep without even realizing, until . . .

When he opened his eyes again, he was alone in the dawn.

It took a few moments for him to realize the listener was nowhere in sight. He scrambled up and looked around, uncertain of where he was. The sound of crashing waves reached his ears, and he stepped off over a rise toward that distant roar. Not long after, he spotted the edge of the thin woods and looked down toward a coastal settlement.

Small boats lined the few narrow docks, and two ships floated in a tiny bay formed by twin streams running into the sea. As he looked upon the settlement, all of the remaining sensation from his last night with the sacred one vanished.

Osha headed down the gradual slope to find passage farther south. . . .

Wynn didn't even realize she'd stopped breathing until Osha went silent and looked down again from where he sat beside her. She took a sudden breath, and any question of what had happened next caught in her throat. All she could think of was that Fay-descended creature that had . . .

"The greimasg'äh, and I . . . and *you*," Osha whispered, "are the only ones I know of who have ever been so close to one of them."

At first Wynn wasn't certain what he meant.

One time in his land, when Leesil had needed to find his mother, Chap had gone off into the wild on his own. Wynn had snuck out after him, even though the an'Cróan forest would quickly confuse her—or anyone not an'Cróan. She was almost instantly lost, but Chap had found her and so had a pack of wild majay-hì, which had included Chap's future mate, Lily.

The only way Wynn had been able to keep up with the racing pack in Chap's search for Leesil's mother was . . .

"You and I," Osha added, "are the only ones I know who have ever been gifted with their aid, in carrying us."

Yes, in Chap's racing search with the pack, a listener had carried her.

Osha hung his head. Whatever tense harshness had shown in his long features since she had first seen him in Calm Seatt appeared to fade.

For just a moment Wynn saw the Osha of past, better days. And though to be Anmaglâhk was all that he had ever wanted, it was his innocent wonder that made him so much better than any of them in her eyes.

"But it left you . . . before you even reached your destination," she said too quickly.

Osha looked over at her, and some brief confusion passed across his face.

"No . . ." he stammered, as if baffled. "It made certain I would hear the waves upon waking."

Wynn wanted to curse herself, and not only for having stalled him now that he was talking. The Osha of old vanished before her eyes, replaced by that harsher, hardened one. It hurt her to see that.

"But you found passage?" she asked, trying to urge him onward.

"Of course," he whispered, looking away. "I was Anmaglâhk. My people would do anything to serve them."

For an instant Wynn hung upon those two words—*I was* rather than *I am*—and then Osha's suddenly cold voice pulled her onward. . . .

Osha had no trouble gaining free passage on a small, single-masted fishing vessel. That was best, for it had no destination for passengers or cargo that would be delayed in serving his need. The following day, when he boarded, the boat's master and her small crew were more than happy to assist an anmaglâhk. He did his best to smile, and he was more than grateful in his manners, though what he had asked of them was not by his choice.

That first day, sailing south down the eastern coast, heading beyond his people's territories, was when he began to truly contemplate the stone inside the pocket of his forest gray cloak.

What unknown reasons did the Chein'âs—the Burning Ones—have for summoning him, of all the Anmaglâhk, a second time?

He could not find an answer.

Worse, over the next two days, now that he no longer clung to the back of the clhuassas, he had too much time to think. He dwelled upon the faces of Leanâlhâm and Gleannéohkân'thva locked in grief with no help or comfort. But on the third day he began watching the shoreline, as Brot'ân'duivé had given him clear instructions regarding what to look for.

When the beach came into view and he saw a distant mountain's peak line up with that place, his chest began to ache. He found it hard to even breathe as he left the bow to approach the ship's master. He was given what meager supplies he asked for without hesitation from the crew.

Osha felt all the more unworthy in that he was here only because a greimasg'äh had broken a sacred oath. And yet the summons could not be refused, or sacred ties to the Chein'âs might be damaged—and Osha would not be responsible for that. If the Chein'âs called to him, he would answer.

So he stepped down into the lowered skiff and allowed himself to be rowed to the shore. Once he was alone again, he turned inland toward the peaks.

He could still hear Brot'ân'duivé's voice driving through his mind like a knife.

The last time he had made this journey, he had been blindfolded while following an elder member of the caste, but he knew it had taken three days. Now he walked with his eyes open as he headed straight toward a mountain in the distance . . . until he saw another, closer one with a broken top.

There were streams along the way, providing both freshwater and fish. He tried not to think beyond his daily needs. He did take the time to find a stout branch, and, using supplies taken from the fishing vessel, he fashioned himself a torch. He knew it would be needed.

It was late the third day when he located the chute. Its bottom end was partially hidden by an overhang. He would have never noticed it without knowing exactly what he was looking for.

He remembered having climbed it while blindfolded, and how he had nearly slipped on the loose, rocky debris in its bottom. After one last hesitation, Osha entered the chute and climbed upward until he reached the mouth of a tunnel . . . where he stopped and lingered.

It was a while longer before he knelt to strike flint against a stiletto to light his torch. He forced one foot in front of the other, inside and downward, until echoes of his steps were all he heard rolling along the dark and rough stone walls. He traveled deeper underground as the tunnel turned this way and that, until he began to feel slightly dizzy and the air grew uncomfortably warm.

The walls were craggy, but the floor smoothed out, and then suddenly he stepped from the tunnel into a cavern. His eyes instantly locked on the space's only prominent feature.

A large oval of shimmering metal, taller than himself, was embedded in the far wall.

Taking shallow breaths in the heated air, he crossed to it. Raising the torch in his left hand, he ran his gaze downward over the metal. His eyes followed the barely visible razor-straight seam. The oval appeared to be split down the center into two halves, but he saw no handle or way to open them. Orange-yellow torchlight glimmered on their perfect, polished surfaces, a bleached silver tone too light for steel.

The portal was made of the same material as his tools and weapons of an anmaglâhk.

Osha stared at it as he thought back to when Brot'ân'duivé had forced him into this journey.

Once in the cavern, you will know what to do. And when you reach the portal of the Burning Ones' white metal—

Osha had cut off the greimasg'äh and not allowed him to finish. Here and now there was no need, for this was not his first glimpse of the doors. The first time he had come here, he had been allowed to remove his blindfold once he stood in this stone chamber. The path here was kept a secret, but all Anmaglâhk were trusted enough to bear witness to what came next.

Osha reached up his left sleeve with his right hand and pulled a stiletto from its hidden sheath. Reaching out, he touched the blade's matching metal to that of the portal.

The portal split down its hair-thin line as it began to open. . . .

"Wynn, are you out here?"

Osha fell silent, looking up as Wynn jumped slightly at Nikolas's call. She barely saw Osha drop his head, and then he called out before she could.

"We here."

Frustration washed through Wynn, and then anger, as she watched Osha's expression close up. It had taken so long to find the right moment to get him to tell her the missing gaps in his past . . . to tell her what had changed him so much.

Nikolas came walking over.

His hair wasn't combed, and he had dark circles under his eyes.

Still angry with him for interrupting, she felt suddenly guilty. At least he was out of his cabin.

"I knocked on your door, but no one answered," Nikolas said. "I couldn't lie there in that bunk any longer, and I . . . I was hungry. Maybe that's good, as I haven't felt that since . . ."

Wynn knew the rest: since the letter from his father had arrived. She tried to smile, to hide any resentment at the interruption.

"It is a good sign," she confirmed as she rose, though Osha hadn't moved. "I have a friend who can't keep any food down while on a ship."

Wynn held one hand down to Osha. It took another moment before he looked up—at her hand and not her. After a few blinks he rose, though he didn't take her hand. And she looked once more to Nikolas.

"Chane is resting, but we'll get Shade and head down to the galley and find some breakfast."

With a quick nod, Nikolas headed off for the door in the aftcastle wall, but when Osha took a step to follow, Wynn touched his arm. Stoic and silent, he looked down at her.

"Later," she whispered, "and . . . thank you."

She forced her hand into his and pulled him along.

CHAPTER SIX

By the middle of the same day that Wayfarer had convinced her companions to allow her to take *some* kind of action, she and Chap stepped out of the harbormaster's office and looked all around the port of Sorάno. She was thankful that, before doing a blind search, Chap had insisted they stop at the office to check on new arrivals. To Wayfarer's great surprise, they now had more of a plan than she had anticipated.

Since Magiere's earlier morning visit to the harbormaster, two ships had arrived, both heading south for il'Dha'ab Najuum. One was a private Numan trader out of Drist called the *Falcon*. The other was a Suman cargo vessel with a strange name she could barely pronounce, the *Djinn*, arrived from the south to exchange standard goods and then return to the Suman Empire.

"Should we try the Numan vessel first?" she asked softly, gripping the end of a rope.

The rope's other end was looped around Chap's neck, and again Wayfarer almost apologized for all of the indignities that had been forced upon him.

Not long ago, at his insistence, she had finally begun calling him by that name. The idea of forcing a name on any creature, let alone a sacred one, had been—was—abhorrent. But she did wish to follow his guidance, and he wished to be called by that name. At the moment, however, he hardly looked like a sacred majay-hì.

Then again, she did not look like herself, either.

Wayfarer took some of the blame for this, for their disguises had mostly been her idea. If only she had realized how far Léshil was going to take her suggestion.

He had insisted that she stuff wads of extra clothing beneath her own to make her look fat. The greimasg'äh had then tasked her to learn to walk like an old, feeble woman. Léshil added an oversized cloak, purposefully made filthy, and a gnarled stick for a walking cane that he had scavenged from somewhere in the large inn.

Getting to the port in that stooped, hobbling fashion had left Wayfarer with an ache in her lower back. But the poor majay-hì . . . Poor Chap was in a much worse state.

He was covered in so much crushed and powdered charcoal that he was almost completely black. And of course he paused often to scratch. Wayfarer more than once warned him to stop or he might reveal his true colors instead.

Worse again, Léshil had wrapped up Chap's muzzle with leather straps to make him appear dangerous to others, so they would keep away. And the straps' ends were tied at the back of his head to pin down his ears. Léshil had also arranged this so that Wayfarer could give a hard jerk on the straps' ends to free Chap's jaws in an instant, should she require protection.

The poor majay-hì—Chap—looked like an untamed beast caught in the wild by savages.

"The Numan ship?" she whispered again in the language of her people, so no one nearby on the busy waterfront might catch even one word.

—I think not— . . . —the Suman first—

Chap's suggestion made her stomach feel cold.

Wayfarer had tried to hide her sadness at being forced away from the *Cloud Queen* and the only two friends she had made in this strange human world. She did understand that Magiere was pursuing an important purpose and that they must move on as quickly as possible. However, talking to people in Numanese was difficult enough without the thought of trying to interact with even more foreign Suman sailors.

Chap did not seem to notice her discomfort and went on.

—The Numan vessel came . . . from Drist— . . . —Its crew . . . and captain . . . may have heard of . . . an altercation there— . . . —A cargo vessel . . . raided after dark . . . by people . . . with . . . a large wolf— . . . —If the captain . . . heard . . . descriptions—

"Yes, I know," Wayfarer answered with a sigh.

She glanced left and right around the edges of her too-big cloak's hood. There were so many people in the crowd pushing about along the waterfront, and she wondered where Brot'ân'duivé might be hiding in all of this. He would not lose track of them, no, but that was both comforting and distressing. Never in her life had anyone watched her quite like the greimasg'äh did. He might view her as an orphan who had become his responsibility, but the lengths he went in meeting that assumed responsibility did not extend beyond making sure she was fed and sheltered and constantly watched.

Osha had been her only true friend on the long journey from her homeland, but he had chosen to remain behind in Calm Seatt . . . with Wynn.

Though that thought brought her fresh pain, she was beginning to find comfort in the reserved but fierce mothering of Magiere, and of all the unexpected others . . . in the company of Chap.

Crouching beside him, she tried to remain resolved, reminding herself again that this little scheme had been her idea.

"When we find the Suman captain, what do I say? What if he does not speak Numanese?"

—He will . . . or one of the crew— . . . —Or he would . . . not . . . sail here . . . so often—

Chap had become more skilled at raising words quickly in her head in her own tongue. He picked them out of any old memory he had caught in her mind at some time. The words sometimes came from too many different voices out of her past and gave her a small headache if he went on too long. Léshil claimed that the more memories Chap caught in someone, the more smoothly he could use them to speak with that same person, given time. It was a relief to her, for Chap was the one she now talked with most often. Still, sometimes it was unsettling to hear a majay-hì.

—Tell the captain . . . you seek . . . passage for four . . . and . . . your dog— . . . —Ask what this . . . will cost . . . and when . . . his vessel . . . sails—

Wayfarer could not help remembering what had happened to some of the last crew that had given them passage. Chap's eyes locked with hers, and she frowned, knowing he must have seen that memory and her worries.

—You can . . . do this—

"Yes," she agreed, trying to sound confident.

Those crystalline sky blue eyes were so intense that she wondered what *he* was thinking. That notion had not passed when he pressed his bound muzzle into her hand, smearing her palm with charcoal dust.

Before recent days, she had been hesitant to even touch him. She pulled her hand away and wiped it on her cloak, which was already filthy. Then she leaned over and, avoiding the soot on his muzzle, touched her cheek to just his nose. It was strange to be so familiar with one like him, after the majay-hì in her homeland had stared at her so often as if to say, *You do not belong here.*

A vivid image flashed in Wayfarer's thoughts. It was so strong that the world around her washed out of her senses for that instant. She appeared to be in the cabin of a ship. And there, to the side of a desk, was the captain of the *Cloud Queen*, sitting on the floor with a stiletto protruding from his shoulder. Suddenly she was rushing across the floor's planks and straight at the desk's front, which was somehow taller than she was.

She felt like she was running—charging—too quickly on all fours, and then she leaped up over the desk.

A snarl ripped out of her throat as she charged at a tall anmaglâhk fighting with Léshil. And Léshil swung upward with one of his winged blades, and . . .

Wayfarer sucked air in a whimpering squeak, fell on her rump, and quickly scooted backward.

Chap jerked his head up, his eyes wide.

They stared at each other as people dodged around them. But Wayfarer did not catch a single word.

What had just happened?

In the past, when Chap had watched and studied her, there had been a few moments when she had felt . . . something. At other times, such as when she had been reading in the little guild annex in Chathburh, she had a sudden sense of not being alone. When she had looked about, there he was in the archway, watching her.

The moment that had flashed in her mind was a mere instant, but Wayfarer was afraid.

—What did . . . you do?—

She scooted back again at those words in her head.

"Me?" she whispered back. "What did . . . what did you do?"

Not a word rose in her head. Still staring at her, Chap dropped on his haunches.

That moment of movement lingered in Wayfarer's head, as if she had been in it, and . . .

"Did Léshil kill . . . one of the caste who was following—?"

—Stop!—

Wayfarer flinched.

Chap was panting rapidly through his nose with his muzzle still strapped closed. He shook in a shudder, and a small cloud of charcoal dust rose from his stiffened hackles.

—We . . . will speak of this . . . later— . . . —Now we must . . . gain passage . . . on the Suman ship—

Wayfarer hesitated and then nodded slightly, relieved at the dismissal of whatever had just happened, and she was not sure she wanted to talk about it later or at all. She struggled up to her feet under the burden of all the wadded-up clothes that made her look heavy, and she picked up the gnarled old cane that she had dropped. When she reached for the fallen end of the rope around Chap's neck, she hesitated again.

"Which one is . . . is the Suman ship?"

Chap started forward, and she quickly backed out of his way.

—The slender one . . . with two masts . . . near the end of . . . this pier—

Wayfarer followed after him at the full length of the rope. He suddenly paused, and she did, too, staying back when his head swung around toward her.

—Lean over . . . and walk . . . as you . . . were taught—

Chap proceeded up the pier, and Wayfarer tried to regain her stooped shuffle. But all the while she watched his back and not where they were going. That moment in her mind that had flashed and then vanished was still fresh with the feel and sound of it.

It was not any moment that Wayfarer herself had ever lived.

Dänvârfij completed her errand, following the two Shé'ith to determine in which inn they were staying. She then returned to the waterfront and spoke briefly with the harbormaster, from whom she learned that the *Cloud Queen* had set sail the day before.

Captains stopping at any port large enough to possess a harbormaster's office were often required to report any passengers who would not reboard. The harbormaster claimed the four passengers had "disembarked" in Soráno.

As she stepped from the office and into the cutway between it and the nearest warehouse, she gained renewed hope. Likely her quarry was still here. Watching the waterfront, she studied every pier in sight and the people moving everywhere.

Dänvârfij did not expect to spot anything worthwhile. Brot'ân'duivé was far too cunning to allow anyone under his protection to wander the docks. Then she crept back to the cutway's mouth, and her gaze stopped upon a heavyset woman, covered in a cloak and leading an enormous black dog down the fourth pier.

Something about the way the woman shuffled was wrong—too affected, too quick for her age . . . too *conscious* in so much effort.

The dog and then the woman—not the other way around—boarded a slender, two-masted vessel. They remained there for a while as Dänvârfij waited, and when they finally reemerged, it was if the large dog pulled the woman along.

At the end of the pier, the dog turned without waiting for its owner and headed south along the waterfront. Both vanished in the crowds.

Dänvârfij's first instinct was to follow this odd pair, but there was still too much to accomplish this day. She glanced back at the vessel.

It was much like the Suman ship that had borne her and her team from the Isle of Wrêdelyd all the way to Drist, so it was likely from the south as well. She hesitated at leaving the shadows beside the harbormaster's office. The traitor might be hiding and watching even now from a rooftop.

Even so, instinct would not leave her be.

Dänvârfij pulled her hood farther forward, stepped out into the sun upon the waterfront, and made her way in, flowing with the crowds toward the fourth pier. After that she strode its length to the slender Suman vessel.

Strange characters were written on its bow's side; she could not read them, though they were the same script that had been on the side of the last Suman vessel she and hers had used. The ramp was down, and she was halfway up when a sailor at the top who was holding a broom spotted her.

Dänvârfij paused. "Pardon," she tried in Numanese, and hoped he understood; her skill with that human language was passable. "I am . . . separate from my friend. I think . . . was she here today?"

The sailor was young, with dusky skin and curling black hair. He looked inside Dänvârfij's hood at her tan face and amber eyes.

"I think you are right," he answered in what sounded like fluent Numanese. "Pretty girl, green eyes, with a dog? She looked a little like you. Thought she was an old woman at first, but she only limped and needed a stick."

Dänvârfij was caught most by that short, telling description—a pretty girl with green eyes who looked like an an'Cróan.

"Yes, my friend. Where she go?"

He shook his head with a shrug and frowned. "She talked to the captain, then left, but the dog got the deck filthy." He made a sweeping motion with his broom. "If you find your friend, help her clean that dog up before you come back. No more soot and black stuff on my deck."

Dänvârfij glanced once down the pier, but the girl and the dog would be long gone.

"Where ship bound?" she asked.

Sweeping again, he appeared mildly surprised. "To il'Dha'ab Najuum. We make the run back and forth. There are no other ports between here and the Suman Empire, just the desert." He frowned. "Look at this mess."

Dänvârfij turned and strode down the ramp, for she now needed guidance from Most Aged Father.

Brot'ân'duivé lay flat upon a warehouse rooftop next to the harbormaster's office. It was the optimal place from which to watch over Wayfarer and Chap. He saw them board the Suman vessel and was mildly surprised when they departed shortly after. They came straight down the pier and headed back into the city without any further stops.

Had they been successful on their first attempt? Or had something gone wrong and Chap rushed the girl back to the inn?

Brot'ân'duivé began inching back from the edge in order to follow them. Later he was uncertain what had made him pause and look back along that pier. A tall, slender figure in a weathered cloak walked up the pier toward the same ship that the girl and the majay-hì had left.

He froze on all fours atop the roof and fixed upon that one person.

The figure was fully covered and hooded, but its smooth gait of soft steps was too familiar. The figure stopped halfway up the ship's ramp for a few moments, appeared to speak with a dark-skinned sailor sweeping off the deck, and then turned around and came back down the pier at a quicker pace.

Brot'ân'duivé debated between following the cloaked figure or making certain that Wayfarer and Chap returned safely to the inn. His purpose here, by his own insistence, was to ensure the safety of the girl and the majay-hì. Frustrated, he backed away from the edge and soft-stepped to the roof's far side to go after Wayfarer and Chap.

Dänvârfij walked into the forest south of Soráno, though it was little like those with which she was familiar. The trees here were mixed somewhat with palms and other tall, broad-leafed growths. She knelt beside a gnarl-limbed tree somewhat like the coastal pines of her land. Her hands shook slightly as she reached into the side of her vestment for an oval piece of smooth, tawny wood no bigger than her palm.

It was often called a "word-wood," and this was the last one left to her team. When pressed against any tree, it let her communicate with her caste's patriarch from anywhere in the world, for it had been created from the very tree in which he now dwelled.

Reaching out, Dänvârfij pressed the word-wood against the tree's trunk and whispered, "Father?"

All of her caste called him Father.

I am here, Daughter.

At his words in her mind, she faltered. How could she begin to tell him what had occurred in Drist, that they had lost two more of their brethren to Brot'ân'duivé's blade? They were now down to four in number, and of those remaining, only she and Rhysís were in proper condition to fight.

"Father . . ." she began. "I require your guidance."

It pained her beyond measure to tell him all that had occurred since they last spoke. The words grew easier once she reached the events of that morning.

"The old woman—the girl who boarded the Suman ship—could only be Leanâlhâm," she said without doubt, "with the wayward majay-hì in disguise. They must have been arranging for passage farther south."

Where is the vessel bound?

She could feel the tightness in his voice within her thoughts. He was disappointed in her for all that had happened, though he would never chastise her. This only weighed upon her more.

"To a place called il'Dha'ab Najuum," she answered. "A sailor on board told me there are no other ports between here and the Suman Empire, only a great desert along the coast." She hesitated for an instant. "How do you counsel us to capture our quarry before they flee again?"

He remained silent for so long that she began wondering whether the link between his tree and the one she touched had been broken. And then . . .

It appears they have been striving to reach this destination all along, since they keep pressing southward. I wonder why and what they seek there.

He was quiet again for a moment.

What of the Suman vessel you commandeered in . . . Drist, was it? You killed the crew before you chose to take the Cloud Queen*?*

"Yes, Father. It was a small Suman ship called the *Bashair*. All aboard were silenced, including the captain."

She wondered why he was asking.

Can you arrange passage from your current location to il'Dha'ab Najuum?

"Possibly . . . The *Falcon*, the Numan vessel we arrived on, is heading south. I could tell the captain that we wish to travel onward."

His train of thought left her doubtful. Her first instinct was to set a trap for their quarry in this city.

Do not attempt capture in Soráno. You are spread too thinly. If the Numan vessel is fast, gain passage and get ahead of Magiere, the traitor, and all with them. Reach il'Dha'ab Najuum first and be ready for their arrival.

She hesitated to question his word, but she could not help asking, "If you feel we are too few, how can we be more assured of capturing them in the Suman port?"

Because you will arrange for assistance from the local authorities, and you are not the first of us to travel there. The Sumans are reputed to be a . . . lawful people. Listen carefully. . . .

* * *

Leesil couldn't stop pacing. His armor and weapons were strapped on, and he was ready to leave in an instant. He both tensed and exhaled in relief when a knock came at the door of their room—and sooner than he'd expected.

Magiere beat him to the door and pressed her face against it with one hand on the latch.

"It is us," said a soft voice from the other side.

Magiere jerked the door open and pulled Wayfarer inside. After Chap trotted in with a trail of charcoal dust in the air, Magiere pushed the door closed . . . almost.

A hand wrapped around the door's edge.

Leesil dropped a hand to grab the sheath tie on one of his winged punching blades as Magiere reached for the falchion on her hip.

The door shoved open, and Brot'an stepped in, shutting the door himself. But the aging assassin said nothing at first.

Leesil carefully watched Brot'an, who was usually hard to read, and Brot'an looked slightly troubled. Leesil glanced at Wayfarer, who was trying to pull the stuffing out of her clothes, and the girl appeared drawn and worried.

"What happened?" he demanded, turning to Chap. "Why are you back so soon?"

"We found passage," Wayfarer answered. "Perhaps."

Magiere lifted a pitcher from the bedside table and poured water into a clay cup.

"Come and sit down," Magiere said, pulling Wayfarer to the bed's edge and handing over the cup. "What do you mean . . . 'perhaps'?"

The girl sank onto the bed, and Leesil cast a glance at Chap. The dog wasn't saying anything, and that bothered Leesil all the more.

"There is a Suman cargo ship in dock," Wayfarer said. "I spoke with the captain, and his ship has come up from il'Dha'ab Najuum. It is here to exchange goods and cargo before returning south again. The captain said he would take us as passengers."

"All right, that's what we need," Magiere replied.

Leesil wasn't satisfied and eyed Chap again. "What's wrong?"

Wayfarer looked at the floor, and Chap still remained silent.

"The ship is not leaving for two days," the girl said, "and the captain wants ten silver pennies a person and five for Chap . . . by tomorrow to ensure our passage."

Magiere's eyes widened a bit, and even Leesil was stunned.

"Forty-five silver pennies?" Leesil asked a bit too loudly. "Just to take us to the next port south?"

When the girl flinched, Magiere shot him a glare, and he shut his mouth.

"We don't have that," Magiere said, and she exhaled, obviously just as troubled as Leesil was by all of this. "We'll have to keep looking for another ship."

"There is one," Wayfarer cut in quietly. "A Numan vessel, but it has too recently come from Drist, and Chap thinks . . . " The girl stalled, and when she looked the dog's way, they both averted their eyes from each other.

"Chap fears," Wayfarer began again, "that the ship's captain or crew may have heard of the trouble back in Drist. And maybe some heard more . . . descriptions of the three of you . . . and a large wolf."

"Trouble?" Leesil repeated. "All we did was free a hold full of slaves. Those killers following us caused all the trouble."

"No one knows that," Wayfarer countered. "They would only know there was violence—maybe some slaves escaped, that crew members were killed, and maybe we were involved. Chap thinks it is too risky." The girl looked up, her large green eyes fixing on Leesil. "He thinks the Suman vessel is our only choice."

Leesil breathed in through his nose and realized why Chap wasn't talking. The dog probably wanted Brot'an to hear directly from Wayfarer about everything that had taken place.

However, this might not have been the best tactic because, to Leesil's surprise, Brot'an nodded once.

"The Suman vessel will suit our needs," the shadow-gripper said. "The only obstacle to overcome is acquiring the fee. I will procure that tonight."

The room fell silent, but a single memory-word snapped in Leesil's mind.

—No!—

Leesil was way ahead of Chap. He could only imagine how the aging assassin would "acquire" such coin. Several local citizens would be left for dead—or actually dead—in some alley.

"No," Leesil repeated aloud. "I'll do it my way."

Magiere came instantly to her feet.

"Oh, no, you won't!" she snarled at him. "That's not going to happen . . . again!"

Chap looked at her intently, and Leesil wondered what passed between them.

"I don't care!" she snapped at the dog. "We find another way somehow."

Wayfarer's head swung back and forth between Magiere and Chap. Her eyes were wide in alarm.

Brot'an raised one eyebrow at Leesil. "I assume you mean to earn the money at cards?"

"I'll have it by morning," Leesil answered flatly. "You said the anmaglâhk would be watching the port, so I should be able to slip out alone and find a game."

—In this quiet city?— . . . —These people . . . do not strike me . . . as gamblers—

"Where there are sailors," Leesil responded, "there's always a game."

"No," Magiere insisted. "What if you get caught cheating—again? What then?"

He took a step toward her. "Fine, then let Brot'an do it," he said. "Let him *procure* what we need . . . his way."

Her expression collapsed, and he hated himself for having caused it.

"I won't cheat unless I have to, and if I do, I won't get caught." He crossed his arms and ran his gaze over everyone in the room. "Then it's settled. I'll go out tonight and have the coin by morning."

No one answered, but no one argued, either.

And even then Leesil noticed that Chap sat to one side of the room while Wayfarer remained on the bed's edge. And the two still didn't look at each other.

Dänvârfij met Rhysís in the same cutway where they had parted ways. He led her into the city to a one-story inn. They did not speak during the walk, as Dänvârfij had much to report and wished to say it only once. Rhysís had never been one for talking, so possibly he did not even notice her silence.

Upon arriving at the inn and the acquired room, he unlocked a door with a key and led her inside. The room was small but neatly organized with a large bed and several chairs. Fréthfâre sat in a chair by the window. Without a cloak now, she looked so odd in her human clothing—a red gown with wide sleeves. Én'nish lay resting on the bed, but she swung her legs over and sat up with a pained effort.

"What have you learned?" Fréthfâre asked without a greeting.

Dänvârfij expected nothing else. She quickly and succinctly related that she had verified that the *Cloud Queen* had sailed without its extra passengers and that she had spotted Leanâlhâm and the majay-hì seeking out the Suman vessel.

Én'nish nearly smiled at the news, but with vicious hunger in her eyes. She was motivated only by revenge against Léshil for the loss of her beloved. Fréthfâre appeared equally pleased in a colder way, though she did not turn her gaze from outside.

"If the tainted quarter-blood girl and the majay-hì are here, then the others are close," she said. "We must learn their location and set a trap by which Rhysís can first kill the traitor with an arrow. Once Brot'ân'duivé is dead, taking the others should not be so difficult."

Dänvârfij drew a long breath, bracing herself. "We cannot."

She paused, and Fréthfâre finally turned her head.

"I have reported to Most Aged Father," Dänvârfij went on, "and he has counseled that we gain passage to il'Dha'ab Najuum and set our trap there. He has given me a possible plan in which we—"

"No!" shrieked Fréthfâre, her normal pallor flushing with rage. "I will not board another filthy human vessel when our quarry is right here!"

Dänvârfij fell silent. She had expected some opposition at first, though few would so foolishly disobey Father. But now the ex-Covârleasa sounded utterly bereft of reason.

Glancing at Én'nish and then Rhysís, Dänvârfij realized she had miscalculated the effect of Most Aged Father's orders. Én'nish's fingers had bit into the bedding, and Rhysís's expression darkened.

"Most Aged Father is not here," Én'nish nearly hissed, though her spite was all for Dänvârfij. "He knows only what *you* report . . . because you have our only word-wood. Give it to me! We will see what Father counsels after he hears *my* report."

Dänvârfij glanced warily about the room at each of those with her. Fréthfâre merely watched her with the barest trace of a smile.

This was close to open revolt, and it left Dänvârfij uncertain, but she could not give in. If she did so even this once, all semblance of order would be lost, and Fréthfâre would lead them all to their deaths in nothing but vengeance.

Hoping for a moment to recover control here, Dänvârfij turned her own glare upon Rhysís. "And what are your thoughts?"

Rhysís remained silent at first. He was deeply loyal to Most Aged Father, as they all were, and everyone knew it, but he was also more practical—dutiful—even with his own motivations for revenge against the traitorous greimasg'äh.

"I think," he finally began, "that Én'nish is partially correct. Additional perspectives might provide Father more to consider, but not because your reports are lacking. In my travels, I, too, am brief in my reports."

"So you think Most Aged Father's counsel is wrong?" Dänvârfij challenged.

"Yes!" Fréthfâre answered for him. "We take our quarry here!"

Dänvârfij was not accustomed to anything so near hysteria and did not know how to respond. But when she looked into Rhysís's eyes, there was no defiance—only the faintest hint of pleading. He knew—could see—that what remained of the team was becoming unstable. When he looked to Fréthfâre, Dänvârfij let him speak.

"I suggest we plan to follow Father's counsel," Rhysís said, "but we prepare for opportunities here. This city is too large to search with so few of us, but Dänvârfij and I can watch the waterfront for our quarry. Sooner or later they will go there. If we see a way to finish our purpose here before we must leave, then we take it. Father would so advise if a clear opportunity presented itself."

Rhysís's words were sound and sensible—and loyal to Most Aged Father.

Én'nish watched for a moment. Her eyes barely shifted to Dänvârfij before she lowered them with a sneer. Even Fréthfâre said nothing, though Dänvârfij was not foolish enough to take that as agreement.

No, the ex-Covârleasa and the grief-sickened Én'nish hesitated only because Rhysís was unwilling to side with them. Dänvârfij's relief was limited, though she kept her expression impassive regardless of the tension in the room.

"This seems wise," she said.

With a nod to Rhysís, Dänvârfij turned to Fréthfâre. She remained outwardly unaffected, as if this were a normal discussion of strategy . . . and Fréthfâre had not been on the brink of rebelling.

"Do you concur?" she asked.

Fréthfâre straightened in her chair, which must have caused her pain. "Yes," she answered, "so long as you actively seek any opportunity to kill the traitor and take our quarry here."

Dänvârfij nodded. "Of course."

Feigning calm, she was well aware how close she had come to losing control of her remaining team. Rhysís had supported her this time . . . but for how long? In her thoughts she recounted all that Most Aged Father had related to her. An idea began forming in the back of her mind as she mentally pictured the inn to which she had trailed the two Shé'ith.

She turned to Rhysís. "You and I will watch the harbor," she said, "but at nightfall I have another task to complete."

CHAPTER SEVEN

The following morning Chap suffered through another coating of charcoal dust. He choked back a growl as Leesil tied up his snout and bound his ears with those straps. Wayfarer put on her disguise as Brot'an stepped to the window, ready to slip out and head across the rooftops. But when it came time for Wayfarer to slip the rope's loop over Chap's head, she stalled and handed the rope to Leesil to do so.

Chap had not spoken to Wayfarer as yet about their strange moment on the waterfront. And he was uncertain whether he ever should.

He had been thinking upon a past incident, the last time they—he and Leesil—had faced down any of the anmaglâhk who had harried them all the way from Calm Seatt. And Wayfarer had jerked away from him, asking: *Did Léshil kill . . . one of the caste . . . ?*

No one had told the girl about that. Leesil didn't even want to tell Magiere, and Chap had agreed. So what had prompted that question from Wayfarer as she sat on the walkway, staring at him in fear?

He was uncertain how to even ask her about this, so he did not.

—Ready?—

She nodded, though she didn't look at him.

This room they all shared was beginning to feel like a prison cell, and the tension was thick. True to his word, Leesil had gone out the night before and returned very late . . . with more than enough coin to pay the exorbitant fee demanded by the captain of the *Djinn.*

Magiere had paced most of the night, and when Leesil had returned, instead of expressing relief at his success and safety, she'd barely spoken to him. Chap understood this.

Leesil was a good cardplayer, though not as good as he thought, and when pressed, he had no compunction against cheating. Occasionally he got caught. Worse, the more he played, the more he wanted to play.

Magiere was not wrong in her concerns, but Leesil had not been wrong that such a tactic was their only option. Brot'an could not be allowed to gain the money his way.

Inside the tense room, it now seemed that questions by anyone for anyone else had become something to be avoided.

Wayfarer picked up her gnarled walking stick, and Leesil handed her a pouch.

"Tuck this inside your cloak," he instructed. "I've put exactly forty-five silver pennies in there." He glanced at Chap. "You stay close to her."

Not dignifying such a comment with an answer, Chap bit back another snarl.

From the window, Brot'an watched all this in silence and then added to Wayfarer, "I will be watching. If you find yourselves in danger, run for the cutway between the harbormaster's office and the nearest warehouse."

"Yes, Greimasg'äh," Wayfarer answered, and as she turned for the door, Chap followed her.

Once they were outside in the morning air, the girl took a deep breath, as if she was relieved to be out of that room. In the not-so-distant past, she'd had to be pried out into the streets of any human city.

She looked toward where the waterfront lay beyond sight. "I did not like the captain of that Suman vessel."

—Agreed—

These were the first real words they'd exchanged since returning the previous day.

Chap hadn't cared for Captain Amjad, either, but Leesil had done his part, and now they must do theirs. Leaning down on her gnarled cane, Wayfarer pulled her hood forward to shadow her face and once again shuffled along in the stooped manner of an old woman . . . with a muzzled and huge black dog beside her.

They never paused until they reached the fourth pier and stood near the ramp up to the *Djinn* as cargo was being loaded. The whole vessel was crawling with activity, and Chap could see that Wayfarer was frightened by the sailors rushing past in their hurried labors.

—We only need to . . . locate the captain . . . and pay him—

Calming slightly, the girl followed as he headed up the ramp and looked around for the captain. A young sailor with curling hair black spotted them and walked over, flashing a set of even teeth as he smiled.

"Hello again," he said with a heavy accent. "Did your friend find you yesterday?"

Chap's ears would have stiffened upright if they could.

"My friend?" Wayfarer asked.

"Yes, she came shortly after you left—tall woman who looked a little like you." His smile widened. "Not such a pretty face, though."

For the third time that morning, Chap choked back a snarl, though a growl still followed, somewhat muffled by the straps on his muzzle. The sailor instantly lost his smile, but Chap's annoyance at a flirting deckhand was outweighed by panic.

They had been spotted yesterday and followed at least as far as this vessel. Brot'an had either not noticed or—as with many things—never mentioned this.

Chap turned his head enough to look up at Wayfarer's green eyes, now fully widened, as she likely came to a similar realization.

—Do not react— . . . —Ask for the captain—

It took Wayfarer two breaths and then, "May we speak to Captain Amjad?"

"Of course," the sailor answered, and, with one wary glance at Chap, he headed toward the prow.

Chap followed, tugging Wayfarer along toward a stout man giving orders, and Chap's mouth filled with the same sourness from the day before. The few Sumans he'd encountered in his travels had been careful about cleanliness, along with exhibiting near-meticulous manners.

Captain Amjad proved a severe contrast.

With a protruding belly that nearly split the ties of his shirt, and a noxious odor and greasy hair, likely he had neither changed nor laundered his breeches and shirt in several years. It appeared that he did not bother to shave, though he could not grow a proper beard. His round face sported sparse patches of dark, straggly strands.

Amjad's surprise at Wayfarer's return quickly shifted to greed in his hard eyes.

"You have it?" he asked rudely.

"Yes," Wayfarer answered, pulling Leesil's pouch from under her cloak. "You will set sail tomorrow?"

"Midday," Amjad said, and, when he opened the pouch and peered inside, he only grunted in satisfaction. "Be on board, or we leave without you. Only two cabins between you, and our cook serves two meals a day, morning and night. You eat whatever he makes."

Wayfarer back-stepped and put her hand over her mouth and nose. "That . . . that will be fine."

—We go—

Chap turned away, and she followed, still gripping the rope. With their transaction completed, he wanted to return to the inn. If they had been spotted and followed the day before, it was possible they had been followed farther than the waterfront. And because of this, once they were off the ramp and onto the pier, he changed their tactics.

—No more . . . playing . . . an old woman— . . . —Pick up the cane . . . and . . . follow me . . . quickly . . . without running—

She obeyed without question, though she was obviously confused and frightened.

"We should go to the greimasg'äh. I promised."

—No— . . . —To the inn—

"But," she whispered, still walking, "if anmaglâhk are watching, we will lead them to Léshil and Magiere."

She was learning and had reasoned the outcome, though this was not what Chap had in mind. He slowed a little to look at her more easily in using memory-words.

—When Brot'an sees . . . us . . . he will know . . . something is wrong . . . and follow closely— . . . —If we are . . . followed . . . he will see. . . . He will . . . keep them from . . . reaching the inn—

Relying on the old, skulking assassin left Chap even more spiteful. Here and now protecting Wayfarer, and Leesil and Magiere's location, was all that mattered . . . and Brot'an would deal with any pursuit.

Dänvârfij lay flat on a warehouse roof two buildings south of the fourth pier. Though she had been successful in her secret task the night before, today she faced a new challenge.

Barely past dawn, she had gone to the captain of the *Falcon* and arranged passage for her team to il'Dha'ab Najuum. She still assumed this was necessary. To her relief, he had agreed, and even appeared glad for extra money in keeping his few passengers. Then he had told her the ship was setting sail today . . . this afternoon.

Dänvârfij was caught in a dilemma, uncertain whether she could convince Fréthfâre to abandon this port so soon. If they missed sailing on the *Falcon*, there was no certainty of when they could find another ship headed south. She might be forced to disregard Most Aged Father's instructions and attempt to capture Magiere or Léshil in Soráno to keep them from escaping yet again.

She did not like being pushed into a decision one way or the other, and then her tension was interrupted.

Up the fourth pier, the short, limping female and her large black dog made their way toward the Suman vessel. Dänvârfij's thoughts cleared and were replaced with a new opportunity as she focused on the tainted quarter-blood girl . . . and the deviant majay-hì.

She waited, though not long. The duo boarded the Suman vessel, but their stay was brief. Within moments they came back down the ramp onto the pier. At first the girl was bent and shuffling in her attempt to feign age, but then she stood straight and picked up the stick. As the dog trotted back up the pier, the girl had to rush to keep up. They were no longer trying to hide themselves in their hurry.

Something had happened.

Still flat on the roof, Dänvârfij scanned every rooftop in sight and the whole waterfront as well. Rhysís was posted somewhere on the waterfront's north end, but she chose not to whistle a signal to him.

Why was this pair now in such a hurry?

Her thoughts turned to the best strategy as the girl and the majay-hì reached the base of the pier and stepped among the people hurrying along the waterfront. If she could capture the girl, then she and her team could lure the others out of hiding with proper bait for a trap.

Perhaps they would not have to sail farther south after all. Most Aged Father had been clear in his instructions, but he would not wish them to waste a perfect opportunity.

Dänvârfij retreated from the roof's edge before she rose into a crouch. Before she had a chance to whistle, Rhysís landed lightly on the roof's south end and hurried to her.

"I saw them," he whispered.

"The traitor may be watching," she whispered back. "We must act quickly and precisely. You will take the girl while I distract the majay-hì, and then we vanish."

Wayfarer would never argue with a sacred being like Chap, but she had made a promise to Brot'ân'duivé . . . and now she had broken it. The manners and customs of her people had long protected them and kept them safe; to break an oath to an elder weighed upon her.

Chap suddenly stopped ahead of her, and she froze as he looked up the busy main street through Soráno. She tried to follow his gaze but saw nothing that should have stalled him. Their inn was two blocks ahead on the right. They had taken the same route on both trips to the port.

Chap's head swung sharply to the right, and then he looked up at her.

—Off this . . . main street to . . . a less traveled path . . . should Brot'an . . . need . . . to intervene— . . . —Quickly—

Wayfarer hesitated. Chap might be most concerned about protecting her, but she feared this change might place Léshil and Magiere in danger. She guessed he had discounted that she and he were leading the anmaglâhk. He placed too much faith in Brot'ân'duivé's ability to both spot and stop any pursuit.

"You should not be more worried about me than about Léshil and Magiere," she said.

When he glanced up, she could see his surprise.

—I am not— . . . —We do not know . . . if we are followed— . . . —If so, then Brot'an is near— . . . —In our last outing . . . anmaglâhk may have followed . . . may know where we stay— . . . —We are in the dark— . . . —We must warn Magiere and Leesil . . . before we are caught— . . . —Anmaglâhk may know . . . the ship we take—

He seemed to pick words from her memories faster and faster with each passing day. In not knowing whether they were followed or not, all they could do was reach the inn as quickly as possible.

Nodding, Wayfarer followed Chap around a turn down an unfamiliar path, deeper inland into the city.

In the cutway beside the harbormaster's office, Brot'ân'duivé was confused and then wary as he watched Wayfarer and Chap leave the *Djinn* and come down the pier. The girl suddenly abandoned all efforts at disguising herself as Chap set a brisk pace toward the shore.

Brot'ân'duivé looked about the port and glanced up once at the rooftop edges above. He had chosen to stay at ground level to move as needed, but now he was limited in looking for whatever had driven the majay-hì into a rush.

Wayfarer had been raised well by his friend, the old healer Gleannéohkân'thva. She would do as she promised and come straight to this cutway if something was wrong. He waited for her to reach the waterfront walkway and then come to him.

She did not. To his disbelief, Chap turned down the waterfront's edge.

Brot'ân'duivé peered around the cutway's corner and watched as the pair turned through the crowd into the first street—not the last—along the harbor. They vanished from his sight into the city.

He turned and ran down the cutway into the broad alley behind the warehouses and then slipped quickly to its end, where it met the next street. But when he peered out, he saw only olive-skinned people in brightly colored clothing.

What had that foolish majay-hì done now?

Brot'ân'duivé spun back into the alley's shadows and scaled the wall to the nearest roof.

Chap led the way for a few blocks until he spotted a narrow, less traveled street leading into the city, and there he turned again. He was well aware of the risk in taking Wayfarer out of the more populated areas, but if Brot'an had paid attention, the shadow-gripper would have freedom to act as he saw fit. And Chap as well.

Such actions had to take place away from public eyes or authorities. He paused for only an instant in looking up at Wayfarer.

—Release my straps—

The girl stalled, perhaps knowing what this implied, but then she quickly pulled on the ends of the leather straps at the back of his head. It was a relief not to have his ears and jaws bound, and he shook the straps off to let them fall.

—Hurry—

Chap broke into a trot, with Wayfarer nearly running beside him. Later he never remembered seeing or hearing the briefest flash of movement.

A tall figure dressed in dark blue materialized from nowhere directly beside them. Before Chap could think or move, the figure grabbed Wayfarer, lifted her off the ground, and veered at a run for the closest building.

Chap had barely glanced at the sudden movement when that figure leaped from a porch railing to grab the awning above with a slender tan hand. White-blond hair fluttered from the side of the cloak's hood. It all happened so quickly that only then did Wayfarer cry out.

Chap's instant of confused hesitation ended.

He swerved after the figure in blue and leaped upward, catching the cloak's hem before he dropped and hit the railing.

He, the anmaglâhk, and Wayfarer all crashed down in a tangle on the street's side. Wayfarer cried out again as her hand latched on his tail, and his panic sharpened.

He had to send her away from this quickly, but there was little time. And their room at the inn was only a few city blocks away.

Chap took only a glance at Wayfarer. *—Run to Magiere!—*

Wayfarer felt the shock of pain as her back hit the street. She could not help crying out, but the strong arm that had lifted her off the ground released. In panic she grabbed for Chap and caught hold of only his tail. At that touch, an image of Magiere and Léshil in the inn's little room rose in her mind and stunned her.

Chap's head twisted until his eyes were on her.

—Run to Magiere!—

The image and those words tangled in Wayfarer's head. She did not snatch her hand away from touching Chap, as she had on the waterfront. Her first impulse was to refuse: she could not abandon him. But Magiere and Léshil were alone in their room and did not know what was happening.

Wayfarer let go of Chap's tail and rolled out of reach as the anmaglâhk tried to grab her. Chap launched into that tall man's chest with his teeth snapping for the man's throat.

Wayfarer turned and ran.

Dänvârfij looked down from a rooftop above Rhysís and was startled at the speed of the majay-hì. It had not occurred to her that the dog would close on Rhysís before he reached the rooftop. Rhysís's hand barely gripped the awning's edge, and Dänvârfij could not grab his wrist in time.

The awning crackled as Rhysís's grip on it broke.

He fell in a tangle with the girl and deviant majay-hì. The girl cried out, grabbing the majay-hì's tail, and the dog turned instantly to look at her. Dänvârfij was about to drop over the edge when Rhysís made a grab for the girl. The majay-hì lunged into him as the girl ran off down the street.

Dänvârfij hesitated between going after the girl and aiding Rhysís.

From the beginning, all her team had wavered at the thought of injuring a majay-hì. But the dog had no such restraint in going for Rhysís's throat.

Dänvârfij pulled a stiletto from her left sleeve and prepared to drop to the street . . . when something on the skyline toward the waterfront caught in the side of her view. A shadow floated—ran and leaped—between two rooftops one city block away. It was coming for them, and fear flooded through her. She vaulted out over the roof's edge before the traitor closed. As soon as her feet hit the ground, she kicked the majay-hì's side behind its foreleg. It let out a choking yelp as it tumbled away from Rhysís, who had drawn a blade, though his hands were bleeding.

The dog righted itself and made to charge.

Dänvârfij grabbed Rhysís by his cloak's shoulder and took off down the street.

"Run! The traitor comes."

She rushed into a cutway to the next street and could hear Rhysís directly behind her. Then she swerved down half the street before veering to another cutway on the street's far side. The traitor was not her main concern anymore, for from up on the rooftops he could not have seen where they ran. Only the majay-hì could track them and might alert the greimasg'äh to where they fled. At the back of the second cutway, she turned left into the adjoining alley, heading away from the path and whatever destination that the majay-hì and the girl had sought. Near the alley's end, she dropped to crouch behind a barrel filled with rainwater and cursed herself for a fool.

Most Aged Father had told them they were too few to attempt anything in this city. He had given her clear instructions about how to acquire assistance in il'Dha'ab Najuum. And what had she done? She had allowed her team to manipulate her into rash actions.

No more.

Ignoring Rhysís's torn hands and wrists, she hissed at him in a whisper, "The traitor will go after the girl and check on his other charges, which gives us time. You get Én'nish and Fréthfâre and all of our gear, including what I brought in last night. Go directly to the *Falcon* and wait."

Breathing hard through his nose, Rhysís stared at her for a moment, but he quickly dropped his eyes with one curt nod.

Brot'ân'duivé heard Chap's snarls and growls from a block away. Abandoning stealth, he ran openly, leaping from one rooftop to the next. Before he reached the roof's edge over the next street, a yelp and then the sound of feet running rose from below. One last snarl followed, and then silence as he reached the edge and looked down.

Chap limped down the street's far side to peer into a cutway. There was no sign or sight of any anmaglâhk . . . or of Wayfarer.

Brot'ân'duivé dropped to the ground and looked all ways as he ran to Chap.

"Where is Wayfarer?" he demanded, growing angrier than he should have allowed himself.

Had the loyalists from his caste taken her?

Exposing teeth and fangs, Chap whirled and snarled at him. Then the dog turned away and loped—struggling—down the street.

Brot'ân'duivé tried to quell his anger as he followed.

Wayfarer ran to the door of their room at the inn and pounded on it.

"It is me!" she called wildly. "Let me in!"

The door instantly opened, and as she rushed in, she nearly collided with Magiere.

Magiere grabbed her by the arms. "What's happened?"

"Chap!" Wayfarer cried amid panting. "He is in trouble! Anmaglâhk!"

"Where?" Léshil demanded.

Wayfarer tried to catch her breath. "They came for me . . . and the greimasg'äh could not have been far behind. Chap sent me to warn you that we have been seen. They may even know of the ship we will sail on."

"What?" Magiere demanded, her mouth dropping open, and she looked to Léshil.

"Where did you leave Chap?" Léshil asked.

"Two streets north," she managed to get out.

Before anyone could say more, Léshil pushed past for the door with a few last words to Magiere. "Stay with her. I'll handle this."

Wayfarer wrenched out of Magiere's grip and shoved the door closed, jerking it out of Léshil's hand.

"No!" she said, flattening herself against the door. "Chap would not want this. The anmaglâhk are after you two most of all."

"Get out of the way," Léshil ordered as he grabbed her wrist.

"No!" Wayfarer shot back. "This was a trick to get to one or both of you. Chap and Brot'ân'duivé can protect themselves, and I will *not* let either of you leave."

Both Magiere and Léshil appeared beyond surprised at her manner, but then Magiere reached for her this time.

Wayfarer felt and heard something scratching at the outside of the room's door.

Without even asking, she spun and pulled it open.

Chap limped inside. An instant later, the greimasg'äh entered as well and shut the door himself. Wayfarer was taken a bit off guard as Brot'ân'duivé glared at her . . . but a sudden relief flashed across his face, and a sigh escaped him.

"Where were *you*?" Magiere snarled, pulling Wayfarer aside and taking a threatening step at the greimasg'äh. "You were supposed to watch them!"

"Only if I could keep them in sight," Brot'ân'duivé replied and then looked to the majay-hì. "Only if they stayed on the agreed route."

Wayfarer glanced at Chap and did not follow the rest of the angry conversation, especially whenever Léshil echoed something from Chap, or not, and everyone else was momentarily confused as to who was truly speaking. Though she trusted that the majay-hì had sensed something to make him change their path, she also remembered that one fleeting moment amid her fright.

She had seen something in her thoughts.

Magiere and Léshil had stood in this very room . . . in her mind. Now that she thought about it, she had been looking at them as if she sat low on the floor. It was the same perspective, the same angle of sight, as when she had lurched away from Chap on the waterfront.

Something the greimasg'äh said pulled Wayfarer back to awareness.

". . . They are too few to try a frontal attack on this inn, if they even know of it," he was saying. "We will be safe here."

"Really?" Léshil retorted. "What if they just set the place on fire?"

"They will not. The risk of killing anyone inside is too great, and they want you and Magiere alive."

After that Wayfarer stopped listening at all and sank onto the bed's edge.

She remembered how easily that one anmaglâhk had lifted her off the ground. She had been unable to do anything about it. And after Chap had pulled her captor down . . .

Her mind slipped back a few years to when she lived on a different continent with her people. She would find herself alone in the forest—and yet not alone. Sometimes she had *felt* eyes upon her and she had turned.

One of the majay-hì would be watching her from the brush.

At the time she had believed that this meant they were judging her . . . that she did not belong among the people. She was mixed blood; she was not welcome in the lands of the an'Cróan. Then there had been the white female who had come to lead her away. The one whom she later learned was Chap's mate . . . and the mother of their child, Shade, who had crossed the world to be with Wynn. In Wayfarer's darkest moment, alone and orphaned, and when she had most needed a guide, Lily had come to her . . . as if somehow knowing of her fear and sorrow.

What did any of it mean? What had happened that morning on the waterfront with Chap?

What had just happened out in the street when in panic she had grabbed his tail?

"Wayfarer, answer me! Are you all right?"

Wayfarer blinked in a shudder and looked up to find Magiere standing over her in worry. She did not know how to answer and only glanced at Chap.

After leaving Rhysís, Dänvârfij went straight to the Suman ship. She knew the traitor would be distracted for a short while by his charges. She had one last preparation to complete before her quarry made its next move.

Most Aged Father had provided the only sound way to fulfill her purpose concerning the monster and her mate, as well as the traitorous greimasg'äh. But Dänvârfij had devised something more of her own.

Striding up the vessel's ramp, she watched as human men loaded cargo into the hold. A filthy one with a round belly shouted orders at the others, and she went straight to him.

When he saw her coming, his expression was one of arrogant authority.

"What do you want?" he asked in Numanese, though his accent was thick.

She needed to exude authority as well for this to work, and she stared him straight in the eyes without blinking and with no emotion on her face.

"To speak . . . you . . . alone," she replied flatly, and then she fell silent, as if expecting compliance.

He appeared taken aback by this. With a tilt of his head and narrowing eyes, he shrugged slightly and gestured to a door in the aftcastle's front wall. She waited until he stepped off before she followed. His stench was enough that she had to stop herself from covering her nose as she headed down the stairs and below deck.

He glanced back once, perhaps suspicious, and then led the way to the last door on the right. She followed and found herself in a small, cluttered cabin that—if possible—smelled worse than he did. He did not shut the door.

"What?" he asked.

She kept her eyes on his and tried not to look at his unkempt, unwashed attire.

"I *hunt* group . . . of thieves . . . murderers. I think they . . . arranged passage on . . . this ship."

That one sharpened word—*hunt*—would be enough to give the impression that she was a bounty hunter, so called among many human cultures. That alone might sharpen his interest if there was money involved.

She was not wrong.

The captain's beady, dark eyes widened slightly.

"You already see girl . . . and black dog," she said, and then she gave the best description of Magiere, Léshil, and Brot'ân'duivé that she could in her limited Numanese. "In Numan water—in port of Drist—they attack Suman vessel *Bashair.* They murder all crew." She paused, granting this slovenly captain a moment to estimate how much profit might be involved. "My words easy prove. Ship found in dock. Bodies of crew . . . in bay, on shore, under dock . . . found dead. You want, check story. All five stayed at place named Delilah's."

There was a risk in blaming her quarry for the deaths aboard the *Bashair*. This captain would obviously pause, worrying about the safety of his vessel—or rather himself. All that mattered was whether his greed was greater than his fear.

Finally, he stepped around her and closed the cabin door. "What do you want from me?" he asked, showing a row of crooked, stained teeth.

"I cannot arrest until they reach . . . il'Dha'ab Najuum. They murder Suman crew . . . so must catch on Suman ground."

"Arrest them?" he echoed. Though filthy, he was not stupid.

"When word of crime reach Suman . . . law officers," she continued, "they offer large reward."

"And you want me to help you once we land? What's my share of the reward?"

"All. I want them . . . nothing more."

His eyes narrowed in suspicion.

"They kill my . . . friends," she said. "I want justice . . . not reward."

She could see he was tempted but still uncertain. Whether he believed her or not, it was time to finish the ploy by tying his greed to a sense of righteousness. Dänvârfij reached inside her vest and removed a folded piece of pale gold cloth that she had hidden there. She unfolded it for the captain to see, and then refolded it when his mouth went slack.

"You are Shé'ith?" he whispered.

She nodded once. "I am in disguise . . . to pursue my quarry."

With no further hesitation, the captain straightened. "And the entire reward will be mine?"

"Yes. I travel ahead on other ship and wait in il'Dha'ab Najuum. Do not let passengers think you know. . . . When you arrive, I contact you for . . . assistance."

"Agreed!"

He did not appear remotely afraid of carrying passengers accused of murdering some other Suman crew. The foundation of the trap had been laid. At first, when Most Aged Father had explained his plan to her, she had wondered about the wisdom of allowing her quarry to be arrested by Suman authorities. She then realized that Magiere and Léshil would be disarmed, most likely separated, and locked up. They would be easy targets for any trained anmaglâhk. No Suman prison would be able to keep her or Rhysís out.

Turning without another word, she left the small cabin, headed up on deck, took a needed breath of clean air, and trotted down the ramp to head for the *Falcon* at a brisk pace.

As she boarded, the captain there smiled, and she nodded to him in turn before descending below to join her team. Opening the door of the first cabin, she peered inside to find Fréthfâre resting on one bunk while Én'nish and Rhysís sat side by side—both working.

Each held a tawny leather vestment with swirling steel garnishes from which they scrubbed away blood. One pale gold sash lay on the bunk beside them, and swords lay at their feet.

"You were careless," Én'nish complained.

"I had to move quickly," Dänvârfij replied.

She did not have to explain herself to anyone here, all of whom had—to one degree or another—sought to ignore Most Aged Father's instructions. And Dänvârfij looked once more upon the folded pale gold sash still in her hand.

She tucked the piece of cloth back inside her vest in case it should be needed once more.

None of them left the cabin that day, and in the midafternoon, the *Falcon* sailed south.

The following morning, still locked inside the room at the inn, Magiere had to bite the inside of her mouth as Brot'an took over all aspects of their short journey to the harbor. She didn't blame him for being overly cautious, considering what had happened—almost happened—the day before. But his manner was coldly insulting, and Magiere wondered how long it would take before either Leesil or Chap—or maybe both—had finally had enough.

"Does everyone know what to do?" Brot'an asked for the fifth time as he pulled up his hood.

Even Wayfarer sighed tiredly as Magiere answered, "I think we are all sure enough, so Leesil and Wayfarer should head out."

If the port was still watched by the two remaining able-bodied anmaglâhk, then four people and a dog walking together would gain their attention instantly. And it seemed those butchers already knew which ship to watch. Brot'an had reasoned that the only strategy was to break into smaller groups. They would stay within sight of one another and move quickly without running when they all reached the fourth pier by separate routes. Once they were all on board, it was unlikely that only two anmaglâhk would move against them.

Magiere agreed, but the aging assassin looked tense, and that made her tense.

Leesil and Wayfarer would go first, heavily cloaked and holding hands like a couple.

Magiere would take Chap next and lead him on his rope.

Brot'an would follow last, keeping everyone in sight, until it was time to quickly catch up.

"All right," he said to Leesil. "Go."

Clearly hating even the idea of following Brot'an's orders, Leesil glared at him. He hefted their travel chest onto one shoulder, took Wayfarer's hand, and left.

Magiere picked up the rope's end. Its other end was tied around Chap's neck, and once again he was covered in soot—which may have been pointless since the anmaglâhk had already seen him like this, but they'd certainly spot a silver-gray majay-hì more easily. She counted to ten and left the inn, making two turns and coming out onto the mainway filled with people rushing or strolling about their days. Chap kept enough of a pace that Leesil and Wayfarer were still in sight.

—Brot'an is . . . insufferable—

Magiere sighed, not even disagreeing, and whispered to Chap, "Let's just get this over with."

The trip to the port felt longer than it was for the tension. But soon they were headed up the fourth pier with most of the distance closed by the time Leesil and Wayfarer walked up the ramp onto the *Djinn*.

Magiere glanced back, and Brot'an was no more than eight strides behind her.

"How uneventful," Leesil said dryly as she and Chap reached the deck.

Then she looked around at the medium-sized cargo vessel upon which they would make the long run to il'Dha'ab Najuum with no stops. It was a bit shabby, and a greasy-looking Suman with a protruding belly came right at them.

"This is Captain Amjad," Wayfarer said politely.

Magiere heard the girl swallow hard with a brief choke, and she smelled . . .

It took no more than one blink to figure out where that stench came from.

However, something beyond revulsion touched Magiere next. The captain's eyes fixed briefly on Brot'an, then Leesil, and finally on herself. He looked her over as if he knew her, though she'd never seen him before now.

"You made it," he said bluntly. "Don't bother complaining about the food or the cabins. No one will listen."

He turned abruptly and headed toward the prow.

"Charming," Leesil said, raising one feathery eyebrow, and then he sighed as he glanced out to sea. "I won't be keeping my food down anyway."

Magiere was worried about more than Leesil's ongoing seasickness. Something here felt wrong.

"I am sorry," Wayfarer said. "This was our only choice."

Altering her expression, Magiere patted the girl's back. "You did well in finding us anything at all."

Still, as the crew prepared to set sail, something nagged at Magiere . . . as if she and her companions should leave this ship right there and then.

CHAPTER EIGHT

Sailing down the coast on *The Thorn*, Wynn couldn't arrange another private moment with Osha until they neared the port of Oléron. It didn't happen the way she expected.

Early one evening, after Chane rose from dormancy and went up on deck, Wynn was alone with Shade in their cabin. She took time to herself to jot notes in a journal, though she no longer recorded anything too critical. The dangerous, important things she dictated to Shade or shared by showing the dog her recalled memories. Shade, as a majay-hì and more, locked those secrets away inside herself beyond anyone's reach.

Wynn stuffed the journal away in her pack and stood up to stretch. "Come, Shade."

Out in the passage, she led the way to the stairs and up on deck to check on her other companions. Pausing in the aftcastle doorway, she was surprised to find Chane and Nikolas sitting side by side on two barrels, with mugs of tea beside each of them. They were intently perusing a text that Chane had brought along, likely one that Kyne had forced on him for his studies.

"No," Nikolas said, pointing at the current page. "This symbol is quite different. If you break down the strokes of its construction according to the methods of the Begaine Syllabary, the Numanese word here is 'confusion.' "

"Why not use the previous symbol?" Chane asked.

"Because that one reads 'puzzlement.' Strokes and marks in a symbol for a word are meant for sounding out that particular word . . . and the term meanings are not what the syllabary is about."

Wynn's gaze fixed on Chane's red-brown hair hanging forward to almost block one eye. Seeing him slightly hunched over that book swept her back to when she'd first met him.

She'd been helping Domin Tilswith, her mentor at the time, in starting a tiny new guild branch in Bela. The branch was the first of its kind in the Farlands of the eastern continent. They'd been given an old decommissioned barracks no longer used by the city guard. Chane often came at night to drink mint tea and pore over historical texts brought over half the world to that place. Sometimes he'd seemed starved for intelligent or at least educated companionship, and Wynn had been secretly flattered by a handsome young nobleman spending so many evenings with her.

At that time Wynn had no idea who—what—Chane Andraso was.

Vneshené Zomrelé . . . "Noble Dead" . . . *vämpír* . . . vampire . . . undead.

That felt like a lifetime ago, though their pasts could never be erased. Not his for his victims and enemies; not hers for what she had done since returning to the guild.

Neither Nikolas nor Chane appeared to have noticed her.

Though the young sage still had dark circles under his eyes, for once, while assisting Chane, he didn't look so bleak and lost.

Chane might be an undead, once a predator of the living. He could wield a sword as if it were part of his hand, and he dabbled in minor conjury of the elements as well, but at his core he was a scholar. No matter what he did—had done—Wynn knew this, and she could never forget it.

Then she noticed that Osha was nowhere to be seen. She pulled back, forcing Shade to retreat down the steps. At Shade's huffing grumble, Wynn didn't stop to explain. She headed down to the lower passage and the farther door of Osha and Nikolas's shared cabin. After a brief hesitation, she knocked.

"Osha?"

"Here," he called in an'Cróan Elvish.

She cracked the door, peeked inside, and asked, "Are you all right?"

Osha was sitting on the cabin floor with his legs folded and his back against the left-side bunk. Tonight his white-blond hair was pulled back at the nape of his neck with a leather thong. The effect made his tan elven face appear more triangular than usual. But he didn't look at her at first.

On the floor before him was a candle. By the way its wick smoked, sending a thin trail curling into the air, it had just been snuffed. Osha finally looked up, as if he had been watching that candle, and he nodded to her.

"Yes," he finally answered. "The young sage looked better tonight, so I left him on his own . . . allowing some privacy for both of us."

"Oh, of course," Wynn said, backing out.

"Not privacy from you," he added.

It was short, startling, direct, and so unlike the Osha she remembered.

Still uncertain, she stepped in, holding the door until Shade followed and flopped on the cabin floor near the right-side bunk.

"Sit," Osha told her, gesturing to the other bunk across the room by Shade.

Wynn tensed slightly as she settled there facing Osha. This small cabin again reminded her of when she and he had sailed down the eastern coast of the far continent and away from his people's lands. They'd often sat upon the floor to talk. It had seemed so normal then, unlike now.

For a silent moment, Osha stared at the trail of smoke from the candle's wick. He suddenly thrust out one finger, appearing to split the trail in two and dissipate it. He sat there, hand still held out with his finger extended as the smoke finally thinned and was gone.

Wynn again saw the burn scars on his hand and wrists.

From where he left off in his tale, she might have made guesses about where those scars had come from—and she didn't want to guess. She wanted the rest of his story, but she couldn't quite find the way to ask.

"You wish to hear more," he said bluntly.

He was not at all like the Osha that she had known, but that part of him was still in there somewhere—it had to be. She nodded.

A flash of something passed across Osha's features. Had it been sadness, perhaps the thought that she was here only to learn his secrets? Then it was gone, as if he didn't care what brought her to him.

"There I was," he said, "standing before the portal of the Burning Ones. . . ."

The white metal doors separated, swinging outward to grind across the cavern's level stone. A wall of heated air rushed out to strike Osha's face and body as the cavern's temperature rose sharply under a stench like burnt coal.

He choked as hot air filled his lungs.

From the last and only time he had been here, he had known this was coming. He stood there, waiting for his body to adjust. After a few more breaths, drawing hot air was still painful but bearable, and he looked through the open doors, raising his torch high.

Beyond stretched a wide passage, and the deeper he looked, the darker it became. There were glistening points of light on its craggy walls, likely from minerals in the stone, for the heat was too much for any moisture. Slipping his blade back into the sheath up his sleeve, he still lingered. Should he strip off his cloak and leave it behind? No, that might be taken below as a sign of disrespect for the covenant between the Anmaglâhk and the Chein'âs. He should be fully and properly attired as a member of the caste.

With his free hand, Osha pushed the cloak over his shoulders to let it hang down his back. There was no more reason to delay, and he stepped through the open portal into the tunnel, working his way down the uneven passage until it narrowed suddenly at the top of a carved stone stairway.

A red-orange glow from below dimly illuminated the stairwell's close walls. There was a small bracket in the wall, and Osha placed the torch inside it. Light from below increased slightly, as did the heat in the air, as he descended. He continued on, down and down, losing track of the passing time.

When it seemed the descent might never end, he stepped down onto a landing and looked through a rough, door-sized opening in the rock to his right. Out there, the orange-red light brightened, making the opening look like the mouth of a hearth in a dark room.

Osha stepped through and halted at the sight he had seen only once before.

A wide plateau ran in a gradual slant away from the entrance now behind him. At its distant edge, red light erupted out of a massive fissure in the mountain's belly, like a gash wider than a river hidden somewhere below from where that light came. Smoke drifted up in glowing red air from deep in the earth.

The heat was almost unbearable.

In slow, heavy steps, he struggled forward until he was halfway to the plateau's edge. There he stopped and reached inside his vestment to draw out the small, dark stone that he could not read. He knew what to do, though he could not bring himself to do it.

What would come of this?

Even for the loss of his jeóin, his mentor, the great Sgäilsheilleache, he still believed in his calling among the Anmaglâhk. It was all he had left. So why had the Chein'âs summoned him—among all anmaglâhk—a second time?

Since the stone would alert those who would come, what if he simply left without casting it over the precipice? He had a life of service awaiting him. With the rift among his caste and his doubts about Most Aged Father, should he turn back to do whatever he could to help?

Brot'ân'duivé had forced him into so many breaches of his caste's and his people's ways. His teacher, Sgäilsheilleache, would not have approved but neither would he have denied such a summons.

Now sweating in the heat, Osha drew a shallow breath as he swung his arm back. He cast the stone and watched as it arced out and over the precipice's edge to fall from sight. Then he froze in waiting, though it did not take as long as he expected.

A soft scraping, like metal on stone, reached his ears before he saw anything.

The plateau's edge looked almost black against the red-orange glare of the chasm below . . . and a part of that dark jagged line appeared to bulge suddenly.

From where Osha stood, at first the bulge seemed no more than a rippling smudge backlit by burning light. Small and blacker than the stone, it crawled over onto the plateau from out of the depths.

Osha made out its legs and arms as it crept forward on all fours . . . no, on threes, as it dragged something behind itself. That object, or bundle, crackled softly like cloth pulled over rough stone, though he also heard something like clicks and scrapes of metal. The closer the figure came, the more Osha was certain that the bundle was made of some strange fuzzy material as dark as the figure itself . . . and thin curls of smoke or vapor rose from the material.

When the figure was no more than a stone's throw away, the chasm's glare cleared from Osha's sight, and he saw *it*, a Chein'âs . . . a Burning One. It was as small as a naked child of six or seven years; Osha could not tell whether it was male or female, and it was covered in leathery ebony-toned skin. It finally halted its crawl and squatted on spindly legs folded up with knobby knees against its chest. Only one hand was visible—the other was still behind its back and clutching whatever long bundle it dragged. Thin digits on that one visible hand curled near its flat cheek, and each ended in a shimmering claw blacker than its flesh.

The little one's oversized head was featureless except for a tightly shut slit of a mouth, vertical cuts for small nostrils, and glowing fire-coal eyes. Where there should have been ears were only two small depressions on the sides of its bald skull.

Osha was not shocked. He had seen one of them before, though the sight of one now unsettled him, and then . . .

More scraping on stone carried across the plateau. The one sat unmoving, watching him with unblinking eyes like glowing metal overheated in a forge. The new scraping sound came from off beyond it.

A second—then a third—small figure crawled up over the precipice's edge.

The last time Osha had come here, only one had appeared to deliver his weapons and tools. He retreated a step as he watched the other two approach, and then the first one scuttled even closer and jerked its bundle out into plain sight.

That burden was long and narrow, made of some dark, fibrous cloth, and thin trails of smoke rose from it.

The two new ones rounded to either side. Each bore a similar but much smaller bundle, small enough to clutch in one clawed hand. Both of those wads of dark cloth smoldered as well.

Without warning, the first one snatched the cloth of its bundle and jerked upward.

A long, shimmering object tumbled out, clanked, and clattered across the stone before sliding to a stop at Osha's feet. All he could do was stare as his mind went blank.

It was a sword, though not like any he had heard described or seen carried by the few humans he had ever met. He did see that the handle was bare and no more than a narrow strut of metal, and that metal . . .

All of the blade and strut was silvery white, like his stilettos and tools, like Chein'âs metal.

The blade was as broad as three of his fingers. Nearly straight, its last third swept back a little in a shallow arc. The back of that third looked sharpened like the leading edge. Where the top third joined the lower part, a slightly curved barb swept forward from the blade's back toward its tip.

The end strut, perhaps needing leather and wood for a hilt, was twice as long as the width of his hand. It curved just a little downward, as much as the slight upward turn at the blade's end. Two more protrusions extended where the hilt strut met the blade's base. The top one curved forward, while the bottom one swept slightly back toward the hilt strut.

Osha did not know how long he stared. Anmaglâhk did not wield such large, clumsy, *human* weapons. They struck swiftly in silence from the shadows by arrow, narrow blade, or garrote, though he himself had never killed anyone.

Unlike many of his people, Osha had no aversion to the sight of that sword. He had spent too much time with humans—with Magiere and Léshil—to be repelled by the mere sight of a foreign weapon. Still, what did it mean?

The Chein'âs had gifted strange weapons, ones made of silver-white metal, to Magiere and Léshil. It was unheard of for any but the Anmaglâhk to receive such gifts. Was this blade to be delivered to one of them? It did not look much like Magiere's falchion.

Why would the Burning Ones summon *him* to carry such a thing away?

Looking up, he shook his head in confusion. "What am I to do? Who is this for?"

That must be the answer. He was so unimportant among his caste that using him as a bearer would cost the caste nothing. But to whom should he deliver this sword?

To his puzzlement, none of the three before him made a sound or gesture.

The one to the right of the first opened its smoking piece of cloth. It flung a cluster of tiny silver-white objects that pinged and skipped across the stone floor at him. Before he even looked to where any of those stopped, the third Chein'âs—to the left of the first—flung a single, slightly larger object, though it was not nearly so large as the sword blade.

That last object clattered and rolled in among the other five small ones.

Osha could not help retreating another step.

The five smaller objects were arrowheads, but not the teardrop points used by the Anmaglâhk or even the military archers who most often served aboard the people's largest vessels. These points were long and diamond-shaped, with harsh angles and thick at the centers.

Osha remembered one of his earliest teachers while he was a mere acolyte. The teacher had shown him and others one such point made of steel, brought back from human lands.

Those were armor-piercing points . . . arrowheads for war.

Osha tried to swallow under a rising panic, but his mouth had dried out.

The final object was again made of shining white metal: a piece shaped like half or maybe more of the circumference of a round tube . . . but its length was slightly curved toward the solid side.

He had no idea what it was at first. It looked a little like the white metal handle for an Anmaglâhk short bow, once the bow's arms were removed to be tucked away in hiding. But this object was longer, open on one side, and slightly curved along its length. Bow arms would never stay in place once inserted into it.

Unlike the sword, everything else before Osha was similar to the tools of the Anmaglâhk, but different in ways that made the pieces unsuited to guardians of the people. The true weapons of an anmaglâhk would not be lying beside a sword, so whom were these objects for?

He raised his eyes to the first Chein'âs as he pointed at the sword. "Where do I take this? Who is this for?"

None of them answered, and he began to wonder whether they even understood his words.

The first one rushed at him.

Osha back-stepped twice, but that one halted at the sword. It scooped the metal with its claws and flipped the blade outward. The sword clattered to Osha's feet again, and the Chein'âs pointed at the blade . . . and then at him.

Fear and revulsion rose in Osha. He could not believe what he guessed.

The first Chein'âs let out a hiss like water striking hot stone. It pointed at Osha's left arm and then at his right.

"What do you want?" he rasped, fighting to breathe the heated air.

It curled its clawed fingers above its opposing arm, as if drawing something down and off that forearm. It whipped that hand outward, as if casting that something aside.

Osha touched his right hand to his left forearm. All he felt there was a sheathed stiletto beneath his sleeve. The agitated Chein'âs mimed the same movement again, and Osha shifted one foot back and set himself.

"No. I am Anmaglâhk! I have my gifts—from *your* people—to prove this!"

At his angry shout, all three rushed him.

Osha faltered, unable to strike at them . . . unable to commit another sacrilege. One of them latched its hand—its claws—around his left forearm, and he screamed.

Smoke rose from his sleeve beneath that searing grip.

Osha struck back as the other two leaped at him. His fist hit the first one, and a jar shot up his arm as if he had struck stone. He heard his flesh sear an instant before he felt it.

Their clawed hands burned him through his clothing as he fought to throw them off. It was like fighting children made of black metal, and everywhere they tore at his clothing, smoke rose with more burning pain . . . until they pinned him down.

Out of his frayed and charred sleeves, they tore off his stilettos, sheathes and all. The pain left him half-blind, half-conscious, and in spasms. He felt them digging for his bone knife and garrote. And then they were gone from atop him, and he tried to roll on his side as he clutched at the plateau's rough stone.

He could barely see while clinging to consciousness. All that he spotted was one of their shadowlike forms far off, as if it now stood at the precipice's edge. That one began tossing things over the edge, and Osha screamed from deep loss more than pain.

His body felt as if he had been burned all over, and he lost sight of everything as the world turned black.

Sometime later he opened his eyes slowly. He did not know how long he had simply lain there in the heat. When he raised his head, he still lay on his side, and one of *them* remained.

The Chein'âs again squatted off beyond reach and pointed at the sword.

Still shuddering, Osha tried to push himself up.

The Chein'âs let out a screech that echoed across the plateau like metal upon stone.

It rushed to the five arrowheads and the other white metal object, snatched them up, and threw them; they fell right beside the blade. The small creature bolted away along the plateau and leaped over the edge.

Osha's sight blurred with tears.

It was not enough that he had been cast out, no longer Anmaglâhk. The Burning Ones had forced upon him something so vile, so human, in the eyes of his people that he would be shunned . . . cast out, should they ever learn of it.

He collapsed on his back. If he lay there long enough in the heat, perhaps he would simply die—and that would be better. He closed his eyes, slipping away in the dark, waiting for the pain to end.

Get up.

Osha twitched in unconsciousness. At first he did not know whether he had truly awoken again . . . until burning pain on his skin and a breath of searing air confirmed it.

Get up . . . now!

He stiffened at that voice and opened his eyes, but all he saw above him was darkness broken only by the chasm's flickering light as it wavered upon the slanted rough stone of the wall behind him. Even that was too hazy in his half-conscious suffering.

We serve . . . even with our deaths. So why waste yourself this way?

Who was there? Who was speaking to him?

Searching for that voice, Osha rolled his head toward the far precipice. The plateau was little more than a blurred black plane that ended in red sky, like sometimes seen before a dawn . . . or at dusk.

Look at me . . . and listen!

Osha struggled to twist the other way, and it hurt him all over. He barely made out the opening he had come through to reach the plateau. Everything around that black pit in the stone was blurred with dim red light. But something—someone—stood in the darker shadows beyond the opening.

What we are is not found in what we are given. What we are called is not why we serve.

Osha could not make out who was there. What little light breached the opening exposed a form of sharper shape than the blurred stone of the chasm wall.

We serve without question . . . or acknowledgment . . . or reward. We serve in whatever way comes to us.

Osha struggled to his hands and knees. That voice was too painfully familiar, though he should not—could not—have truly heard it after so long.

What he could make out through the opening appeared to be a man. There was a hint of a cowl or hood, almost colorless, and perhaps a cloak with its corners tied up across the waist over a tunic. All of that attire was the same colorless tone down to leggings and high felt boots . . . perhaps of forest gray.

Do not forget what little I was able to teach you. Honor me in that . . . not in memory or mourning . . . or a worthless death.

Osha pushed up, somehow climbing to his feet amid the pain, and squinted at the shadowed figure.

"Jeóin . . . Teacher?" he tried to say, though it came out a hoarse whisper.

The figure did not move or speak again. Perhaps the too-dark pit of its cowl shifted, as if looking beyond him.

Osha teetered as he turned enough to peer at what still lay upon the stone. Even the sword, the arrowheads, and the split tube were blurred in his sight, and when he looked back . . .

No one was there beyond the opening.

Osha rushed over, stumbling, and looked up the steps leading back to the white metal portal.

"Sgäilsheilleache!" His scream tore his throat, though it did not stop him. "Please . . . Sgäilsheilleache . . . come back."

The only answer he received was the echo of his own torment, and he crumpled upon the first step. When he had no tears left, he crawled back out upon the plateau. On his knees, he stared at what had been given to him in place of what had been taken from him.

He had to accept it all. He might no longer be Anmaglâhk, but he could not disrespect the covenants. He could not shame his lost teacher.

Spreading out his tattered and charred cloak, he fumbled to place all of the objects upon it . . . even that hiltless sword. He could not tie it all together and was forced to gather it all in his arms. That only made his flesh sting as he crawled up the stone steps out of the searing depths. . . .

Wynn sat on the bunk. She ached inside as she watched Osha, who only stared at the dead wick of the candle that no longer sent a trace of smoke into the cabin's air.

"I have told no one but you," he whispered, expressionless.

Wynn began to shudder, and the room became a watery blur before her eyes. But she would not cry, not let one tear fall. Nothing she felt could match what he had been through.

Most Aged Father, Brot'an, and then the Chein'âs . . .

What had they done to the Osha she had once known?

She slipped off the bunk's edge and knelt on the floor before him, though the dead candle was in her way, and she didn't know whether she should—could—move it to reach him. Only then did Osha blink once and look up at her.

"I can't imagine what . . ." she started, and looked at his hands, cupped one in the other in his lap; the sheen of burn scars was visible below the sleeve cuffs. "I can't imagine," she repeated.

"No, you cannot."

"What . . . what then?"

"I made my way to the shore. . . . I am uncertain how. . . ."

Osha remembered waking to the sound of waves crashing and the sight of the ship's master standing over him, her wide eyes filled with fright and worry.

"Be careful," she said, looking aside at someone else. "He has been burned."

Osha almost cried out as two of the ship's crew gripped and lifted him. As they stepped into the water to place him in a skiff, he must have fallen unconscious again. When he next awoke, he lay on his stomach upon a bunk aboard the ship. For all that he could tell, he was naked, covered only by a thin blanket. But he could feel cold, soaked cloths wrapped around his forearms and draped across his back. Nearby on the floor lay the wrapped bundle of what had once been his cloak and what was held within it.

He did not want to see or think about it.

Days passed, each the same, and the ship arrived at the enclave where he had first boarded it.

The crew found clothes for him from among their own people—in various shades of brown. He managed to dress himself, as he would not let anyone do so for him. He did not want them staring at his burns.

It had been so long since he had worn anything but the forest gray of an anmaglâhk. When he looked down at himself in those strange yet familiar clothes of his people, he did not feel like himself; he did not feel like anyone at all. And then he gathered the hated bundle to go up on deck.

"Take me ashore," he said.

Two of the crew immediately prepped the skiff.

Once ashore, Osha walked to the very back of the settlement, near the edge of the tree line, as he thought of that shadowy figure . . . the one he had thought had been . . .

No, it could not have been Sgäilsheilleache. His jeóin would have been ashamed of all the breaches into which his student had been forced, of the Chein'âs casting him out . . . of their taking his gifts as an anmaglâhk to force a human weapon upon him.

His sorrow suddenly smothered under anger.

"Valhachkasej'ú . . . Brot'ân'duivé!"

Osha cursed the greimasg'äh by name in the foulest way of his people. Dropping his bundle of burdens, he ran into the forest and searched for any open space among the trees. He tried to think—imagine—how to call to the clhuassas, the listener, so it might take him away. . . .

Everywhere among the thinned coastal trees, there seemed no place like the one in which the twisted greimasg'äh had first called the sacred one. Osha panted in pain as his clothes rubbed his burns.

Then a sharper rustle rose in the branches above him. It was too loud for the shore breeze.

Before he halted or even looked up, a large black feather flipped and rolled down into the scrawny grass before him.

It looked to be that of a raven . . . a very large one. Osha tilted his head back.

Something peered down at him with round and glassy black eyes in a black face.

Between the leaves hid something—*someone*—larger than a mere bird. *He* would have been no more than half Osha's height if he stood upon the ground instead of squatting on a thick, low branch.

The séyilf—a Windblown one—gazed fixedly down at Osha as he flexed his folded black wings just once.

Though he was slight-boned and narrow of torso, if he had opened those wings fully, they would have spanned five times his height. From his pinion feathers to the downy covering on his body and face, he was a shiny shade of black.

The only séyilf that Osha had ever seen was at Magiere's trial before the people's clan council of elders. He had never heard of a black one.

Instead of hair, larger feathers combed back from the top of the séyilf's head. The same were visible on the bottom edge of his forearms and the sides of his lower legs. He pushed farther out of the leaves above and cocked his head like a raven.

As Osha continued looking up, all the anger, sorrow . . . everything washed out of him. He knew the Windblown did not speak as he did, but he had to know what it was doing here. They were responsible for carrying message stones to and from the mountain of the Chein'âs. How was unknown, and beyond this, they were seldom seen. The Windblown, like the Burning Ones, were protected in alliance with the an'Cróan.

Before Osha could think of a way to pose a question, the male began plucking more of his feathers. He dropped each one, and, five in all, they fluttered to the ground before Osha. The séyilf pointed to the feathers and then out and north along the coast.

Osha looked down at the shining black feathers, and when he looked up, the séyilf was gone.

Five feathers . . . and five white metal arrowheads . . . for war.

The meaning was clear.

Osha began to pant again, as if he could not catch his breath, until he went numb. He watched as one feather rolled twice under the coastal breeze . . . and he waited.

Let them all blow away, and he would not have to look at them again. But not another one moved.

Osha gathered the feathers and slowly returned to retrieve the bundle of his other "gifts." He returned to the enclave to find that there was already another, larger vessel anchored offshore, and when he asked about it, he was told that it was bound for Ghoivne Ajhâjhe—Edge of the Deep—his people's only true port and city far to the north.

A hesitant knock came outside the cabin door.

Wynn started slightly, still on her knees facing Osha over the dead candle.

"Wynn . . . are you in there?"

At Chane's voice outside, she stood up—having no wish for him to walk in and find her kneeling before Osha.

"Yes, we are here," she called.

The door cracked open halfway, and Chane peered around its edge. He glanced from Shade to Wynn and then back to her before his eyes found Osha.

"We near Oléron and should gather our things. I could not find you in our cabin, so . . ."

He trailed off, and Wynn watched his expression darken. But her thoughts were churning with everything she'd heard. Osha suddenly rose, snatching up the candle, and he tucked it away in a small satchel.

Ignoring Chane, Wynn asked softly, "Are you all right?"

Osha nodded once without looking at her, but she didn't believe him.

"You should get packed," she said for lack of anything better.

Lying near the bunk's other end, on the floor, was the long and narrow canvas-wrapped bundle. She had already seen his bow and his black-feathered arrows, though she didn't know what had become of the tube of Chein'âs metal that he'd mentioned. But there could only be one thing left in that canvas.

The sword.

She wondered where he'd gotten the bow that she'd seen him use with shocking skill . . . a skill he'd never displayed in those early times she'd been with him. But she'd never seen him nock an arrow with a white metal head.

"I am packed," Osha answered, though he'd not moved from where he sat.

CHAPTER NINE

The port of Oléron was small compared to others Chane had seen: it was not even large enough to boast a harbormaster's office. Even at night, it looked shabby and unnoteworthy. A knot formed in his stomach as he led the way into its smattering of structures, for he kept thinking back to the moment when he'd opened that cabin door.

Wynn's expression had betrayed something like guilt as she stood inside with Osha. What could she have to feel guilty about? A small part of Chane wanted to know. The larger part did not.

At Nikolas's vocal yawn, Chane looked down at his side.

The young man had circles under his eyes that had grown darker with each passing day. Clearly the homebound sage was exhausted and not sleeping well. Nikolas looked around at the little town, which must be familiar to him. There was nothing exceptional about Oléron to Chane's eyes; yet Nikolas appeared haunted by the sight of it.

"I can't re-remember if there's an inn . . . here," he stuttered.

Chane glanced back at Wynn following behind him, and she frowned. She, too, caught Nikolas's misconception, and she stepped ahead with Shade at her side. As Osha tried to follow her, Chane sidestepped in the way.

His distrust of Osha only continued to grow.

"We need a wagon and horses," Wynn began, "to get started on our way to Beáumie Keep."

"Tonight?" Nikolas asked, a squeak of shock in his voice.

"Yes," Wynn answered. "You know about Chane's . . . skin condition."

Chane looked away at the small dwellings and faded shops. For some reason Wynn's mention of a "condition" bothered him, as if he had some weakness that others had to accommodate. He could see that Nikolas needed rest.

"Chane cannot be exposed to sunlight," Wynn went on. "I told you we needed to travel by night once we reached land."

"Yes, but . . ." Nikolas stammered, "but I didn't think we'd do so the instant we landed."

Until recently Chane had been able to resist falling dormant during the day through the use of an inky violet potion—though he still had to remain protected from direct sunlight. But he had used the last of that draught back in Calm Seatt and had been unable to prepare more. One primary ingredient was a rare flower that in his native tongue, Belaskian, was called *"dyvjàka svonchek,"* or "boar's bell." There was a superstition that only wild boars and other hearty beasts could eat it and survive. It was deadly, and a difficult component to acquire.

So for now he was stuck falling dormant the instant the sun rose. Chane spotted a possible small tavern or inn up the central street, little better than a wide dirt road. He quick-stepped to touch Wynn's shoulder before he pointed out the place.

"Take everyone there to rest," he said quietly. "Give me your travel orders and enough funds for a wagon and horses, and I will find a stable or livery here . . . somewhere. You speak with the inn's owner and see if there is fresh food to purchase somewhere for the journey."

She nodded, and he immediately felt a little better. They had traveled long ways together since he had found her again. She knew that she could rely on him.

Wynn halted, as did everyone else, as she swung her pack off her shoulders. She handed her staff to Chane and began digging in the pack.

"Do you want Shade to come with you?" she asked, pulling out a small black leather pouch.

The pouch bulged more than Chane expected. "No, keep Shade with you."

Chane trusted Shade to protect Wynn—and Nikolas—more than he trusted that sulking elf.

"I will not be long," he called in his harsh rasp as he headed up the street.

It wasn't long into the night before Wynn was aboard a wagon heading south down a rough coastal road. The moon was bright, and, while sitting beside Chane on the wagon's bench, she looked out and over the cliffs at the ocean. White-foam ribbons of waves below lapped toward the rocky shore.

Chane had insisted on driving, and Osha, Nikolas, and Shade were all in the back.

True to Chane's claim, he had procured a sturdy wagon and a team of young bay geldings. Even better, the stable master had acknowledged the letter from Premin Hawes as a domin of the guild, and agreed to hire out the wagon and team instead of expecting a full purchase. The guild was well trusted in such things, and Chane signed for the property with the promised return of both wagon and horses once they returned to Oléron.

All things considered, the journey had gone well so far.

If only Nikolas didn't appear to dread his homecoming so much.

If only Chane and Osha would at least try to tolerate each other.

If only Osha weren't suffering from mysterious burdens placed upon him by the Chein'âs.

In the last of all that, Wynn hoped that once Osha had told her everything, she'd understand the changes in him and why he—and Leanâlhâm—had come all this way with Brot'an. Instead she was now even more confused.

"Are you all right?" Chane asked.

Wynn turned to find him looking down at her. Her expression must have given away her worries.

"Yes," she answered too quickly. "I'm only wondering what we'll find at this duchy."

Though she said this to put him off, perhaps it was better to push down the issues with *all* of her companions and focus on the tasks to come.

It seemed that a messenger—either a tall woman or a slender-boned man—wearing a black cloak and a mask and gloves had brought a package with a letter for Nikolas from his father. Therein was another sealed letter, the content of which Nikolas didn't know, for Premin Hawes. The premin had then packaged several suspicious texts—one on transmogrification—as requested for delivery to Master Jausiff Columsarn upon his adopted son's return to Beáumie Keep in Witeny. And the old master sage had also mentioned to Hawes that something was wrong with the young duke of the keep, and there were unexplained changes in the land, people, and even wildlife and livestock in the surrounding villages.

The nature of those texts, especially that one, left Wynn wondering what was happening in the villages . . . or to the duke, a childhood friend of Nikolas Columsarn.

And then, one night after the double letter arrived, someone matching the description of the messenger had somehow breached the dwarven underworld.

That interloper had been stopped only upon reaching the wall through which Wynn had been taken through earth and stone to see the ancient texts she had brought back from the far eastern continent. That hidden place, accessible to only the Stonewalkers, was also where Ore-Locks had hidden the orb of Earth.

If the messenger and the would-be thief were the same person, how could she—or he—possibly be connected to Nikolas's father? And how could that someone know where the orb had been hidden?

It still bothered Wynn that she'd been forced to set aside locating the orb of Spirit. But this possible attempt to steal the orb of Earth was more pressing, and so Premin Hawes had sent Wynn after their only lead.

Glancing into the wagon's back, she saw Osha sitting cross-legged with his back against the wagon's left sidewall. Shade lay right behind the wagon's bench with her eyes half-closed. Nikolas had drooped where he sat, flopping sideways onto two stacked packs by the wagon's right wall.

"We should stop well before dawn," she whispered to Chane. "Nikolas is done in already. He's not used to shifting time frames, day to night, like the rest of us."

Chane raised an eyebrow but nodded. "We should put another league or two behind us, perhaps go on until the high moon, but I will watch for a suitable place to camp. We can make the young sage comfortable once we stop. I asked the stable master to loan us canvases, poles, and blankets along with the wagon."

Wynn glanced sidelong at Chane, who kept his eyes ahead on the road. She couldn't clearly make out his irises in the dark, but perhaps they had lost all of their color, and their pupils widened to see far better in the dark than the living could.

He had changed in strange ways over the past season. Much as he had always watched over her and even Shade, his devotions as a protector had spread to any member of the guild as well . . . even for all the misery and obstacles the premin council had heaped on her.

"Thank you," she said quietly, looking back over the cliff.

"You do not have to thank me."

As promised, and well before dawn, Chane spotted an adequate clearing off the road. They stopped there, and he allowed himself to get lost in mundane tasks, such as tending the horses and setting up two makeshift tents. These chores kept him busy until the moon was past its highest point. Only when Chane went to see whether Wynn needed help with the fire did he notice something else.

"Where is the elf?" he asked.

Shade lifted her head where she lay beside Wynn and peered all around the clearing.

Wynn straightened up on her knees from blowing on embers inside moss laid over spindly branches.

"I thought he was helping you," she said, looking about as well.

Nikolas had already crawled into one tent, but Osha was nowhere to be seen.

As Wynn got to her feet, Chane focused on listening to every sound around them as he let hunger slip through his flesh to increase his hearing. Beneath the sounds of surf over the cliff and wind in the trees, he heard the gurgle of water, like a stream. Perhaps the sullen elf had gone for freshwater.

Chane did not actually care where Osha went. His purpose was to protect Wynn and aid in her pursuits. But any member of their current group who suddenly vanished without his awareness unnerved him. And then he heard the light footsteps approaching.

In less than a breath, Osha came around a near tree into camp. With his hood down, his long white-blond hair hung loose and bright in the dark. His sleeves were pushed up, exposing his tan and scarred arms, and he carried three large silver fish on a cord strung through their mouths and gills.

He could not have been gone long, and he had no hook, line, or pole. Had he caught the fish with his bare hands? More annoying was that Chane had not even heard the elf's approach until the last instant.

Wynn sighed, which pulled Chane's attention in time to see her smile.

"Oh, good," she said, closing on Osha. "I managed to buy some bread, cheese, and a few apples, but those will help our supplies last."

She was praising Osha for providing food.

Chane hated most human emotions. They were beneath him. He especially hated anything petty, even when he heard himself saying . . .

"There is still plenty of time before dawn. Shade and I will hunt for other game."

Osha looked him up and down, held up the fish, and said in Belaskian, "Wynn does not like meat. She likes fish."

Chane went cold. The beast inside him, the monster of his inner nature chained down within him, thrashed at its bonds as if wanting blood. He struggled to hold himself in place.

Perhaps his own hunger was why his emotions surfaced so easily. How long had it been since he fed?

Wynn stepped up to him, placing herself between him and Osha, and touched the sleeve of his shirt. "You've been looking paler the past few nights," she said quietly. "There should be . . . wildlife here. Perhaps you could go and . . ."

Chane dropped his eyes from the elf to her. Some time ago she had made him swear never again to feed on a sentient being. He had kept that promise so far, and she believed he subsisted on the blood of livestock and large wild game.

This was half-true.

"I'll cook the fish," she said. "You go while you have time."

She was correct, though it felt as though he was being dismissed. Still, before they reached the duchy, he needed to be at full strength.

When traveling, he always carried two packs: one was his own, and the other had belonged to his old mentor, Welstiel Massing, now dead for the final time. No matter how long Chane possessed that second pack, he would always think of it as Welstiel's.

Without another word, Chane grabbed the second pack from the wagon's back and walked off into the trees. He felt Wynn's eyes upon him but did not look back.

Osha watched Chane vanish into the woods, and he fought to keep his own expression still.

Wynn ran a hand over her face. When her hand dropped, her eyes flashed with anger.

"You did that on purpose," she accused. "You tried to humiliate him." Then her tone softened. "That's not like you."

No, it was not, but it was unthinkable that one such as she would keep company with that *thing*. Obviously she had also changed.

"Where is he going?" Osha asked in his own tongue, perhaps too sharply. "What is he doing?"

"Hunting for himself," she answered, keeping to Belaskian.

Osha knew that was not the whole truth.

She stepped closer, looked at the fish he held, and sighed. "Nikolas is already asleep. We should cook and eat some ourselves, saving one for when he wakes. I'll share mine with Shade."

Grateful for a simple focus, Osha nodded. While she stoked the campfire, he scavenged and whittled until he had forked branches planted at the fire's sides and a thicker green bough stripped of bark for a skewer. He cleaned one fish and handed it to her, and while she skewered and set it over the flames, he started on the second one.

"You always were good at catching fish," she said.

He looked up. "It is not difficult," he answered in an'Cróan Elvish.

"Not for you." She glanced away, lingering in looking to the wagon.

His curved bow rested on the wagon's end with his quiver.

"You've become quite the archer," she said. "But that's not the bow of a . . ."

Osha turned his attention back to cleaning the fish. No, it was not an anmaglâhk's bow, which would be assembled from parts hidden away in the back of a forest gray vestment beneath a matching cloak. He no longer possessed any of those things.

He had told her most of his story, at least for what had happened before he left his people. But he was uncertain that it had done her any good. It had not done anything for him.

"Why did you leave?" she asked, and then hesitated. "Why did you come all the way here . . . with Brot'an . . . after what he did and . . . What possible reason could you and Brot'an have for bringing Leanâlhâm?"

"What is it you want?" he snapped, growing angry now. "After all that I have told you—the shame of it—and still *you* want more from *me*?"

Her face calm, she rocked back on her heels. "Yes, I want all of it."

Frustrated, he let his mind roll back to what had happened the night his ship reached Ghoivne Ajhâjhe.

"When I left the ship and was about to step off the dock, I saw

Brot'ân'duivé standing there in the sand . . . waiting for me! He was the one who forced me to answer that summons, who sent me to the Chein'âs! And there he stood. But before I could curse his name, I heard someone cry out . . . and I looked down the shore to see Leanâlhâm being assaulted by three of my caste." He gazed into Wynn's shocked face. "Yes, they attacked her. One of them lifted her off the ground." He shook his head. "They were willing to hurt one of our own people, a helpless girl."

"Why?" Wynn gasped.

"Because of Brot'ân'duivé! I did not know at the time, but a small team of the loyalists had murdered Gleannéohkân'thva. In retribution the greimasg'äh made an attempt on Most Aged Father's life. This sent the loyalists into madness. They were going to take Leanâlhâm hostage and use her against Brot'ân'duivé."

Wynn's mouth fell open. "Anmaglâhk murdered Gleann? Oh, poor Leanâlhâm. Why would they do such a thing?"

There Osha paused. He could not bring himself to tell her that the old healer was killed over a journal that Wynn herself had sent—a journal that Most Aged Father had desperately wanted, as he believed it contained information about the first orb.

"Gleannéohkân'thva was a dissident," he answered flatly, instead of giving her the whole truth. He hoped she would stop questioning him. He had questions of his own that *she* needed to answer.

"So Leanâlhâm was attacked there on the shore?"

"I went to rescue her, and . . . I had to accept help from the greimasg'äh, for I could not take three of them alone without my weapons. The greimasg'äh had wounded all three before I went for Leanâlhâm's captor. Once I had her, Brot'ân'duivé drove off the trio. But by then . . . it did not matter."

Every scar upon Osha stung anew, as if burned by the memory, as he turned his eyes again on Wynn. "Leanâlhâm is now seen as an enemy of Most Aged Father, and, through his lies, an enemy of the people. I marked myself the same in attacking my . . . the anmaglâhk . . . in company with the greimasg'äh."

"So you had to run," Wynn whispered, "from your own caste, your people."

"Because of Brot'ân'duivé! He had a new *purpose*—to hunt those who hunted Magiere and Léshil, and to kill them. I joined the greimasg'äh on his journey and later . . . had no choice but to join in his purpose, for I had to protect Leanâlhâm from his obsession."

Osha fell silent, idly turning the fish on the skewer—and still Wynn would not relent.

"What happened on the voyage . . . to my homeland?"

He could not even bring himself to look at her; it was a moment before he said another word, and finally he began to speak. . . .

Osha, along with Leanâlhâm, followed Brot'ân'duivé, who somehow gained them passage on a civilian an'Cróan vessel willing to sail into human waters. If that crew had only known what the greimasg'äh had done, would do . . . but they did not. And who among the people would deny aid to an anmaglâhk, let alone the great Brot'ân'duivé, greimasg'äh and master of silence and shadow?

The people were grateful, for the Anmaglâhk served them, protected them. So it was said and believed. The ship took them around the point and south toward the Outward Bay and Bela, capital city of the human nation of Belaski. That voyage unto itself was painful.

For all that Osha had suffered, he stayed inside a cabin on board as much as he could, for Leanâlhâm would not leave the place, even for meals. Whenever he left to seek out food and water, when he brought such back, he saw panic in her eyes, as if she feared he might not return. Also, he noticed that she flinched every time he said her name.

It was longer still before Osha suspected there was more to this than Leanâlhâm's loss of home, Sgäilsheilleache, and then Gleannéohkân'thva, but he did not press her.

There were some things one did not demand—or take. So Osha cared only for her needs and did what he could for her suffering. Yet even amid this,

Brot'ân'duivé insisted upon examining Osha's "gifts"—as he called them—from the Chein'âs and the black séyilf.

As Leanâlhâm looked anxiously between her companions, Brot'ân'duivé demanded that Osha tell him what happened in the fire caves.

Osha said nothing. And so the greimasg'äh took the sword only and left the cabin that all three of them shared. Osha did not care whether he ever again saw that human thing that had severed him from the life he had wanted in service to his people.

Brot'ân'duivé came back without the sword . . . until the fifth following day, when it was in his hand again. He thrust it at Osha.

The hilt strut had been fitted with tawny, smooth, and shimmering wood like that of the living ship of their people that carried them—a Päirvänean. The same wood was used for the hilts of Anmaglâhk blades, though it was not always grown out of a ship. Those hilts were also wrapped tightly in straps of leather, obscuring what was beneath the wrap, for a sure grip.

"It is yours," the greimasg'äh declared, "made for you by the Chein'âs. You must learn to use it . . . though I cannot be your teacher for this."

Osha wanted nothing to do with that cursed thing. He touched it only long enough to wrap and hide it from his sight. More than once he thought to cast it overboard, but each time he faltered, unable to do so.

Once the ship reached Bela, Brot'ân'duivé learned that the team hunting Magiere and Léshil had already set sail.

It took two days to arrange passage and board a human ship sailing to the central continent. Osha balked at that, though the thought of Leanâlhâm alone in some foreign land with only the tainted greimasg'äh was more than he could tolerate. Even if he had not cared for her as if she were of his own blood, she was the last kin of his jeóin, his teacher.

He tried to consider any option besides forcing her onto a ship bound for another continent.

"She cannot stay here among humans," Brot'ân'duivé stated flatly, "and you cannot take her home. You would both be seized for treason."

And why? Because they both had ties to the greimasg'äh, and thereby they were both of use to Most Aged Father.

So they boarded the human vessel and crossed the ocean.

That journey over seemingly endless water felt like a lifetime. Osha found some comfort in caring for Leanâlhâm and in the fact that Brot'ân'duivé often left them alone. It gave Osha a reason—a purpose—not to think on all that had happened to him.

When they landed in a stinking and teeming human city on the central continent's eastern coast, Brot'ân'duivé's demeanor changed. He settled Osha and Leanâlhâm in an inn and vanished for a while that night. The following dawn he returned . . . with a longbow, a number of bare arrow shafts, black crow feathers, other odd materials, and even some steel arrowheads.

"The loyalists head west, across land," he said. "We will track them."

Osha did not know or care how Brot'ân'duivé learned this. But he could not help thinking that if the loyalists hunted Magiere and Léshil, they might also hunt any of the pair's past companions . . . such as Wynn. She had written the journal via which the greimasg'äh and Most Aged Father had started open war among the people.

That fear goaded Osha into obedience to the greimasg'äh. The next day began another long journey, this time overland. And Brot'ân'duivé would not leave Osha in peace.

As they made camp at the end of their first day, the shadow-gripper stood over him and demanded, "Give me the white metal bow handle."

Osha was confused, not knowing what the greimasg'äh meant. When he did not respond, Brot'ân'duivé went to Osha's belongings and began searching. Osha was on his feet in an instant, for he had had enough meddling for a lifetime.

The greimasg'äh rose, and in his hand was the split tube of white metal that was slightly curved.

Osha stared at the thing.

"It was likely made to fit the handle of a bow carried by our ship's soldiers," the greimasg'äh explained. "I did not realize this soon enough."

He crouched again and retrieved the curved bow he acquired in that long night in the city. With a bit of pressure, he snapped the tube over the back side and around the bow's handle. "It is not a proper fit, but it will do once it is properly wrapped."

Brot'ân'duivé settled to the earth, dug in his own pack, and pulled out a long strip of thin black leather. He began by packing the strip's end in between the tube and the handle with the tip of a stiletto, so that the tube was not loose. Then he set to wrapping and binding the white metal tube around the handle.

Osha settled to the ground. Not wishing to watch, he looked away to where Leanâlhâm had fallen asleep upon her bedroll. He hoped she did not dream of the recent past as much as he did.

"You will learn to use this bow," Brot'ân'duivé said.

"No," Osha replied.

Even if he could not cast aside the burdens given to him, he would not use them. He would not submit to more loss of himself in what had been put upon him as well as taken from him.

"It will be unfamiliar," Brot'ân'duivé went on, as if Osha had not spoken. "The bow arms are longer and far more curved than those of an Anmaglâhk bow. It has greater range and power but will be more difficult to draw, and hence—"

"No," Osha repeated.

Something cracked sharply across his chest and upper right arm. Pain made his sight flash white as he toppled over, and then anger brought him around in a crouch.

Brot'ân'duivé sat cross-legged on the earth with his left arm outstretched to the side, and he still gripped the unstrung bow he had used to strike. The greimasg'äh's eyes, one caged by the four slashing scars, fixed on Osha.

"Enough self-pity!" he ordered. "The stretch we must cross for more than a moon is called the Broken Lands by those in the city who speak adequate Belaskian. There are creatures out here that neither of us has ever seen. Any merchant caravan crossing either way travels heavily armed and guarded. And we are only three."

"Then we turn back and find a caravan!"

"I will not lose time in tracking my quarry or have them double back to find you, should you think to turn back on your own. You have one choice, here and now."

Osha clenched all over as his fingers dug into the earth. Only a fool would assault a greimasg'äh, but he was beyond caring.

"If not for yourself," Brot'ân'duivé whispered, "then what of the girl?"

Osha froze before he could lunge and glanced toward Leanâlhâm's sleeping form.

"When a moment comes when I cannot protect you both," the greimasg'äh added, "how will you protect *her*? If not for yourself, that is a reason to accept what you have been given."

Osha hung in stillness.

"And since I cannot teach you the sword . . ." And the greimasg'äh's extended arm whipped forward.

Osha scrambled back out of reach, but instead of striking him again, the bow tumbled to his feet.

"You will make yourself useful," Brot'ân'duivé said.

Again Osha found he had no choice. He could not let Leanâlhâm suffer for his burdens or the bloodlust of Brot'ân'duivé. But he burned inside at the way the greimasg'äh manipulated him through using someone else . . . like Most Aged Father so often did.

In the following days, when they stopped before dusk, he learned how to fletch, but he would work only with the steel arrowheads and the black crow feathers that Brot'ân'duivé had brought. Osha would not touch the white metal heads or the five black feathers dropped by the séyilf. As he fletched, Leanâlhâm watched him. Once, she tried to offer to help, but the greimasg'äh forbade her, saying that only Osha should attend his own weapons.

However, while Osha worked upon the arrows, often starting over for mistakes, the greimasg'äh frequently slipped away, sometimes not returning until dawn. Brot'ân'duivé said nothing of where he had gone, though Osha knew the greimasg'äh was tracking the team of loyalists.

When Osha finished with the steel arrowheads and would still not touch the five from the Chein'âs—or the black feathers from the séyilf—Brot'ân'duivé fashioned those himself in less than an evening.

"Do not use these in battle unless necessary," he instructed. "There is some purpose to them that I—you—have yet to understand. But you will learn to use them."

Osha had no intention of doing so. When the moment came to learn the bow, he strung it with only a little effort, for he had been "adequate" with an Anmaglâhk bow. As he reached for a steel-tipped arrow from his quiver on the ground . . .

"That is not an anmaglâhk bow," Brot'ân'duivé said, "but you will learn as if it was, and by what is taught later to even those who . . . barely managed to gain a jeóin."

Osha heated under that slight.

"You will learn what Sgäilsheilleache did not have the days to teach you," Brot'ân'duivé said.

Osha was at a loss as to what that meant. Yes, he had lost his teacher too soon after gaining the only one he had wanted—and the only one who might have accepted him. More baffling was that this new training did not begin with an arrow.

It began with a lit candle.

At first he wondered whether he was to shoot at it. Even Leanâlhâm blinked and frowned at this strangeness.

"Sit ten strides off and watch the flame," Brot'ân'duivé instructed as he lit the candle and set it upon the ground. "Listen to *everything* around you, but keep your eyes on the flame at all times."

And so Osha did, but only on those evenings when the wind was no more than a breeze that could not snuff the candle out. How many dusks and dawns did he do this each time until the greimasg'äh told him to stop? And one morning, instead of fluttering in the changing breeze, the flame blew out.

A trail of smoke from the wick quickly dissipated.

"What did you hear?" the greimasg'äh asked.

Osha scowled. "Wind, a breeze . . . in the grass . . . in the trees."

"What did you feel on your body, your exposed skin, your hands and face?"

"Wind!" Osha snapped.

"Enough to blow out a candle?"

"Yes, enough to . . ." Osha paused, staring at the wick ten strides off. "No . . . not enough."

"What is the difference between you and the candle? What did you hear that you did not feel?"

The difference became obvious, though he had never thought of this before. The wind did not blow with the same strength in each place where it passed—even with as little as ten paces' difference.

Training continued with two, then three, and finally four candles in line out beyond him. It grew harder to know for certain, to hear the differences in the air's movement farther outward. After that the greimasg'äh added a change whenever the wind was too strong for candles.

Brot'ân'duivé took Osha into stands of woods along the way. He gathered leaves that had fallen beneath a near tree and walked out across an open space to another distant one. He turned and, dropping a leaf every few strides, traced his steps back.

"Draw an arrow and aim for the far tree," he said. "Watch the leaves until an instant comes when you are certain all of the leaves are still."

Osha did so and hit the tree the first time, though it was only twenty to twenty-five paces off.

"Now wait until you see only one leaf turn, and then shoot."

Again he hit the tree, though a little off center. This continued every morning until they camped early near some tall oaks and the wind was more brisk than a candle could bear. That evening the greimasg'äh laid out the leaves, some of which turned or flopped immediately.

"Take aim, note the movement of the leaves for three breaths, then close your eyes and shoot."

Osha scowled at such a ridiculous practice, but he did as instructed. He never heard the arrow hit the tree.

"Retrieve the arrow and repeat . . . always with the same arrow."

Osha went wandering off after the arrow. He spent until dusk trying to hit the tree with his eyes closed—and never did. He cheated and tried it with his eyes open, and hit the tree only half of the time. When the sky darkened too much, he turned back to camp, where Leanâlhâm had finished cooking a squirrel that the greimasg'äh had likely caught.

"So, why did you miss . . . even when you opened your eyes?" asked Brot'ân'duivé.

Osha glanced back along the way he had come. The greimasg'äh could not have seen him from camp, so how would he know?

"Because I listen," Brot'ân'duivé said, "and you do not. Obviously you only hit the tree when your eyes were open. Return to the candles at dawn. You will use the bow and leaves only at dusk. And this time you will *listen* as well as look."

The greimasg'äh fixed Osha with an unblinking stare.

"When aiming for a distant target, you will not have leaves and candles to mark the varied movements of the air at different points along the arrow's path."

Leanâlhâm let out a sharp sigh before Osha could. The greimasg'äh did not look her way, but Osha did. Leanâlhâm appeared as mentally weary of all this as Osha felt.

A whole moon passed before he hit a tree at least half of the time at twenty, then thirty, and finally forty paces. In that time the greimasg'äh often disappeared for a whole night. One dawn Osha and Leanâlhâm awoke, had a fire going and oats boiling in a small pot . . .

And Brot'ân'duivé had not yet returned.

Osha wondered whether to go searching, but he could not leave Leanâlhâm alone. She, too, stared off into the distance with panic in her quick breaths. And perhaps that panic sharpened when she glanced at him looking off into the distance. And then Osha started at the sound of leaves crushed underfoot, and he quickly pulled an arrow and drew it back as he turned left.

He relaxed a little even before Brot'ân'duivé stepped out of the trees. If the greimasg'äh had wished, he would not be heard until too late. Then Osha tensed again and heard Leanâlhâm gasp.

Brot'ân'duivé's tunic and sleeves were rent and torn. One side of his hood had been sharply split, and the forest gray cloth was splattered with dark stains . . . from blood. Without a word, the greimasg'äh stripped off his tunic, cloak, and hood, dropped them in a pile, and settled cross-legged on the ground beside the fire. He looked at Leanâlhâm. "Can you wash and mend these?"

Wordlessly she nodded, but Osha studied the greimasg'äh.

There were other old scars, besides the ones on his face, on Brot'ân'duivé's torso and arms. A line of bruises had formed along the left side of his chest and on his right forearm, but more disturbing was what was not there.

There was not one bleeding wound for all the blood on his clothes.

Osha knew then that they had caught up to the loyalists . . . who were now at least one less than they had been.

"How far?" he asked.

"A day's walk," Brot'ân'duivé answered, peeking into the pot over the flames as if interested only in its contents.

Osha blinked repeatedly, looking west, not believing that even the great Brot'ân'duivé could have gone so far and returned in one night.

Leanâlhâm crouched before the pile of stained and torn garments, but she still had not touched them. With her green eyes fully widened, she looked up at Osha, and Osha turned to the greimasg'äh.

"Will they not find—"

"No," Brot'ân'duivé said as he poured water from a flask to rinse his hand with stains long dried and crusted. "The body is hidden. Once they know one of theirs is gone, they will not willingly linger against their purpose in trying to find it."

"You left one of our—" Leanâlhâm began, but she was silenced by the greimasg'äh's stare.

"He . . . she . . . whoever," Osha added, "is still one of our people. How could you leave even one of them with no way back to our ancestors?"

"There is no time for sentiment," Brot'ân'duivé whispered at first and then barked, "or do you believe these fanatics would give you such a thought?"

Yes, Osha did . . . or he hoped. Without that, at least, what was left of their people, no matter who won this conflict? And still Leanâlhâm would not touch the bloodstained clothing.

Osha took those clothes and walked off into the trees to search for a stream or pool or even a puddle that was far from Leanâlhâm's sight. And when he returned with the soaked clothes and hung them over a tree branch to drip in the night . . .

"You do nothing for her in hiding the truth of our state," Brot'ân'duivé said, lying on his back in the dark near the fire's dying embers. "Her innocence and your denial of what is . . . are a danger to you both."

Osha ignored this, though he sat up half the night and watched Leanâlhâm sleep fitfully.

In the morning his training changed again.

"You will use only an arrow with a Chein'âs point," the greimasg'äh ordered. "We will see if its secret can be uncovered."

"No."

"Do as I say!"

To his shame, some part of Osha could not continue to rebel. All that previous night he thought on Leanâlhâm, and then worried about the loyalists still at least a day ahead. It was not hard to imagine what they would do once they arrived on the western coast. Somewhere in the city of Calm Seatt was one known place—and person—from where that journal had come.

Wynn Hygeorht would be easy to find at her Guild of Sagecraft as a starting point in a hunt for Magiere, Léshil, and the wayward majay-hì called Chap.

Osha pulled a white metal–tipped arrow from his quiver and drew it in his bow. His heart was not in the first shot, and he missed. The arrow vanished among the trees.

"Find the arrow," ordered Brot'ân'duivé. "And continue."

Osha set down his bow beside the quiver to go searching for that arrow . . .

one he was reluctant to find. The morning continued, though he hit the tree only three times. When he did so, the greimasg'äh held him off with a raised hand and went to stare at the embedded arrow. Each time he returned with that arrow, his frown had deepened.

It appeared there was nothing special about the white metal arrowheads.

On the last shot of that morning, Osha missed again. The arrow glanced off the tree's trunk and disappeared from sight.

"It is time to move on," Brot'ân'duivé said, exhaling long and slow. "Gather your equipment, retrieve the arrow, and return to camp."

Tiredly, Osha picked up his quiver, and, with bow in hand, he stepped off toward the tree to gauge the strayed arrow's trajectory. Slinging the quiver over his shoulder as he walked, he raised the bow and prepared to pause at the tree and unstring it.

The bow suddenly felt wrong in his grip, and it tilted to the right as if unbalanced.

He stopped at the tree's right side, where the arrow had struck, and looked the bow over. He wondered whether he had somehow warped it. Perhaps it was not as resilient or as soundly made as an Anmaglâhk bow. But he could not see anything wrong with it.

"What is the delay?" Brot'ân'duivé called out.

"Nothing," Osha answered, pivoting left to get a sight line from the gouge in the tree's bark.

The bow tilted sharply to the right in his loose grip. Warmth beyond that caused by holding it all morning grew in the handle's leather wrap. His mind flashed with a memory of being assaulted by the Burning Ones.

Osha dropped the bow and backed away.

"What?"

He flinched at the greimasg'äh's demand, too loud in his ears, and Brot'ân'duivé now stood beside him.

"It . . . moved," he whispered. "It grew hot . . . and then moved."

"Pick it up!"

Osha did not move, and Brot'ân'duivé barked at him, "Now!"

He reluctantly did so. Nothing happened until the bow was fully upright, and then he felt the warmth growing. Before he could drop it again, the greimasg'äh's hand clamped over his grip on the bow's handle.

"They would not give you something that would cause enough harm to be useless."

Osha was not so certain, but the bow's handle warmed only a bit more.

"Now turn both ways in holding it upright."

He did so, first back toward the tree, and he felt the bow try to tilt to his right. As he turned the other way, the force of its torque lessened.

"Let it lead you . . . and follow it."

He did so, turning as it urged him, and when that feeling of a tilt stopped altogether, Osha was nearly on top of a bramble. The greimasg'äh stomped and ripped at the thorny vines.

There inside the bramble was the lost arrow.

Brot'ân'duivé picked it up and eyed the white metal point. "Partially useful, as at least you will not lose one gift in learning to use the other."

Osha did not see what real use this could be. Why would the Burning Ones force such a thing upon him . . . a thing that was so clearly not of the Anmaglâhk?

Each day became too much like the last as they walked onward. Much as Osha watched the land around them, out to the craggy, barren mountains to the north, he never saw a sign of anything. Whatever the humans feared in these so-called Broken Lands, it had yet to make itself known.

He divided time between practicing with his bow and caring for Leanâlhâm, who had been sheltered all of her life by Gleannéohkân'thva and Sgäilsheilleache. In spite of the shame forced upon him—that he was no longer Anmaglâhk—he would protect her as they had.

He did notice that she had begun to flinch less often when he used her name, but he remained determined not to ask her about this until she herself wanted to tell him.

There was one evening when he returned from practice that he found the greimasg'äh sitting cross-legged on the ground and facing Leanâlhâm.

Brot'ân'duivé leaned in close to her, though she had her hands over her face as she wept.

"What have you done?" Osha shouted, closing quickly on the greimasg'äh.

Brot'ân'duivé ignored him, though Leanâlhâm turned her face away, hiding from everyone. The greimasg'äh rose on one knee, gripped the girl by the shoulders, and gently settled her upon her bedroll to cover her with a blanket. But when he stood and turned, Osha stepped in his way.

"Answer me!" Osha demanded.

Brot'ân'duivé eyed him in silence, and then said, "I have done nothing but listen. As to what, that is her confidence with me—unless she tells you otherwise. It is not your place to even ask."

It was another moon before Osha saw the city of Calm Seatt in the distance, though even then he was not certain whether that city was the one until they entered late one night. But along the way, he cared for Leanâlhâm and waited for her to say something about the night he found her crying before the greimasg'äh. She never did.

As well, each morning there was always training.

Osha, whose name meant "a sudden breeze," shot arrows through the wind until he lost count of how many struck a tree without his ever missing.

Wynn was at something of a loss after all Osha said. She didn't know what to say about all that had happened between him and Brot'an. And so . . .

"Back in Calm Seatt, you let Leanâlhâm leave with Brot'an. If you were protecting her, why did you leave her with him?"

It was a mistake, though she realized it too late.

Osha looked stricken. "I did not leave her with Brot'ân'duivé! I left her with Léshil and Magiere, and Chap . . . and Magiere had sworn to Sgäilsheilleache to protect Leanâlhâm. My place was to protect you . . . from everything that greimasg'äh started with Most Aged Father. Even if Brot'ân'duivé fulfills his chosen purpose, it will not end Most Aged Father's desires."

"I'm sorry," she whispered, dropping her gaze. "That was a stupid question. I think it is hard for me to understand all that you have been through . . . all of the changes."

"Then instead of questions, what are your answers?"

She looked up to find him watching her.

"Tell me of your life since we parted," he said, tilting his head. "I know I am not the only one who has suffered."

This wasn't the first time he'd stunned her since he'd reappeared in her world. No one had ever asked her about this—though Chane didn't need to. He'd been there since she'd first uncovered the truth that there was more than one orb.

"What did it cost you to find this orb of Earth?" Osha asked. "I can see its cost . . . in everything about you."

Wynn grew more uncomfortable under his gaze. "I don't know where to start."

"When you left me on the waterfront of Bela."

The mention of their parting made her flush. She reached out and turned the spitted fish over, as on nights long gone when they had huddled by the fire in sharing their pasts.

Out in the forest Chane wrenched a young stag by its tineless antlers.

He threw it to the ground, pinned its neck with his knee, and struck once with full force against the back of its head. The animal went limp upon the damp forest mulch, though it was still alive, as he wished. He then went back to where he had stowed Welstiel's pack before his hunt. When he returned, he dug inside of the pack, pulled out an ornate walnut box, and opened it beside the limp stag.

Inside were three hand-length iron rods with center loops, a teacup-sized brass bowl with strange etchings, and a white ceramic bottle with an obsidian stopper. All of these rested in burgundy padding. Every time he performed this act, he remembered Welstiel instructing him. . . .

There are ways to make the life we consume last longer.

Welstiel had used the cup to feed upon humans, and Chane had taken the process a step further by his word to Wynn. He intertwined the iron rods into a tripod stand and placed the brass cup upon it before lifting the white bottle with its precious content—thrice-purified water. Pulling the stopper, he half filled the cup and remembered Welstiel's clinical explanation.

Bloodletting is a wasteful way to feed. Too much life is lost and never consumed by our kind. It is not blood that matters but the leak of life caused by its loss.

Chane glanced at the deer.

The very idea of the cup revolted him, aside from the unwelcome necessity of feeding upon animals. But he needed life to continue protecting Wynn, and he could not risk feeding on a human: she might hear of someone missing or worse.

Chane drew the dagger he kept in his pack and made a small cut on the stag's shoulder. Once the blade's tip had gathered a bead of blood, he carefully tilted the steel over the cup.

A single drop struck the water. The blood thinned and diffused.

He began to chant, concentrating upon the cup's innate influence. When finished, he watched the water in the cup for any change.

Nothing happened at first.

The stag let out a low sound. It was nothing more than the last bit of air escaping its lungs as its hide began to dry and shrivel. Its eyes collapsed inward, and its jawbone began to jut beneath withering skin. In moments it was only a dried, shrunken husk as vapors rose briefly over its corpse.

Chane turned his attention back to the cup.

The fluid within it had doubled, brimming near the lip, and it was so dark red it appeared almost black. As always, he was relieved and revolted by the sight, for he knew what awaited him in drinking the conjured fluid. The first time, Welstiel had warned him with only two words: *Brace yourself.*

Chane downed half of the cup's contents. For a moment he tasted dregs of ground metal and strong salt.

Then he gagged and collapsed.

His body began to burn from within.

Too much life, taken in such a pure form, burst through his dead flesh and swelled into his head. Jaws and eyes clenched, he curled upon the earth until the worst passed and his convulsions finally eased.

In feeding this way, it would be a half moon or more before he needed to do so again.

He slowly pushed himself up with his arms and sat staring at the shriveled husk of the young stag. He waited until his false fever subsided. Then he pulled a small bottle from the pack, poured in the remaining liquid from the cup, stoppered the bottle, and carefully packed everything away.

Strong and sated, in control of his senses, he headed back for camp, leaving the carcass where it lay. He smelled—heard—the sizzling fish long before he arrived.

Dawn was not far off.

However, when the campfire came into sight through the trees, he saw only Wynn and Osha huddled by the fire in close and quiet conversation. Both Nikolas and possibly Shade must be asleep in one of the makeshift tents.

Chane purposefully crushed a fallen branch under his boot heel.

At the snap of wood, Wynn looked back and up. "Did you . . . ?"

"I am fine."

He stepped fully out of the trees as Wynn turned her back to him to look at Osha. The elf merely stared into the fire. And as Chane passed by, he could not help noticing the sudden disappointment on Wynn's oval face, as if he had interrupted something that she wanted back.

CHAPTER TEN

The next few nights proved awkward. Wynn had hoped that time together would push Osha and Chane into a grudging acceptance of each other, but if anything the tension between them increased, and, worse, the farther south they traveled, the more Nikolas withdrew from everyone.

Wynn began to worry more about him than about Chane or Osha. Nikolas looked more disheveled and haunted each day. She often had to place food in his hands before he remembered to eat.

When Nikolas had first arrived at the Numan branch of the guild, she'd been off with Domin Tilswith, trying to lay the foundation of a new guild branch on the eastern continent. And then she'd gotten tangled up with Chap, Magiere, and Leesil. Only when she returned to Calm Seatt a year ago did she meet Nikolas Columsarn for the first time, though she'd been too wrapped up in fighting with her superiors to learn much about him. What few comments he'd made had led her to believe he was an orphan—and perhaps he was—but it had surprised her to learn his adopted father was a master sage, let alone the counselor for a duchy in Witeny.

Wynn sat on the bench as the wagon rolled along the rocky coastal road with Chane silent at the reins. Suddenly there was Nikolas climbing up on her other side to kneel on the bench's end.

"We're getting closer," he said. "I know this area well."

To make things more crowded, Shade shoved her head in on Wynn's other side and jostled Chane's elbow as she started sniffing the air.

"How far?" Osha called from the wagon's back.

"We'll reach Beáumie Keep tomorrow night," Nikolas answered, his tone making it sound like a sentence after a trial.

Wynn grew frustrated on the now-crowded bench and tilted back her head to look up at the fading stars. "Dawn isn't far off. Perhaps we should make camp."

"I have been looking," Chane answered.

And then Osha was at Wynn's back and pointing out over her head. "There."

Wynn grabbed Shade's muzzle to shove the dog back. "Would you all *please* give me some room?"

As Nikolas and Osha returned to the wagon's back as well, Wynn saw the outline of a grove in an open space beside the road. Chane turned the horses before she said anything, and soon they were all busy setting camp—all except for Nikolas, who sat on a downed tree as he stared up the road.

Wynn had had enough. She needed to know more about what they were heading into. Chane, tending to the horses, was a good distance off.

"Osha, could you gather some firewood? I'll get Nikolas to help me with the tents."

Osha raised an eyebrow, casting a doubtful glance at Nikolas, but he nodded and headed off into the woods. Wynn pulled a heavy folded canvas out of the wagon's back.

"Nikolas," she called, "come grab these stakes and give me a hand."

He jumped slightly as if startled. By the one cold-lamp crystal she'd ignited and left on the wagon's bench, his eyes looked a bit glassy. But, after gathering stakes and rope, he came to her. Shade leaped out the wagon's back to follow them.

"The ground looks most even here," Wynn said, kneeling down.

"What do I do?" he asked quietly, just standing there beside her.

Through the darkness she studied the white streaks in his hair.

"Nikolas . . ." she began, ignoring the tent stakes. "Premin Hawes asked me to deliver some texts to your father, so we'll probably be staying at the keep for a few nights before heading back. I'd like to know more about the place. Besides your father and the duke, who else lives there?"

This seemed an innocent enough question with which to begin, but he winced as if she'd asked something painful. Wynn took one furtive glance at Shade and wondered if the dog caught any errant memories suddenly rising in the young sage. In spite of invading Nikolas's privacy, Wynn rather hoped so.

"Nikolas?" Wynn prompted.

He hung his head, and his straight hair fell forward. "The duchess."

"The duchess? Then the Duke Beáumie—your friend—is married?"

"No."

Wynn frowned. "His mother?"

"His sister," Nikolas whispered. "Sherie."

That last word, a name, came out almost too quiet to hear. Before Wynn could figure out how to ask for more about this new detail, Nikolas went on. "My father and Karl . . . they promised me . . . I would never have to come back."

Wynn put aside everything about her assignment, the orbs, or possible minions of the Ancient Enemy on the move. She grasped Nikolas's forearm and pulled him down to kneel beside her.

"What happened?" she whispered. "I won't tell anyone else, but please tell me, whatever it is. I can see what it's doing to you."

Shade slipped in close and sat down. Wynn carefully released her hold on Nikolas's arm, and as she dropped her hand into her lap, she let it slide down to touch Shade's paw.

An image flashed into Wynn's mind.

She saw a beautiful girl, perhaps sixteen years old, with a serious expression. A mass of blue-black hair fell down her back and shoulders. Her dress was made of dark red velvet, which set off her pale skin and brown eyes.

Inside that memory passed by Shade directly from Nikolas, Wynn glanced downward, seeing through Nikolas's eyes into the past moment. Her—his—hand was tightly clasped with the girl's.

"Did something happen between you and . . . Sherie?" Wynn asked.

Wordlessly Nikolas nodded, the white streaks in his hair shimmering under the moon. She waited quietly, hoping Chane would take his time with the horses.

"We grew up together," Nikolas whispered. "Me, Sherie, and Karl."

A different memory came, something further back than the first one.

Two children, a boy and a girl, ran along a rocky beach on either side of Wynn—Nikolas—as they squealed and laughed without care. Both had blue-black hair and pale skin. And then the moment was gone.

"I don't know exactly when it happened," Nikolas said. "Sherie and I became . . . more."

Wynn clenched her jaw against a gasp as Shade echoed another moment to her.

She—Nikolas—was kissing the dark-haired girl, once again about sixteen or so. Wynn saw the girl's eyes open too close to hers—to Nikolas's—as she caught something of what he'd felt in that moment . . . or perhaps something from her own past told her more of what the young sage had felt.

It was so intimate, so full of longing, and almost fearful of losing what was in that touch.

Wynn's mind spun suddenly as two moments tangled: that of Nikolas's memory and . . .

So long ago, believing she might never see him again, she had thrown herself at Osha. She pushed that thought away to remain in control and not have to jerk her hand from Shade's paw.

"We were too young," Nikolas went on, "and too foolish. I was nothing . . . the adopted son of a sage with no money and no title. I shouldn't have let it happen."

The memory of him kissing Sherie went on as his hands moved down Sherie's sides to her hips, and the passion building in the moment stirred the pain of Wynn's own memory again.

A door opened—inside Nikolas's memory—and shattered that reminiscence of Osha, almost to Wynn's relief.

Standing in the open door in a wall of masoned stone was a tall middle-aged man with black hair who was dressed in a fine, dark red velvet vestment. His eyes widened in shock, and then rage spread over his angular features.

"We never thought . . ." Nikolas stammered. "Then one night her father, the elder duke, walked in on us. . . . He found us when . . ."

Wynn jerked her hand away from Shade's paw when the memory showed a quick flash in the corner of her sight . . . of a bed in that dim room. A young woman had risen in the dark, clutching a thick quilt, and that was all that covered her.

It was another moment, another hard breath, before Wynn had enough control to speak.

"Did he send you away?" she asked.

But that didn't make sense. If Nikolas had been sent away for only this, why did he dread returning now? Certainly after years away, and with Karl now in power at the duchy, the matter was long done with.

"No." Still looking at the ground, Nikolas shook his head. "The duke arranged a marriage for his daughter—for Sherie—to a wealthy local baron over twice her age."

"Marriage? How old was she?"

"We were both sixteen, but among the nobles it's normal to marry off female titled heirs at that age, to strengthen alliances and maintain . . . pure bloodlines."

Wynn felt the chill in the night sink into her. Witeny had long past given up rule by monarchy, but there were still nobles who clung to the old ways in this country.

"She and I decided to run," Nikolas went on. "Karl was two years older and had access to money, so he wrote us letters of travel. He didn't want Sherie—or me—to be abused that way. He helped us slip out of the keep. He was going to get us to safety and then go back. But . . . somehow his father found out and came after us."

When Nikolas's eyes flickered, Wynn clenched her jaw again and took hold of Shade's leg.

She—Nikolas—was running through the forest at night and holding Sherie's hand tightly, as the younger man with blue-black hair to match his sister's led the way. Wynn heard them—felt herself—panting with exertion. She didn't have to imagine the fear of being caught, for she felt it.

A horse charged out of the trees ahead.

The young man in front skidded to a halt. Before Nikolas could change directions, the elder duke, with a long dagger in hand, slid from his stomping horse.

"You ungrateful viper!" he shouted at Wynn—at Nikolas. "This is your thanks for a life in my household . . . to ruin my daughter's life and bring scandal upon my family?"

As he strode straight at them, Sherie pulled away, holding out both hands.

In terror, Nikolas reached out to grab her, to try to get her behind himself. For an instant he lost sight of the old duke as he half turned his back. And then Nikolas saw Sherie's eyes go wide as she screamed.

"Karl! No!"

Wynn—Nikolas—spun, still trying to keep Sherie back.

Karl and his father were on the ground, thrashing and struggling. At a wet, gurgling sound, the younger man scrambled backward across the forest floor. He then jumped to his feet, and his father lay prone on the ground.

"What have you done?" Sherie cried. "Karl! What have you done?"

The old duke didn't move; his eyes—and mouth—were open and slack. The younger one, Karl, stood staring as he shuddered . . . and the now-bloodied dagger was in his hand.

Wynn had to let go of Shade again to remain in the present, and Nikolas had put his hands over his face.

"When Sherie's father caught us out there," he whispered, "I think . . . I think he meant to kill me. Karl tried to stop him and . . ."

"He killed his father?" Wynn asked.

"No," Nikolas said, shaking his head vehemently. "The old duke fell on his dagger. It was an accident."

Wynn's eyes fixed hard on Nikolas. In his memories she had seen only Karl rise with the dagger in his hand. What had truly happened in that moment when Nikolas's back was turned? Any story concerning the elder duke's death that had been told to those back in the keep would have been at least half a lie.

Nikolas appeared to truly believe it had been an accident when a son had tried to keep a father from murder.

"Everything changed," he whispered. "It was my fault, not Karl's. I had tried to . . . would have . . . ruined Sherie's life. Karl told me to run, though Sherie wouldn't leave with me. Only after I reached the guild of my father—well after—did I learn what he and Karl had arranged for me there. I never heard a word from Sherie since I left."

Nikolas closed his eyes and slumped where he knelt.

"How can I face her again . . . or Karl? How can I sleep in that place and eat at a table with them knowing I was the cause of it all?"

Wynn didn't know how to answer. This tale was darker than she'd expected, even given how Nikolas reacted to being summoned home.

"Does your father love you?" she asked.

He looked up with visible shock on his face. "Of course."

"He'll be there—I'll be there," she said. "I would guess no one who knows any of this has shared the full truth of the secret, and neither will I."

Nikolas didn't say anything, but the tension in his shoulders appeared to ease. Then Shade whined and huffed once, and Wynn glanced aside.

Chane came toward them, possibly to help with the tents, which hadn't been set up yet. He looked down at the three of them just sitting there.

"Everything all right?" he asked.

Wynn noticed the sky lightening to the west above them. They needed to get a shelter up for Chane.

She nodded at him and began unfolding the canvas.

If it hadn't been for Shade, she wouldn't have learned the whole truth even from Nikolas. Something more might have happened on his last night near the duchy's keep. And there was no telling what had happened since then at Nikolas's lost home.

The following night Wynn got them back on the road as soon as possible once Chane awakened at dusk. If they were indeed going to reach the duchy tonight, she did not want to arrive too late.

But the sky wasn't even completely dark yet when Chane looked up ahead. "I can see the outskirts of a village." As usual, he was driving the team.

Wynn couldn't make out anything that he might have seen.

"That will be Pérough," Nikolas said quietly from the wagon's back. "It's only the first along this road. We have another league before reaching Beáumie Village below the keep."

"The village was named after the family?" Wynn asked.

"Yes, like the keep," Nikolas answered, his voice strained. "It might have been called something else once, but the Beáumie line goes back more than two hundred years."

The wagon lurched, and Wynn gripped the bench's edge. Chane pulled up the pair of horses, as the right-side horse had shied and lurched away, almost drawing the wagon off the road. Chane hissed at the team and jerked the reins with more strength to bring the wagon to a halt.

Wynn lurched forward. She grabbed the bench with both hands as someone grasped the back of her cloak and pulled her upright.

"What was that about?" she asked.

When she looked to Chane, he was glowering over his shoulder and behind her. The grip on her robe released, and she already knew at whom that look had been aimed.

"A hare," Osha said from behind her and pointed ahead.

Shade pushed in on Wynn's other side, at the bench's left end, and let out a low-throated growl. Before Wynn could even ask . . .

"It not right," Osha whispered in his broken Numanese. "Shade knows, too."

Wynn might have been pleased to find Shade more accepting of Osha's presence, as the two stood close together behind her. But as Shade's hackles rose, Wynn looked ahead. At first she didn't see anything but the road in the dark.

"To the left . . . near the road's edge," Chane whispered, and now he was staring as well.

She followed his gaze . . . and something moved on the road's packed earth.

A small, furry creature half hopped, half dragged itself across the road. It didn't appear wounded, though it favored a rear leg. Slowly Wynn made out that a good deal of its fur had fallen out. Its back looked malformed, twisted, as if it had been born with some deformity. The sight of it made her uneasy, and as it approached the road's far side, she shuddered.

When it hobbled into the brush, she spotted something worse protruding from its backside: not a tail, but a shriveled fifth leg.

"What happening here?" Osha whispered.

No one spoke, and Chane got the horses started again and drove them onward. In less than a hundred yards, Wynn saw the first huts, made from logs or planked wood with thatched roofs.

When they rolled through the village of Pérough, only a few people were out and about. But those few seemed in a hurry, as if they did not wish to be outside any longer than necessary, though it wasn't raining.

There were several dozen structures, at a guess. One nearest the road had to be a smithy with an attached livery and stables, though Wynn didn't see or hear any horses. The wagon soon passed a broad area that could have served as an open market when needed. However, Wynn didn't see any stalls.

And neither did she see nor hear any animals—no dogs, let alone mules, goats, or cattle brought in for the night.

"Is it always this quiet?" Chane asked, looking around.

Nikolas was slow in answering. "Not that I remember."

Wynn noticed a young man ahead dragging a small girl child along the roadside beyond the village's far limits. They were perhaps hurrying toward the nearest dwelling. The man stalled, likely spotting the wagon, and he veered sharply, jerking the girl along as they ducked into a stand of trees. Neither of them made a sound.

Wynn pulled out her cold-lamp crystal and swiped it harshly across her thigh to ignite a pale light from it. It wasn't until the wagon passed near the trees that she saw anything more.

The man peeked out at her from behind a tree.

He looked pale in the crystal's dim light. His face was more heavily lined than she'd have guessed, as his quick movements moments before and his fully dark hair suggested a younger man. His right eye twitched at the sight of her, as if she frightened him.

"Shade?" Wynn whispered, and immediately memory-words rose in her head.

—Not—you— . . . —He—remembers—dark robe—but not like—your—blue one—

In a blink both man and child vanished deeper into the trees.

"Another sage?" Wynn asked. "Has he seen someone else like me?"

Shade rumbled but didn't huff or raise memory-words in Wynn as an answer; that meant Shade didn't know.

"Something is wrong here," she said, feeling foolish for stating the obvious. Master Columsarn had alluded to that in his letters. But it was likely not a good idea to go poking about right now.

Once the village was too far behind to see, and Wynn was still lost in worry and thinking of the deformed hare, Osha tapped her on the shoulder.

She almost squeaked in fright.

"This place . . . land . . . sick . . . die," Osha whispered.

He didn't have to point at anything, for she saw the brush, bushes, and trees along the road. Too many appeared wilted or dying. Wynn closed her hand over the crystal to smother most of its light.

No one spoke for a long while, until they approached the outskirts of another village.

"Beáumie," Nikolas whispered.

In size it was similar to Pérough, though this place appeared nearly deserted, with even fewer people visible as the wagon rolled through. They ran for doorways while holding hoods low over their heads to hide their faces.

"I don't like this," Nikolas said. "It's nothing like I remember."

As the wagon passed beyond the village, a cold drizzle began to fall. Shivering and pulling her cloak tighter, Wynn tried to clear her head to form a proper question for Nikolas about anything else that was different from in his youth. Then she heard him suck in a breath, and she glanced back.

He was crouched low, looking up ahead of the wagon.

"The keep," Chane said, and Wynn turned forward again.

The road rose up a thinly forested slope, growing steeper near the top, and she heard the sea from somewhere beyond. But her gaze locked on what was visible at the crest far ahead. The first thing that caught her eye was the light of flames. In the deepening darkness, she spotted the keep's outline first, constructed on the rise and likely with its back to the sea below it. Some form of gate in a surrounding wall faced the road's far end. Whatever braziers burned there were on the inner side and set high upon the gate's sides. She made out only one large square structure beyond the gate, rising to about twice its height. As they rolled up the incline, even closer, she spotted a single tower that rose above the keep's left corner. The whole place looked so stark—so unwelcoming—against the starless skyline.

Chane suddenly pulled up the horses, and as the wagon halted, he sat there gazing upward. "Do we go on?"

Right then, instinct told Wynn to tell him to turn around. "We have to."

Chane flicked the wagon's reins, urging the horses up the road's rise toward the gate in the darkness haloed by orange-red light.

As the wagon rolled up to the iron-lattice double gate, several things surprised Chane and several did not. He did not find it odd that the gates were closed and that two guards stood peering out at newcomers with unwelcoming suspicion. He was surprised to find no gatehouse or tunnel or portcullis.

Beáumie Keep was surrounded by a stone wall some four yards high, encompassing its inner dirt courtyard; the entrance was framed by two pillars rising barely higher than the wall. As Chane reined in the team of geldings, he looked through the gates' iron lattice and straight to the keep's double doors—which were up a rise of six broad stone steps. At a guess, the keep's rear wall faced the cliff over the ocean shore. Likely it had been built here due to the solid stone of the knoll and cliff for a sound foundation.

A little more disconcerting were the astonished and angry faces of the two guards looking out at him. By the light of the braziers on the pillars' inner tops, both men wore leather armor with riveted steel plates under gray tabards and cloaks. Chane could not make out the emblem on the tabards, but neither man wore a helmet beneath his cloak's hood. Both began whispering to each other until . . .

"Stay where you are!" one called out.

Chane could not be certain in looking through the gate's iron slats, but the second guard might have reached for a sword at his hip.

"Turn back and leave . . . now!" the first guard shouted.

Chane considered doing so, there and then, but Wynn's hand closed on his forearm. Wynn had faced much in the past few years and would not be intimidated by a pair of guards—admirable but sometimes unwise.

"We have an invitation," she called out.

Then one of the keep's far double doors opened.

A tall figure emerged and stepped down the stone stairs to the dirt yard. Chane could not make out a face, but by the heavy folds of a full-length skirt below a long wool tunic and cloak, he could see that it must be a woman. As she came toward the gate, he realized why her face had been difficult to see in the night. She had dark skin—darker than anyone he had ever met, with brown-black, tightly curling hair all the way to her shoulders.

Taking in her large eyes over a flared nose and very full lips only slightly lighter than her skin, he wondered who she was. She was dressed like neither a servant nor a noble.

The dark-skinned woman paused halfway to the gates as both guards looked back. One guard left his post to go and meet her, saying something so low that Chane could not catch it. After looking out through the gates for an instant longer, the woman turned and vanished back into the keep. The guard who had gone to her went running off toward what appeared to be a barrack on the courtyard's north side.

Chane was about to advise that they leave.

From out of the barrack came a short, muscular man with a nearly shaved head. He was dressed like the two guards—except that his hood was thrown back. The way the messenger guard followed two paces behind suggested that the short one had authority over the others.

"What is this about?" he barked before he even reached the gate.

"Nothing, sir," the first guard answered, straightening stiffly. "We're just turning a wagon away."

As the short man—apparently in command—neared the gates, he peered out through the lattice, and his eyes roamed over all in the wagon.

"Captain Holland," came a voice behind Chane, and he turned halfway on the wagon's bench, as did Wynn.

Nikolas stood behind Wynn and between Osha and Shade in the wagon's bed.

"It's me," Nikolas continued, pulling back the hood of his cloak. "My father sent for me."

The short one squinted and then frowned. "Master Nikolas?"

"Yes, please let us in. We have come a long way."

Chane heard a tremor in the young sage's voice, but perhaps Nikolas's speaking up might disarm the tension here.

"I'm sorry," the captain said, polite but firm. "There's been plague in the villages, and I have standing orders not to let anyone through."

"Plague?" Wynn repeated. "We saw no signs of plague."

Indeed, what Chane had seen in passing through two villages was strange but not indicative of disease.

The captain's eyes narrowed as he fixed on Wynn, and a scowl rose again on his face. "Turn the wagon around and leave. I have my orders."

"Captain Holland! Open those gates . . . now!"

At this new voice shouting from somewhere in the courtyard, the captain turned about, as did the two other guards. All three stiffened to attention as a small young woman walked brusquely toward the gate.

She was pale, though beautiful, with a narrow jaw, a heart-shaped mouth, and a high brow of perfect skin. A mass of shiny, straight blue-black hair fell over the shoulders of a velvet gown of dark emerald green. She wore no cloak and gave no regard to the rain. Behind her followed the much taller dark-skinned woman.

"My lady?" said the captain, with his back to Chane.

The small woman stopped and looked through the gate from about five paces off. Her eyes locked on someone other than Chane, and the harshness of her gaze faltered for a blink.

"Open the gates," she repeated. "Master Columsarn has asked to see his son, and I doubt this small group stopped in either of the villages."

Her dark eyes shifted focus, possibly to Wynn, and then slightly upward as she studied Chane.

He felt Wynn's hand touch his arm.

"Duchess Sherie Beáumie . . . the duke's sister," she whispered.

Chane glanced at Wynn and wondered how she knew this, but she kept her eyes forward.

The woman—the duchess—approached the gate as the captain quickly stepped aside. But when the captain turned to follow her, he appeared worried and took a hesitant glance back toward the keep. The darker-skinned woman stopped three paces behind all the others.

Duchess Beáumie continued looking at Chane on the wagon's bench. "Did you stop at either village along the road or speak to anyone?"

"No," he answered.

If she found his near-voiceless rasp odd, she did not show it as she turned her head toward the captain. "As you see, they came in contact with no one."

Chane, born into a minor barony with a mother fragile and weak in both body and mind, had met but a few noblewomen who gave orders as if they never expected to be questioned.

The captain nodded instantly to his duchess and then to his men, though he still looked troubled. One guard swung the rotating gate bar, and both men pushed the gate's halves outward.

Chane flicked the reins, and the horses passed through as the duchess and her companion stepped aside. The guards closed the gate immediately once the wagon entered the courtyard.

"Everyone out," Chane whispered, setting the brake as he reached back for his packs.

Wynn reached for her own pack and pulled her sheathed sun-crystal staff from beneath the bench before she hopped down. Osha and Nikolas gathered their belongings and got out the back as Shade leaped over the side to join Wynn.

In the cold, wet night, and under the red glare of the gate's brazier, Nikolas appeared almost ill as he rounded the wagon's back. Chane caught the duchess's eyes on the young sage.

There might not have been hatred in her stare, but Chane recognized pain and resentment when he saw it.

"You came," she said simply, looking away.

Nikolas said nothing, and the young woman glanced over the rest of the group while appearing to regain her composure. Her perfect brow wrinkled slightly at the sight of Osha and the overly large black wolf standing beside Wynn.

She addressed Nikolas again. "Your father and I did not expect an entourage."

Her haughty tone appeared to catch Wynn off guard. Wynn might not be intimidated by a pair of guards, but she had little experience with arrogant nobles.

Chane understood them only too well—as he had been one of them. Drawing himself to full height, he stepped in next to Wynn.

"The guild sent this sage with some texts for Master Columsarn," he returned with equal disregard for the duchess's position. "Two sages could not travel such a distance without protection." He lightly brushed back his cloak's folds, exposing his longsword on one hip and his shorter sword on the other. Osha's longbow was also in clear view.

"Please," Chane said, "take us inside before one of them catches an illness in this rain."

The young woman's veneer was well practiced, not taken aback even in recognizing someone of her own kind—by his bearing and manner.

"Of course," she said coldly. "Come. Someone will see to your horses."

Turning, the duchess led the way toward the keep. The dark-skinned female lingered until all of them passed by, and then she followed behind.

Chane did not care for that, though when he glanced down, Wynn was looking up at him with an expression that clearly asked,

What have we gotten ourselves into now?

Shortly after, Wynn found herself in the keep's central hall, with Shade pressed up against her leg. The open chamber was surprisingly bare, with no tapestries and only one long table and eight tall wooden chairs at the room's far end. But the table was dusty, as if it hadn't been used or tended in a while. At least a fire, providing warmth and light, burned in the great hearth to one side of the hall.

The duchess—Sherie—took a dry stalk from a bucket near the hearth and touched it to the flames. She lit a few candle lanterns and set them on the table.

"Rooms will be made ready immediately," she said. "Dinner is past, but I will have the kitchen prepare food as well."

She seemed different than she had in the courtyard: slightly less sure of herself and almost in a hurry to get them settled. Even before she set down the third lantern, she gestured with curling fingers toward the taller, dark-skinned woman. That one came close in long, firm strides and, after a whisper from the duchess, she left the hall.

Wynn wondered about the sudden subtle change in the duchess, though there was much she could guess as she glanced at her companions. Chane appeared almost cold and disinterested, though his gaze roamed over everything. Osha was clearly ill at ease as he looked over the bare stone walls. He hadn't said a word since they reached the gates.

Nikolas's face was pallid, and he wouldn't raise his eyes.

Wynn found it hard to imagine how Nikolas and Sherie had ever taken to each other, considering the way they were now. Then again, lost love, betrayal, and perhaps even murder could change people drastically. After what Nikolas had told her and unknowingly showed Shade, Wynn couldn't imagine how he must feel.

Sherie hardly appeared glad to see him.

"I want to see my father," Nikolas said, and his voice sounded too loud in the hall after the moment of silence.

Sherie looked up from setting the third candle lantern on the table. Her pale skin was flawless, and Wynn had never seen anyone with such an abundance of shining hair. It was not hard to imagine a sixteen-year-old Nikolas being attracted to her, though it left Wynn wondering about what Nikolas had been like back then for her to want him.

"He is being checked on," the duchess answered. "If he is well enough, you may see him."

Nikolas took a hesitant step toward her. "Is he that ill? His letter suggested that . . ."

He never finished, as swift footsteps carried into the hall. Wynn turned the other way as a young man strode in from a side archway, and she recognized him immediately.

Although Sherie was small with soft curves, her brother, Karl, the current Duke Beáumie, was tall with hawkish features. Their coloring was identical, though he was dressed all in black, with silver fixtures and adornments from his tunic to his pants and high leather boots. The young duke wore vambraces on both forearms above heavy leather gloves on his hands. But in some details his appearance was different from the memories Shade had passed to Wynn.

His skin looked stretched over his face with a feverish shine. His blue-black hair lacked its previous luster from Nikolas's stolen memories and hung flat, combed but perhaps in a hurry and not washed in a long while. And more . . .

His sister lost her composure, as if she was beyond surprised by his sudden arrival.

"Karl . . ." she started and didn't go on.

Wynn noticed three men standing at attention outside the hall's main entrance. Their presence didn't surprise her, but their appearance did.

Most nobles employed as many armsmen as they could afford, but these three were dusky skinned with dark hair—not as dark as that of the duchess's companion, but they were all obviously Suman. Instead of armor, they wore long silk tabards of deep yellow over white muslin shirts and loose pantaloons—and they had curved swords in hand, the blades resting against their shoulders. One was about the height of Nikolas but much more muscular in build. The other two were tall and slender.

Why would a duke of Witeny employ Suman guards?

"What is going on here?" the duke demanded. "Who gave permission to open the gates?"

"They were opened for me," Nikolas said quietly.

The duke turned, looking past Wynn as he spotted Nikolas. In turn Nikolas hesitantly studied the friend of his youth.

The duke stood frozen in silence at the sight of the young sage.

A cascade of erratic shifts passed through Karl Beáumie's expression: first shock and then confusion, followed by a shudder of panic. It ended in a sudden, possibly forced smile.

"Nik?" he said, and the smile turned to a manic grin as he strode over, grabbed and embraced Nikolas. "I had no idea. . . . Why didn't you send word? I would have sent an escort to bring you through the villages."

Nikolas tried clumsily to embrace him back, but Wynn could see he was troubled. Pulling a step away, he looked up at his old friend's face. Though concerned, Nikolas also appeared somewhat relieved, and she could hardly blame him.

Karl's welcome—forced or not—was far warmer than Sherie's.

"My father sent for me, and I . . . I had protection," Nikolas said, briefly gesturing to Chane and Osha. "The guild felt it best."

Karl straightened, turning to inspect Nikolas's companions one by one and finishing with Shade. His expression darkened.

"I had no idea the guild would employ hired swords and archers," he said with an edge.

"They are with me as well," Wynn added before Chane took offense. "I travel extensively and require guards. Master Jausiff Columsarn requested some rare texts. I was charged with delivering them."

Karl looked her midnight blue robe up and down before turning to his sister. "So, Nikolas relates that his father 'sent' for him? How did that come about?"

His tone held such a coldly implied threat that Wynn half expected the duchess to falter, but Sherie was once more the commanding noble who had first appeared in the courtyard.

"I sent for him," she replied. "Jausiff has not been well . . . as you would know, if you were more aware of your staff."

The first statement was a lie; Wynn knew firsthand that Nikolas's father had written both letters.

"And how?" Karl wavered. "The keep is on lockdown due to the plague . . . by my order. Who would deliver such a message?"

Wynn waited anxiously for the answer. Would she learn the messenger's identity this easily?

Sherie showed no reaction at all. "I am duchess here, at least until—if—you marry. I communicate with whom I like and how I like. Or will you take it upon yourself now to read my private letters?" She paused, waiting, and though her brother became agitated, he didn't answer. "An ailing father has a right to see his son. And you . . . have been unavailable of late."

At the last of that, the duke's mouth dropped partly open. He quickly closed it again.

Wynn pondered this odd situation. Young noblemen who inherited titles normally took wives as the titled lady of the household. Young noblewomen were married off elsewhere, often for land, wealth, political influence, and more. Here brother and sister both remained unmarried and possibly vied for control of a little-known duchy far from anywhere of note.

"If you hadn't locked down the keep," Sherie continued, "I would not have been forced to circumvent you."

"I had no choice," Karl returned. "Not after that fool of a counselor went into the local villages along with his outlander servant, once the plague was—"

"There is no plague, as neither Jausiff nor Aupsha has come down with it . . . even after secluding themselves for a quarter moon as a precaution."

Wynn turned her head as little as possible in watching the exchange. Whatever was wrong with Jausiff, the counselor here, it was not this "plague" the duke continued to mention. And who was this "outlander" servant, considering the oddity of Suman guards under the duke's command?

If possible, Karl's expression darkened further. "Neither you, sister, nor the counselor are a trained physician, let alone a healer—"

"And how is any physician to come here when you let no one in?" Sherie challenged.

"Father?" Nikolas called out.

The unseemly argument between brother and sister halted as all eyes turned to Nikolas. An instant later Wynn followed the young sage's gaze.

An aging man entered the hall with the assistance of the dark-skinned woman whom the duchess had sent off. He was in his late sixties at least, and leaning on a cane, though when he moved the cane, it struck the hall's floor with solid certainty each time. Dressed in the gray robe of a cathologer, as he had once been in the guild, Master Columsarn's shoulders were broad, his face was nearly unlined, and his silver-white hair was cropped evenly at his collar. His eyes were light blue, and they panned slowly through the hall and took in everything before stopping upon his adopted son.

"Nikolas!" he said with a smile.

In contrast, the woman at his side . . .

Wynn fixed on the woman she had first seen with the duchess, and studied this one more closely now. She had heard of people who lived south of the Suman Empire in the savannahs and jungles there. They were reported to be dark skinned, but Wynn had never imagined how dark, as she had never seen any of them. The woman's hair was brown black and fell in tight, almost kinky curls to her shoulders. The long, heavy skirt and undyed wool tunic looked somehow awkward and improperly fit on her tall frame, as if they were borrowed and not entirely comfortable.

Nikolas hurried to his father. "Are you all right? What is ailing you?"

"I informed him that you were not well," Sherie said quickly.

Wynn took note of this strange comment as Jausiff blinked and then nodded.

"Thank you, my lady," he replied as he gripped Nikolas affectionately by the arm. "Nothing is wrong, my son, just old age catching up with me." Then he lifted one eyebrow with a wry smile at the duchess. "She dotes on me too much. That is all." Half turning, he handed his cane to the tall woman beside him. "Aupsha, take this for me, please. I have my son to lean on now."

With a respectful half bow, the woman did so, and it was obvious to Wynn to whom the duke referred as the "outlander" servant. Everything here was getting more tangled by the moment between Nikolas's past and the present.

"And were you expecting Nikolas to arrive in such . . . company?" Karl asked.

For an instant Jausiff's fatherly joviality slipped as he took in all the newcomers, finishing with Wynn . . . and his gaze lingered on her, dropping and rising at the sight of her midnight blue robe. Suddenly Master Columsarn did not appear pleased.

"I brought the texts you requested from Premin Hawes," Wynn explained.

"Yes, yes," he said, instantly regaining his good nature as he looked to the duke. "My lord, I *was* expecting an emissary from the guild with some texts." He smiled at Osha. "I did not expect Lhoin'na archers but am glad the guild sees to my son's well-being."

Wynn glanced up to her left. Osha nodded politely, and perhaps he followed the situation better than she realized—as she was barely following it herself.

"So my sister requested these texts for you?" Karl asked.

The number of interlaced lies and half-truths grew by the moment, and Wynn had trouble keeping up. But the young duke was being handled carefully in his sister's efforts to protect the family's counselor.

"Of course," Sherie answered, much calmer now. "At his request, and while he and Aupsha were quarantined. Master Jausiff so rarely asks for anything, so I was glad to assist him . . . as you would be, brother."

Karl's mouth tightened at the barb. "Forgive all this fuss, my old friend," he said to Nikolas. "The plague has caused such caution of late. But it *is* good to see you again."

"Well, then . . ." Jausiff said, taking his hand from Nikolas's arm and pressing his palms together. "We shall need to find you all rooms and arrange for a late supper. I am sure you are tired and hungry."

"Rooms?" Karl repeated, glancing once at Chane and then at Osha. "For them all . . . in the keep?"

"Of course," Sherie repeated. "They cannot stay in the villages, and, as lord here, I know you would never refuse hospitality to an old friend, an emissary from the guild, or their assigned guardians."

Her tone was polite and matter-of-fact, as if no question was at stake and she simply spoke the obvious. Still, her brother eyed her for a moment.

"No . . . no, of course not," he agreed. "Please see to their rooms, as I have other . . . business to attend."

"Of course," she answered, and that echoed phrase began to sound like mockery to Wynn.

"Nikolas," the duke called out in striding off the way he had come. "You and I must catch up soon."

"I fear I must rest a bit, son," Jausiff said. "Perhaps you should go and get settled now."

The young duchess recovered, drawing herself up.

"Come with me, please. Rooms were being prepared even as we were delayed."

She said this with such clear distaste that Wynn felt somewhat embarrassed. She'd never enjoyed being an unwanted guest, and she and hers were certainly that, it seemed. Osha especially looked uncomfortable, though Chane simply cocked his head after the duchess to signal Wynn to follow. He didn't care what anyone thought of him; it was one of his greatest strengths and weaknesses.

Wynn dropped her hand on Shade's neck. "Come on."

As they headed into a side archway, Wynn saw the three Suman guards fall in behind. Along the way, three Numan guards dressed like those outside joined the procession. For better or for worse, Wynn and her companions were now well-protected guests locked inside this keep.

CHAPTER ELEVEN

Chane could not help being alarmed by the number of guards "escorting" a small group of guests to their rooms. And what were Sumans doing in this remote place? All six guards remained a discreet distance behind, but he glanced back more than once, and noticed that Osha did the same. The elf, Nikolas, and Wynn each carried one of the three candle lanterns from the main hall.

Duchess Beáumie, holding her velvet skirt in one hand as she began climbing a flight of stairs, led the way as if the guards did not exist.

She stepped off the landing upon reaching the third floor.

"I apologize that we have no true guest quarters," she said, not sounding remotely apologetic. "The keep is small; however, we have three spare rooms in the upper servants' area. Though they are sparsely furnished, you should find them comfortable."

Down the passage, Chane spotted three open doors. Two female servants in white aprons hurried out of the far one.

"Is all prepared?" Sherie asked.

The second girl halted, turned, and bowed her head. "Yes, my lady."

The duchess stopped at the first door and gestured inside as she turned to Wynn. "Mistress . . . ?"

"Hygeorht," Wynn supplied. "Journeyor Wynn Hygeorht."

"Of course, Journeyor, you may have this first room," the duchess went on. "Your bodyguards can take the second, and young Master Columsarn the third and smallest . . . for his own."

Chane detected a note of spite in her designation of the last room, as if Nikolas was only a guest here and she meant to remind him. The young sage did not respond. Chane, however, fought against a sudden urge to balk at the arrangements as an unpleasant realization hit him.

Wynn, as a female emissary of the guild, could certainly not share a room with one of her guards. As the counselor's son, Nikolas also should have a private room. And it was unusual that two "bodyguards"—which was the ruse Chane and Osha played—would even be housed here instead of in the barracks. So the duchess probably thought she was offering a favor by housing them inside the keep. That meant he would have to share a room with the elf.

The very thought pushed him to refuse, until Wynn caught his eye and shook her head once, very slightly.

"That will be fine, my lady," she said. "Thank you."

Appearing relieved, as if an unpleasant duty here was done, the duchess swept back down the passage for the stairs. "A meal will be ready soon," she said over one shoulder.

Chane glanced uncertainly at Wynn, but Nikolas spoke up first. "I think . . . I will get settled."

As the young sage headed for the last door up the passage, Wynn looked to each of her other companions. Once Nikolas entered his room, she tilted her head toward the nearest open door, her room.

"Come, help me get settled," she said loudly, and then slipped inside with Shade right behind her.

Both Chane and the elf went for the door at the same time. Chane halted at one side, but Osha back-stepped and stood silently watching him. With a glare, Chane raised a hand, ushering the elf to go ahead. Osha did not move.

Wynn's harsh whisper carried from within the room. "Both of you, get in here . . . now!"

Chane stepped in, immediately meeting Wynn's irritated expression. Shade grumbled and hopped up on one of the narrow beds. Even when Wynn eyed Osha the same way as the elf entered and shut the door, it was not satisfying to Chane. He stood waiting for Wynn's rebuke over the standoff in the passage, but she only looked away with a shake of her head.

The room was simple but serviceable, with two plain single beds—one near the front wall by the door and one at the rear. A worn, short table stood by each, and a water pitcher and basin rested on the nearest one.

The only light in the room was from the candle lantern that Wynn held, and she set that on the rear empty table as she dropped her pack and staff on the far bed.

"What is going on in this place?" she asked suddenly.

Chane held up a hand to halt any further comment. He stepped back and cracked the door. From what he could see—and hear and smell—the Suman guards had left, but a keep guard remained at each end of the passage, one near the stairs and another at the other end, where an archway led to somewhere else on this level.

Chane quietly closed the door. "It appears we are not to go walking around on our own."

Osha frowned. "Many guards are not . . . normal?" he asked in Belaskian.

Chane realized the elf would have little experience with human castles or keeps or the ways of human nobility.

"No, the number is normal," Wynn answered, "but they aren't usually used to keep guests locked inside their rooms." She sank down beside Shade on the far bed. "At least we can speak freely in here."

That was true. Without Nikolas, they could speak as they pleased.

"I have not been long in this land," Chane said. "Are Suman guards often hired for local forces?"

"Not that I know of," Wynn answered. "And what did you make of Jausiff's servant, Aupsha? She's not Suman, though I've heard of other peoples farther south described like her."

"I cannot place her, either," he answered. "But she, as connected to the duchess and the master sage, might be the likely messenger that we seek."

Wynn shook her head. "Not if she was sequestered for fear of plague after she and Nikolas's father went into the villages."

"One of . . . Suman guards could be . . . messenger," Osha put in. "They move free in keep."

"Maybe," Wynn said. "But they appear to be more the duke's men than the duchess's. Still, it is possible." She turned to Shade. "Did you pick up anything from any of them, some memory as a hint?"

Shade did not even lift her head from her paws as she huffed twice for *no.*

"Well, this is where we start," Wynn went on. "We need to establish the identity of the messenger, if it was someone inside the keep." She looked at Chane. "I don't need to consult your sense of deception to know that everyone in that hall was lying about something."

Yes, Chane had slowly developed his "talent," though such differed for each Noble Dead. At a guess, some abilities depended upon who the person had been in life.

He had lived on the fringe of Belaski's gentry and nobility, where truth was to be guarded, an asset not shared except for advantage and gain. What had only recently manifested was his ability to sense deceptions and lies in spoken words, if he focused and let the beast of his inner nature sound its warnings to him. Many lies had passed in the main hall, though there was one that had made his inner self rattle its chains.

"Good place . . . start," Osha said, still struggling with his Belaskian. "Who lie to who . . . and why?"

"Well, the duchess seemed to be taking a good deal upon herself," Wynn said, "if she sent the message while Jausiff and Aupsha were in quarantine. Both letters that arrived at the guild were written in the same hand, and since Nikolas never mentioned anything odd in that, we can assume Jausiff wrote both of those. So either the duchess is covering for Jausiff or she somehow got the letters and sent them without the duke's knowledge."

"She did not send the letters herself," Chane put in.

Wynn glanced up. "You're certain?"

That was the moment the beast had stirred inside of Chane.

"When she told Karl that she sent them *for* Jausiff, she lied. Yes, I am certain."

Wynn eyed him a moment longer and then nodded.

"That leaves Jausiff as the one who arranged for the delivery," she said. "Somehow he found a way to send the letters through someone, but there's another problem in that. We don't know if that person was the one who went all the way to Calm Seatt . . . or if the letters were handed off to another messenger. Anyone here traveling that far would be missing for so long as to be noticed. The duke would know that much by now, and he was certainly surprised by all of this."

"And we do not know if a messenger has even returned," Chane added, "be it one from the keep or a second one confirming the delivery. There is also the need to confirm if the messenger and infiltrator at Dhredze Seatt are one and the same."

Wynn's expression fell.

Chane was uncertain whether her sudden frown was for the whole tangled problem, or his merely stating it, or both.

He understood and shared her fears, for the messenger and/or would-be thief was the key to all this. Someone had breached the dwarven underworld, the realm of the Stonewalkers, even though the infiltrator had not reached the orb of Earth. There was the fear that an agent of the Ancient Enemy had learned where they had hidden an orb. If Jausiff was connected to such an agent, then he could not be trusted, and the master sage's agenda had to be rooted out.

It was also possible that the thief had nothing to do with Jausiff and had acted on his or her own and not returned here. If so, then Wynn and the rest of them had wasted time in coming here.

"Messenger first," Osha said, pushing himself back into the discussion. "Maybe-thief we find next, unless same."

Wynn nodded. "Yes, that still seems our only path forward." She placed a hand gently on Shade's head, and the dog's ears pricked up. "And we have a few extra methods to use in searching."

"Anything?" Chane asked. "Anything at all, even seemingly unconnected?"

"Shade said no already." But then Wynn twitched slightly, her eyes appearing to lose focus.

"What?" Chane asked a bit too sharply.

Wynn blinked, frowned, and looked down at Shade. "Just a flash . . . an image of two of those Suman guards standing in front of a door in a dim, windowless passage. Maybe . . . maybe underground."

"Whose memory?"

Shade rolled her eyes up at Wynn.

"The duke . . . Karl," Wynn whispered, still looking at Shade. "But that's all she saw. I think everyone was so focused on the moment at hand that Shade couldn't catch anything else." She stroked the dog's soft, charcoal-colored head. "It's all right. You keep trying."

The door suddenly swung inward without a knock.

Chane dropped his hand to his longer sword's hilt as he turned.

In the opening stood the tall and dark-skinned female servant, who looked only at Wynn.

"Master Jausiff wishes to see the texts you brought for him," she said, her accent smooth and rolling.

Wynn studied the woman in the doorway. She looked so out of place here, regardless of the common wool tunic and long, heavy skirt for a cold, dank climate. And she hadn't dropped her eyes, as had the two serving girls making up the rooms.

"Now . . . please," the woman said, her full lips exposing starkly white teeth.

"Of course," Wynn answered, and she dug in her satchel containing the books.

"I will come as well," Chane stated.

"No," Aupsha answered flatly, though she never looked away from Wynn.

"It's all right," Wynn told Chane. She needed to speak to Master Columsarn—Jausiff—as soon as possible. Perhaps she might gain some further clues by a few tricks, and she looked back to Aupsha. "May I bring my dog? She gets restless if I leave her alone too long."

After a brief hesitation, Aupsha nodded once, making her hair shift stiffly on her shoulders. Chane was still watching Wynn with concern as she slipped out behind the tall woman. As Wynn did so, she heard another door open, and looked up the passage.

Nikolas stepped out of his room and paused at the sight of Wynn with his father's tall, foreign servant. And, now that Wynn paid attention, she realized that Nikolas had obviously never seen Aupsha before.

"I'm going to see your father," Wynn said, holding up the texts.

"So am I," Nikolas responded.

"He has not sent for you," Aupsha said coldly, taking one step up the passage and halting between Wynn and the young sage. In truth Wynn hoped Aupsha might prevail here, as she needed to speak with Jausiff alone.

Nikolas stood his ground. "He is my father, and I *am* going to see him."

When he took his first step, Wynn turned her eyes on Aupsha's back . . . and dug her fingers into Shade's scruff. She wasn't even sure whom she should send Shade to block off, but Nikolas stepped past the tall woman unchallenged. Surprisingly, he didn't appear frightened.

Aupsha turned slowly, keeping her eyes on Nikolas until he stood beside Wynn. Only then did Wynn see the twitch of Nikolas's eye, like the old Nervous Nikolas. The tall woman silently stepped around all of them to lead the way to the stairs and past the keep guard waiting there.

The passage was wide enough that Wynn, Shade, and Nikolas walked side by side past the guard's watchful eyes. At the stairwell they had to fall into single file, with Shade in the lead and Nikolas behind Wynn.

Aupsha took them one floor down, to the keep's second floor, and stepped off down another passage almost all the way to its end. One large door there was already open.

As if he had heard them coming, Master Jausiff Columsarn stepped out as the tall servant arrived. In contrast to Aupsha, he looked perfectly at ease in his clothing—a gray sage's robe—and he didn't have his cane in hand. He did have a rather intense, serious expression even before he turned his eyes on Wynn. That quickly changed when he looked beyond her.

At the sight of Nikolas, Jausiff appeared slightly startled, though he recovered quickly with a warm smile.

"Settled already, my son? You weren't always so efficient."

"I just wanted to see how you were," Nikolas responded.

Whatever he'd expected from his father, it wasn't a playful jibe about his past youth in this keep.

"Of course," Jausiff answered with a chuckle. "We'll have a good long talk, you and I. But first I must see what the journeyor has brought me from the guild. If you wouldn't mind, son."

Wynn was taken aback by this, though it was the way she preferred things. As she glanced at Nikolas, he appeared a bit stunned as well.

"Um, that's fine," Nikolas tried to answer. "I'll . . . wait."

Jausiff's smile broadened, and he looked to Aupsha. "Is their dinner prepared?"

"I will check," she said, and she turned and left.

Jausiff, still smiling, studied Wynn for a breath before waving her in. She'd barely entered with Shade when he solidly closed the door.

"My private study," he said, stepping slowly around her.

The chamber had all the fixtures and messy qualities of a longtime office, with shelves covering every available wall. Ink bottles, quills in old cups, open ledgers, and stacks of papers were half-organized across a solid, dark wood table serving as a workspace.

However, something about it struck her as sad.

Perhaps because of an overabundance of shelves, the master sage had tried to make them look filled by placing scrolls lengthwise and spreading out various books and volumes in small sets, as if he could not stand the sight of too much empty space. There was a good bit of dust on most of the collection, as if little had been taken off the shelves in a long while. In one back corner stood a small unmade bed, suggesting that this room served as his living quarters as well: one room for his library, office, and bedchamber.

What had kept him here all these years?

Sages by nature were curious people who loved to be either lost in their research or off on a journey of discovery. Something had anchored him here. But as Wynn's attention turned from the chamber to its occupant, now standing behind the messy table, any personal questions vanished from her thoughts.

Master Columsarn's warm good humor was gone as his gaze locked on Shade.

"Unusual for a sage to travel in the company of a pet, especially a wild . . . animal of such size. How did you acquire her?"

Wynn tensed. She could be standing before someone in league with a minion of the Ancient Enemy. Also, he'd hesitated at mentioning an "animal" as a companion, as if he might have used another word.

As a master sage, Jausiff would be well educated and possibly even know about the majay-hì. But unless he had traveled in the lands of the Lhoin'na, it was unlikely he had ever seen one. She had no intention of offering any information about Shade unless he commented more specifically.

"She found me, after finding herself wandering Calm Seatt," Wynn answered lightly. "She's proven an able companion I wouldn't be without." This last was added with some emphasis, and Jausiff crossed his arms.

"Indeed," he said, and then pointed at the bundle in Wynn's arms. "I assume those are for me?"

"Yes." Glad for the shift of focus, she approached to place the satchel on the table. "Premin Hawes sent everything you requested."

"And a few things more," he said dryly while opening the delivery. "I did not expect an *emissary* from the guild, and certainly not some hired sword and a Lhoin'na archer. Did Premin Hawes have a reason for not sending the texts with my son?"

Wynn had faced down her own superiors more than once and had lost any tolerance for intimidation, subtle or not. This master sage exuded an unusually strong presence, and, in truth, he was not wrong. Premin Hawes had exceeded his precise request.

Searching for an answer, Wynn fell to a half-truth. "Nikolas seemed . . . hesitant to return home, perhaps distraught. Given the rarity of some of these texts, the premin thought it best if one of her order transported them, and with proper protection for the remote destination."

Jausiff's eyes narrowed. The explanation was plausible, and since he knew everything of Nikolas's past, he would believe in his son's reluctance to return. The aging sage's intense gaze drifted downward over Wynn's midnight blue robe.

"You must be a very trusted student," he said. "Perhaps one of the premin's most favored, to be given such a task."

"Of course."

"You could have no better teacher, then. And you've studied under her for years in the order of Metaology?"

Wynn swallowed. "Yes."

Where was the old sage going with all of these questions that weren't really questions? Something was wrong, and she needed to turn her own questions on him instead.

And then Jausiff slipped the first text out of the satchel. For one blink, lines of age softened on his face as he looked at it. It brought Wynn a stab of pity. How lonely he must be here, so far from the guild's archives and library to fulfill his needs and wants. Here there would be few if any scholarly chats with peers.

When he opened the text in his hands, Wynn again saw the title on the cover:

The Processes and Essence of Transmogrification.

"It has been many years since I've perused this," he said. "Of course under Hawes, you must have read it at least once. Can you refresh my memory on the sections relating to the mutation of flora?"

In spite of his conversational tone, Wynn knew she was in danger. He was not some lonely scholar seeking discussion. He was testing her, and she had no way to answer. Until recently she had been in the order of Cathology, devoted to the preservation of knowledge—and she had never read the text he held.

"I read it once a long time ago," she replied.

Jausiff's gaze rose slowly from the opened book. "Yes, some sages have better memories than others." He laid the text down, picked up another, and opened it, and again Wynn caught the title.

The Three Aspects of Existence.

"Now, this one Hawes has students turn to regularly," he continued. "Even apprentices of other orders study it. Do you agree that it is the three Aspects, and not the five Elements, in which we find the strongest grounding for the magical ideologies? And what about the processes—spell, ritual, and artifice—used across all three arts? Do those hold a stronger connection than the ideologies to the Aspects . . . at least for you? Of course, there's the whole misnomer about cantrips being simple spells. Certainly you've come to that realization, for as far as you have progressed . . . Journeyor?"

Wynn kept her eyes on the text. Except for the most basic practices of thaumaturgy, and one botched ritual that still plagued her with mantic sight, she knew next to nothing about magic. And certainly she didn't know enough for a passing philosophical debate under the master sage's sudden barrage.

That hesitation ruined Wynn. Jausiff snapped the book shut and rounded the cluttered table more quickly than he should have as he closed on her.

"You are no student of Frideswida Hawes, and perhaps not even a sage. What are you doing here in your little masquerade? And how did you come by these texts and my son's company?"

"I assure you, I am a sage," she stated flatly, meeting his eyes and trying not to waver. "You can ask your son, if you—"

"I am not blind—yet—girl! My son obviously knows you, accepts that you *claim* to be a sage, but that does not explain the robe you wear. Nor is it enough for *me*!"

"Nikolas and I . . . we've become friends . . . at the guild," she stumbled on. "Until recently I was a journeyor of Cathology. I applied to change orders less than a moon ago and was very recently approved . . . by Premin Hawes herself."

"That is the extent of your story?"

"Not a story but the truth."

He pointed to the texts on the table. "And Premin Hawes entrusted you to bring me those, particularly the first volume? I do not think so. At least one is only for the eyes of masters, domins, and above! Which is partly why I asked that they be sealed from my son's eyes."

For a sick old man he stepped much too swiftly past her, though she barely had time to note this before he jerked the door open. And there was his missing cane, leaning against a casement's end behind the door.

"Nikolas, come," he called, and then glanced back at Wynn. "Thank you for your service. Since your duty is complete, there's no need to linger. You can return to . . . your new order in the guild."

Wynn went numb at being so quickly undone and dismissed. With little choice, she collected herself and left, passing Nikolas just outside the door. Poor Nikolas still appeared lost, confused, and likely worried about his father. The last of those concerns was unnecessary, from what Wynn had seen.

Jausiff was no sick, frail old man, so why had Nikolas been called home?

Shade's tail was barely out the door when it shut.

Wynn flushed for a moment before she could even ask, "Did you catch anything useful?"

—No . . . memories— . . . —from old one . . . Not . . . slip . . . once—

Wynn ran her hands over her face. The old sage had even outdone Shade. Now they were both suspected by one of the few here who might have some answers. This had become a terrible blunder.

—I try . . . when . . . he . . . not know . . . see . . . me—

Wynn dropped her hands and looked down into Shade's crystal-blue eyes. Those broken and halting memory-words, and Shade's reluctance for language, often distracted from how much Chap's daughter had begun to comprehend human ways strange to her. Wynn ran both hands over Shade's large head and down her neck, and then looked to the door shut tight against her. She heard muted voices inside the master sage's chamber, but she couldn't make out what was said. Perhaps Jausiff might tell Nikolas things he would tell no one else.

She and Shade were still alone in the passage, and, after brief reluctance, Wynn crept closer and crouched before the door. Hoping to hear what transpired inside, she leaned close to the keyhole.

"Father, you . . . you tricked me into returning?" Nikolas stuttered. "You are not ill at all, are you?"

"I had my reason for deception, out of concern about the duke. You saw the changes in him, yes?"

After a long pause, "I saw . . . something."

"He has locked down the keep," Jausiff continued, "and some sense of normalcy must be reestablished. The duchess and I thought a guest—a reason to force him to play host—might help bring him back to himself. We could think of no one but you for whom he would open the gates."

"Me?"

Another pause followed, and Wynn imagined the aging counselor nodding.

"I know I promised that you would never have to return here," Jausiff went on, "but will you, to assist us? The duchess needs you. . . . I need you. Nothing else that we have tried has reached the duke, and now he might be shaken enough to respond to his childhood friend. He always trusted you."

It was hard to be certain from outside the door, but Wynn thought she heard Nikolas expel a shuddering breath. She clenched her fists at the old sage's cruelty in reminding Nikolas of trust, especially given what Shade had shown her of the night Nikolas tried to flee with Sherie. Wynn wondered what story had been provided to explain the old duke's death; certainly it had not been the truth.

Whatever Sherie and Karl had decided to say, perhaps Jausiff had been given the same lies as everyone else regarding that night. But Nikolas blamed himself for the elder duke's death, accident or not.

"Will you stay and help?" Jausiff asked again.

Again a long pause, and then a quiet, "Yes."

The sound of footsteps came toward the door.

Wynn scrambled away, pulling Shade a short distance down the passage before the door opened and Jausiff looked out.

"Journeyer?" he asked. "Is there something else?"

"I thought to wait for Nikolas. With guards placed near our rooms, it seemed better not to walk about without someone known here."

The wrinkles of Jausiff's brow deepened. "Guards?"

Nikolas came out, breaking the moment, but he was almost as ashen gray as his robe.

"And you two are friends at the guild?" Jausiff asked, suddenly good-humored again. "For some time now?"

Wynn kept silent.

"Yes," Nikolas answered absently.

"Splendid," Jausiff said. "Go find some supper, as a meal should be ready by now down in the kitchen."

Eager to be far from this study, Wynn took Nikolas's arm. "He's right. Let's go find something to eat."

She hurried him away without looking back until she heard the door close. The old sage was nowhere in sight, and only Shade trotted after them. Halfway down the passage, Nikolas exhaled, and Wynn slowed.

"Are you all right?" she asked.

He came to a complete stop and closed his eyes, and a little of his color returned. "My father wants me to help him and Sherie with Karl. I said I would . . . but . . . I can tell she's sick at the sight of me. I don't know how long I can stay here."

Wynn hesitated again. As of yet Nikolas had no idea what she was really doing here, but if he had access to the family, he might be able to help her.

"You can see there is something very wrong here, can't you?" she asked, and when he didn't answer or open his eyes, she went on. "If you want to help the duke, you need to find out what has happened to bring about the change in him—his odd behavior, according to your father; his insistence on a plague; his refusal to let anyone come or go, even for messages to be sent. Once you know more, you'll have a better idea what to do."

Nikolas opened his eyes, and when he looked at her, he appeared so tired and locked in dread.

"You think I should talk to Karl? Ask him about these things?"

"No." Wynn shook her head, and this was the tricky part. "I think you should talk to Sherie."

Nikolas's body stiffened.

"You said she and your father want your help," Wynn rushed on. "If so, then she'll talk to you. Ask her how this all started, and see . . . see if she knows anything about why Karl stopped all messages being sent to or from the keep. And given that, how your father managed to get a letter to you."

Nikolas frowned, but he was paying more attention now. "How my father sent a message? Do you think that's important?"

"Aside from some obsession over a plague, real or not, why would your old friend not send for help with that . . . or let anyone else do so? That alone is worrisome, and maybe a sign that whatever is wrong is getting much worse."

Wynn gave him a few breaths to mull that over, though it was only a half-truth.

Finally he nodded. "I'll try. Maybe tomorrow."

Wynn took a careful breath in relief, but after her exchange with Jausiff, something else still bothered her. Though she hadn't known what to expect upon meeting him, he didn't strike her as the type of man to have actively sought to adopt a child, especially considering his profession. If she was to succeed here, she needed to know more about his character.

"Nikolas," she began, not quite certain how to word this. "How did you . . . How did you come to be adopted by Master Jausiff?"

For once Nikolas wasn't averse to speaking of his past. "I don't remember any of it. I was only an infant, but Father told me that my parents were apothecaries down in the village, and he was fond of them. They were the closest things he had to friends at that time. A fever passed through the villages, and though my parents did all they could to help, they were struck down themselves. My father brought me to live up here . . . the same year that Sherie was born."

His expression became pained again, and Wynn did not press him further. His explanation did help her understand Jausiff a bit better: he was loyal to those he considered friends, enough to adopt their orphaned child. Then again, that didn't mean much in the end. She assumed even minions of the Enemy might be loyal to some friends.

Taking Nikolas by the arm, she urged him on. "Let us find this promised supper, considering how late it is. I'm starving, and Shade, well, she can always eat."

Her thoughts turned back to Nikolas's promise to speak to Sherie—to try to learn the identity of the messenger. Whether he could learn anything of use was still to be seen, but at least it was a start after her horrible blunder with his father. She was determined not to let *that* happen again the next time.

All she needed was some reason to go at the master sage again, and it might depend on Nikolas acquiring some answers first.

* * *

Chane paced the small room he was forced to share with Osha. The elf sat in silence on the bed closest to the door. Not that Chane minded silence, for their having to speak to each other would be worse, but he hated the present situation.

Wynn had been escorted away at the master sage's request and had been gone too long. Chane rebelled against the very thought of her alone with anyone here, for no one in their group knew whether some new minion of the Ancient Enemy might be hiding among the residents of this keep.

Finally he could stand it no longer.

"I am going out," he rasped.

Osha rose instantly. "I come, too. She gone too long."

Chane stalled at the door, with Osha an arm's length behind him. "No. You stay. I will be back."

He had no idea how he might search for Wynn, given the guards at both ends of the passage, but he did *not* want the elf along. Yet a fight to put the interloper in his place was out of the question. Wynn would not forgive him for that.

Osha merely stood there, slightly taller than Chane—which was beyond annoying—with his ridiculously long white-blond hair hanging loose. In exasperation Chane opened the door, stepped out, and of course Osha followed.

They both stopped upon seeing the woman called Aupsha pass by the guard near the stairs and come straight toward them. Her dark eyes flickered slightly in surprise at the sight of them outside of their room.

"A meal has been prepared in the kitchens," she said. "I am to bring you."

"Where is Wynn?" Chane demanded.

Aupsha remained stoic. "I will bring her and Nikolas when Master Jausiff has finished speaking with them."

"Nikolas is with Wynn?" Chane asked, looking past her toward the stairs.

"Take us to her," Osha said.

The woman said nothing to this. She simply turned and headed back the way she had come.

Chane hesitated for only an instant. Was she leading them to Wynn or to whatever late meal had been prepared? Either way he would get out of this passage, past the guard without incident, and then choose what to do next. He followed, hearing Osha two steps behind him, and he made a brief peripheral assessment of the guard as they passed. The man appeared armed with only a sheathed longsword—no visible knives, daggers, or other secondary weapons.

As they neared the second floor, Chane heard familiar voices. He reached the next landing, and relief came at the sound of Wynn's voice. Then he saw her with Nikolas coming down the passage, and Shade trailed behind them.

Aupsha paused, blocking Chane from going to Wynn.

"Chane . . . Osha?" Wynn said at the sight of them. "We were coming to find you before heading to the kitchen."

Chane cocked his head toward Aupsha. "We have an escort."

Asking Wynn about what had transpired with Nikolas's father would have to wait for privacy.

Aupsha turned back, heading to the next flight of stairs downward. Chane let Wynn and Nikolas slip by, but before he could step in behind her . . .

Osha took advantage of his rearward position and did so, even pushing in front of Shade.

Chane clenched his jaw as he followed behind.

The tall servant woman led them down to the main floor, but instead of heading into the main hall, she turned right down a dim passage lined with several narrow archways. They passed rooms filled with casks and crates, and Chane assumed these were extra stores, though it was odd that they were stored in the keep's main building. A short way onward, they emerged into the heat of a kitchen with food and simple place settings on a long wooden table ringed with stools.

"We are to dine in here?" he rasped, unable to keep distaste out of his voice.

Aupsha ignored him, but Wynn glanced back. "What's wrong?"

"Nothing," he covered quickly.

In his youth, when he had visited other noble families with his father, he had never once been expected to eat in the kitchen. He had rarely even seen such places where only servants went to bring a meal to a main hall or more formal dining chamber. However, his and his companions' status here was uncertain.

Cutting Osha off, he followed Wynn to the far end of the table. Soon she, Chane, and Nikolas were seated, which put the elf at the far end near the entrance. Shade dropped her rump to the floor at Wynn's side and snuffled repeatedly while starting to drool.

"I will return when you are finished," Aupsha said, and she abruptly left.

Only two other people remained: a fat woman in a stained apron and one of the girls who had helped prepare their rooms. She looked to be about sixteen, overly slender with dark blond hair, and she kept her eyes down. The fat woman glowered first at Wynn and then at Chane from where she stood by the wood-burning iron stove.

Chane had no idea why she should be so insolent.

"We are sorry to have disrupted your schedule," Wynn said to the cook. "We were delayed. I'm sure you were already cleaning up for the night."

Their journey had not been delayed, for they had to travel by night, but Wynn's apology seemed to have the proper effect. The stocky cook grunted with a nod and began dishing out boiled potatoes, glazed carrots, and what might have been roasted beef onto plates.

"Can't be helped. You need to eat," she said somewhat grudgingly.

Chane noted that she did not defer to Nikolas at all. So far the only person outside the family who had acknowledged the young sage had been Captain Holland out at the front gates. Something about this seemed relevant, but as of yet Chane was not sure why.

The shy girl brought them their filled plates, and Wynn smiled at her. "Thank you. What is your name?"

At first the girl did not answer. She cautiously set a plate in front of Osha while glancing up as if trying not to stare at his pointed ears and large, slanted eyes.

"Eliza, ma'am," she said quietly.

"Thank you, Eliza," Wynn responded. "Could you spare a plate for my dog?"

The girl's posture relaxed slightly with a glance at Shade, and she nodded. "Yes, of course, ma'am."

Chane always noted how strangers were either frightened or fascinated by the sight of a large black wolf kept as a "pet." Either reaction could be useful, and even Shade took advantage of this at times. The serving girl appeared to fall into the latter category, and Chane knew exactly what Wynn was up to.

Servants knew secrets, whether useful ones or not. Befriending them was thereby useful as well.

"You ain't giving that dog my good roast," barked the fat cook at the stove, and she pointed to the kitchen's rear chopping table. "There's boiled bones over there."

At that Eliza stalled with a plate already in hand. She set it aside to hurry in gathering stewed bones for the "dog."

And an awkward meal began.

Chane knew that, given a choice, Wynn did not care for meat, but she dove into her potatoes and carrots. As a result she was too busy to speak. Osha was silent as well, and ate like someone uncertain where his next meal would come from. Nikolas would not look at anyone and pushed his food around his plate.

Chane looked down at a plate loaded with food he could not eat. He waited until the cook turned her back. When the girl spotted him sliding a gravy-soaked slice of beef over the plate's edge—over the table's edge—she smiled slightly and looked away as Shade snapped up each slice before it hit the floor. Then he forked his vegetables over onto Wynn's plate. Eliza came around with a pitcher of ale to fill the clay cups, and Wynn took her own two slices of meat and passed them under the table as well—most likely to avoid offending the prickly cook. Shade had the best meal at the table and much better than a few stewed bones.

"How was your meeting?" Chane asked as softly as possible.

Wynn shook her head, whispering, "Later."

Nikolas picked up his cup and downed half of its ale. He had not touched his food. Osha's plate was empty, though he ignored the ale after taking a puzzled sniff.

"I think we are finished," Wynn called to Eliza.

The girl nodded and darted out into the passage. She returned a moment later, led by Aupsha.

Chane found the entire situation odder and odder. Were they guests, prisoners, or simply a notch above the keep's staff? Aupsha stood near the archway as the girl hurried about in cleanup.

Chane looked down at Wynn. "It appears our escort awaits."

Wynn's mind was busy as Aupsha led them up to the third-floor passage and their rooms. She was eager to speak with Chane and Osha but did not want Nikolas in on the conversation. Upon reaching her door, she feigned a yawn.

"I'm exhausted. Good night, everyone."

Openly relieved, Nikolas nodded and hurried off toward his door. As Chane passed by, Wynn tugged his sleeve, tilted her head toward her door, and mouthed, *Come in a little while.*

Chane eyed Nikolas entering the far room and then nodded as he headed off to the second door. Osha followed him, though not before a quick, deep look that made Wynn swallow before she slipped inside her room.

She waited along with Shade until certain that Nikolas would be settled for the night, and then she changed her mind. It would be less notable to the guards if she went to the other room instead of Chane and Osha coming back out to enter hers, so she cracked the door open.

Both guards were still in place at each end of the passage. Both glanced her way. She stepped out and ignored them as she went to the second door and knocked.

"I forgot to give you instructions for tomorrow," she called out.

The door cracked open, and she stepped in to find Osha behind it. Before he said a word, she put a finger over her lips.

Wynn listened carefully as Chane closed the door after her. She heard no footsteps in the passage outside, so both guards had remained at their posts. Apparently they didn't care about the guests' movements so long as no one left the upper floor without an escort. With a sigh, she turned to Chane and Osha, and noted that the small room was much the same as her own.

"How was . . . meeting with old sage?" Osha asked.

"A disaster," she answered honestly. "Jausiff came at me with questions about my new *order* that I couldn't answer. That ended everything, when I was exposed as some type of fraud in this robe."

Chane frowned. "You learned nothing?"

"Well . . . he's not ill or infirm from age, and I do think he's genuinely concerned about Karl. His loyalty to the family isn't in question, or he would've left this place years ago. But something else is going on here." She mulled over the rest of the encounter. "It appears Jausiff called Nikolas back to help with issues concerning the duke. Even that didn't seem to be all there was to it. Once I was alone with Nikolas, I suggested that he speak to the duchess . . . to see if Sherie knows any more about how the messages were sent."

Chane stepped closer. "Will he . . . or, rather, can he?"

Obviously Wynn wasn't the only one doubtful of Nikolas's usefulness. "I think he'd do anything so he can leave here. He told me he'd try tomorrow."

"Good," Osha said, nodding to her.

She deserved no such praise after being so poorly prepared to deal with Jausiff.

"I hate to use Nikolas like this," she said, "but I couldn't see any other way. The duchess is unlikely to talk to me, let alone either of you. She might not even know anything of use. We need to know if the messenger was sent from here, as that's our only hope of learning if that person and the would-be thief are one and the same. And how Jausiff is connected, if at all."

"As you say, and it's more than we had upon our arrival," Chane replied.

He moved around her to the door; Osha sidestepped away as he grabbed the latch. "There is nothing more we can do tonight, so you should sleep now."

His abrupt manner—almost as if he wanted her to leave—caught her off guard. Perhaps he was right on both issues. Feeling somewhat off center and frustrated by failures, she headed for the door as he opened it.

"All right," Wynn agreed, still puzzled by Chane's eagerness to see her off. "Osha, I will see you in the morning."

Did Chane really want to spend the night alone, watching Osha sleep?

CHAPTER TWELVE

Not long past nightfall, a figure garbed in a full-length hooded black robe and cloak materialized in one small room of the keep's underground chambers and passages. Inside a voluminous, sagging hood—where there should have been a face—was only darkness. Though the chamber's air was still and stale, both robe and cloak shifted subtly, as if upon a breeze.

Sau'ilahk awakened from dormancy, fully aware and alone, for the man who usually awaited him was late.

It did not matter yet.

He raised one arm, and his sleeve slid downward. For an instant he stared at his own thin arm, hand, and fingers all wrapped in strips of black cloth. Even to him, his arm looked so real, so corporeal, but it was not. Anything might pass through it, as if it were a mirage upon the great deserts of his homeland. Focusing with intent, he turned his hand solid as he drifted across the chamber without the sound of a single step. He paused at the one small table, worn and bleached with age, and looked down upon the single object lying there. . . . A circlet, broken by design, made of ruddy metal.

It was thick and heavy, slightly larger in circumference than a great helm, and about a fourth of it was missing. From its open ends, protruding knobs pointed straight across the gap at each other.

Some might call it a *thôrhk*, a neck adornment worn by few honored dwarves, but it would more correctly be called a key.

Sau'ilahk picked it up with his willfully solidified hand and turned slowly away from the table. This chamber, carved from solid rock, was not large, but it was private, secure, and suited to his needs. It had perhaps once been a storage room or a cell for prisoners. One solid but aged wooden door behind him would open into a main subterranean chamber lined with similar doors that could also be locked.

To the right of the door was an iron tripod stand.

Three legs supported a like iron ring, which held the only other object in this locked room.

The globe resting in the stand was slightly larger around than the object he held, but it was not made of the same ruddy metal. Rather, the globe appeared fashioned from some unknown material, neither metal nor stone, and it was dark as char, with a surface faintly rough like evenly chiseled basalt. A spike of matching material pierced down through the globe's center; its broad tapered top was wider from side to side than a clenched fist. The spike's pointed tip also protruded through the globe's bottom between the stand's legs. But both spike and globe appeared formed from a single piece.

The very sight of it still caused Sau'ilahk to quiver with elation after a thousand fleshless years of yearning. Oh, how long had he suffered in his search for . . .

The orb—"anchor"—of Spirit.

His impatience growing, Sau'ilahk glanced at the door and then raised the *thôrhk* before the hollow of his dark hood. This object had been his salvation—once he'd finally realized it could serve a purpose beyond opening an orb . . . an anchor.

Earlier this year, he had been led by Wynn Hygeorht on a futile chase all the way to Bäalâle Seatt, a vast, forgotten, and long-fallen mountain stronghold of the dwarves in ancient times. He had hoped to find this very orb in that place, but the one hidden in the deepest depths was not the one he had sought for a thousand years.

Desperation had almost broken him in that moment and nearly pushed him into eternal grief and madness. That orb beneath a forgotten seatt was useless for his need to regain the flesh—his physical form—cheated from him by his god, who had promised him eternal youth.

Immortality—eternal life—was not the same as eternal youth.

One served the spirit while the other served the body, though the mind could cling to and go on with either. If only he had known then . . .

His spirit, that essence of self and a shadow of life, had gone on, but his body had aged and withered and died just the same. It had been even longer until his dead flesh decayed to dust, and he rose from his mountain tomb as only a spirit, an undead.

How he had screamed in horror and then raged that first night.

Nearly a thousand years later, in Bäalâle, in a dead-end tunnel far beneath the dwarven seatt, all that had been left to him was spite and the need to flee his pursuers. Before they caught up and found the false orb that meant nothing to him, he took the *thôrhk*—the key—he had found as well and hid it within the cave's stone wall. He fled that place in the same anguish and betrayal that he had felt upon the first night he arose in death—but also in a growing hatred for his god.

How many days had followed in which he'd writhed in the grip of Beloved during his dormancy? How many following nights had he awoken, until one night came with a whispered hint from his god. . . .

Back to Bäalâle . . . back to the key . . . That is your hope of salvation.

This made no sense. It was the wrong key . . . for the wrong orb. Both were worthless, and he believed this urging to be another of a thousand lies from his god. He ignored that whisper, but in the nights that followed, Beloved teased him and beat him down in the dark.

The key is your only salvation . . . servant.

What other choice did he have? To find that little whelp of a sage yet again and hope she stumbled upon the true orb of his need?

Sau'ilahk relented and returned to Bäalâle Seatt. More whispered hints followed once the key was in his possession. And through Beloved's teachings, he learned one thing he had never realized.

Any key could be used for any orb.

He also learned how to use the one that he had like a compass, and it led him to the hiding place of the anchor—the orb—of Spirit.

Since a time just past the end of what was now called the Forgotten History, that orb had been hidden away in an underground sanctuary in the mountains above the great desert. Beloved told him next to nothing of the strange sect that guarded it or of how they had even acquired the one anchor he sought.

It did not matter then, for taking it from them had been easy, and his joy could not be measured.

But it mattered now.

Sau'ilahk?

At the hissing voice inside his thoughts, he choked down hatred and obediently answered, *Yes, my Beloved?*

That very title stoked ire that he quickly quelled.

You teach the duke to use the anchor—its power—to gain your promised reward?

Yes, Beloved. I will have flesh again soon . . . as you promised.

A knock on the door cut him off . . . and then brought puzzlement. The man he awaited was the lord of this keep, and he never knocked.

However, outside the door were some of the Suman retainers—mercenaries—that Sau'ilahk had acquired to help gain the orb and move it to this place. He had instructed them all to serve the duke as needed.

The door opened.

One of Sau'ilahk's Suman servants stepped halfway around the door's edge and bowed his head at the sight of his master.

He was tall for his kind, and slender, and the other Suman guards viewed him as their leader. Also unlike the others, this one wore a close-trimmed beard along his jawline; with one center peak that ran up to his lower lip. His curved sword was still sheathed, so no immediate threat was likely.

"Master, forgive the intrusion. . . . I have news," Hazh'thüm said, his eyes still lowered.

The very air around Sau'ilahk vibrated under his conjury to give him a voice. *"What news?"*

"Visitors in the keep. The duchess ordered the gates be opened, and she allowed strangers inside."

The absurdity of this did not fully register at first.

Sau'ilahk had made it clear to the duke that no outsider was to be allowed into this place until their work together was completed. Likewise, no one here was to leave. Sau'ilahk would not risk anyone beyond the keep learning of his presence or the changes in the duke.

"One visitor is the son of the old counselor," Hazh'thüm continued. "The duchess would not leave him outside, but he was not alone."

"What of the others?"

"A young female sage, a tall swordsman, and a Lhoin'na archer. There was also a large black dog."

Sau'ilahk stalled for an instant. *"A female sage with a black dog . . . or do you mean a wolf?"*

Hazh'thüm hesitated. "Perhaps, Master, but I have never seen such an animal with my own eyes."

"What color was the woman's robe?"

"At first it seemed black, like the dog . . . or wolf. Once the wagon passed under the gate's braziers, perhaps blue but still very dark."

None of this made sense, from all that Sau'ilahk knew of sages. If this one was a metaologer, then she could not be Wynn Hygeorht. But another female sage with a black "dog" seemed too unlikely. Then again, to his knowledge, Wynn had never traveled with an elf of any kind.

"What does the sage look like? And what of the swordsman?"

Hazh'thüm faltered, as if struggling for a description. "I could not clearly see her face, but the Numan male was tall, pale, with brown hair that tinged red. Perhaps that was only the brazier's light. He was plainly dressed, though his clothes were finely made, from what I could see."

The hiss from Sau'ilahk's conjured voice began even before the servant finished a description that could fit Chane Andraso . . . an undead of flesh rather than spirit.

A female sage with a black "dog" in the company of Chane Andraso could only be Wynn Hygeorht!

How had she found him?

His first wild instinct was to find and kill her, but he hesitated.

"Does she carry a staff, perhaps with a covered upper end?"

Even with eyes still down, Hazh'thüm nodded. "Yes, Master."

"You are dismissed!"

Hazh'thüm backed out, never looking up, and closed the door.

Sau'ilahk wallowed in fear and hate. The staff's crystal emitted light that emulated the sun in the hand of that whelp of a sage. He had been burned out of existence once by that tool and had survived only because of Beloved's intervention . . . and then he had suffered long for his failure.

Of course, that failure had not been his fault.

Wynn Hygeorht was nothing compared to him, but she was gifted with luck beyond belief. And she had a penchant for attracting or acquiring unusual allies, from an undead guardian and a majay-hì—a contradictory combination—to Stonewalkers, foreign sages, and more. How did a Lhoin'na archer fit in?

And how had Duke Beáumie reacted to this forced intrusion at the hand of his sister?

Slowly Sau'ilahk forced a state of calm reason.

The wisest path was to remain hidden and proceed with his current plans while he worked to learn more. Wynn could not reach him down here . . . and the young duke's body was almost ready. A matter of a few nights at most.

The clack of an iron lock cut him off, and he heard the chamber's door creak in opening. Sau'ilahk waited, still and silent with the *thôrhk* gripped tightly in his solidified hand.

The door swung open.

Duke Karl Beáumie quickly stepped in. Though tall, young, and handsome, with hawkish features and high cheekbones, he was not as beautiful as Sau'ilahk had been in life.

Dressed all in black with silver fixtures and adornments, the duke wore vambraces on both forearms above heavy leather gloves on both hands. Half turning his head, he ordered one of the Suman guards in the outer chamber to relock the door as he finally closed it.

None of Sau'ilahk's Suman retainers would open that door again until the duke called to them to do so—as he always did.

That is, unless Sau'ilahk said otherwise.

He took in the sight of his nightly visitor.

The duke's complexion had lost some of its luster since Sau'ilahk had first made his presence known to the young noble. His blue-black hair hung in an unkempt, unwashed tangle and his flesh was stretched tightly over his face. Dark circles of fatigue surrounded his eyes.

These lesser effects of the work they did together could not be helped.

Sau'ilahk bowed his cowled head in false respect.

My lord.

Since the first night of their secret work, a bond had formed between them, and the duke could hear Sau'ilahk in his mind as if the words were spoken aloud. But the young man did not respond to the greeting, and his haunted eyes fixed upon the orb.

"How much longer?" he asked, with a slight tremor in his voice. "How long until I need never fear death?"

Not long now, my lord.

Sau'ilahk's pretense of continued servitude had served him well. He would not have found this place, or Karl Beáumie, without Beloved's assistance. He knew he should be grateful, but gratitude was nearly impossible among the mounting deceptions and betrayals of his god.

And yet the young duke was nearly perfect for Sau'ilahk's need.

Once Sau'ilahk had stolen the orb, Beloved had whispered that he must take it far from the southern territories. As he had fled north, he realized that what he sought next would be difficult to find. That obstacle had not occurred to him before in his obsession to merely find the orb of Spirit.

Sau'ilahk's own flesh had long ago become dust. He needed a living body.

First and foremost, he needed someone young and beautiful. That went without question, for he had been so in his own time. Others had stared at him in awe, and he would have that again.

Second, he needed someone with enough power and position to hide, safeguard, and protect the orb until he found a way to make his new flesh immortal. He would not be cheated by Beloved again in asking for only "eternal life" . . . and then watch his new flesh wither as his own body had.

Third, he needed someone who feared death over all else, for whatever reason—someone willing to believe anything for the prospect of eternal life. Such a man was not as easy to find.

Beloved had whispered again to Sau'ilahk: *Go to the coast of Witeny, to Beáumie Keep.*

How his god had known of this place had made Sau'ilahk wary. Was this another manipulation, trick, or task to be followed by another and then another? In the end he could not take the chance of ignoring his god, not since he had finally gained the correct orb.

With newly acquired servants, plied with promises and threats and one death as an example, he had sought out this unknown place and the young duke. The rest had been a surprisingly easy seduction, and Sau'ilahk had always been gifted in that.

"There has been a development," Karl said, the tremor in his voice increasing. "The keep has been breached. We have strangers among us."

I have been informed. Can you not send them away?

The duke stared at him. "Not easily. One of them is . . . an old friend, not just of mine but of my sister."

And he brought others?

Mild surprise, followed by a twist of frustration, rose on the duke's pallid face. "Yes, an emissary from the guild . . . with bodyguards. She is delivering books to my counselor, but I cannot turn her out into the night."

Sau'ilahk pondered this and wondered about these texts. Perhaps Wynn Hygeorht's arrival was pure coincidence.

The duke's expression shifted again to desperation, and he whispered sharply, "We must finish! We cannot let this interrupt the work—our work. I want no more haunts in my dreams . . . no more fear of retribution for what I did."

Sau'ilahk would have smiled if he had a face that anyone could see. Karl Beáumie was as determined as Sau'ilahk to make the same body immortal and a vessel that could not be killed. He would never again fear death or what vengeful spirits lay in waiting on its other side.

"I cannot fail," the duke whispered.

Sau'ilahk did not know the whole story, but he had gleaned bits and pieces over many passing nights. The elder duke had died by the hand of his son. Whether by accident, intent, or perhaps both in a moment of opportunity did not matter, for Karl Beáumie was desperate never to follow his father.

Shall we begin?

Duke Beáumie took a labored breath. With his left hand, he pulled off his right glove, exposing a grotesque transformation.

That right hand was deformed, slightly twisted in shape. The nails of his thumb and first finger had distended and yellowed, as if slowly changing to pale talons night by night. Patches of skin here and there up to his wrist were brittle, flaking, and sallow. In places there were hints of scales like a reptile's. And in one spot tiny follicles of fur appeared to sprout, while two other places were almost downy in a sickly brown, like a fledgling that had not yet gained true feathers.

Sau'ilahk was unconcerned by such temporary imperfections. These were only side effects of their work together, and all such could be corrected in time.

Beáumie's attention remained fixed on the orb. His features were flooded with both longing and loathing.

Sau'ilahk held out the *thôrhk* to the duke. *Take the key . . . my lord.*

"We must accelerate our efforts," the duke said. "Can we finish tonight?"

Nothing would have pleased Sau'ilahk more now that Wynn Hygeorht had come again. But he had no intention of failing for a lack of patience. The process of emptying the duke's body of his spirit was a delicate matter. The essence of Spirit was an animating force that gave life to physical organisms. If the spirit was ripped out too quickly, rather than thinned and severed at only the final instant, the body might be uninhabitable.

It is best to give your flesh time for each increment of the transformation. Each small step toward immortality must stabilize before proceeding to the next.

With an expression of anger, the duke blindly extended his deformed hand, and Sau'ilahk placed the *thôrhk*—the key—into the man's grip. Without even looking at his tutor, Duke Beáumie slid in toward the iron stand and the orb.

Proceed as I have taught you so far.

Beáumie reached out with his misshapen hand holding the key. Knobs at its open ends fit perfectly into two grooves in the protruding spike's head. With a now-practiced ease, the duke lowered the key's open ends around the spike's head and slid its knobs along the grooves, and they settled fully into place. The key fit perfectly like a handle made for this.

Sau'ilahk merely waited, for the young duke had repeated this act many times. He knew the precise fraction to pull the spike enough to let a whisp of the orb's power reach out for him, supposedly to strengthen the bond between spirit and flesh.

At least so he believed.

Even Sau'ilahk was uncertain how much of the orb's power a human body could withstand all at once. This endeavor was only slightly less trial and error for him than it was for the duke. In fear of having to start over, Sau'ilahk would take no chances.

Karl Beáumie twisted the key handle one quarter turn to the right and then back, as Sau'ilahk had taught him—as Beloved had taught Sau'ilahk. He then rotated the handle downward until it was level with the floor, all without letting the key's knobs slip out of place.

Sau'ilahk began to whisper a spell, a conjury, only in his thoughts. It was one that had taken him many nights like this to contemplate and construct, in order to control the specific effect the orb would now release upon the duke. But Sau'ilahk lost his focus as something changed in the young duke's expression.

My lord?

Beáumie's eyes twitched repeatedly as he stared not at the key under his grip but at the orb—at the place where the spike would separate from the whole. Some terrible longing filled his face, like . . .

Sau'ilahk remembered being trapped for years—decades—in the cave of his burial.

In that first night of his death, some thousand years ago, he had not known that desiccation and small insects, which came to feed on his rotting corpse, would eventually free his eternal spirit. He had known only the torment of not being truly dead but trapped forever, unable to turn his head to see where stones had been piled in the cave's mouth to inter his remains.

Sau'ilahk knew—saw—that desperation on Karl Beáumie's face.

No!

The duke jerked the spike from the orb, and scintillating light filled the chamber as he screamed.

Wynn lay under the covers in the far bed of her guest room and no longer tried to sleep. Her mind was too filled with worries, self-recriminations, and mysteries. Huddled close for warmth, Shade lay beside her, and though she tried to sort out her tangled thoughts, Wynn's eyelids finally drooped. Without warning a flash of dizziness and nausea welled inside of her.

It felt as if she'd mistakenly invoked her mantic sight. A yelp echoed in the room as something thrashed and pushed off the bed.

The straw mattress bucked, and Wynn lurched upright.

The sudden movement threatened to make her vomit potatoes and carrots all over the bedclothes. She clamped a hand over her mouth and reached out for Shade. The dog was gone, but a mewling growl rose in the pitch-black room. Wynn fumbled for the cold-lamp crystal left on the near table, and she rubbed it for friction.

Soft light from the crystal filled the room.

Shade stood in the room's center, between the beds, with her hackles raised and her ears flattened as she faced away toward the door. But she quickly turned—and kept turning—and looking all ways.

"What?" Wynn barely got out before her dinner threatened to rise again.

Shade twisted her head to look directly at Wynn. *—Fay!—*

Wynn came fully awake, scooting back up the bed into the room's corner. She groped for her staff nearby, not that it would do anything for her, but it was all that she had.

Sniffing and snarling, Shade raced around the room, and Wynn looked everywhere, not even knowing what to search for. From what she remembered of the two times she'd faced a Fay manifestation, and from what little Chap had told her of his communion with his kin, a Fay—the Fay—had to inhabit something physical in order to come at her.

And the dizziness and sickness would not stop.

—Wynn . . . stay . . . hide . . . here—

Shade rushed the door, rose with her forepaws braced against it, and clamped her jaws on its handle. She tried to twist it by rotating her whole head.

"Wait!" Wynn choked out, and stumbled across the room to help.

Shade whirled off the door and charged. Both the dog's forepaws hit Wynn's chest and knocked her over the nearer bed's foot, and Shade lunged in on her with a snarl.

—Stay—

The door suddenly opened.

"What's all this—?"

Shade spun with a snap of jaws as Wynn spotted a guard peeking in through the open door; one hand was pressed against his stomach. His eyes widened at the sight of Shade, and his other hand released the door's outer handle to reach for his sword.

Before Wynn could grab for Shade, the dog rammed the guard's legs. The man toppled over Shade as she bolted through the door. Wynn struggled over the bed's foot.

"Shade!" she cried as she stumbled for the door and then slowed as the world swam before her eyes. She stepped through the opening, and the whole passage seemed to suddenly burst with sight and sound in her head.

The second guard came weaving from the passage's back end; his sword was drawn, but he hit the side wall with his shoulder. Chane and Osha burst out of their room, and then Osha gripped the door's frame as if he needed to grab something to stay on his feet.

"What is happening?" Chane rasped, spotting Wynn.

She wasn't certain, but all of the color had drained from Chane's irises. Shade raced by, perhaps trying to reach the passage's back end. Chane saw the approaching guard try to step in the dog's way with his sword raised.

"Get away from her!"

Chane's broken voice grated in Wynn's ears as he lashed out, fingers curled like claws. The guard's body lurched backward as his feet left the floor. Osha sank down against the next door's frame as Shade darted up the passage.

Only Chane appeared unaffected . . . except for his eyes.

Dizziness overwhelmed Wynn. She collapsed as the passage vanished from her sight.

Unbidden thoughts rose in her mind: memories of childhood, growing up at the guild . . . sailing with Domin Tilswith to a new continent . . . the first time she saw Chane . . . the long trek homeward with Magiere, Leesil, and Chap . . . Shade's appearance in the night streets of Calm Seatt . . .

Images kept coming, one dying under the next. This was nothing like Chap or Shade calling up memories. It felt as though pieces of her were being torn away. Terror made her try to scream out. . . .

"Chane!"

Wynn never even heard her own voice as her mind went dark and silent.

*   *   *

Sau'ilahk slammed his solidified hand down on the duke's grip and the raised key. The force drove the spike back into the orb. All of the scintillating and blinding light escaping the orb vanished from the chamber.

Karl Beáumie collapsed and lay still upon the floor, though his eyes had not fully closed.

Sau'ilahk felt emptied . . . hungry . . . starving . . . and as if dark dormancy might swallow him whole in the night instead of at dawn. When he looked at his own hand, wrapped in shreds of black cloth, it flickered, with the stone below showing through from one moment to the next.

It took all that remained of him to crouch over the duke and not feed upon him right then. He did sense a spark of life still within Karl Beáumie's limp form. Relief flooded through Sau'ilahk, followed by anger and sharpening hunger. What a fool, to risk everything out of impatience born of fear!

Sau'ilahk examined his prone subject more carefully. The duke's right hand was further twisted, the talons longer, and misbegotten scales and wisps of fur and tiny feathers had spread farther up his forearm. Would the glove even fit anymore to hide such effects?

Sau'ilahk turned for the door and drew close so that his conjured voice might vibrate in the air beyond it.

"Hazh'thüm, assist me."

No one entered.

Sau'ilahk tried to solidify his hand to grab the door's handle. His effort failed. He had been drained when the orb had been fully opened, perhaps in the wrong way. And so he slipped straight through the door.

In the outer chamber of six doors, he found Hazh'thüm and another of his Suman guards trying to push themselves up off the floor. Hazh'thüm was gasping, and his eyelids fluttered.

Sau'ilahk wondered how far the orb's effects had been felt.

"Get up!"

"Master," Hazh'thüm choked. "Forgive me."

"The duke requires care. Take him to his room and avoid being seen, if possible."

Hazh'thüm shuffled to the door, fumbled as he unlocked it, and then entered. But Sau'ilahk remained, watching the second guard. That one still braced against a far door as he gained his feet, and then lowered his eyes before his master.

What was his name again? It did not matter.

Sau'ilahk struggled under intense hunger and tried not to fade from the world into dormancy. He needed life's energies if he was to remain for the night. . . . He needed to feed.

Osha had seldom been truly frightened in his life. But waves of fear washed through him beneath dizziness, sickness, and unwanted memories of his entire life flooding his head. He had lost control of his body as everything darkened before his eyes and left only those flashes of his past rising into his awareness to then dissipate like smoke in the dark.

For anyone with his training as an anmaglâhk, to be this helpless was worse than anything imaginable.

As suddenly as it started, the horrifying sensation ceased.

Osha found himself lying on the passage's cold stone floor as his head began to clear.

"Wynn!" someone rasped.

After that the passage was quiet.

Osha did not even hear the majay-hì snarling as he pushed himself up. There stood Chane with his back turned as he lifted Wynn's limp form from the floor as if she weighed nothing.

"Wynn?" the undead rasped.

Osha wanted to shout at that *thing* to put Wynn down. He tried to speak, but nothing came out. Then he heard struggling behind him. He spotted the young sage, Nikolas, trying to pull himself up in the opened doorway of the third guest room. Both guards who had been in the passage were down but conscious and visibly shaken.

Besides the undead holding Wynn, only the majay-hì was mobile. Turning circles as if searching, Shade paced the passage and then rounded in a trot straight toward Wynn and Chane.

"I'm all right. . . . Put me down."

At Wynn's whisper, Osha struggled up and hurried toward her.

Chane slowly set her on her feet, though she wobbled in trying to step around him, and the undead turned as well.

Osha saw that Chane's eyes had no color at all. He grabbed Wynn by the wrist and jerked her away behind himself as he pulled a dagger from his tunic.

"Back!" he snapped, pointing the blade at Chane.

He knew enough of such monsters—from his time with Magiere, Léshil, and Chap—to know what those colorless eyes meant. No matter what it cost him, he was not letting that *thing* anywhere near Wynn in such a state.

The majay-hì suddenly lunged between him and the undead.

Shade turned on Chane with a low rumble as she bared her teeth, and then Osha felt Wynn grab for his outstretched arm.

"Stop it!" she said. "Chane would never . . ."

When she did not finish, Osha took one fleeting glance. She was staring at the undead, so at least now she saw what had happened.

Chane lowered his eyes and backed away, and the majay-hì's rumble lessened.

Wynn jerked upon Osha's arm. "Go help Nikolas . . . now!"

Both guards appeared to be recovering like everyone else. Only the majay-hì had been unaffected by whatever had happened . . . and Chane had succumbed in a different way. But as long as Shade was aware of the additional danger . . .

Osha finally relented, retreating rather than turning his back, until he could take hold of Nikolas and pull the young sage to his feet.

Chane, his face still averted, whispered in Belaskian, "What happened?"

Osha glanced once at both guards rising. Likely the undead spoke in his own tongue so the guards and Nikolas would not understand. Any moment, those guards would have questions of their own, before or after driving everyone back into their rooms. Osha spun his dagger and flattened the blade against the inside of his wrist to hide it at the ready.

"Shade sensed a Fay," Wynn answered quietly—also in Belaskian. "That's all I know . . . so far."

To Osha this did not seem so bad. "Fay?" he repeated to her in Elvish. "Not an undead? I felt . . . I felt as if my life was being pulled from me."

Her eyes bleak and shadow ringed, she pivoted to look up at him. The last thing he wanted was to cause her more worry or pain.

"She said it was a Fay," Wynn confirmed as she knelt beside the majay-hì.

How strange it was that a sacred one would be so familiar with a human.

Shade refused to be stroked or comforted, and padded away, still looking up and down the passage. Then she darted halfway past one dazed guard to peer into Wynn's room.

"A Fay . . . here?" Chane asked sharply, and his colorless eyes turned on Wynn. "Why? There are too many people present."

"I don't know," she answered.

One guard jerked his sword from its sheath and pointed it at Chane. The second guard stumbled closer as he commanded his partner, "Take that wolf out of here now! And all of you . . . back in your rooms."

Before Osha could grab Wynn, she stepped between Chane and that outstretched sword.

"Shade is not dangerous to anyone here," she argued, "but she sensed something wrong, perhaps a predator in the keep. That's all. No one is taking her anywhere."

It was a weak explanation, and neither guard appeared to accept it.

Osha pulled Nikolas behind himself in preparation.

"Or would you like to wake the duke or duchess and explain your actions?" Wynn went on.

Neither guard said a word. Perhaps losing control over "guests" during whatever had happened was not something for which they cared to answer in the middle of the night.

"Get that animal out of sight, and get back to your rooms," the first guard barked, and then looked to Osha. "You two, as well."

Osha had expected this and longed to speak with Wynn. Whatever had happened here was nothing he had ever experienced before. Apparently neither had she, and what it had to do with "Fay," as humans referred to the sacred nature of the world, left him baffled.

"We should do as they say," Nikolas said weakly.

The young sage did not look any better than Wynn did . . . any better than Osha felt. He nodded politely to the young man, and Nikolas wearily turned in to his room.

"I am staying with you," Chane stated.

Osha turned back and found the undead looking down at Wynn with those colorless eyes.

"No!" Osha snapped, unable to keep quiet this time. "I stay . . . with Wynn."

Chane's expression twisted into sheer hatred.

Osha stepped in behind Wynn. That *thing* would not stand over her—watching her—while she slept.

"Get to your rooms!" the guard ordered.

"I'll be fine with Shade," Wynn said over her shoulder. "If I need you, trust me: you will hear me."

Then she grasped the front of Chane's shirt with one hand and whispered something Osha could not hear.

The undead turned his face away from her. An instant passed before he nodded, stepped around her, and headed for the second door.

Wynn looked to Osha. "There's nothing to fear from him."

Osha did not believe her and clenched his teeth as he, too, turned away. The guards watched him as he headed for the second chamber along the passage. There was nothing more for him to do except spend the remainder of the night locked away with Chane.

Unless there *was* something more to be done, he considered, as his thoughts turned over what had just happened to all of them.

* * *

Back inside her room Wynn felt far less certain about anything than she'd claimed to the others. Shade refused to settle and kept pacing. Still feeling sick, Wynn knelt and stopped Shade. When she placed her hand on the dog's back, Shade was trembling.

"Are you sure you sensed a Fay?"

Shade stood there for an instant before one memory-word popped into Wynn's head.

—Fay—

The dog began pacing again, leaving Wynn kneeling on the floor in fear and uncertainty. As frightened as she was, she could not understand why a Fay would manifest near or inside this keep and then suddenly vanish. For that matter, she still remembered the time the Fay had attacked her through trees, back in Osha's homeland. Chap had come to her aid with a pack of wild majay-hì, including his future mate, Lily.

She hadn't succumbed to any sickness or blacked out then, though she'd nearly died. If a Fay—the Fay—had manifested here, perhaps Shade's presence had warned it—them—away. She, like her father, was not a normal majay-hì.

Still, that didn't explain everything that had happened.

Chane knelt in the room's far corner and dug quickly into his pack. He heard Osha enter and close the door, but all that mattered to him was that he found what he needed to quell the gnawing hunger inside him.

It was as if all the *life* that he had gained in feeding upon the deer had been torn out of him. The beast within him strained against its chains, and its starved howls and screeches tore at him inside.

And the smell of Osha's *life* thickened in Chane's fully expanded senses.

He did not need full light to find the bottle in the pack's bottom, though; desperate for the remaining black-red fluid he had gathered using the brass cup, he fumbled with it in his panic.

Chane almost downed all of the bottle's contents.

He stopped, for doing so would affect him too much. He had no privacy, and with Osha present—watching—he did not dare become that incapacitated for even a few moments. He took only a sip, and even that was punishing, as he quickly replaced the stopper in the bottle and shoved it into his pack.

"What you do?" Osha growled.

The acrid tang of ground metal and heavy salt coated Chane's mouth as he swallowed. He did not collapse in convulsions this time, but still a burning like acid filled his gut as concentrated life trapped by the brass cup spread through him. He clenched his jaws and waited for it to pass, though he heard leather squeak before he realized his grip on the pack had tightened too much. And he began to shake.

"Answer!"

Chane ignored the elf and waited for the shallow convulsions to pass. He could still feel the hunger, but he would not drink more and leave himself vulnerable while that forest whelp was present. Finally the beast within him settled to a low, growling complaint.

When he rose and turned, Osha still stood before the door.

Chane had no intention of discussing anything and decided to simply wait for Osha to fall asleep.

Instead of pressing matters, all the elf did was settle on the bed nearest the door and light another of his little candles upon the side table. He leaned back, fully clothed with his boots on, and reclined against the wall behind the bed's far side. Osha closed his eyes as if resting.

Chane turned away, settling on his own bed in annoyance, which quickly shifted to worry. He had no idea what was happening inside this keep—what had happened moments ago—and the blind ignorance quickly wore on him.

What had caused Shade to claim that she sensed a Fay? What had caused Wynn and the others to fall ill and then recover so quickly? What had left him upon the edge of losing his control to the feral nature that hid within him?

His thoughts drifted back to something Wynn had said earlier . . . about a single memory Shade had stolen from the young duke:

Just a flash . . . an image of two of those Suman guards standing in front of a door in a dim, windowless passage. Maybe . . . maybe underground.

Why would the duke order two Sumans to guard an underground door—if it was underground as Wynn or Shade had claimed? If this door had been the one thing to pass through the duke's thoughts, then what lay beyond it?

Chane watched Osha, still reclined with his eyes closed, and knew that he would have to wait until the elf fell truly asleep. That had not happened yet, judging by the sound of the man's forced breathing. The next obstacle would be getting past the guards in the passage. A diversion or distraction was needed if Chane was to seek this door perhaps somewhere below the keep.

To his frustration, Osha opened his eyes a little, glanced at the burning candle, and then closed his eyes again.

Desperation, impatience, and still-nagging hunger goaded Chane.

He rose and went to the door to put his ear against it. Listening for any sounds outside, he heard nothing. He assumed both guards would still be at their posts even after the turmoil, but without peeking outside, he could not know for certain.

"Not yet."

Chane glanced back to find Osha watching him, and he then looked to the lit candle. Had the elf been waiting—timing—something of his own?

"Do not tell me what to do," Chane answered.

Osha merely closed his eyes. "If any need go out, I go. I am . . . was anmaglâhk. No one see—hear—me."

Chane hissed before a dry reply. "And how would you get past two guards?"

"I will," the elf answered, "when time right."

Chane paced back toward his bed but did not sit. "Fool! Go to sleep."

Neither of them spoke again for some time. Osha opened his eyes infrequently but always to look at the candle while ignoring Chane. And then, at another, later glance at the candle . . .

Osha rose off the bed. "I go."

Chane was on his feet before the elf finished. "You are staying here, out of my way."

Osha turned toward the door at the foot of his bed.

Chane almost lunged to grab the elf, but then stopped himself. "And how are *you* going to get past those guards?"

Soft footsteps rose in the passage outside.

Osha froze, cocking his head.

Chane realized the elf heard them, too, and he took a step. When Osha twisted toward him, he froze. Raising both of his hands, open and empty, Chane slowly pointed at the door. Osha sidestepped to the corner behind the door and then along the room's side wall. Chane cracked the door open to a sliver and peeked out.

With the door opening inward, and its hinges toward the passage's back end, he could see along the door to that end of the passage. The guard stood with his back to the far wall and stared straight across the passage.

Chane looked back at Osha and then nodded toward the candle. Osha rounded wide and snuffed out the flame. The passage outside was very dim, and, as Chane pulled the door farther inward, he did his best to keep inside the frame and out of the rear guard's sight line. When he had pulled the door open enough, he took a quick peek toward the passage's front end, retreated, and quietly closed the door.

"What you see?" Osha whispered.

Reluctantly Chane told him. "The guard near the stairs is missing."

Osha nodded. "I overpower guard . . . without him know too soon. I move fast; he not . . . remember."

Chane scoffed. "Even so, he might be found when the other returns. And if one of us is found missing, we will be blamed, no matter if he remembers who put him down or not."

"Then what you do?" Osha challenged, folding his arms.

"A distraction first," Chane rasped. "Be quiet and let me focus, but be ready to crack the door open."

He went to his pack and dug out the gloves he used as part of his coverings for withstanding daylight. Returning to the closed door, he focused upon it and then along the chamber's front wall as he imagined the passage's end toward the stairs that he had just seen.

Chane stilled his thoughts and held out his right hand with the palm turned up. In his mind he drew lines of light and slowly crafted symbols to overlay his sight. First a circle, then around it a triangle, and he scrawled the needed glyphs and sigils stroke by stroke into the corner spaces between the two. He prepared to aim . . . as a small wisp of fire ignited in his palm. Then Chane felt his flesh begin to sear beneath the glove as Osha sucked in a sharp breath.

"Now!" Chane whispered.

Osha stepped in and pulled the door slightly.

Chane crouched, lowering his hand. Throwing the flame was not possible, for it was fueled into existence by only his concentration. Even fire could not hang in the air without something physical as fuel to feed it. But making the flame move might work. When the back of his hand flattened on the stone floor, he shifted his mental pattern slightly into the passage and . . .

The flame crept off his fingers and around the door's frame.

"Close it," he whispered, and Osha silently shut the door.

Chane clung to concentration as he moved the pattern in his mind's eye along the wall of the room, parallel to the passage. The bed in the way did not help in that. When his gaze reached the room's corner, where the passage would turn down the stairs, he heard noise outside. Perhaps the flame had died the instant it was out of his sight.

"Fire!" a voice shouted out in the passage.

Osha pushed at the door, but Chane raised a hand. "No danger," he barely whispered, and already the steps of running feet had passed the door's far side. "The flame will go out."

Then he regretted having explained it at all.

Chane dug inside his shirt and pulled out a cold-lamp crystal. It was a spare that Wynn had given him in their journey to find the orb of Earth, but he did not ignite it yet. Opening the door slightly, he heard the guard descending the stairs, and then came mute voices from somewhere below. He quickly slipped out, and, as he was unable to stop the elf, Osha followed him.

The situation rankled Chane as they hurried up the passage the other way to find another route to the lower floors.

Sau'ilahk was alone in the small stone chamber with the orb.

Hazh'thüm had already removed the body of the other guard—the one Sau'ilahk had drained of life—and the duke had been carried away to his private chamber above in the keep. It was inconvenient for Sau'ilahk to have sacrificed one of his small contingent, but it had been necessary to recover from the orb's unexpected influence. If nothing else, the remainder of his servants would be that much more cowed into obedience.

What mattered most was whether the duke would recover.

Any effects upon his flesh could be dealt with once the process was complete. Sau'ilahk dwelled instead on the almost-certain presence of Wynn Hygeorht.

Why was she here, and what had truly called her to the keep?

He had to know, and in thinking, he gazed at the orb. The act he had in mind would cost him much of the energy sapped from one guard—not as much as the fully opened orb had taken from him—but there was little choice if he was to remain undetected until he learned more.

Floating to the chamber's center, Sau'ilahk focused inward.

In midair, he envisioned a glowing circle the size of a splayed hand for Spirit. Within this he formed the square of Air, and in the spaces between the nested shapes, he stroked glowing sigils with his thoughts. He fixed upon this grand seal for his first conjuration as a small part of his energies bled away in a passing wave of weariness.

He needed something more than what one element could provide, for Air only recorded sound and so would be worthless in the night when everyone was asleep. He needed something capable of sight, capable of slipping through stone rather than limited to following passages.

A silent breeze grew inside the chamber.

Sau'ilahk called the breeze into the seal's center. The room's temperature did not change, but the pattern's center space warped like air over a searing desert at noon. That nearly invisible distortion held its place, and he solidified one hand to cage it in his fingers. Then he conjured yet again for the element of Fire.

A yellow-orange glow began emanating from within his grip.

Next came Spirit, for the necessary connection with it, though this would also give it a will and make it harder to control. And last came Earth. . . .

Exhausted, Sau'ilahk slammed the servitor into the chamber's stone floor.

The square for Earth via Stone rose in umber lines around his splayed hand and then the blue-white circle for Spirit as he embedded a fragment of his will. More glyphs and sigils of iridescent white filled the second pattern upon stone.

All the glowing marks in his sight vanished as he whispered in thought, *Awaken!*

A glow rose in the stone beneath his hand and began to rush about as if light swam beneath the chamber floor. He closed his fingers like hooks, and he straightened, making a motion as if drawing something to the surface.

The floor bulged like a bubble erupting from gray mud.

One glowing eye like molten glass winked at him as his servitor heaved its oblong body out of the floor and stood up on four three-jointed legs of stone that ended in sharp points.

Go!

It skittered up the chamber wall and sank through the ceiling above him. Sau'ilahk lost all sight of the orb's chamber as his servitor swam through the keep's stone.

Here and there, darkness broke as it surfaced upon the ceilings of passages, rooms, and chambers, one after another. He saw through it, catching sight and even sound as a servant here or a guard there went about duties late into the night. Not one ever looked up to spot the small monstrosity that submerged back into the ceiling and moved on through the keep.

The duke had not been present when the "guests" had been housed, but there were few spaces in this small place for such. Sau'ilahk had already wandered the keep himself in the last quarter of some nights. He guided his servitor to the third floor and the only spare chambers he had found with beds.

When the servitor surfaced again, he looked down at a young male with white streaks in his hair. Over the end of the bed lay the gray robe of a sage. Something about this one struck Sau'ilahk as familiar. As if struck by some recurrent nightmare, the young man murmured and gasped in his sleep.

Sau'ilahk drove his servitor across the ceiling and through the wall to the next room.

It was empty. Though someone . . . perhaps two people were clearly lodged here. Two cloaks hung on pegs near the door. Two packs, one near the other, were at the foot of one bed. A bow and quiver with black-feathered arrows, as well as something long wrapped in canvas, lay on the floor beside the bed nearest the door.

Sau'ilahk stalled too long in looking about the room. Where were the occupants, considering how late into the night it was? He finally drove his servitor on to the next room.

The servitor froze upon the ceiling as Sau'ilahk succumbed to pure hatred.

Wynn Hygeorht sat on the floor below and watched the black majay-hì pace about. Neither was doing anything comprehensible, and nothing in the room offered a clue as to why they were here. And she was garbed in a midnight blue robe.

Sau'ilahk had no idea why, and he did not care. There was no doubt that the previous room housed the undead called Chane and likely the unknown Lhoin'na who had come with them. But if so, where were they?

A sudden wave of weariness overtook Sau'ilahk. He was being drained too much in maintaining a continuous connection to his servitor, and he would need his energies for the next night to come. Once he had finished his work here and achieved his long-awaited desire for living flesh . . .

Wynn Hygeorht would never leave this keep alive.

Osha continued after passing through the archway at the back of the passage. He led the way, with the undead creeping too close behind him. It stood to reason that there would be stairs somewhere else on this level of the keep.

"There," Chane whispered, pointing past Osha. "A landing."

Squinting in an unlit passage, Osha took several more steps before he saw it. He flinched at a sudden pale light rising behind him and looked back to see a crystal, much like the ones that Wynn carried, in Chane's hand. It was glowing softly.

Chane stepped ahead.

Osha was admittedly relieved not to have the undead at his back, and admittedly his unwelcome companion could walk in relative silence. So far they had heard no one raise an alarm, and as long as any guard returning to the guest quarters' passages did not look into the second room, they would not realize anyone was missing.

Chane quickly descended all the way to the main floor and then paused as he closed his hand over the crystal. Osha listened as well and heard no movement or voices. Carefully Chane stepped out, rounding quickly into a wide passage, and then Osha heard something.

Chane halted, and they both listened for a moment.

Osha heard the distant, muted sound of waves breaking on a shore.

"We are somewhere near the keep's back wall," Chane whispered, opening his hand slightly to let the crystal's light escape. "And some opening to the outside, from what I hear."

Osha nodded. The area was cold and appeared deserted. He noticed old cobwebs above in the corner where one wall met the ceiling. This passage must not be a main path used in the keep. At his best guess, they were facing northward, and possibly the passage led out of the keep's north side.

Chane crept onward until they reached where the passage continued ahead but also had a branch to the left, likely leading toward the keep's front. He stalled there and closed his hand on the crystal, and as he put that hand behind his back and retreated one step, Osha was forced to retreat as well.

When the undead flattened against the passage's left wall, Osha shifted to the right side to do the same. Ahead and beyond the left-side passage, where the main passage they followed continued straight, a small light glowed faintly. It was not large enough for a torch or lantern, and did not flicker, either.

Osha slowly shifted forward along the wall. His people could see better in the dark than humans could, but without a moon or stars in an open sky, that was not enough illumination to tell where that light came from . . . and then it vanished.

Osha froze.

The light reappeared and had moved, perhaps farther along the passage's far half. He heard soft scrapes of footsteps down there, and then something poked his shoulder.

Osha slapped at the contact and quickly reached behind his back for his dagger, and then he heard a soft hiss. Chane leaned close enough for Osha to see his scowl.

Chane looked down to where his fist holding the crystal was now beside his rearward hip. With his other hand, he pointed at his fist and then toward that other light.

Osha looked along the passage in the dark.

He did know how Chane had made the connection. Only three other people that they knew of in the keep might have a sage's crystal. Had Wynn slipped out to go searching for something on her own before they had? No, the majay-hì would have never tolerated that, and Nikolas Columsarn doing so seemed as unlikely.

That left only the elderly counselor, the young sage's father. Then again, Chane had acquired a crystal, so . . .

Osha waved Chane back and then slid forward along the wall until he could peek down the side passage.

It appeared to run all the way to the keep's front. There were two doors and at least one archway that he could see along the length. He held his breath and slipped across that passage, and flattened himself at the far corner where the hallway met the one he had left. Before he could peer around that corner, the undead slipped across and flattened beside him.

Chane quickly raised his fist; the crystal's light made it glow faintly. He held up two fingers on his other hand and pointed toward the corner.

Osha scowled, but he would not ask how Chane knew there were two people near that other light. He peeked around the corner with one eye, and, indeed, he made out two shadowy figures. Both were muted in form by bulky cloaks and hoods. When the shorter one turned slightly, a soft light appeared in the hand of the other one and illuminated an elderly face inside a hood.

Jausiff held out some strange metal object in his hand.

Osha could not make out the other person's face, but from the height alone it might be Aupsha—as she was taller than Jausiff and claimed to be his servant. The elder sage appeared to be studying the floor, and when he turned up the passage, Osha lost sight of what the sage was doing. The other figure turned as well in following the old man, and the pair slowly continued onward, stopping every few steps. In another dozen of their paces, Osha noticed something more.

At the passage's far end was a door with some sort of small opening at head height. Perhaps it had small bars across it, but Osha knew that was from where the sound of the waves came. The door had to lead out to the northern side of the keep's courtyard. And, more, the right side of the passage's end near that door was too dark compared to the walls of the passage.

There was a turn or archway there, though the layout made no sense if the passage ran along the keep's rear wall.

What would the old sage be doing here, studying the passage's floor step by step?

Osha heard other steps more clearly, and quickly turned the other way to find Chane staring down the side passage. Those footfalls were hard and rhythmic, at least three pairs, perhaps four.

Light began to grow in the archway down the side passage.

A gusting breeze suddenly rushed out of the main passage, and in curling around the intersection's corner, it whipped Osha's loose hair.

Instinct and old training took hold, and Osha slipped around the corner. He barely had time to note that all light in the main passage, all the way to the far door, was gone. Osha planted one foot against the passage's far wall as he pushed against the near wall, and he hand-and-foot-walked up both walls to hide against the passage's ceiling.

At those sounds of footfalls down the side passage, Chane was caught between ducking back the way he and Osha had come or trying to catch whoever was down the main passage's far end. He barely heard more than felt a sudden movement of air behind him, and when he turned . . .

Osha was gone.

Chane ducked around the near corner. Even with his senses still fully widened, he saw no one in the passage all the way to where it ended at a heavy wooden door with iron fixtures and a barred sentry window. There was no sign of the two living beings he had smelled . . . or of Osha.

He heard that those other footfalls had already entered the side passage.

Hoping to slip outside and hide until whatever guards came and went, Chane ran to the passage's end door. It was not only bolted within by a heavy bar—the bar itself was fixed in place by a padlock.

Where was Osha, let alone anyone else who had been in this passage?

Chane quickly peered out through the door's small barred sentry window and saw no one outside between the grounds' outer wall and the barracks off to the left. When he turned, there was an archway to the door's right side. Stepping through there and down two steps to a landing revealed only another short flight of stairs, parallel to the passage, that ended at another heavy door. He checked it and found it locked. He was trapped with nowhere to go.

Chane returned to the passage's end and the door leading outside.

He could smell Osha, though perhaps that lingered from the elf's passing. A vulgar dwarven word came to mind—*yiannû-billê*—heard once from Ore-Locks addressing a pompous Lhoin'na shé'ith who had gotten in their way.

Where had Osha, that gangly, interloping "bush-baby," gone to now?

Three keep guards rounded the far corner in the passage. The one in the lead held an opened oil lantern. All three stopped at the sight of Chane.

Fighting his way out of this would do no good and only get Wynn thrown out of the keep.

"Forgive me," Chane said, forcing modesty. "I seem to have taken a wrong turn. Could you direct me to the privy?"

Hidden in the dark against the passage's high ceiling, Osha watched as Chane was marched off. He waited until the sound of footsteps and any semblance of light faded completely.

Only then did Osha drop softly to the floor. He believed he could still make it back to the guest quarters on his own, but instead, he soft-stepped to the passage's end and the door.

Neither Chane nor the guards had found anyone else here, but the old sage and the tall companion had to have gone somewhere. Most likely, judging by the sudden breeze, they had slipped out the door. Yet that was not possible. He would have heard any attempt to open the heavy iron lock with a key. And, likewise, he looked through the right-side archway and down a short flight of steps to another door. Since the undead had quickly returned to the main passage, then that lower door must be locked as well.

Osha lingered longer in looking up the passage. Where had that sharp breeze come from? Where had the elder sage and his tall companion gone?

Why had they been inching along and peering at the floor, and what was that object the sage held while the companion handled the old one's crystal?

Osha found himself at a loss for any answers. The guards would most likely return Chane to the guest rooms. The moment they did so, they would notice one other guest was missing upon putting him in his room.

Wynn had specifically warned them not to cause trouble. Raising an alarm among this place's inhabitants and causing a full search would certainly qualify. Still, if Osha chose to, he could evade the guards until morning and look about further before simply reappearing at the morning meal.

So little, mostly more questions, had been gained in this search, but Wynn had her purpose to fulfill. He wanted her to believe he served that—for her—and not to cause her even minor failures. She, and whatever she needed, was all that he had left of value in a life without purpose.

With a sigh, Osha crept back the way he had come.

CHAPTER THIRTEEN

Far down the coast, aboard the *Djinn*, Magiere had soon realized her initial instincts about Captain Amjad had been right—after it was too late to act. With no stops between Soráno and il'Dha'ab Najuum, she and her companions were trapped. When they'd boarded, her doubts had been only whispers in her mind. When supper was served the first night aboard, her worries had grown. She, Leesil, Chap, Wayfarer, and Brot'an were given four small pieces of flat bread and what appeared to be dried fish to share.

The flat breads were about three bites each and tasted stale. When Wayfarer tried to chew the fish, she paled. Magiere tasted it herself and found it overly salted, old, and almost leathery. Chap spit it out, and he would eat almost anything. All of them went to bed hungry that night.

Magiere mentioned that the cook was probably busy setting up stores and hadn't had time to make a proper meal. But she suspected that no one believed her, and the next morning they'd been given four pieces of flat bread and dried fish for breakfast. When they ended up with the same for supper that second night, Leesil privately expressed concern. Wayfarer already wasn't looking well. Her people lived on fresh fish and fresh or dried fruits and vegetables.

They never saw the cook, for all meals were delivered by a skeletal boy who didn't speak any Numanese and always looked at the floor. Complaining to him would be pointless if not cruel.

And now, a good number of days into the long run down the desert coast, the ship's cook hadn't provided anything better. They were all beginning to weaken, especially Wayfarer.

More than once Magiere had considered finding the captain, but he'd made it clear that any complaints would fall on deaf ears.

However, sitting on his bunk and looking down at another "breakfast," Leesil finally shook his head.

"That's enough. I'm having a word with the captain."

Chap lay beside him on the bunk. Wayfarer and Brot'an were still in their own cabin. The girl had emerged looking hopeful at each meal, and Magiere could barely stand the thought of seeing her disappointed again.

Leesil was right, warnings or not.

In the small, shabby cabin, Magiere had to slouch when she stood up. "I'm coming with you."

Both Leesil and Chap eyed her, and even the dog appeared to frown. Their anxious worry that in a heated moment she might lose herself . . . to her other half only made her feel worse. She both needed and resented them for this.

"I'm fine," she said coldly. "And if I throw the cook over the side, it'll be a conscious choice."

One corner of Leesil's mouth twitched, and he nodded at the bad joke. Chap rumbled, though he didn't lift his head from his paws.

"All right, since you speak Numanese better," Leesil agreed, and he flipped his hand toward the flat bread, showing traces of mold, on the bunk. "There have to be other food stores on board, as I doubt the captain eats this refuse. Chap, stay here, and when Wayfarer comes, tell her that we'll be back shortly."

Chap's crystalline blue eyes rolled toward Leesil, and Magiere wondered what the dog had to say about this. When Leesil only shook his head and stepped toward the door, Magiere followed.

They'd all spent much of their time below deck, going up for fresh air only when necessary. The crew was as bad as the bread, hard and filthy, and Magiere didn't want any more to do with them than necessary. The only good luck they'd had on this voyage was Leesil's usual seasickness passing more quickly than ever before, likely because he'd been stuck on some ship for so long.

Magiere followed him up on deck, and they emerged into a bright morning. Several unwashed sailors looked over, but she ignored them. Of the entire crew, only one had struck her as worth the bother. He was young, with dark, curling hair, and seemed determined to keep the ship a bit cleaner, or at least try. She'd spoken to him a few times, and he was polite enough. A few days ago she'd learned that his name was Saeed.

Looking around, she spotted him once again scrubbing the faded deck with a bucket of dipped seawater. He actually smiled as she and Leesil approached, but his smile faded when he saw her expression.

"Where's the captain?" she demanded.

"Magiere!" Leesil whispered.

She took a long breath to calm herself, but she was too angry. Back in Soráno, Leesil had had to go out gambling to pay the very high passage fee, and now Wayfarer was slowly starving.

Saeed rose from his knees with his breeches soaked, and studied Magiere's face with his dark eyes before pointing toward the prow. "There . . . but he will not hear you."

"Oh, yes, he will," Magiere answered, turning away toward the prow.

As she rounded the front mast, there was Captain Amjad sitting on a barrel and stuffing his face with a handful of plump dried figs. Two large, equally well-fed men stood nearby with curved blades tucked in their ragged sashes.

Magiere's breathing started to quicken and deepen.

Amjad was repulsive from his looks to his odor, from his greasy hair to his round face of sparse patchy, straggly strands in place of a real beard. Several of his front teeth were blackened.

Magiere closed on him so quickly that she left Leesil a few steps behind.

"You need to do something about those *meals* your cook sends us." She started right in. "Even our dog can't eat that swill!"

Amjad didn't flinch or react, and only spat a fig pit out across the deck. "You eat what the crew eats, as I told you before we left port."

Glancing around, Magiere noticed the crew didn't look any better than she and hers felt. Were they all living on nothing but molding bread and hardened dried fish? Then she felt Leesil's grip latch on to the back of her belt.

"Girl with us ill," he cut in, attempting his best Numanese as he pointed to the bowl of figs on the barrel beside the captain. "She needs fruits . . . vegetables."

Amjad turned away. "All foodstuffs in the hold go to market in il'Dha'ab Najuum. If you wanted better, you should have bought your own back in port. You paid for passage . . . only."

Magiere realized further talk was pointless, as this wretch wouldn't do anything to help Wayfarer. The day grew suddenly too bright in Magiere's eyes. Her irises must have turned black as she felt her teeth begin to change, pressing against the clench of her jaw.

And she didn't care.

Her left hand shot toward Amjad's throat . . . and didn't connect as Leesil jerked on her belt.

Amjad came off the barrel in a spin. When he came around to face her, there was a small knife in his right hand as both of his guards pulled their curved blades. But when he looked her in the eyes, his own widened a fraction and then narrowed.

Leesil kept a tight grip on Magiere's belt and held out his other hand. "No trouble."

Magiere stiffened, stopping herself from striking back to break Leesil's hold. She felt tears running down her cheeks from sunlight burning her widened irises, and she fought to pull herself under control.

Most people cringed in fear at first seeing her like this. Amjad did not, though the two men behind him stalled, perhaps waiting on their captain.

"No docks, no ports for many days to come," Amjad said, still gripping his knife. "If you wish, you can swim for shore and walk the rest of the way. Maybe you will survive long enough to see il'Dha'ab Najuum from somewhere in the distance before you perish."

Magiere wanted to take his knife and ram it down his throat. He hadn't even mentioned before leaving Soráno that they should bring their own food. He'd only warned them not to complain about the food, and she'd had no idea what that had really meant. She slid one foot back, easing the tension of Leesil's grip, before she turned her head just a little toward him.

Leesil looked calm on the outside, but his amber eyes were hard. And when facing a threat, he was at his most dangerous when he was silent, still, and apparently at ease. Magiere clung to that, and it helped her regain more control.

"Thank you for time—we make do," Leesil said quietly, turning away and pulling Magiere along.

Once they reached their cabin, and the sunlight no longer burned her eyes, Magiere became herself again. When she entered the cabin behind Leesil, both of them ducking to get through the door, they found Wayfarer on the bunk with Chap. Brot'an wasn't there, and the girl looked pale and tired, even though she'd been sleeping a good deal.

"Did you speak with the captain?" Wayfarer asked.

Obviously Chap had somehow told the girl, and Magiere's anger was smothered under desperation. "It didn't do any good."

Wayfarer dropped her eyes and swallowed with effort.

"Chap," Leesil said, soft but sharp, "take Wayfarer up on deck for some air."

As the dog lifted his head and stared, so did the girl, and old fears rose on her face.

"Must I?" Wayfarer asked.

"Yes," he answered flatly. "You need the air. Chap will watch over you."

Chap studied Leesil for a long moment and then hopped off the bunk.

Magiere wasn't certain why Leesil was sending them both away, though likely it had something to do with her near loss of control with the captain.

Wayfarer struggled up and followed Chap, and Leesil closed the door behind them. When he turned around, he didn't mention the scene with Amjad and only tilted his head toward the nearest bunk.

Magiere settled there, watching as he came to join her and pull off his old head scarf to let his white-blond hair hang loose. She could feel the warmth of his thigh against hers.

"Some of this is our fault," he said. "I had a bad feeling about this ship the moment we stepped on board."

Perhaps he just wanted to talk, and part of her was relieved. She couldn't stand for him to express any "concerns" about her nearly grabbing the captain by the throat.

"So did I," she agreed. "When he said not to complain about the food, I thought it meant meals would be simple."

Meals on the *Cloud Queen* hadn't been fancy, but the cook often served freshly boiled oats in the morning, and fish stews—with vegetables—late in the day. They had traveled on many ships over the past two years. Adequate though simple meals had always been part of passage.

"We're trapped . . . and Wayfarer is growing weaker each day," Leesil said, grabbing her hand without looking at her. "For the rest of the voyage, you'll have to trust me."

Magiere tensed at this, for she didn't know what he really meant. Then he turned on her almost too quickly, released her hand, and took her face with both of his hands.

"Do you trust me?" he whispered.

She trusted him in all things except for his seeing to his own safety.

"Leesil—" she began, and he stopped her with the press of his mouth on hers.

She knew what he was doing—trying to distract her. At first she almost pushed him off for such a weak ploy . . . until his mouth slowly moved against hers.

He pulled away slightly, brushing his lips along her cheek.

"That's a cheap trick," she growled at him.

"Is it working?"

With a rumble in her throat, Magiere grabbed Leesil by the shirt and pinned him on the bunk.

Wayfarer did not remain on deck for long. She felt dizzy and weak all of the time now and did not think Chap would force her to stay out longer than she wished. Neither she nor Chap was a fool, and Léshil obviously wished to speak alone with Magiere.

The fresh air did feel good, but this vessel's crew was more frightening than any she had encountered. By the way Chap watched every movement, he did not care for most of them, either.

"Can we go below?" she asked. "To my cabin . . . if you can tolerate Brot'ân'duivé."

—Better than being up here—

With relief she followed him to the aftcastle and down the steep steps, but when she reached the lower narrow passage . . .

"Wayfarer."

Turning in alarm, she looked up to find Saeed leaning through the short doorway above, and he quickly climbed down. Of all sailors on this ship, he was different.

There had been a time when being trapped in a narrow space with any human male would have frightened her speechless. But Saeed was always polite and well mannered and had been the one to inadvertently warn her in Soráno that the team of anmaglâhk had arrived, though he had not known who and what they were. Chap was familiar enough with him not to snarl or snap in warning.

As Saeed stepped down into the passage, he reached into his loose shirt. "I snuck these down for you."

Wayfarer's breath caught. In his hands were two large red apples, and the thought of fresh fruit made her want to snatch one and bite it. She looked up at him. From what she had seen on this ship, he had probably not eaten any better than she had. The captain fulfilled all of the lesser evils she had been taught about humans.

"It is all right," he said, holding them out as if he guessed her thoughts. "Sailors who make this run with Captain Amjad learn the hard way to buy—and hide—food before leaving a port."

"Hide it?" she questioned.

"Or it will be stolen halfway through the journey. Some making their first voyage on this ship are unprepared. Fights—and even some deaths—have occurred."

She cringed at the last of that, but he only shrugged.

"Most do not make more than one voyage on the *Djinn*. The captain hires new sailors often when in Suman ports. No one is paid until he returns to il'Dha'ab Najuum, so most have no coin for food along the way. You must be careful."

Wayfarer glanced once at Chap, who appeared to listen closely, but Saeed's words confused her. He seemed so much better than the other men here.

"Why have you stayed?" she asked.

For an instant any kindness in his face faded.

"It is a good place to hide." And he held out the apples again. "Take them. Eat one today and hide the other. I do not have much to share, but I am homebound. You need these more than even your companions."

She hesitated only a breath before taking the apples. "Thank you."

"Eat one quick," he said. "And do not let anyone see the other."

In a flash he was up the stairs again.

More grateful than she could express, Wayfarer looked down at the apples. But she had no intention of eating one by herself and hiding the other.

Stepping down the passage past Chap, she was about to open the door to her cabin.

—Wait—

She jumped slightly at that memory-word popping into her head, and, when she turned, Chap still stood farther up the passage.

—We must . . . talk . . . about . . . Soráno—

"What do you—"

—On the docks . . . when we went . . . to find passage . . . for this ship—

More and more of his memory-words in her head were becoming clearer over time—perhaps because he had been sneaking a peek at her memories far too often. She did not like that, but here and now she was still at a loss for . . .

—When you touched . . . me . . . and pulled . . . away—

Wayfarer backed down the passage, away from the cabin door—away from Chap.

What she thought she had seen in her head had been a mistake, only a flash of imagination. Perhaps he did not even know about the second time, when the anmaglâhk had tried to take her and he had stopped them.

In all the times she had thought about him—how different he was inside compared to the way he looked—she had tried to see through his eyes and imagine the world of a majay-hì like no other. That was all it had been . . . that one flash of something on the docks of Soráno.

She did not want it to be anything more.

—There has been no proper time . . . since then . . . when we were alone— . . . *—I need to know—*

Everything that had happened to her had started after learning of those watchful eyes in her people's forest. Even when she did not catch them staring from the brush, it was as if they were always there, looking at her . . . as *he* did now.

Chap stepped closer, and Wayfarer—once called Leanâlhâm—flattened her back against the passage's wall.

—*Touch me . . . now*—

"Please . . . stop."

—*Now*—

Even standing, she was short enough that he could have shoved his head into her stomach and knocked her down. But he simply stood there, looking up at her . . . looking at her as so many others of his kind had once done.

Wayfarer took a shaky breath as she shifted the apples and clutched them to her chest with one arm. As she reached out, she flinched once before her fingertips touched his head between his ears.

At first nothing happened as she stared into his crystalline eyes, as blue as clear sky. And then she smelled . . . something . . . like a forest floor after a light rain. A flash of white appeared in her thoughts.

The white majay-hì stood in a space between tall trees in Wayfarer's homeland. Sunlight caught in a coat of pure white fur, making the female hard to look upon as she padded ahead through the brush. It was not until the female paused, turning her head to look back, that Wayfarer realized . . .

Flecks in the female's eyes appeared to turn those blue irises green like her own. She was looking directly into those eyes as if she sat on the forest floor, but she was standing. And when she looked down . . .

At the sight of paws where her hands should be, Wayfarer's breaths stopped.

This had never happened when she had followed the white majay-hì.

The ship's corridor reappeared, along with Chap, staring up at her. With a gasp, as if drowning, she pulled her hand back from his head. Then she turned too quickly, trying to get away, and bounced off the passage wall.

Wayfarer hit the floor. One apple fell from her grip and went tumbling farther down the passage. She rolled over, scooting backward in fright away from Chap . . . and again when he took a step, still staring at her.

—*What did you see?*—

She looked at her hands to make sure they were not paws. Why was he doing this to her?

—*Answer . . . now*—

"A forest . . . my people's," she began. "But something . . . someone else who—"

—Lily . . . You saw Lily?—

Wayfarer lost her voice. It was not that he put a name on another sacred being; she had come to tolerate that through him. But she had heard that name before in reference to the white female . . . Chap's own mate, on the other side of the world.

"What did you do to me?" Wayfarer finally whispered.

This time he was the one to back away.

—No . . . not me— . . . —Only you . . . somehow—

That was even worse.

"Well, what do we have here?" said a male with a thick accent.

Wayfarer twisted on the floor to look toward that voice down the passage.

A spindly and tall Suman sailor stood where the passage's far end turned to another set of stairs down to the ship's cargo hold. He grinned, half-toothless, as he tossed the apple she had dropped up in the air and caught it again. His eyes closed halfway in a hardened glare.

Still gripping the apple, he jerked his head to one side and took a threatening step. "Get out of my way!"

Wayfarer was too shaken and did not know what to do. A rumble, followed by a snarl, rose behind her.

Chap lunged forward. Before she could throw herself aside, he pushed off, leaping over her. She twisted back again to see him land and charge.

The sailor with the apple back-stepped to the corner. Chap cut him off before he could run, so instead he pulled a knife that Wayfarer had not noticed before from his belt.

Chap, all of his fur on end and his ears flattened, lunged in anyway. He snapped once toward the hand holding the apple.

Wayfarer thought she heard a door open behind her, but all of her fear was wrapped around the apple in the hand of the thief. Scrambling to her feet, she rushed in behind Chap. She shouted at the sailor, and, amid fearful anger, it came out in her own tongue.

"Give it to him!"

The man just stared at her until she pointed at the apple and then Chap. For an instant the sailor might have thought to hold out the apple, but he simply dropped it.

Chap snatched it in his jaws before it hit the floor. He backed up, still growling, and the man raced off, heading down for the cargo hold.

"What in the seven hells is all the noise?"

Wayfarer turned at the foul words normally used by Léshil, but it was Magiere who stood, with her falchion in hand, halfway out of the nearer cabin's door—and she was naked.

Wayfarer flushed in staring.

Magiere swallowed and then almost toppled against the doorframe.

Léshil, one winged blade in hand, shoved past her, and . . . he was naked as well.

Wayfarer's breath caught in her throat as she spun away, scrunching her eyes closed. She heard scuffling and more awful language behind her, until . . .

"What happened?" Magiere barked.

"Nothing . . . nothing," Wayfarer answered, though she did not know why she had lied. She hesitated before turning, barely opening one eye to peek.

"I . . . I dropped an apple," she added, "but Chap retrieved it."

Magiere was now half-covered with a blanket, and the greimasg'äh must have come out of the other cabin, as he was standing closer with a stiletto still in hand. Both looked beyond Wayfarer and likely at Chap, with the other apple in his jaws. Wayfarer was thankful that Léshil was no longer in sight, though she still heard him muttering angrily inside the nearer cabin.

"An apple?" Magiere asked, and then she saw the other one, which Wayfarer still held. "It looks like you two have something to tell us."

Wayfarer was uncertain what that referred to, the apples or her lie, but Chap came up beside her with a snort muffled by the apple he had in his jaws.

Magiere's brow furrowed. "Wait. We'll be ready . . . in a few moments."

Ducking into the cabin, she slammed the door shut. The last to turn away was Brot'ân'duivé, but he eyed both Wayfarer and then Chap before returning to his own cabin. Wayfarer was again alone with Chap, but another long moment passed before she could look down to find him watching her.

—We will learn . . . why . . . this is happening to you. . . . I promise—

Those memory-words did not comfort her as she took the second apple from him. Still, she believed that he had not done this to her. It was not Chap's fault that she had seen—been forced to see—a memory he had chosen for her.

It was something further wrong with her.

Chap scooted closer, and Wayfarer numbly watched as he stuck his nose out toward her hand holding the second apple. It was he this time, and not she, who flinched once before he touched her hand.

She saw nothing in her head and only heard his words called up from her own memories.

—Say nothing . . . of . . . what you did . . . with me . . . to Brot'ân'duivé—

Brot'ân'duivé was still puzzled by whatever had happened in the passage. It could not be something as simple as the attempted theft of an ill-gotten apple.

When he had returned briefly to his cabin, it was only because he knew nothing would be said by the girl or the majay-hì while he remained. Certainly Brot'ân'duivé would hear nothing Chap said unless someone else repeated it. At that, he wondered. . . .

Leanâlhâm, "Child of Sorrow" . . . Sheli'câlhad, "To a Lost Way" . . . and now Wayfarer might not even tell him what had truly transpired in the passageway.

It was clear to Brot'ân'duivé that, in whatever had happened, the majay-hì had adequately seen to the girl's safety. In that, he trusted Chap.

For a while he waited in his cabin and listened until he heard a door open. It did not surprise him that the girl and majay-hì had gone to Magiere and

Léshil first. When he heard that door close again, he stepped out for the same destination.

At his knock it was Léshil who opened the door, scowled, and turned away.

Brot'ân'duivé ducked in, closed the door himself, and the room was so quiet that it was obvious that he had interrupted a conversation.

The left-side bunk where Magiere sat, now hastily dressed, was in disarray: the altercation in the passage had interrupted something else. But any leftover anger was gone from Magiere's face and posture. Instead she appeared . . . shaken.

Léshil as well looked shocked and distracted where he stood beyond Magiere in the small cabin's left rear corner. However, Chap lay on the right-side bunk with his head hanging on his forepaws over the bunk's edge. His eyes were half-closed as he stared at the floor, as did Wayfarer beside him.

The apples were still untouched in the girl's lap.

"Where did you get those?" Brot'ân'duivé asked.

Wayfarer blinked twice before looking up at him, as if the question was out of context for whatever was on everyone's mind.

"A sailor gave them to me," she said.

At that, some of the ire and suspicion returned in Magiere's expression.

Wayfarer immediately noticed this as well. "It was Saeed. You know he is very polite . . . and kind."

Magiere straightened on the bunk, and Léshil turned to look at the girl. Even Brot'ân'duivé was somewhat surprised at this, considering the way the girl had always reacted to unknown humans, especially males. Only Chap did not move or look up.

"Léshil," Wayfarer said calmly, "let me borrow your knife."

Brot'ân'duivé watched as she took the knife and began cutting the fruit into slices to be passed out.

Wayfarer fed a slice to Chap, who wolfed it down in two bites. "Saeed told me that sailors on this ship buy their own food in ports and then hide it," she continued. "He said that men sometimes fight, even kill, over food."

She offered Brot'ân'duivé a piece, which he consumed rapidly, and then passed slices to Magiere and Léshil before biting a piece of her own. Whatever heavy thought had preoccupied her and the others melted in their relief. But a few bites of an apple would not solve the current problem.

Brot'ân'duivé noted the angry hardness that filled Léshil's face as he watched the girl sag in exhaustion once the last of the apples was consumed.

He had joined with Magiere and Léshil—against their wishes—for several reasons, one of which was to learn more about these orbs and why the Ancient Enemy had gone to such great lengths to have them guarded. What he needed most was to learn more of the power the orbs held . . . and whether they could truly be used as a weapon.

And as to whatever had transpired in this room in the moments before he had entered, that was a more immediate problem to solve. Secrets were a matter of life to Brot'ân'duivé, and he had always been patient in their acquisition and use.

Leesil was still edgy, even after the old shadow-gripper left on some excuse about looking into "purchasing" more food from the crew. When Magiere's lips parted to say something, Leesil quickly shook his head. Before she could even frown, he stepped in front of Chap and crouched down.

"Is he really gone?" he whispered.

Wayfarer looked up in puzzlement.

With a grumbling huff, Chap climbed off the bunk and stalked over to the cabin door. He sniffed the space between the door's bottom and the floor and then pricked up his ears as he stood there a moment longer.

Chap turned back and huffed once for *yes*.

And now that they were certain Brot'an was gone . . .

"Are you sure?" Leesil asked with a quick glance at Wayfarer before he eyed Chap again. "Could it have just been—"

—No— . . . —Not memory-words . . . I called up— . . . —And not as . . . Wynn hears . . . my thoughts spoken to her—

"Maybe you did something that—"

—No— . . . —She saw . . . my chosen memory . . . of my Lily . . . through her own touch— . . . —She . . . relived . . . a moment . . . she could not have had—

Leesil eyed Wayfarer, and the girl dropped her gaze.

"How . . . Why?" Magiere demanded.

This time Chap spoke aloud with three huffs for *uncertain* or *unknown.*

Leesil shook his head and sat down on the floor as Magiere sighed while watching Wayfarer. Still the girl wouldn't look at anyone.

Did this have something to do with Wayfarer's visiting the spirits of her people in name-taking? Had they done something to her, or was it something else about her?

Leesil, and Magiere, had already tested that the girl couldn't catch a memory from them through a touch. So was this something that only worked with Chap because he was . . . Chap? They didn't have any other majay-hì around, such as Chap's daughter, Shade, so they couldn't test whether it worked with other majay-hì.

Some might have thought such a thing quite wonderful, but those people would be idiots. The girl had been through enough—too much—and now she was a potential tool, from what Leesil saw of what she could do.

Chap had been right to keep this from Brot'ân'duivé, for if he had not, Leesil could only imagine how the old assassin might have tried to use the girl. Chap knew things that no one else did—could—including Leesil himself and Magiere.

Such as where two orbs were hidden far up north.

If Chap ever let such a memory slip out while Wayfarer was touching him . . .

Leesil exchanged a worried glance with Magiere, and then he reached out to poke Wayfarer's leg. Startled by that, she finally looked at him.

"Well, it could be a good thing," he said wryly. "Chap can show you some things better than he can describe them with broken words pulled up from our memories. At least in that, the bothersome mutt has less reason to prattle in *my* head."

Chap curled his jowls, and Wayfarer cast Leesil a reproving look—probably over what she considered to be his disrespect to a *sacred* majay-hì.

"I'm just saying," Leesil added quickly, raising both hands in surrender.

CHAPTER FOURTEEN

When Wynn awoke the following morning, her dizziness was gone, but she still felt weak and tired, as if she hadn't slept. She found Shade stretched out beside her on the bed, but facing the other way. Wynn sat up and stroked Shade's head and noticed that Shade's eyes were open and fixed on the room's closed door. She wondered whether the dog had done that all night.

"No more time to lie about," she said. "We have to make better progress after I messed things up yesterday."

Pushing down the covers, Wynn reached for her sage's robe on the bed's end.

Jausiff would not get the better of her today. She knew his approach now: to go on offense and stay there. She could play that game herself. Once dressed, she tied her hair back, but when she went for the door, Shade growled softly, hopped from the bed, and cut her off.

Wynn was in no mood for this. "We have work to do. Now get out of the way."

Shade didn't budge, so Wynn stepped around her with *almost* complete certainty that the dog would not bite her and pull her back. She was thankful to be proven right. Though Shade snarled as she followed, Wynn stepped out and immediately saw something more was wrong.

In addition to a standard guard at each end of the passage, there was now a Suman guard in a long yellow tabard standing in front of Osha and Chane's door.

What happened during the night?

With growing alarm, she walked up to the Suman blocking the second door along the passage. He was young and clean-shaven and stared straight over the top of her head.

"Please step aside," she said. "I need to speak to my guards."

He didn't even look down, as well as acting as if he had heard nothing.

"You cannot keep me from my companions," Wynn insisted. "Please move aside."

He continued staring over the top of her head.

As Wynn looked around in frustration, her gaze stopped on the next door, the one to Nikolas's room. She strode there, with Shade following closely, and knocked.

"Nikolas, may I come in?"

No one answered, and Wynn's confusion and alarm grew. She tried the door's handle and found it unlocked. Hesitantly she cracked it open.

"Nikolas?"

Again no answer, and she pushed the door inward to find both beds made and the room empty. Nikolas's pack was still on the floor at the end of the far bed.

What was going on?

Turning around, she fixed on the Suman guard blocking Chane and Osha's door. And she started toward him again.

Footsteps carried up the passage from the stairs, and then Nikolas stepped up and around the corner, with Aupsha right behind him. Both looked exhausted. At the sight of Wynn and Shade, Nikolas halted just short of Wynn's room.

Looking over his shoulder at Aupsha, he said, "You have delivered me. You are dismissed."

His tone was surprisingly cold, almost regal, and it left Wynn wondering what position Nikolas had played growing up here—perhaps not one of the nobility and yet not a servant. His manner was quite different from that of the young man she'd come to know at the guild.

Without a word or any visible reaction, Aupsha turned and left back down the stairs.

Nikolas walked right by the Suman guard and whispered to Wynn, "My room."

Puzzled even more, she followed him in, and after Shade entered, she closed the door.

"What's going on?" she asked. "Why is that Suman guard out there?"

Nikolas ran a hand over his face, and perhaps a bit of the old Nervous Nikolas resurfaced. "It seems Chane and Osha somehow slipped out of their room last night and went . . . exploring. Chane was caught somewhere near the back of the keep, though not Osha, who came back on his own later. They are both in trouble."

"Slipped out? Those idiots!"

Yes, Chane, always thinking he knew best, had a tendency to "go exploring," but Osha should have known better. He'd understood that they could not give the duke a reason to throw them out—or so she'd thought. Then something else occurred to her.

"Nikolas . . . how did you learn of this?"

"Sherie," he answered, and then swallowed, looking miserable. "Try not to worry. She won't let you be sent away—or at least she'll do what she can. I did what you asked, and I tried to speak to her, but apparently Captain Holland was informed of Chane's and Osha's wanderings . . . and he informed Sherie. There's tension between the keep guards and these new Sumans, who've been here only a few moons."

Wynn found that suspicious, but she had more important questions. "Did you learn anything else from the duchess, anything about how the message was sent and who carried it?"

Her persistence with that one question might soon be suspicious as well, but she had to ask.

"Not much," Nikolas answered, with a shake of his head. "It's all so strange. Either she doesn't know or won't tell me, but I get the impression she's at a loss for how it was done." He glanced away. "It's . . . difficult to speak with her, but at least she thinks I'm here to help Karl."

"What else did she say?"

The pain in Nikolas's face faded slightly as he frowned. "My father decided to send for me while he and Aupsha were in a self-imposed isolation. Apparently they'd gone into the villages to see if they could help. When they returned, Karl ordered the guards to open the gate for them, but then he had a fit. He was so angry that my father placed himself and Aupsha in a quarantine to end the matter."

"So the duke didn't know they had left the grounds . . . or how?"

Nikolas shook his head again. "I would guess not."

Wynn found that another odd puzzle, but, not wishing to interrupt Nikolas's thoughts any further, she remained silent.

"While they were locked away," he continued, "servants left their meals by the door. One night my father spoke through the door and asked a servant to bring Sherie. Of course she came, but when she arrived, she found a small paper-wrapped package outside the door. My father asked her through the door to take it to the north wall and throw it over."

"Wait—what?—throw it . . . ?" Wynn began, and then said, "Never mind; go on."

"She did as he asked, but why would he ask this? It must have contained the message for me and the one for Premin Hawes, but how could anyone know it was there, outside the wall? The only people who could have were Sherie, my father, and perhaps Aupsha, since she was locked away with my father."

Wynn sank onto the bed nearer the door. What she'd heard did explain how Jausiff got the message past the gate guards but not how it was retrieved and delivered to Calm Seatt. Aupsha had the right height for the messenger and the would-be thief who breached the Stonewalkers' underworld. But there were others here of the same height and build, and she had been locked away with the master sage.

"I'm sorry," Nikolas said. "I want to help my father with Karl, but that seems to be all Sherie knows."

"That must have been difficult for you," she replied. "You did your best, and now we need to get Osha out of that room."

Then she realized she'd omitted Chane. She was used to his lying dormant until the sun set, and thankfully Nikolas didn't seem to notice the slip.

"I can't help with that, but Sherie might," he said. "She was going to speak with Karl, so I'll try to catch her."

Wynn nodded in relief, for she couldn't think of anything better or safer. She and Shade followed Nikolas out into the passage and as far as her own door. He walked swiftly to the guard at the top of the stairs—a different one than Wynn remembered from the night before. This one had broad shoulders and graying hair.

"Lieutenant Martelle," Nikolas said. "I need to see the duchess."

The guard nodded once.

That Nikolas knew the keep's people by name and position told Wynn that he must be respected here, at least, for being Jausiff's son. The guard stepped out of sight onto the stairs as he called down, "Comeau? You there?"

A moment later Martelle stepped back up into view with another guard and nodded to Nikolas as he gestured to his companion. "Guardsman Comeau will escort you to the duchess, Master Nikolas."

Wynn sighed in frustration, for even Nikolas was not allowed to walk around by himself. As the young sage and the new guardsman vanished down the stairs, she turned to face the Suman guard. Perhaps she could try something a little . . . louder?

She ignored the guard and called out, "Osha! Are you all right?"

The guard barely had time to scowl when the door jerked inward and opened. Osha tried to take a step out, but the Suman had already whirled, with a hand on his sword's hilt.

"Get back," the guard ordered in Numanese.

Osha didn't move.

"Oh, for goodness' sake," Wynn exclaimed, tired of all this, and then remembered Nikolas's mention of odds between the Sumans and the keep's guards. "Lieutenant Martelle?" she called toward the stairs. "May I please speak to my personal guards? I promise that we all shall remain in the guest quarters."

The lieutenant stalked a few steps down the passage, eyed her once, and looked at the Suman guard in obvious annoyance. "Let her in."

The Suman glowered back but hesitantly stepped aside.

Wynn wondered about the chain of command in the keep. Was the old guard still considered the final authority? It seemed so . . . as long as the duke wasn't present.

Wynn waved Shade ahead and hurried in as Osha stepped back and closed the door once they were all inside. Chane, fully clothed down to his boots, lay stretched out on the far bed. Without breathing, he looked dead for all practical purposes.

Osha looked as exhausted as Wynn felt.

"What in the seven hells were you two doing last night?" she whispered harshly in Elvish. Likely their little excursion had been Chane's idea, but he wasn't awake for her to chastise.

Osha ignored her bit of temper and answered calmly, "Looking for the guarded door Shade saw in the duke's memory."

That just irritated her more. By what Shade had shown her, the door was probably underground, and Osha and Chane clearly hadn't made it that far before being caught. Still, what had they found? And when she asked . . .

"Not a door . . . or not the one you described for the majay-hì." Osha ran a hand through the messy hair at the crown of his head to push it back before he continued. "We reached a passage at the keep's back near its rear wall. I heard shore waves close by and saw a light down the dark passage ahead. The undead . . . Chane . . . said it was a sage's crystal. I saw the elder sage with a metal object in hand, and he appeared to be searching the floor, though he stopped often, as if looking at the object he held. Another tall person was with him and holding the crystal, though I did not see that one's face. Both were fully cloaked and hooded. Then footsteps rose in a side passage. I looked around the corner toward that sound, and a sharp breeze struck me from behind. When I turned back in to the main passage, there was no light, and no one appeared to be there anymore."

He went on to explain how he had evaded capture and inspected a locked door with a sentry window at the passage's end, and how there was also an archway to the right and another locked door down a parallel set of stone stairs.

Sometimes Wynn forgot he'd once been an anmaglâhk trained to be a spy if not yet an assassin.

"And you found no one left in the passage?" she asked.

Osha shook his head.

Tired as Wynn felt, she knew all this was somehow important. "Close your eyes," she told Osha, "and try to remember as much as you can of what you saw." She reached down to touch Shade at her side. "Show me."

A dim passage appeared in Wynn's mind as Shade passed whatever Osha strove to remember. In a matter of moments, Wynn saw most of what Osha had described. She felt the wind, and then, indeed, Jausiff and the tall companion had somehow escaped. When she saw the dead-end passage and the locked door leading outside, she was certain it was not the same door that Shade had seen in Karl's memory.

"That's enough." Wynn shook her head. "Nikolas told me that when Jausiff and Aupsha were in quarantine, Jausiff called for Sherie. She was told to take a package left outside the door and throw it over the north wall. Whoever the messenger was retrieved it before heading for Calm Seatt. That's how the two-letter message got out of the keep without the guards or the duke knowing."

Osha absorbed her words, turned, and took a few long paces. "I would guess that the companion in the passage must be the old sage's servant, Aupsha. As to the message being thrown over the wall, I cannot see what this means."

"Well, we know Jausiff and Aupsha are up to more than helping Karl," Wynn countered. "And he and she are the ones sneaking around, searching for something that the duke and possibly the duchess know nothing about." She crossed her arms in frustration. "Somehow Jausiff and his companion got out of a passage with two locked doors . . . one leading downward, perhaps under the keep."

"How long were Aupsha and Jausiff isolated?" Osha asked. "Who was outside the keep and could retrieve and deliver the letters? Someone from one of the villages, perhaps contacted while Jausiff was there?"

Wynn uncrossed her arms. "Yes, there might be—"

"Why does Karl not want anyone going into the villages?" Osha cut in. "Because of plague or fearing the lack of that being uncovered? If the latter, did Jausiff know there was no plague? If not, then why not send the message while he was outside the keep? And—"

"Enough, Osha!" Wynn interrupted. "I know we have a lot of unknowns."

He asked all the right questions but simply too many at once. He also tended to change whenever Chane wasn't part of the discussion. He became more certain, more willing to throw out thoughts and ideas . . . more forceful and more impatient. Yet somehow all of this felt like a distraction to Wynn, as if Osha wanted to make it all seem futile in the moment.

But why? Was there something else he wanted from her?

"Perhaps Karl's reaction upon their return caused Jausiff to send the messages," she suggested. "If so, that would be a reason why he did not send them until he came back. It would also mean he might not have thought to arrange for someone to retrieve the package thrown over the wall."

Osha shook his head. "No, if he had discovered there was no plague and then wanted to call for his son in dealing with the duke, he would . . . *I would* have arranged the messenger before returning to the keep. There is also the possibility that the duke might have known there was no plague, using that lie to control the movements of everyone here. If so, the duke would have known the old sage's reason for self-quarantine was a lie as well."

For an instant Wynn felt as if she were arguing with Chane again, and she fell silent to look at Osha. Much more had changed in him and left her wondering how a year with Brot'an might have altered him in other ways.

"Yes, much has changed," he whispered, "for both of us, it appears."

A sudden sadness washed over his long features . . . except for his eyes. His gaze flicked once toward Chane.

"You know most of why . . . for me," he added, "but as for you . . ."

Wynn began to ache inside.

There was too much to tell, most of it hard to explain, and some of it she didn't dare try. And here and now wasn't the time.

"You have overstepped your authority!"

At that harsh female voice outside in the passage, both Wynn and Osha looked to the door, and Shade went for it first. Wynn rushed over, relieved by the interruption. She cracked the door enough to look out without the risk of anyone outside seeing Chane's current state.

Both Nikolas and the duchess stood outside as the latter tore into the Suman guard, who had at least sidestepped away from the door. Lieutenant Martelle, with poorly hidden satisfaction, stood a few paces behind the duchess. And there was Aupsha, stoic as usual, two steps farther down the passage toward the stairs.

"I do not care what your superior ordered," Sherie continued, closing on the Suman guard. "You are not part of the keep's forces. You are dismissed—now!"

In profile, the Suman was expressionless, but he glanced at Martelle, who in turn settled a hand on the hilt of his sheathed sword.

It was obvious to Wynn that the keep's standard guards obeyed anything the duchess commanded. Perhaps they trusted her judgment more than they did her brother's, considering the foreign interlopers that the duke had brought to this place.

With a slow bow of his head, the Suman guard turned and walked away toward the stairs. Lieutenant Martelle watched that one's every step. Maybe there was more than simple tension between the keep's guards and the Sumans?

Wynn was about to thank the duchess for the assistance, when something else caught her eye.

As the Suman guard passed Aupsha, he turned his head toward her. Even with his back to Wynn, he obviously kept his eyes on Aupsha until he passed beyond her. She did not return his glance and remained attentively watching the duchess.

Wynn was too caught up in that brief moment and was startled when the duchess turned on Martelle.

"You and your man are dismissed as well," Sherie said. "I will take responsibility for our guests."

"Yes, my lady," the lieutenant answered with a nod. As he left, he waved to the guard at the passage's back end to follow him. The duchess turned to face Wynn in the half-opened door.

"I apologize. After speaking with Nikolas earlier, I went to see my brother, who is . . . unwell this morning. I came as soon as I could."

She, too, appeared tired but was pristine in attire and bearing. Her blue-black hair was combed to hang evenly over the shoulders of a burgundy gown. She also seemed less rigid this morning, regardless of formality. When she'd spoken Nikolas's name, there was almost no bitterness. Then again, perhaps that was only because of so many other complications she had to address. Either way, it appeared that Nikolas's attempt to speak with her had not been the disaster he'd envisioned.

"Aupsha and I will walk you down to a late breakfast," the duchess added.

Wynn was still uncertain about her status here. "So . . . you've dismissed our guards, but for how long?"

The duchess stood with her back perfectly straight. "With my brother indisposed, I am in charge. You will be treated as guests, so long as you remain within the keep's upper floors or the courtyard. Do not try to go anywhere else and avoid the duke's private Suman guards. They are . . . protective of his privacy and act quickly, without consulting Captain Holland or Lieutenant Martelle. As long as you avoid the lower levels, this should not be an issue."

Wynn was relieved that she and hers were free to move about the keep, making her tasks easier to accomplish. After Chane's and Osha's foolishness from the night before, this was far more than she expected. She shooed Osha and Shade out before she pulled the door closed and wished she could lock it behind herself.

The duchess looked Osha up and down. "What about your swordsman?"

"He's a late sleeper and usually remains awake for my needs at night," Wynn answered, knowing it sounded ridiculous in the middle of all this noise and chaos.

"As you wish." Sherie turned down the passage, with Aupsha and then Nikolas behind her.

As Wynn took a step, she stalled at one thought and let Osha and Shade slip out ahead of her. Yes, she was now free to move about except for anywhere below the keep.

As Osha entered the kitchen, he took a little satisfaction in having Wynn to himself until dusk. She had come to him to exchange ideas, to think through obstacles in seeking his help, and then he succumbed to bitterness again. It was not right to press her about her own past since they had parted, now that they faced hidden threats amid seeking the identity of a messenger and a thief, one and the same or not. But he hoped to know soon why she, too, had changed so much.

For now Osha had this day to show her exactly how much help he could be to her.

Sgäilsheilleache had not taught him the traditional methods of Anmaglâhk interrogation, for he had not believed in the use of torture. But he had started to teach Osha other things, such as how to ask unexpected questions, ones seemingly disconnected, and how useful silence could be as well, even after an answer was given.

Osha never had the chance to practice any of this, but by nightfall, before that undead rose again, he would turn any opportunity he found to Wynn's favor. As he sat down at the kitchen's table, his only discomfort was the way the dark-skinned woman glanced too often at him.

If Aupsha had been in the passage with the elder sage, had she seen him there?

"You may go, Aupsha," the duchess said.

With a bow of her head, the tall woman departed the same way they had all come. This left Wynn, Osha, Shade, Nikolas, and the duchess alone, sitting at the table. Everyone looked at one another in an awkward moment of silence.

The bad-tempered cook came stomping through an archway at the kitchen's rear.

"I've got breakfast ready, my lady," she announced angrily, "but that girl, Eliza, can't be roused. I'll have to serve you myself."

"Is Eliza ill?" the duchess asked.

"Just lazy," the cook growled. "Says she can't seem to wake up."

The duchess frowned at the cook's manner. "We will be glad to have you serve us, Martha."

Osha exchanged a glance with Wynn, who looked tired as well. They had both experienced the same thing this morning, and only Wynn's calling his name through the door had brought him to his senses.

With a grunt, the unhappy cook served strong tea with milk, eggs, potatoes, and bread that was too white. Osha did not care for the latter, as it felt like paste compared to his people's rich, wild grain breads. Wynn fixed a plate for Shade, and no one chastised her. Osha found the rest of the food better than what he had eaten at the sages' guild or while sailing across the far ocean. He ate three eggs.

Wynn kept glancing at him, and he sensed that she felt limited or hampered by the duchess's presence. Then, as the meal neared its end . . .

"Sherie, you said Karl was unwell this morning?" Nikolas asked. "Is there anything to be done for him?"

The duchess looked across the table at the young sage. For an instant her expression filled with a sad longing that Osha knew only too well.

"I was about to see that the fire has been lit in the main hall," she said. "Perhaps you could walk with me to talk of this."

Nikolas stared at her as if he had not heard her correctly. "You want me to . . . ?" He nearly jumped to his feet and then looked to Wynn. "Will you and Osha be all right on your own?"

"We'll be fine," she answered.

Nikolas followed the duchess out and left Osha with Wynn and the majay-hì, who still licked her plate on the floor, as the cook stomped about and irritably muttered near the ovens.

Osha said nothing, merely waiting on Wynn.

She finally blinked and leaned in to whisper in his tongue. "I can hardly believe it, but it seems that we are free to move about as we like."

He could hardly believe it, either, and whispered back, "Where do we start?"

Wynn glanced at the cook. "I should try Jausiff again and hopefully catch him off guard about what he was doing last night."

"Do you have any reason to fear speaking to him alone?"

"No. Even if he was in league with a minion of the Ancient Enemy, knowingly or not, he'd never openly risk harming a friend of his son or an emissary of the guild."

Osha nodded, though he was not as certain as she was. "I will seek out Aupsha. More and more she seems the likely one with the elder sage last night. If nothing else, I will find a way to confirm that first . . . and if I can, there may be more to learn."

Wynn's expression grew anxious. "Are you sure? We don't know anything about her, and her allegiance to this house, and especially Jausiff. She might not have any reluctance to injuring one of us."

"I will be cautious," he assured her. "We will meet in our rooms afterward, the easiest place to find each other . . . in privacy."

Wynn nodded and stood, and then she looked toward the cook as she spoke loudly in Numanese. "Thank you for breakfast, Martha. Could you tell us where we might find Aupsha again? We need some help getting about the keep without mistakes."

"That foreigner?" Martha grunted, holding a pot in midair. "It's not my job to keep track of her comings and goings." Then she set down the pot and faced Wynn. "I heard she don't like it much indoors, and spends mornings in the courtyard. Try there first."

Wynn nodded and turned back to Osha, whispering, "Shade and I will try Jausiff's study first, while you look to the courtyard."

For the first time, Osha did not feel so much like an outsider in Wynn's world . . . in her life.

CHAPTER FIFTEEN

After leaving the kitchen, Wynn steeled her resolve as she made her way toward Jausiff's study. In recent years she'd managed to face down premins, nobles, Stonewalkers, and the undead. So what was it about Nikolas's father that left her feeling like a stuttering little guild initiate? She wasn't going to let that happen again, and she stroked between Shade's ears as they climbed the stairs to the keep's second level.

"Jausiff's a guarded one, but try to catch anything that slips out of his memories."

Shade huffed once for *yes*.

Upon reaching the second floor, they stepped off down the passage, but Wynn faltered at the master sage's door and paused for a deep breath.

"Ready?" she whispered.

Shade huffed again, and Wynn knocked on the door—and she waited longer than expected.

For some reason Jausiff hadn't come down to breakfast, and so Wynn assumed he would be in his chamber, but that might have been a mistake. She knocked again, harder, and this time heard a faint rustling or movement beyond the door. A moment later it opened.

Jausiff's gray robe was rumpled, as if he'd slept in it. His eyes were mere slits behind strands of uncombed silver-white hair, but at the sight of Wynn, his eyes opened fully.

"How may I help you?" he asked.

All of Wynn's confidence drained away.

A cloudy sky and drizzling rain met Osha as he reached the keep's courtyard and looked around. Straight ahead, three standard guards were on watch at the large gate. To his left was a stable and to the right the barracks. There were no Suman guards in sight.

Neither did Osha see Aupsha, and the courtyard was not large. As he stepped onward, movement near the stable caught his attention.

Aupsha came around its far corner toward the courtyard's front and stopped upon spotting him. He nodded politely in turning toward her.

He had never before seen a human like her, with such very dark skin and eyes like stained walnut wood. Her tightly curling hair was even darker. With long and slender limbs, she was easily as tall as the average human male—perhaps taller. She wore no cloak and seemed unaware of the falling rain, but she watched Osha without moving as he closed the distance.

"May we . . . speak?" he asked in Numanese.

During the past moon he had worked hard on his Numanese and had become slightly better with it than he was at Belaskian, but he could not remember the word for "privately." Instead he swept a hand toward the stable, and by that she should take his meaning. He hoped the structure was empty of anyone but horses.

Only Aupsha's dark eyes shifted once toward the stable's open central bay doors. The barest crease of her brow signaled suspicion.

That gave Osha a strong suspicion of his own. If she had been the one with the elder sage in the passage last night, it was possible she had seen him as well. She turned for the stable, as if he was no concern to her, and he followed.

Something more caught Osha's attention—something he should have heard but did not.

He dropped his gaze down the back of her wool tunic and down the low, full skirt. He saw the back of one boot push up against the skirt's hem. There was no extra layer at the heel and the sole was flat, thick leather worn smooth over time. When that foot moved forward in another step . . .

It did not make enough sound in landing as her other heel-less boot came up.

The packed-dirt courtyard was drenched by rain. There were puddles of water everywhere, even along her path. He should have heard at least the soft smack of footfalls, but no. She walked with more silence than the average person would, almost . . . like an anmaglâhk.

Once inside the stable, alone and out of sight of the gate guards, she turned as he stepped in, three paces behind her.

"What do you want?" she asked clearly, with only the trace of an accent he had never heard before.

Her bluntness, and that walk, and the look she had given him when he had first spotted her called for a change in approach . . . as Sgäilsheilleache would have done.

"I saw you and the old counselor in the passage last night. You were there and then not. How?"

Her expression flickered with sudden wariness, as he knew it would, and he remained silent in waiting for her answer. She would not answer his actual question, but she would say something to change directions.

"There are secrets . . . within secrets in this place," she said. "They are not mine to share, and none of your concern."

That brief falter—catch—after that third word told him she perhaps lied in a quick second thought. He had learned of such the hard way as he had waded through all of the much better lies of Brot'ân'duivé. That she had not given him a direct lie as to how they had left that passage said something more.

However she and Jausiff had vanished last night, it had nothing to do with the secrets of the keep. It had to do with her. When she said no more, he knew further silence on his part would not induce her.

"What object did Counselor Jausiff hold?" he asked. "What did he do with it?"

Aupsha glanced beyond him toward the stable's bay doors or somewhere outside.

"Where are the female sage . . . and her wolf?" she asked.

Osha realized his mistake. Except for Nikolas, Wynn was the only other visitor who had been in the kitchen with him. And Osha had come alone in looking for Aupsha, one of two people seen in the passage last night.

He should not have focused so suddenly on the elderly sage. When he did not answer, Aupsha's eyelids drooped, half closed as she watched him.

She leaped backward.

Before Osha could charge, Aupsha ducked around a support post laden with gear and straps for wagons and horses. A sudden breeze rushed into his face and blew his hair upward. An instant later a foot struck his lower back.

Osha lashed back to grab a booted ankle, and pain exploded in his left temple as his head whipped under a blow.

He lost consciousness before he hit the stable floor.

As Jausiff pulled the door wider, Wynn walked into the master sage's chamber and tried to regain her composure. There was too much at stake for her to be rattled so quickly. She couldn't let him put her on the defensive this time.

A few steps into the room, she stopped with Shade close by her side. As she heard the door close, she buried her fingers in the fur of Shade's neck.

"Would you like some tea brought up?" Jausiff asked, as he rounded her toward his cluttered desk.

"No, thank you."

His bed in the corner was unmade, and he slipped around the desk to where four of the texts she'd brought him lay open. She watched as he closed them one by one. Had she awakened him by knocking, or had he been delving into what Premin Hawes had sent him?

"I heard two of your companions had an outing last night," he said casually, not even looking up.

Wynn stiffened and then shook off that reaction; that was his mistake, not hers, and it gave her an opening.

"They said the same thing about you."

Jausiff raised only his eyes, not quite closing the last book, and Wynn rushed on before he had a chance to think.

"What was the device you were carrying? What were you and Aupsha looking for in that back passage?"

She didn't really expect an answer, and she didn't need one. As Shade's neck muscles tightened beneath her hand, an image appeared in her head.

Wynn—Jausiff—stood in a passage so dark that a nearby pale light barely revealed a ruddy metal object in her hand. Her—his—hand obscured the object too much, though its ends stuck out beyond his closed grip. Something about the metal itself seemed familiar. Were there markings on it?

She—he—was bent over it and staring at the passage's stone floor and creeping along in small steps. He then leaned even more, lowering the object, and . . .

The memory vanished.

Wynn was careful not to flinch, as either Shade lost that memory or Jausiff dismissed it.

"Why hold the object so near the floor?" she asked.

Still he stalled. Perhaps he wondered or worried how much had been seen by her companions but did not know that he had just shown her and Shade even more.

Jausiff recovered, flipping the last book closed. "That object is just an old keepsake, gifted by a metaologer I once knew at the guild. It locates other objects made of metal, and the duchess recently lost a favored ring."

"In a back passage with only a padlocked side door?" Wynn asked dryly. "Maybe she *dropped* it on her way down below the keep?"

Wynn heard the door's handle ratchet behind her. Shade twisted backward out of her grip as the door slammed open against the wall, and Wynn started to turn.

A yelp broke Shade's snarl as Jausiff shouted, "No, wait!"

Before Wynn could finish turning, someone's hand clamped over her mouth, jerked her head up and back, and she felt an edge of cold steel press suddenly against her throat.

Osha groggily pushed up off the straw-strewn stable floor. When he touched the side of his head, it only made the pain worse, and he struggled to his feet.

Aupsha was nowhere to be seen.

He remembered that she had somehow gotten behind him, though it should not have been possible. He should have spotted her coming around either side of the tackle and post, but he had not. He had felt only the strikes that came at him from behind, but before that . . .

There had been a sharp breeze, like in the passage last night.

Even so, he had no doubt of where she had gone.

Stumbling out of the stable, Osha made it halfway across the courtyard before finding his feet enough to run. He slowed only long enough to open one of the keep's front doors and then bolted toward the main hall. But once there, he stalled at a voice.

"I don't know what to do." The duchess stood near the burning hearth with Nikolas nearby as she went on. "He has always been difficult, but at least I understood him. Now he is a stranger."

"I'm so sorry," Nikolas breathed, "but I don't know what—"

"Duchess!" Osha shouted as he ran for the stairs. "Nikolas! To your father's room—now!"

* * *

Wynn took shallow breaths and tried not to move, feeling a hand over her mouth and a blade against her throat. Someone tall was pressed up against her back, but she hadn't seen who it was.

Shade was snarling, her claws raking the stone floor as she came around into Wynn's view.

Jausiff stumbled around his desk as he shouted in a language Wynn didn't know. The words sounded somewhat close to modern Sumanese.

A memory rose in Wynn's mind as she found Shade's eyes fixed on her. She recalled the first time she had seen a tall, deeply dark-skinned woman come out of the keep into the courtyard. Shade's gaze shifted slightly, and Wynn knew it was Aupsha behind her.

Aupsha shouted in the same tongue the master sage had used.

It wasn't hard to guess that Jausiff ordered her to stop what she was doing, but nothing came of it. Instead, Wynn stumbled, trying to keep her feet and avoid being cut as Aupsha sidestepped, perhaps to get her back away from the open door.

Shade mirrored their movements, and Wynn raised a hand to hold Shade off.

"Stop this—it accomplishes nothing!" Jausiff commanded, this time in Numanese.

"Lock the door," Aupsha answered likewise.

"And then you will release her?"

No answer came, and Jausiff finally headed for the open door. Aupsha turned, forcing Wynn to do so as the master sage passed. Jausiff gripped the door to push it closed . . . and it bucked out of his grip as he stumbled back.

Osha lunged into the room with a dagger in his hand. He halted at the sight of Wynn's situation, and his gaze shifted up above her head.

"Let her go!" he ordered.

Shade's snarling grew louder, and the blade at Wynn's throat pressed until it made her skin sting. Jausiff stepped between Wynn and Osha, though he flinched when Shade snapped at him.

"Put your weapons away, both of you!" the old sage commanded.

Neither Osha nor Aupsha moved.

Wynn wasn't exactly afraid—though she knew she should be. In her searches for the orbs, she had been in worse positions than this.

Osha was positioned squarely before the door, and he'd left it open without even looking back. The sounds of fast footsteps and voices carried in from the passage outside. Sherie and then Nikolas, followed by Captain Holland and two standard guards in gray tabards, rushed in as Osha shifted around the room to stand beside Shade's left hip.

The cluttered chamber became quite crowded.

Osha held his dagger out as all of Shade's hackles rose.

Wynn hoped no one would be stupid enough start something now.

The duchess looked at Osha and then Aupsha and finally at Wynn with her mouth still covered by Aupsha's free hand.

"They are treacherous, my lady," Aupsha said. "The Lhoin'na cornered me with questions he should not know to ask, and this sage"—she jerked sharply on Wynn's face—"did the same with your counselor."

Sherie's normally pale face went white, and she turned toward Nikolas. "Is that why . . . why you were being so kind? To separate us so your companions could go at my staff one by one?"

"No!" Nikolas answered, shaking his head so hard that his streaked hair swung.

"Then what are they really doing here?" Sherie demanded. "Why did you bring them?"

"Everyone stop!" Jausiff called in a booming voice that belied his age.

Even Shade ceased snarling and settled to a rumble as Jausiff followed up with a labored sigh.

"My lady," he added, turning to the duchess, "please dismiss the captain and his men . . . and lock the door. We have matters to discuss in private, and Aupsha may have misread the situation."

Sherie fixed her regal glare on him, and Wynn watched as mixed confusion and doubt passed across the duchess's face.

"Please, my lady," Jausiff urged.

Sherie barely turned her head to speak over her shoulder. "Captain, take your men and wait outside."

Holland hesitated with a glance at both Osha and Aupsha before he obeyed.

Without moving, Sherie commanded Nikolas next: "Lock the door." Once he did so, she turned her scrutiny back on the master sage. Clearly she felt betrayed but was uncertain whom to hold responsible.

"And now?" she asked, though there was a slight tremor in her voice.

"Aupsha, release the journeyor," Jausiff said. "And you, Master Elf, put that blade away. Both of you disarm—now!"

Osha's eyes were moving in watching anyone present. He still hesitated when the hand came away from Wynn's mouth, though he looked directly at her.

"Do it, Osha," she said.

She watched his jaw clench as he lowered the dagger. The blade's edge at Wynn's throat released some of its pressure. Osha's large amber eyes widened as some incensed fury twisted his long features.

"You . . . bleed!" he hissed.

Osha raised his blade again and took a step as Shade's jaws clacked around a snarl.

Wynn and Sherie shouted in the same instant.

"Put it away!"

"That is enough!"

Osha froze and Shade stood her ground. Only when the blade's edge fully left Wynn's throat did Osha reluctantly put the dagger behind his back. It was a moment longer before he revealed an empty hand. Despite losing his Anmaglâhk stilettos, he had somehow rigged the dagger to be drawn and returned to concealment as needed.

Wynn touched her throat where it stung, making it worse. Her fingers came away with a smear of blood. Even then she could barely move in trying to catch her breath.

When Aupsha sidestepped toward the door, Sherie shouted, "Do not move!"

Aupsha froze, and to Wynn it appeared that Jausiff was not the only one whom Aupsha served. There was far more collusion here than she would have first guessed, but it appeared that not all of them knew everything about . . . whatever this was about.

"What is happening here?" the duchess demanded of the elder sage.

"A moment, my lady," he answered, and his gaze hardened as he studied Wynn. "Before we proceed, you will prove to my satisfaction that you are who and what you claim to be, a true sage and a cathologer. Succeed . . . and we continue speaking in here. Fail, and the duchess will call the guards back in."

Wynn had lost control and realized she would have to play Jausiff's game. Worse, she and everyone but Chane were now trapped in this room. If she failed, someone would soon enough find Chane "dead" in the guest quarters. After that, being thrown out of the keep would be the best and least likely outcome for failure.

Before she could even agree or disagree with the terms, Jausiff shot the first question at her.

"Who is the assumed creator of the symbolic system used to catalogue and shelve texts in the guild's libraries and archives?"

Wynn raised one eyebrow. The youngest apprentice of any of the five orders could answer this.

"Kärêm al-Räshìd Nisbah," she answered. "It was his own system as an imperial scholar, and used in the libraries of the Suman Empire some six hundred years ago."

Jausiff said nothing, and then, "If I needed to search the archives for Spirit by Air, what symbols would I seek *and* what texts would I find?"

This was a more complex question, suited to a journeyor, for even apprentices were not generally allowed in the archives. The guild's emphases of orders were often represented by geometric symbols associated with the prime Elements of Existence: Spirit, Fire, Air, Water, and Earth. In turn, any works that fell into an order's fields of endeavor were marked and shelved by those symbols. Columns of such symbols on casements, and even on some shelves and texts, were used to classify, subclassify, and cross-reference their subject matter.

"You would look for a square above a circle," she answered, "where you would find material on myths and legends shelved by delineation of historical context."

This time he nodded once. "How many lexicons are there at the Calm Seatt guild for the pre-Numanese dialect of Êdän?"

Wynn almost answered "two" but stopped herself.

Êdän was pre-Numanese, yes, but it was an elven dialect no longer spoken and not a precursor to modern Numanese. So old, in fact, that it predated the Lhoin'na tongue and even the old dialect of the an'Cróan, Osha's people.

A trick within a trick that only an advanced journeyor of Cathology might know, but still Wynn wondered. . . .

Jausiff likely hadn't visited the guild for many years, probably since before her time. Shortly after she achieved journeyor status, the Lhoin'na guild branch had gifted a second, updated Êdän lexicon to High Premin Sykion. Jausiff wouldn't know this.

"One," she answered.

He took a step back toward his desk. "It seems you are *what* you claim to be."

"I told you," Nikolas said irritably.

"Seems!" Jausiff repeated as he turned and snatched a book off his desk. "As to *who* you claim to be, through whom you serve . . ."

In his hand was one of the texts Wynn had brought to him; she knew it by its cover.

The Processes and Essence of Transmogrification.

Wynn grew nervous again, not knowing what Jausiff was up to now. She hadn't even finished skimming that book, let alone studied it enough to answer any questions about its content.

"You said three questions," she challenged.

He ignored her. "Where would I find this text—by its subject matter—shelved in the library?"

Wynn stalled, though she knew the answer. That text wouldn't be found in any openly accessible library. He would know this as well, because of the person who had received his request for it . . . *through whom you serve.*

No, mentioning Premin Hawes wasn't the real point.

Jausiff was apparently as paranoid as Wynn about sharing anything with anyone. No one in collusion with any minion of the Enemy would do all of this in sharing information. And that actually made Wynn trust him a little more.

"Well, where is it shelved . . . in the library?" he repeated.

"It isn't," she answered. "Such a text would only be in the archive under the control of a domin and master archivist . . . or in the private holdings of a domin—or premin—of Metaology."

The old sage dropped the book on his desk with a thud and, with a scowl and snort, he nodded once to the duchess.

Lady Sherie was not so easily assured. "Someone explain what is happening here!"

"These interlopers are a danger," Aupsha insisted.

Everyone else appeared to ignore her.

Wynn dropped—almost fell—to her knees beside Shade and rested her hand on the dog's back. For all the talking going on in this room, few people seemed to be speaking to one another.

"You asked me your questions, Jausiff," Wynn said clearly. "May I do the same?"

His eyes glittered. "By all means."

"You called Nikolas here to help with the duke, but you didn't want him to see the texts you'd requested. Why?"

Jausiff's eyes narrowed once again. "How do you know that I . . ." He trailed off, perhaps realizing the answer before he finished the question. "Hawes showed you my letter. Who are you that a premin of Metaology would trust you this much . . . send you here?"

"Someone she felt was qualified to understand whatever is happening."

Jausiff walked to a nearby cabinet and opened it quickly to remove something from inside. He returned holding a little cork-capped glass jar smaller than his palm. This he handed to Osha, who just stared at it.

"Put some on her throat," Jausiff instructed, gesturing quickly to Wynn.

As Osha knelt by Wynn and fiddled to open the jar, the old sage glanced at the duchess and nodded, though he still ignored Aupsha, who watched everything warily. Wynn flinched when Osha applied the salve to her cut, but she felt a rush of hope. Would Jausiff finally be candid?

Nikolas could no longer contain himself. "Father? You called me home, telling me you were ill! Then you said you wished me to 'help' with Karl, but except for Sherie, I don't see anyone trying to help him."

"Maybe your father is trying to help in his own way," Wynn interjected, and apparently having gained some cooperation, she turned to her own questions. "Why those specific texts? I know it has something to do with the duke's behavior or with what's happening in the villages and the surrounding land."

Jausiff folded his hands behind his back. "Yes, in the villages, I saw things . . . unnatural. Not a simple sickness among the people, but . . . other things in the land around the keep."

"Many dead, dying trees," Osha interrupted. "Hare . . . with five leg."

"When did you first notice?" Wynn asked Jausiff.

"About a moon ago."

"And when did you first see changes in the duke?"

"Half a moon before . . . perhaps earlier," Sherie answered this time, her noble sternness fading. "He went out one night, claiming to settle a fence line dispute in an outlying village and that he'd spend the night there. I thought nothing of it, but when he returned late the following day . . . the Suman guards came with him. He wouldn't say why or from where, but it was eight more days—nights—when he took to wearing gloves. He looked exhausted, if and when he was up at all during the day. Later, when I went to his room past supper for some issue, I found it empty. I checked every night after that, and he was never there. I would guess that had begun long before I noticed."

"Where he go?" Osha asked.

The duchess slowly shook her head. "Somewhere in the lower levels. All the stores below were moved to the main floor, though he never gave a reason. After the Suman guards appeared, no one was allowed down there but Karl and them."

Jausiff took over from there. "Both the duke and the effects in the surrounding land are worsening."

Wynn knew that the time frame between changes in the duke and the land was too close for coincidence. Obviously the others here shared this conclusion. Something else too disturbing for coincidence struck Wynn.

Last night Shade had gone berserk in claiming that a Fay had manifested somewhere near or inside the keep. Wynn looked to Jausiff, and without warning . . .

"What *were* you doing in the back passage last night?" she asked. "What was that device you were carrying?"

She knew this might cause confusion and worse, and she wasn't wrong. Sherie and Nikolas both started in surprise and asked at the same time, "What is she talking about?"

Aupsha hissed and stepped in on Jausiff.

A string of words erupted from her in that unknown language, and Jausiff snapped back at her in kind.

Wynn didn't know what they quarreled about and only guessed that Aupsha did not want the questions answered. However, Wynn knew enough to let the initial outburst pass, and even as Osha rose tensely, she placed her hand on Shade's back.

"Shade," Wynn whispered, and an image rose in her mind.

It was so intense that she clenched her eyes shut.

Wynn found herself running through a dim cave more swiftly than she could have. And her hands—the hands—pumping in rhythm with her strides had long, slender fingers with dark skin.

The memory Shade had caught was from Aupsha.

An agonized sound of pain escaped Wynn's—Aupsha's—mouth.

Dark-skinned, similarly dressed people—bodies—were strewn about the floor. Some had their throats torn open or their heads at severe angles from broken necks. All of their eyes stared blankly out between limp eyelids.

Wynn—Aupsha—cried out in pain again.

She slowed, looking to the cave's rear, where a heavy door appeared to have been shattered outward from within. Just inside that smaller space was an empty pedestal with a round hole in the center.

Inside the memory, Aupsha screamed as she rushed through the door.

Someone lay beyond the pedestal inside the small chamber. At the elderly man's moan, she rushed over, falling to her knees. His abdomen and light cotton shift had been torn open. He was covered in his own blood and would not live much longer.

Wynn—Aupsha—scooted closer to cradle the old man's head. His features were Suman, as was his hair, but he was darker than any Suman she had seen. Perhaps he was of mixed heritage. His long and curly chin beard was fully gray. When he whispered in his own tongue, Wynn picked out meanings in the words through Aupsha's remembrance . . . or perhaps it was something in the way Shade passed this memory.

"Father," Aupsha sobbed.

"It is gone," he whispered, looking up at her in panic, though he struggled to keep his dark eyes open. "After so many hundreds of years, the artifact has been taken from us. . . . We have failed our sect's sacred duty to safeguard it." When he coughed, blood seeped over his thick lips. "Get a compass piece and find it. . . . You must find it . . . and bring it back!"

"Who took it?" she asked, weeping openly. "Father, who did this?"

The old man went still in her arms.

Wynn jerked her hand from Shade.

All of Aupsha's grief and anger threatened to overwhelm her . . . and then came her own fears, her suspicions, and she grew sick inside.

"What was stolen from your people?" Wynn asked before she even opened her eyes. "What is this . . . compass . . . you used?"

The chamber had gone silent, and when Wynn's eyes opened, everyone was looking at her.

The curved knife reappeared suddenly in Aupsha's hand as she charged. Wynn cringed back as Shade lunged outward and Osha stepped in with his own dagger somehow in hand.

"Hold your place!" the duchess shouted.

Aupsha barely hesitated, but it was enough for Jausiff to step in and grab her arm.

"Stop this!" he shouted. "Remember that you came to me for help . . . not I to you!"

Aupsha turned on him, and Wynn reached out for Shade, but the dog wouldn't retreat. Neither would Osha.

"You *will* keep your place," Sherie ordered Aupsha. "Or you are gone! Now, what is happening here?"

Jausiff remained fixed on his tall, dark attendant, though he raised a hand to the duchess to hold her off. "I promised to help you," he said to Aupsha, "and you trusted me once you learned who and what I was . . . a sage, a preserver of knowledge." He pointed at Wynn. "So is this young woman. Though I had reason to doubt her at first, I believe she might be able to assist. Enough nonsense!"

Aupsha remained rigid, her face a mask of anger. Finally she stepped back, and Wynn waved Osha off as well.

"Master Columsarn!"

Wynn flinched at that sharp utterance, and the duchess stepped slowly and steadily up to the master sage.

"You will explain all of this immediately," Sherie added, "including everything you have kept from me."

Jausiff swallowed and glanced sidelong down at Wynn. "Able to assist or not, *you* are a good deal of trouble."

"I've heard that before," she answered, and even before she asked the next two questions, she feared she already knew the answer to the first. "Now, what was stolen from Aupsha's people? And what is the compass and the device you held in the passage?"

Jausiff took a step away from Aupsha, though he kept his eyes on her.

"Aupsha is a member of an ancient sect . . . worshipers of a long-forgotten saint, for lack of a better term. They have been hidden away in the mountains above the great desert for countless years in protecting an artifact. Though she has not been completely forthcoming, she assured me her ancestors acquired this artifact to keep it from the wrong hands, and their only purpose is to guard it. It was stolen from them earlier this year, and she tracked it here."

"How did she track it?" Wynn asked.

Jausiff paused. "The compass, as you say, and the device in my hand last night are one and the same. We were using it in trying to determine where below the keep this artifact has been hidden."

"It's here?" Wynn whispered.

Nikolas stood staring at everyone as he stepped in behind Sherie. "Father? What is going on?"

A brief scowl, or maybe a flinch of pain, crossed Sherie's face at his closeness. "Continue," she ordered the old sage.

With a frown of his own, Jausiff pulled a cord around his neck from out of his robe. Dangling from it was a small key. He rounded behind his desk to a heavy chest at the back wall and unlocked it. After digging inside, he turned back with something wrapped in an oilcloth.

Wynn rose quickly, stepping in to face him across the desk as he opened the cloth.

There inside the cloth, across his hand, lay a slightly curved piece of ruddy metal, though it looked sound for appearing so old. It was a little longer than the width of his palm, thicker than it was wide, and perhaps the width of two of Wynn's fingers.

"Aupsha's people cut up a secondary object said to have been found with the artifact," Jausiff explained. "They did so to keep it from ever being a tool to use the artifact, but they discovered its pieces still had an affinity for that artifact. This is how she tracked what was stolen."

That was all Wynn needed to jog her awareness and strip away all doubt. Judging from the slight curve of its length and the metal itself, she now knew where it had come from . . . what that other object had been.

Wynn began to tremble, for Jausiff was holding a piece of an orb handle . . . an orb key.

Last night Shade had sensed the Fay, just as Chap had once when Magiere used her own *thôrhk*—key—to open the first orb of Water. Everyone in the guest quarters other than Chane and Shade, and perhaps more throughout the keep, had lost partial control of their bodies and their memories. In those few panic-driven moments Wynn had felt as if her awareness—her *self*—had been draining away.

And each night the duke vanished into the depths below the keep.

Another time, another way, Wynn might have been relieved at the realization. But not this way, here and now, for there was an orb below the keep.

"This is what you've been doing without telling me?"

Wynn flinched at Sherie's sharp words and turned to find the duchess shaking her head at the aging sage.

"And you already knew!" Sherie accused Jausiff. "You . . . knew what was harming my brother."

"Forgive me, my lady," he answered. "I strive in my own way to save the duke, but I vowed to Aupsha and her people to keep silent on all of this . . . in exchange for her assistance."

"A promise worth nothing!" Aupsha snarled at him.

"We have to get the artifact back," Wynn interrupted. "At any cost."

Aupsha turned on her. "We have already sought to do so but cannot penetrate the lower levels. The door is impassable, and only the duke and his foreign guards go below. And there is more to uncover."

Aupsha closed on Wynn, which drew a warning growl from Shade.

"How was it found among my people at all?" Aupsha asked, as if suspicious of everyone now. "I have subtly engaged each Suman guard. None seem clever enough for what was done. It could not have been the duke himself, for he was here when my people were assaulted. Someone else stole our . . . charge."

Wynn wondered about all of this as well. Who had the ability and knowledge to locate an orb, and more so one hidden for centuries by generational guardians? She was also curious about how this "sect" had procured an orb in the first place. But *someone* had located it among Aupsha's people.

When Wynn had gone looking for lost Bäalâle Seatt, an ancient city of the dwarves from the time of the Forgotten History, Chane and Ore-Locks had been the ones to actually find the orb of Earth. But they'd found no *thôrhk* or key with it. Sau'ilahk had gotten ahead of them, and for some reason he hadn't taken that orb.

Every orb uncovered so far had a handle—a key. Even the deceptively frail and ancient undead Li'kän had possessed one in guarding the first orb. Why hadn't there been one in Bäalâle Seatt? Or perhaps there had been.

Had someone taken a key instead of the orb?

It made no sense until Wynn looked at the "compass" object in Jausiff's hand. Could a key as a whole be used to track down an orb? If so, and if Sau'ilahk had gained a *thôrhk* left with the orb of Earth . . .

The bodies in Aupsha's memory showed no signs of the way the wraith killed. None had been aged, left shriveled from devoured life, or even marked like young Nikolas with streaks of gray in his hair. Such details might not matter, though. Sau'ilahk might have arranged for human assistance.

"In your attempt to reach the underlevels," she said to Aupsha, "how close did you get?"

Aupsha's eyes shifted toward Osha. "To the door around the end of the passage where he saw us. We have not found a way through it."

"The only key to that door was taken by my brother," Sherie added.

Wynn turned. "I need to get to that door. I need time there undisturbed to . . . to study it. Can you arrange this for me?"

Sherie watched Wynn for another three breaths. "And if this artifact is recovered, what would *you* do with it?"

Wynn couldn't tell if that was a threat hiding behind a suspicious question. "I will take it far from here to where no one, including your brother, will ever see it again."

Aupsha spun toward Wynn again, but Wynn looked away to Shade and then Osha.

"I'll need you and Shade as well," she added.

Neither of them responded, though a worried frown marred Osha's expression.

There was only one way Wynn could determine whether the orb was below the keep. As to Sau'ilahk, if he was here, she wouldn't be able to find him yet . . . not until nightfall.

Shade wasn't going to like what Wynn had in mind, but at least Chane was still dormant and wouldn't be there to argue.

CHAPTER SIXTEEN

The day after the incident with the apples and just before dusk, Leesil was up on deck at the side rail with Wayfarer when the girl fainted from hunger. He carried her down to the cabin he shared with Magiere and Chap and laid her on a bunk. Both Chap and Magiere sat close in concern, and the anguish on Magiere's face was the last straw for Leesil.

Wayfarer's long brown hair spread out around her now-pale face and closed eyes. She murmured twice as if caught in a dream, and Magiere was about to charge off for freshwater and a rag when Leesil assumed that task himself. It took some arguing with one of the crew to get the extra ration of water, but on his way back below, he took a moment to sneak all the way to the passage's end.

Down a set of stairs to the next level was a door where a passage cut left toward the ship's kitchen. By the door's position, Leesil reasoned that it must lead into the cargo hold. He pulled out a steel probe and another tiny pick earlier hidden in his boot, and he set to opening the door's crude iron lock. When he finished and twisted the lever handle, the door still wouldn't budge.

Something blocked it. It couldn't be cargo; that made no sense. Obviously the door was barred from the hold's side, though that didn't figure, either—not at first. Leesil realized that blocking the door from the inside meant none of the crew could get in or out to take anything, even if one them managed to steal a key. With a slight grimace, he stepped back. For what he had in mind now, he'd have to go up on deck to get into the hold . . . and all before Magiere caught on.

With no immediate way to raid the cargo, Leesil hurried back to the cabin.

He sat on the floor as Magiere dabbed Wayfarer's head, and, when night finally settled, the room grew dim around him. Since the day before, Magiere had been watching him like a hawk, but now she was preoccupied.

It was time to do as he'd planned, and he stood up.

"You and Chap stay with Wayfarer. I'll let Brot'an know . . . see if he has any ideas to help."

That was a foolish comment. If Brot'an could have done anything to help, he would have done it by now. Luckily Magiere was distracted with worry, and only nodded. Chap appeared equally focused on the girl's condition, and Leesil slipped out.

However, as he made his way up the passage, he didn't stop at Brot'an's cabin door. Instead he went straight for the steep steps and paused at the top, at the door out leading to the deck. In a way it was sadly fortunate that Wayfarer had fainted and thereby kept Magiere and Chap occupied.

Cracking the door slightly, Leesil peeked out. Dim, dirty lamps hung upon the ship's masts, but he saw no one across the deck. Two low, muffled voices carried from somewhere above him on the aftcastle, so likely the night watch was up there. He looked to the rope mesh covering the hold's central opening out in the middle of the deck.

At its nearer end was a small hatch he'd seen opened a couple of times for access to a ladder down into the hold. Each time, the captain had stood close by, watching and checking crew members coming back up to make certain they hadn't pocketed anything while below.

Leesil carefully widened the door enough to slip out. With his back against the aftcastle's wall, he sidestepped toward the ship's rail and then crept out a short way to peek back and above. Whoever was up on the aftcastle was too far to its rear to be seen—or to see him. Likewise, he saw no one toward the bow. He crouched and crept to the nearest mast, then ducked in front of it before glancing around its far side and up.

He just made out the heads of two men at the aftcastle's rear. They were engrossed in talking to each other, and so he crawled to the small hatch near the hold's opening.

Leesil froze, for the padlock that typically held the hatch's bar in place lay to one side and was still opened from being unlocked. He'd expected to have to pick the lock, for that oily sewer rat of a captain would never leave the hold open while he wasn't watching.

Whoever had forgotten to set the lock again was going to suffer by morning.

Carefully sliding the lock bar out of its brackets, Leesil grasped the hatch's handle. As he lifted slightly, the hinges creaked and he froze, this time listening for a sudden silence.

The two on the aftcastle were still chattering away. They hadn't heard anything.

He opened the hatch quickly, with a creak from its hinges, and dropped onto the ladder's rungs. Then he listened again for silence or any footfalls. All he heard were the muffled voices of the watch.

Leesil stepped a few rungs down the ladder and let the hatch close softly above him. It was a dark climb down the ladder, but once he reached the hold's floor, the full moon's pale light filtered though the rope mesh above. To his relief, he could see well enough to move about. The hold was crammed with crates and barrels and smaller boxes. The first thing he searched for and found was an iron hook to wrench open containers. Nothing was clearly labeled—or at least not in a language he could read—and he had to work by trial and error.

Gripping the hook, and about to pry open the closest crate, he *felt* rather than heard something behind him. Whirling with the hook poised to strike, he saw an unusually tall, familiar form standing near the ladder.

"Brot'an . . . what are you doing?" he hissed. "Did you follow me?"

"I am assisting you," Brot'an whispered back, soft-stepping closer, and in his off hand was a large, empty burlap sack. "I saw your face yesterday and knew you were planning something. I assume you did not tell Magiere?"

Leesil kept his voice low, barely enough to be heard. "Magiere is no thief, not even in the worst situations. She might have swindled people in the past, but she doesn't accept charity, and I've never seen her steal anything. It's not in her."

Brot'an studied his face. "But it is in you?"

Leesil had had enough of this conversation and turned away. Clearly it was in Brot'an as well, or he wouldn't be down here.

After that they moved deeper into the hold, almost to the edge of where moonlight could reach. Quickly and quietly, they both searched the crates and boxes. Leesil was astounded by the variety of food down here, considering nearly everyone on board was starving. Between himself and Brot'an, they loaded the burlap sack with crocks of olives, small wheels of wax-sealed cheese, apples, dried onions, and jars of what looked like some kind of orange fruit.

Leesil set to opening another crate, and even before he finished, he could smell jerked beef. The crate was packed with it. Beyond hungry and unable to stop himself, he shoved some in his mouth. So fresh and tender, it nearly came apart on his tongue.

His anger at the captain grew as he loaded a good amount into the sack.

When he finally looked up and about, Brot'an was stuffing various food items inside his own shirt. Leesil ignored him and kept to his task. As he finished filling the sack, Brot'an approached, looking at it curiously.

"What will we do with all of that?" he whispered. "We cannot risk bringing it into your cabin."

"Not to mine . . . To yours." Leesil paused. "Yesterday, when you were up on deck taking some air, Wayfarer was with Magiere in our cabin, and I went into yours. I pulled up three floorboards and found a space beneath. I put the boards back but removed the nails. We'll hide the food under there."

Brot'an was quiet for a moment. "Like your mother, you are ever resourceful."

Leesil stiffened. Brot'an was the last person he'd ever want to talk to about his mother. Putting down the hook, he turned and made his way toward the ladder with the now-heavy sack in hand.

"Let's just get this hidden before we're caught."

"Not that way . . . at least not for you," Brot'an said. "Look where we are standing. These food stores have been placed near a lower access point into the hold, so that supplies can be moved more easily to a kitchen or elsewhere below . . . through a door."

Leesil turned around. "I tried coming in that way. The door was barred."

He thought he heard the old assassin sigh, just barely.

"Yes," Brot'an whispered, "but at least one crew member has come or gone from the hold by using a key on the door. How and why else would one have come up into the passage at the noise made by the girl and the majay-hì? Or did you not remember this while picking the door's lock from the outside . . . and too noisily?" Brot'an turned, heading even deeper in the hold's rear. "Enough talk. Come."

Leesil wanted nothing more than to get this food to Magiere, Chap, and Wayfarer. With a glance up at the hold's opening, he crept after the master assassin. It still made no sense that any food would be placed near a hold's lower door.

"This captain doesn't care about supplying the crew," Leesil whispered.

Again he barely heard Brot'an sigh. "A ship is constructed like any structure for efficiency of use, not a single captain's deviance. A glutton and miser still wants discreet access to his hoard, preferably in a way that does not display it before all whom he considers potential thieves."

The crewman who'd appeared in the passage might have been secretly trying to move more food to the captain's quarters—and maybe sneak out some for himself. Unfortunately Chap and Wayfarer had gotten in the way. That also meant someone else would have had to block the door from the inside—after it was locked—and then climb up the ladder to the deck.

There must be a few crewmen Amjad either trusted or had terrified enough to allow them inside his precious hold without worrying about theft.

"Here," Brot'an whispered.

"What? Where?" Leesil asked.

Inside this far, it was too dark to see much. But as he closed behind Brot'an, he heard the scrape of wood on something hard, perhaps metal.

Leesil realized that Brot'an was removing whatever barred the door from the inside. At the soft click that followed, a little light showed the stairs beyond the open door.

"Go," Brot'an said. "I will bar the door and return the way we came in."

Leesil stepped out, glancing down the side passage along the outside of the hold's wall. Down the way, light spilled from the entrance into the kitchen. Perhaps the cook was still up, but he rarely seemed to leave his stench-ridden cabin.

So far Leesil had been successful. There was nothing left to do but sneak up the stairs and hide the bulk of the food in Brot'an and Wayfarer's cabin. And then he had to hope the theft was not discovered anytime soon, and, when it was, that no one connected it to the ship's passengers.

He stalled briefly as he heard the wooden brace slide home beyond the hold's door, and then he slipped up the stairs to the passage lined with cabin doors.

Brot'ân'duivé swiftly scaled the ladder. He understood the greater necessity for the actions that he and Léshil had undertaken, but he had no desire to be caught. When he reached the ladder's top, he balanced on a rung and cracked the hatch open with his head to keep both hands ready to strike. Upon seeing no one on deck, he climbed out to crouch behind a mast.

Almost instantly two forms stepped out from around the mast's far side. Two sets of eyes glinted by the light of dim lanterns hanging above, and they saw him. The first looked down at the bulging front of his shirt as the other drew a cutlass.

Brot'ân'duivé did not move.

"I thought I heard something," the first said in Numanese.

The night watch could not have heard his own descent. Had they heard the hatch creak earlier when Léshil had come down into the hold?

The first man, now with his own cutlass drawn, pointed the blade's tip at the bulging shirt.

"I know what you have," he said, his eyes wide with longing. "Hand it over, and we won't tell the captain."

Brot'ân'duivé knew both sailors assumed he had stolen food.

He never pondered what to do, for there could be no witnesses. Locking eyes with the first sailor, in order to distract the man, Brot'ân'duivé's left fingers curled upward. He pulled the tie string at the inside of his left wrist. A stiletto sheathed beneath his left sleeve began to slide down, and he closed his hand on its hilt.

The cutlass's tip rushed in toward his abdomen. Brot'ân'duivé turned so slightly. As the cutlass slid sharply away along his side, he spun the stiletto in his off hand and thrust. The thin, silvery blade pieced the sailor's heart and slid out again, dark and wet, before the man's eyes could widen. He turned on the second sailor before the first began to drop.

Brot'ân'duivé did not need to see the second cutlass swinging for his head. As he ducked left, he rammed his shoulder into his first crumpling target and pinned the body against the mast to keep it from hitting the deck with too much noise. He dropped the stiletto from his left hand and caught it with his right.

The second man tried to reverse his sword, and his mouth opened to call out.

Brot'ân'duivé thrust upward, piercing flesh at the top of the sailor's throat below his jaw and sinking the stiletto deeply. The worst of it was that the man instantly dropped his cutlass, and it clattered on the deck.

Brot'ân'duivé released his hold on the embedded stiletto and grabbed the second dead sailor. He quietly lowered both bodies to the deck and crouched there for an instant.

All was finished in less than a moderate breath, as it should be.

He pulled a handful of jerked beef and a clay crock of olives from his shirt and scattered the first around the bodies and dropped the second on the thighs of one sailor. When he drew his stiletto out of the second man's jaw and skull, he took a moment to disguise each man's suspicious wound with a thrust of the other's cutlass.

On a ship like this, those wasting away in hunger would draw no suspicion for killing each other over stolen food. Brot'ân'duivé silently stepped on toward the aftcastle door to below. By the time he reached the passage to the cabins, he no longer thought of bodies left upon the deck. He thought only of surviving the remainder of the voyage and keeping all those under his guardianship alive as well.

Even when Wayfarer finally awakened, Magiere continued to sponge the girl's head and give her sips of water. Magiere felt helpless for the most part—and she hated feeling helpless.

Something had to be done. Perhaps she could speak to Saeed in the morning about buying any possible food hidden among the sailors. That was a slim chance at best, as food was more precious than coin on this slop bucket of a ship. But she had to try anything.

—Leesil . . . has been gone . . . too long—

"What?"

Magiere glanced over as she realized Chap was right. How long could it take to locate Brot'an?

"Where is Léshil?" Wayfarer asked weakly from the bunk.

"He went to find Brot'an, but he'll be right back."

Just the same, Magiere began to worry. She'd vowed to keep a close watch on Leesil, and she had no idea where he was. Right then the door opened, and, as if he'd been called, Leesil slipped inside.

"Where have you been?" she asked. "Where's Brot'an?"

He didn't answer, and his amber eyes fixed on Wayfarer. "You're awake," he said in relief.

Before Magiere could press him for answers, he hurried over, dropped to his knees, and pulled a rolled cloth from inside his shirt. He unrolled it on the bunk's edge next to the girl.

Magiere's voice caught as she gasped, "Leesil?"

Inside the cloth were loose olives, small bits of broken-up cheese, jerked beef, and what looked to be some kind of orange fruit. Leesil picked up one olive and held it to Wayfarer's mouth.

"Eat . . . but mind the pit."

As Wayfarer took the olive, Leesil tossed a large piece of jerky to Chap, who rose up on his hindquarters to catch it with a clack of his jaws. Leesil then handed another strip to Magiere.

She was starving, but none of this made sense. "Where did you get this?"

He glanced at her. "Brot'an and I stole it from the hold."

Tearing the cheese into even smaller bits, Leesil encouraged Wayfarer to sit up so that she could eat it herself. Then he tossed Chap another strip of beef, as the first one was gone, and he looked up at Magiere.

"Eat," he ordered, taking a bit of cheese himself. "We should finish this as quick as we can."

Magiere started picking out olives. If he'd stolen food from the ship's hold, the captain might find out, so the evidence had better disappear quickly. Watching Wayfarer gobble down cheese, Magiere took a bite of jerky. It was good, tender and easy to chew. Then she eyed Wayfarer.

"Don't eat too fast," she warned the girl. "You'll make yourself sick."

To her surprise, she wasn't angry with Leesil for taking such a risk—and for stealing. She was too relieved at watching Wayfarer eat, and then she looked at Leesil.

"You didn't take much. Maybe it won't be noticed."

Leesil glanced away. "The rest is well hidden," he mumbled. "Enough to keep us until we reach port."

Magiere stopped chewing.

"I told you to trust me," he added, frowning and still not looking at her. "Now eat."

For once Magiere didn't feel like arguing. They shared the olives, fruit, and cheese until it was gone. She wasn't certain what to say or how to feel.

Leesil had placed himself—and probably the rest of them, should they be found out—in danger, but she hadn't come up with anything better. The thought of Wayfarer having decent food until they reached land again almost made her want to weep.

Then . . . a loud noise outside of the door made everyone turn.

Leesil twisted around on one knee as the door began to open—without anyone calling out an invitation. Of course he'd expected to be questioned sooner or later. Once the theft was discovered, everyone would most likely be questioned. But that it happened so quickly alarmed him.

He rose in the same instant as Magiere. Her falchion was within reach, leaned up against the bunk's end. She didn't grab for it, but he saw her glance to mark its place as the door opened.

Captain Amjad stood there with his jaw clenched. His two hulkish bodyguards peered over his shoulders from out in the passage.

Leesil remained purposely passive but wondered why the captain had focused so quickly on the ship's passengers.

Amjad took one step into the cabin, and Chap began to growl. The captain stopped, blocking the door before his bodyguards could slip in.

"Have any of you been in the hold?" Amjad demanded.

Well, he was to-the-point if nothing else.

"You mean . . . ship cargo hold?" Leesil asked, feigning confusion.

"We've all been in here since dusk," Magiere returned sharply. "The girl is ill."

Amjad's anger wavered with one quick glance at Wayfarer on the bunk. Maybe he had a sudden doubt as he looked around the small cabin and perhaps searched for something he did not see—like the remnants of food, which he did not find. He shook his head slowly as his anger returned.

"Someone was in the hold tonight, breaking crates open and stealing food. None of my men would dare. Any who do so without permission are thrown overboard. And I sometimes toss one over on the voyage up . . . just so they know I mean it."

Now, *that* Leesil had not known.

"There are two dead watchmen up on deck," Amjad spat out. "Do you know anything about that?"

Leesil tensed—Brot'an must have run into trouble after leaving the hold.

"None of this has to do with us," Magiere said.

Leesil glanced sidelong at her. Anger was her only real way to sound convincing, since she was a terrible liar. But he was instantly on guard when she grabbed her falchion, though she left it sheathed.

"Care to try throwing one of us overboard?" she asked, as if inviting it.

Chap snarled loudly. Whether that was for Magiere or Amjad, Leesil wasn't certain. He was too fixed on listening to the sound of the bodyguards in the passage—the sound of hands clenching on leather-wrapped blade hilts. Then he spotted an awkward shift in the captain's expression.

Something mixed with the greed and spite in Amjad's eyes, as if he was suddenly reluctant or had overplayed what all this was really about. For just a breath Leesil wondered if all of this was just for show and the captain wouldn't throw them overboard no matter what they did . . . as if he wanted them alive for some reason.

Amjad half turned in the doorway. "Where's the other one? The big Lhoin'na?"

"He went to rest in his cabin," Magiere lied. "He's been in here all evening, too."

"Search the other cabin!" Amjad barked at one of his bodyguards.

Leesil's tension increased. What if Brot'an hadn't returned to his cabin yet?

From where he stood, he could only listen as one of Amjad's men stomped up the passage outside. To Leesil's relief, he heard a muttered word or two briefly exchanged, so the old assassin was in his cabin. A few moments later, the guard reappeared outside the doorway beyond Amjad and shook his head.

That the guard hadn't forced his way in to search Brot'an's cabin made Leesil even more suspicious.

Amjad turned to glare at Leesil.

"Maybe," Leesil said, struggling with his Numanese, "your men too hungry . . . take chance. You feed them, problem is solved."

With one last black look, Amjad spun out of the cabin and slammed the door shut.

Leesil listened as three sets of footfalls headed up the passage to the stairs without pause. At least Magiere, Chap, and Wayfarer had enough food for the rest of this voyage. That was all that mattered . . . for the moment.

CHAPTER SEVENTEEN

"How long will this take?" the duchess asked, leading the way. Apparently she knew exactly where Osha and Chane had gone last night.

"I don't know," Wynn answered. "Or if I'll learn anything of use."

Osha and Shade followed behind Wynn.

The duchess had suggested leaving Jausiff, Nikolas, and Aupsha out of this excursion. Aupsha had argued vehemently to be included, but Jausiff had denied her.

But in this way, should their small group be caught by any of the duke's Suman guards, Sherie could simply say she'd been giving her guests a tour of the keep and taken a wrong turn. No one would believe her, but Karl's guards wouldn't challenge her, either. She would take responsibility for "the mistake," and the only repercussion would most likely be an immediate escort away from any restricted areas.

It wasn't a perfect plan, but it was the safest thing the duchess could come up with—and Wynn had not argued.

Sherie turned a final corner and paused to lift the lantern she held a little higher. Aside from a small barred window in the door at the far end, this passage at the keep's back had no other lighting.

Wynn thought she heard the ocean's surf echoing faintly through the thick wall, and the air felt cold and dank.

"I have spent little time back here in recent years," Sherie said quietly, still facing forward. "Karl and I . . . and Nikolas . . . sometimes snuck outside this same way."

Wynn heard a slow, shaky breath in the silence that followed, and the duchess stepped onward. Suddenly Osha slipped past, and Shade came up beside Wynn. Osha was the first to reach the passage's end, though he didn't stop at that door leading outside. Instead he ducked to the right and vanished into a side way. Wynn did stop briefly at the door—for she could hear the waves below the keep's back side more clearly through the door's small window bars.

On an impulse, she tried the door and found it locked, as Sherie, followed by Shade, stepped past through the right arch. Wynn joined them and found Osha standing before another heavy door two steps down a short stairway that led the other way, parallel to the passage.

Osha crouched before the door and eyed its iron lock plate.

"I don't suppose you can open it?" she whispered.

He shook his head without looking back as he answered in Numanese, "I not learn . . . not time."

At this, the duchess frowned, looking between them.

Wynn was not about to explain Osha's past, what he had been, or that he had never left his people's land until she had gone there. But she understood that he'd never had a chance to learn skills such as picking locks.

However, Osha gripped the door's handle and twisted it slightly until it stopped—probably just to be sure it was locked.

Wynn flinched at the soft click, for the last thing they needed was anyone below hearing someone at the door. She waved everyone back up to the passage, where they could talk more easily.

Aupsha's device had led her and Jausiff here, and soon after, guards had come this way, caught Chane, and forced Osha to hide.

"Whatever you are going to do, do it quickly," Sherie whispered.

"You should leave, as this will take a little time," Wynn countered. "It is one thing to be caught walking about the keep with the lady of the house . . . but something else entirely to be found lingering near that door by your brother or his men. Anyone caught here might need someone in authority still free . . . who wasn't involved."

"Exactly what are *you* going to do with a locked door in your way?"

Wynn faltered, for she certainly wasn't going to explain the curse of her mantic sight. Even if the duchess believed her, it would take too long and raise more questions—and possibly suspicions. And in a silent war with an opposition seeking the same secrets as she did, Wynn had learned never to share any secrets of her own with anyone until necessary.

Sherie still watched her, and Wynn didn't answer the question as she waited.

"Very well," the duchess said. "I will expect to hear from you . . . soon."

As the duchess turned away, she offered the lantern. Wynn shook her head and held up one of her cold-lamp crystals. She waited until Sherie was fully gone from sight.

"Osha, I'm going to do this while sitting," Wynn said, and she handed him the crystal. "Do you remember how to use it?"

He nodded and brushed it once with his other hand. A soft light rose inside the crystal.

"Don't make it too bright. Too much light might be seen under the door . . . or interfere with what I'm going to try. If I start to topple, catch me before I hit the floor and make any noise."

Osha looked up from the crystal, asking in Elvish, "What do you mean? I thought you had been honing your ability while at the guild."

"Yes . . . but once I start, it can be difficult the longer I go on," Wynn answered. "Shade may have to help me end it, if I can't do so myself."

Even Shade rumbled in displeasure as Osha shook his head in doubt.

"No more time for arguments," Wynn warned, hooking a finger at them as she turned to the door. "Both of you be quiet and let me focus."

Her mantic sight was a hard-won blessing forever caged in a curse. It was not a true talent or a metaologer's ability based on years of training and knowledge. This wild taint had been left in her from tampering with a mantic form of thaumaturgy. Once the sight was engaged, she could see the presence of the Elements, one at a time, in—and through—all things. So far Spirit was the only one that she could see well, but that was the one she needed to see now.

She went down the two steps and knelt before the door, leaving herself a little room. Osha dropped to one knee behind her on the left as Shade settled near to her right. Extending the first finger of her right hand, Wynn traced the sign for Spirit on the floor and encircled it.

At each gesture, she focused hard to keep those lines alive in her mind's eye, as if they were actually drawn upon the stone. Then she scooted forward to sit atop the pattern and traced a wider circumference around herself.

It was a simple construct, but it helped shut away the outer world as she closed her eyes to seek out the elemental essence, rather than presence, of the world and let it fill her. Starting with herself, as a living being in which elemental Spirit was strongest, she imagined breathing it in from the air as well. Then she felt for it, as if it could flow up into her from the floor's stone.

Wynn held inside her head the first simple pattern she had stroked upon the floor, as she called up another image. Chap—Shade's father—appeared in the darkness of her closed eyes, and she held on to him as well.

Shade huffed once beside her, and Wynn's concentration faltered at the sound. She managed to pull both pattern and image back into focus. She envisioned Chap as she'd once seen him before with her mantic sight.

His fur shimmered like a million silk threads caught in blue-white light, and his whole form became encased in white vapors that rose like flames from his fur.

Vertigo rose inside her.

"Wynn?" Osha whispered.

She threw out her hands to support herself against the stone floor. When she opened her eyes, nausea lurched upward from her stomach.

Wynn stared at—through—the door.

Translucent white, just shy of blue, dimly permeated the old wood. The door's physical presence still dominated her sight, but there was more, something beyond it. Pale and blue-white, the ghostly shapes of stairs continued downward.

Shade whined so close that the noise was too loud in Wynn's ears. Without meaning to, Wynn glanced aside at the dog.

At first Shade was as black as a void, except for too-bright crystal-blue eyes staring back. A powerful glimmer of blue-white became clear, permeating Shade more than anything else in sight. Traces of Spirit ran in every strand of Shade's charcoal fur and burned in the dog's eyes.

Shade was aglow with her father's Fay ancestry, and Wynn had to look away.

"Are you all right?" Osha asked, again in an'Cróan Elvish.

"Yes," Wynn choked out as she stopped herself from looking at him.

Because Osha was one of the an'Cróan, an Elven people associated with the element of Spirit, it might be nearly as bright in him as in Shade. She couldn't break her focus again, and instead concentrated on what was beyond the door.

At the stairs' bottom, a straight passage ahead was no more than inverse shadows, as though she was looking into a space where all edges and corners were outlined with a blue-white glow stronger than that on the surfaces. Farther on was a large chamber, though deeper and farther than her sight reached. The layers of bluish white made any details difficult to pick out.

She spotted six tall outlines, three to each side, inside the chamber. In focusing on those, she found them a little brighter than stone as they sharpened into upright rectangles. They had to be doors, perhaps made of wood. And there were three blurs, almost as tall as the doors, of an even brighter blue-white positioned about the chamber.

One shifted slowly, moving a short way to join the other two. Those had to be living beings—Suman guards, most likely. And that one stopped near the other two before the second door on the right.

"Do you see anything?" Osha whispered almost too faintly to hear.

"Six doors." Wynn struggled to answer. "Second door . . . on the right. Three guards."

Nausea began to cripple her.

She quickly fought to see anything more, but she couldn't reach past any of those doors. When she tried, there were too many layers of Spirit outlines, and her stomach clenched as if she might heave up her breakfast.

The one thing she hadn't seen—wouldn't see during the day—was the black shadow of an undead's presence.

Everything in Wynn's sight blurred and twisted, and vertigo overwhelmed her as her will failed. She shut her eyes and crumpled.

Two hands caught her shoulders as she fell.

"Wynn!" Osha breathed in her ear.

At Shade's soft, short whine, Wynn felt herself pulled back against Osha's chest. She barely opened her eyes and then regretted doing so.

There was Shade, a glistening black form haloed in blue white, and the dog's irises burned with so much light that everything else in Wynn's sight began to spin. A sudden memory rose in her head.

Not an image—a sensation like a warm wet tongue dragged repeatedly over her face, as if her eyes were closed, though she still stared at Shade's burning blue irises. Her eyes had been closed—at another time—when she'd used mantic sight to track Chap in the forest of the an'Cróan.

Shade lunged in so quickly that Wynn grabbed the dog's neck in panic—and Shade's tongue lapped her face as she shut her eyes. Wet warmth dragged over her eyelids.

Nausea lessened as Wynn leaned against Osha while clutching Shade's neck.

She had never learned how Shade knew Chap's trick for smothering mantic sight. Perhaps Shade had learned of it from one of Wynn's own memories, and it had become useful several times. As the last of the vertigo faded, disappointment welled in its place.

"Not enough," she whispered. "I didn't see enough."

"Quiet now," Osha whispered.

Before Wynn could move, she was picked up and carried off as any light from the cold-lamp crystal winked out when Osha's hand closed over it.

Wynn doubted those three supposed guards, so far down in that main chamber, could hear them. But it was better that Osha was being cautious, and she waited to speak again until he settled her on the floor halfway down the back passage.

"Only three guards below?" Osha asked as he opened his hand and let the crystal's light out. "Do you think the guarded door is where the duke goes?"

Wynn nodded. "Perhaps, but we should leave here. Whatever is down there, no matter what we think, is important enough to be guarded at all times. And we don't know when or how often the guards are rotated."

Trying to get up, Wynn braced a hand on the passage wall, and Shade ducked in to give her additional support as Osha grasped her other arm.

"There is nothing more we can do until Chane wakes up," Wynn added.

Osha's expression darkened. "Why?"

"Because he grew up in a keep and might know something of use . . . because he's stronger than any of us . . . and he cannot be killed by normal means."

Osha's scowl only deepened, though Shade rumbled at him.

"This is all dangerous, more than you can imagine," Wynn warned. "And it will get ugly. We need our numbers . . . everyone."

Osha appeared no less sour, but he finally nodded.

Chane opened his eyes.

"Oh, finally!"

He squinted and then flinched in his bed upon seeing Wynn hanging over him with a lit cold-lamp crystal in her hand.

"What's wrong?" he asked immediately.

Chane sat up too quickly, swinging his legs off the bedside, and almost hit Wynn's forehead with his own. He was still slightly disoriented as he glanced around the room. Beyond Wynn was Osha, watching him. Shade sat on the floor a little closer, and then there was Nikolas. . . .

Chane's fingers closed tightly on the bed's edge.

The young sage stood flattened against the room's closed door, and his eyes stared back in fright.

"Nikolas," Wynn said softly. "I told you, there's nothing to fear from Chane."

Chane turned to her. Even sitting on the low bed, he barely had to look up to see her face.

"It's all right," Wynn said. "He knows. It was necessary to tell him because of what might come . . . for there's an orb in the keep . . . we think."

Confused and stunned, Chane's eyes never blinked as she rushed onward. By the time she finished telling him about Aupsha, Jausiff, the duchess and duke, and all else concerning a sect that had protected and lost an orb, he almost forgot she had revealed what he was to a young, somewhat unstable sage. *Almost.*

Chane was not pleased and glanced at Nikolas again.

After what the young sage had suffered from Sau'ilahk, the last thing Nikolas needed to hear was that he had unknowingly kept company with another undead and led it to his home. Then something else Wynn had said sank in regarding what she had done.

"You used mantic sight . . . without me or Premin Hawes," he accused.

"Osha was there," Wynn answered defensively. "And Shade brought me out with no trouble. If anything, it went better than ever before, so enough!"

Chane chilled inside. He knew he should focus on the important things she had told him, that there was likely an orb here. That should have been more critical than anything else, but he could not let go of other issues.

So much had happened, far beyond his possible imaginings, and while he lay dormant and useless all day, Osha had been the one at Wynn's side. And Wynn had revealed his nature without his knowledge or permission. Life, or any semblance of it for him among the living, kept becoming more complicated around her.

Something in his mouth tasted acrid.

"What did you see beyond the door?" he asked.

"Three guards, likely Suman, in the level below the keep."

She went on, though there was little more to tell.

"You believe the duke has an orb?" he echoed. "And he is . . . using it to some purpose that is affecting him and the surrounding area? What is he doing?"

Wynn shook her head. "I don't know, but I think what we suffered last night might have been from the orb being opened . . . or opened too much or too long. For what little we've overheard, no one here has experienced such effects before last night."

So far no one else present had spoken. That was no surprise from Nikolas, for what Wynn had done. Shade seemed the least disturbed, but one could never be certain of her reactions until she demonstrated such. As to Osha, he simply watched, narrow eyed.

"We have to get the orb," Wynn said. "So I've been waiting for you to . . . wake up."

At least she had been sensible in that.

"How many Suman guards, total, throughout the keep?" she asked. "I've seen different faces, but never more than two or three at a time."

"Sherie says eight . . . that she knows of," Nikolas answered, and when everyone else turned his way, the young sage swallowed. "I asked her, after you told her what you'd learned."

Chane ran a hand over his head and pushed hair back from his face. He hated the thought of accepting help from the elf, but there was little choice. Shade could harry guards—even highly skilled ones—and keep them in a panic, even if she could not put any of them down. But that would not be enough for the numbers they faced. They would need Osha as well.

"All right, first we must—"

At rushing footfalls in the passage outside, Chane lost his train of thought. Before he could react, Wynn went for the door as Nikolas backed out of her way. Wynn barely opened the door when it was shoved wide.

And there stood the young duke dressed all in black.

His pale face glistened as if from a cold sweat, but his ringed eyes fixed coldly on Wynn. He latched a hand on the doorframe as if to steady himself. There were others—three Suman guards and two keep guards with readied crossbows—standing close behind him.

Chane rose very slowly, waving Nikolas farther away from the door.

"My lord?" Wynn said.

Duke Beáumie ignored her as his glare roamed the small room: first to Osha, then to Chane, and lastly to Nikolas. Some of his anger wavered at the sight of the young sage, and he dropped his gaze for an instant before he returned it to Wynn, and his expression hardened again.

"I have been unwell," he said, "and have just awoken to be informed of your invasion into a restricted area last night. You will relinquish all weapons and remain confined to this one room until further notice."

It took a breath or two before Wynn answered. "The duchess lifted all limitations on us this morning and removed the guards. We would never do anything without—"

"My sister is not in charge here," the duke interrupted, and he looked beyond her at Chane. "Turn over your weapons."

Shade began to growl softly, and Osha slipped his right hand behind his back.

Chane's dwarven-crafted longsword and his makeshift shortsword were sheathed and leaning against the wall beyond his bed's foot. His first instinct was to lunge for them, but Wynn was too close to the door. As the duke shifted to one side in the doorway, one guard pointed his crossbow at Wynn.

"Don't," Nikolas whispered, stepping in behind her.

Chane did not know whether that was a warning for Wynn or someone else. He could not risk either of them being killed by his own attempt to charge the door. Raising both hands in plain sight, he carefully sidestepped to the bed's end and reached for his swords.

"Give him your bow and quiver," he told Osha.

Osha turned a scowl on him.

"The bow and the quiver," Chane repeated with emphasis.

Osha's expression turned briefly confused, and then it cleared as he nodded once. As long as none of the guards searched any of them, they would not find the dagger Osha kept hidden beneath the back of his tunic. That would leave one weapon in their possession. But after that brief hesitation, the guards with crossbows forced Wynn back and stepped inside. One aimed at Osha and the other at Chane himself. A third, a Suman, stepped in to collect all visible weapons.

"Am I to be confined as well?" Nikolas asked.

The young duke would not look at him. "Just for now . . . Nik. I'll . . . I'll come for you later."

The guards retreated, and the duke himself closed the door. At the rattle of a heavy key ring outside, the door's lock bolt clacked home in the stone frame.

Wynn spun around, fury and frustration on her oval olive face. As Chane was about to speak, Osha put a finger to his lips. The elf rushed to the wall shared with the next room, Wynn's, and put his ear to the stone as he closed his eyes and listened.

Chane did not need to do the same as he let hunger rise to sharpen his senses. He heard the next door down the passage open, and then movement in Wynn's room. There was a rough clatter of objects being dropped, and possibly the creak of the bed's frame. Then the door was closed again, and footfalls faded down the passage to the stairs.

"They put our weapons," Osha said, "in room for Wynn."

Chane merely nodded.

"My sun-crystal staff is in there," Wynn said quietly, as if no one else here was aware of that. "What are we going to do?"

At least she had looked to him and not that elf.

"We will think of something," Chane answered.

* * *

Sau'ilahk rose from dormancy to manifest like a black shadow in the center of the small room that housed the orb. He was alone, and his normally forced patience was thin tonight.

He did not know whether Karl had recovered from having opened the orb fully for an instant. The last time he had seen the young duke, the man was being carried upstairs in a state of unconsciousness.

Sau'ilahk slid nearer the door and raised his conjured voice of twisted air to be heard outside of it.

"Hazh'thüm?"

No answer came, not even the sound of the door being unlocked. Three of his Suman servants were outside at all times. Perhaps those present were reluctant to answer after finding one of their own drained and dead following the duke's impetuous mistake.

Sau'ilahk slipped straight through the wall into the outer chamber of six doors, three to each side. All three guards stiffened, one back-stepping, as all dropped their eyes in obeisance. Hazh'thüm was not among them.

"Where is your captain?"

"With the duke, my lord," the closest answered. "There have been developments."

"What has happened now?"

"We do not know."

"Is the duke awake, recovered?"

"Yes, my lord."

That brought some relief. Sau'ilahk would have despaired at needing another suitable candidate and having to begin all over again. He drifted back through the wall without a further word to his servants and waited in the orb's room. His patience grew as thin as his incorporeal presence.

Finally the familiar sound of booted footsteps rose outside, and the door opened.

The young duke entered, pale to the point of being ashen, with shadows like faint bruises beneath his eyes. The glove on his misshapen right hand showed signs of strain along its seams as he closed the door with his other hand.

"This visiting sage and her guards are more than they pretend to be," he announced with labored effort.

The last thing Sau'ilahk wanted to hear of was Wynn Hygeorht's meddling, and he no longer needed his air-conjured voice to ask,

What has happened?

"Last night her swordsman was caught in the passage outside the upper door to this lower level. The Lhoin'na with him evaded capture . . . and later returned to his quarters on his own." The duke's voice then edged with rage and panic. "How could they know where to go?"

Sau'ilahk's anxiety sharpened. He had not expected Chane Andraso to get so close so quickly.

Where are they now?

"I've locked them all in a single room on the third floor. They have no weapons and are under guard."

Sau'ilahk pondered for a moment and then drifted closer to the orb.

They no longer matter for the moment, my lord. We may proceed.

The duke stepped closer as doubt rose in his features. "They do not concern you?"

Not as they are.

At that, Karl Beáumie breathed heavily as if finishing a hard run. "Yes, you are right, and I will keep them locked away." His voice took on a manic edge. "We are so close now that . . . that I can *feel* it. Death drifts farther from me each night."

Yes, my lord. We are close to the end.

But Sau'ilahk's thoughts belied those soothing words. Wynn Hygeorht would not sit idle. Chane Andraso had already come much too close. And the majay-hì, that anathema to any undead, could not be allowed to sense anything.

The duke had shown himself to be unstable and unpredictable, although last night's rush had not destroyed his body.

Sau'ilahk knew that he must act quickly, or what he desired most could yet be stolen from him.

Come, my lord. Take up the key and let us begin.

* * *

Chane grew more desperate as time crept by. But to escape this room, he would have to break the door. In doing so he would lose the element of surprise.

Wynn sat on the end of Osha's bed nearest the door. Her chin rested in her hands with her elbows propped on her knees. If there were more than two guards posted outside, the chance of injury to her—before Chane could clear a path—was too high.

"What are you thinking?" she asked.

"That I wish I could see out into the passage . . . or into the next room to know if our weapons are truly there." He thought he had heard them dropped in there, but he wanted to be certain.

"Weapons are there," Osha stated flatly where he leaned against the wall. He had not moved since listening to the guards enter Wynn's room.

Wynn looked up at Chane. "Do you want me to try?"

The question confused him at first and then he understood. "No! Even one use of your mantic sight has always left you incapacitated."

"I'm better."

"Twice is foolish!"

Shade rose from where she lay, sat before Wynn, and growled at her. Clearly the dog agreed with him.

"Only way," Osha butted in. "She can do."

Chane turned on him. "You do not know anything about it!"

"I know her," Osha added, stepping away from the wall.

Before Chane could think of putting the elf down . . .

"Stop it, all of you!" Wynn ordered, even grabbing Shade by the muzzle as she fixed on Chane. "I only need a moment, maybe two, to get the count and position of the guards, and maybe glimpse where our weapons and my staff are. If there are too many out in the passage, then nothing is lost anyway. And it's better than just sitting here!"

Beyond the far bed—Chane's bed—Nikolas silently eyed everyone, though his gaze flinched away when Chane looked over.

No one spoke for too long, and Wynn pushed her way around Shade to head for the door.

Both Chane and Osha started after her for differing reasons.

"No," Osha said before Chane could, and the elf pointed to the room's front corner at the foot of the first bed. "Best—short—to look from passage to room."

That was not what Chane would have said, and he wanted to put Osha down right then. Wynn got in his way as she ducked back around the bed and crawled atop it to the corner.

Shade started growling again, but Chane knew it would not matter.

"Shade, enough!" Wynn snapped over her shoulder. "I don't have a choice." And she began tracing with a finger atop the bed.

"What are you doing?" Nikolas asked.

Chane found that the young sage had crept closer, not flinching now as he watched. No one answered Nikolas, and the sooner this was over, the better.

Wynn scooted forward over whatever she had traced upon the bed. At another pass of her finger around herself, she closed her eyes.

Nothing happened at first, and then she gagged.

Chane hated this, but he did not touch her yet. He only stepped around Shade for a better angle to see.

Wynn opened her eyes and shuddered as she peered at the wall between the room and the passage outside. Her head turned slowly, as if she followed something along the wall. Then she stopped, her sight line aimed roughly toward the passage's back end.

"Two guards . . . keep guards," she whispered, and then swallowed hard as if choking something down. "Both outside our door . . . with crossbows."

She turned slowly the other way until Chane could no longer see her eyes. She stalled, then wobbled, and Chane almost rushed in. Wynn caught herself with one hand as her head turned further, and she faced the corner of the wall between their current room and hers.

"Bow . . . quiver . . . swords . . . are . . ."

Chane heard her gag, though she just sat there, facing the wall.

Then she began to topple back.

"Wynn?" Osha almost shouted, reaching for her.

Chane leaped onto the bed and dropped an instant before Wynn fell back across his knees and thighs. Her eyes were closed, and her mouth was slack.

"Wynn!" he rasped.

Her eyelids did not even flutter.

Sau'ilahk pushed Karl Beáumie longer and harder than ever before.

A quiver ran down the young duke's arm to the deformed hand gripping the key, which held the spike out of the orb by the barest fraction. Lines of perspiration, all sparkling in the harsh, scintillating light escaping the orb, ran in rivulets down the man's face and jaw.

"Must . . . stop," he whispered. "Enough."

A moment more, my lord. Only another moment . . . to gain eternity.

Sau'ilahk solidified his right hand and, without warning, gripped over the top of the duke's deformed one.

Karl Beáumie lurched backward, slipping halfway through Sau'ilahk as he tried to pull free.

Sau'ilahk twisted his grip upon the duke's hand and the key.

CHAPTER EIGHTEEN

Osha knelt beside the bed and studied Wynn's pallor and closed eyes for any sign that she might awaken. Chane had been right about one thing: Osha did not understand enough about Wynn's mantic sight.

Whenever Chane was awake and involved, Osha felt as if he was secondary, and he had let this get to him. He should not have claimed certainty of Wynn's success. He should not have let the undead's interference push him to spite. Even worse, Wynn's sacrifice had gained them little beyond what he had already determined by merely listening to the movements of the guards.

Osha adjusted the blanket over Wynn as the majay-hì hopped up and wriggled along the wall to lie beside her. Shade occasionally licked Wynn's face with a rumbling whine, but it had no effect upon her.

"We need to get out," Chane rasped as he paced. "We must overcome the guards and reach our weapons."

Osha turned his head and scowled over his shoulder. Chane paused his pacing to return the look in kind.

"It is what she would want," the undead added, "rather than waiting for her to awaken."

This time Shade instead of Osha snarled at Chane.

"No!" Osha said for the majay-hì. "We wait. . . . Guards grow tired . . .

easy to surprise. Wynn sleep, so I need carry her and you fight only. Not wise."

Chane stopped pacing, as if pondering these objections, but he turned quickly at another voice.

"I can carry her."

Osha spotted Nikolas standing quietly in the far back corner. For most of their time locked in this room, the young sage had remained silent. Osha looked him over with some reservations, for Nikolas's build was slight.

"I am stronger than I look," Nikolas added, perhaps with a bit more force. "And Wynn . . . well, she's not very big."

No, she was not, and, lying there on the bed, she appeared even smaller. There might be more to Nikolas than Osha had yet seen.

"Even so," Chane said, his near-voiceless rasp now a hesitant whisper. "Perhaps Osha is . . . Perhaps we should wait a little longer."

Osha said nothing as he returned to watching Wynn.

Sau'ilahk opened his eyes.

That sensation alone made him shudder. He *lay* upon the floor and *felt* cold, hard stone beneath his back. He went numb in thought until the pain came. All his joints and muscles felt as though they had been torn loose . . . but he did not have joints and muscles.

Everything rushed in on him as he fought to lift his left hand until he could see. . . .

A perfectly fitted glove of black lambskin covered the duke's left hand. When Sau'ilahk thought to close his hand . . . the duke's fingers curled. He cautiously tried to touch his face—and did so.

By the power of the orb, he had taken Karl Beáumie's body.

As he tried to roll onto his side and push himself up, he grew suddenly concerned. How much damage had been done to the duke's flesh in shaking loose the last vestiges of the man's spirit? Sau'ilahk had had to claim that flesh in the precise instant.

Why was he so weak . . . and would this pass?

What of his abilities and powers honed over a thousand years, now that he was once more housed in living flesh? He had wanted this in ways beyond imagining but had never considered the costs until now.

Advantages began returning in his thoughts.

He was now the duke of Beáumie, lord of everyone and everything for the leagues of this remote province. That sliver of authority and earthly power was nothing compared to what he had once wielded in a long-lost life as Beloved's high priest. Given time, he would build upon this, but his first task was to secure his new identity. That included removing all evidence that he was not who he appeared to be.

The orb had to be taken somewhere beyond the reach of Wynn Hygeorht and any who might believe her claims. And then this body had to be made truly immortal beyond the false promise by which he had seduced the young duke.

Looking down, he saw Karl's slender form dressed all in black felts, wools, and leathers. The first wave of pure joy overtook him, but the flesh itself had been neglected. He was unwashed, and his clothing smelled as if it had not been changed, let alone laundered, in many days. He needed a bath, sandalwood soap for his hair, and of course fine clothes, but such things could wait a little longer. Sau'ilahk went to the pedestal—still troubled by a weakened and damaged body—and checked on the orb.

The spike had fallen into place and become one with the orb again, and the key—the handle—lay on the floor near one pedestal leg. He had to brace himself on the pedestal while leaning down to retrieve the key, and the other hand—the deformed one inside the stretched glove—was clumsy in its grip.

He shuffled to the door and called out, "Open!"

The sound and ease of a true voice were startling to him.

After the scrape of a key and the clack of a lock, the door opened, and all seven of his remaining Suman guards were waiting outside as instructed. Their rapid, hushed chatter barely abated, and Captain Hazh'thüm stood farthest away, toward the passage to the stairs.

Not one of them dropped their eyes. They stared at *him*.

The one who opened the door bowed his head slightly. "My duke, do you wish an escort to your room?"

Growing furious, Sau'ilahk glared at the man. Then he calmed in a fit of amusement.

"You do not recognize me . . . do you?"

The guard frowned, blinked twice in confusion, and glanced back at his captain.

Stepping closer, Hazh'thüm pushed through the others as he, too, frowned.

"You are . . . Duke Beáumie," the nearest guard said hesitantly. "Are you unwell, my lord?"

Sau'ilahk could not help but smile. Then he searched his own thoughts, his own memories, just in case. No, nothing lingered of Karl Beáumie in this flesh. That might be a difficulty, not knowing all about the past of the duke for a proper masquerade. Yet now he faced a different problem.

How much would it take to prove who he truly was to these base underlings?

How much of his former nature still remained, now that he had taken flesh?

Both the closest guard and Hazh'thüm peered beyond Sau'ilahk through the door. Perhaps looking for a tall, black-robed and cloaked form, their gazes roamed the orb's chamber.

"Sire, you should rest," Hazh'thüm suggested. "Let me take you to your room."

The others appeared relieved by him taking charge.

Sau'ilahk had no time or desire to reason with them. There was a quicker way to test something he needed to know. He lashed out with his left, good hand and snatched the nearest guard by the throat.

At the sight of him attacking one of their own, the others all pulled their swords.

Even Hazh'thüm lunged at him—and stalled in the last instant. His eyes widened as his mouth gaped.

The one guard barely had a moment to struggle and claw at Sau'ilahk's grip.

Satisfaction followed by relief flushed Sau'ilahk as his captive's hair began to bleach and his face withered with rushing age. All of the guards froze where they stood as they watched their comrade's life being drained away.

That life filled up Sau'ilahk. The pain in his new body lessened, and he straightened to full height as he released his grip. The guard crumpled like an old man breathing his last, and Sau'ilahk succumbed to euphoria amid relief.

He could still feed.

What other remnants of his previous existence had carried though to this new one?

The dead guard hit the floor. All six remaining men stood frozen until Hazh'thüm stepped back and lowered his eyes.

"Now do you know me?" Sau'ilahk asked.

All six men dropped to one knee and bowed their heads low.

"When we are in public, under the eyes of the unknowing, you will serve me as the duke," he commanded. "At all other times, you will show *proper* respect for who I am."

"Yes, my lord . . . Yes, Eminence," Hazh'thüm whispered.

Sau'ilahk smiled. "Prepare the orb for transport. We leave this place tonight."

Chane sagged in relief when Wynn's eyes opened. He had told himself over and over that she had merely collapsed from exhaustion. When she struggled to sit up on the bed, he did not even interfere when Osha assisted her and then put a cup of water to her lips.

"Are you all right?" Chane asked.

After a swallow, she nodded weakly. "Still dizzy . . . and . . . what happened?"

Her braid had come partially loose, and her wispy brown hair was a mess around her oval face. Her olive-toned skin appeared slightly pallid, but he was further relieved by how coherent she sounded—almost herself.

"You fainted," Nikolas said. "What were you doing?"

No one answered him, and Chane stepped to the door to listen for a moment. "It has been quiet out there for some time," he whispered, and then looked to Wynn. "If I break the door, Osha, Shade, and I can rush the guards. One of us, at least, should break through to our weapons . . . and your staff. Can you run yet?"

"Wait," Osha said. "She need more time."

Wynn waved him back and swung her legs off the bed. "I can walk," she said, struggling to her feet. "I'll get better soon enough."

Chane nodded. He would have preferred to give her more time as well, but if there was an orb in this keep, they had been locked in here too long. He knew she would not want to wait.

"I will break through," he whispered to Osha. "Once I have drawn the guards' fire, and they have no chance to reload, you and Shade must rush for the other room." He looked to Shade. "Agreed?"

Shade huffed once as she dropped off the bed to step around Wynn and closer to the door. Osha slipped his hand behind his back, and it came out again with the dagger.

"Nikolas, come here near me," Wynn said, but he didn't move.

"Where exactly are we going once we get out?" Nikolas asked. "Karl controls all the guards, not just the Sumans. Even if you get this artifact out of the lower levels, the front gates are locked down."

Chane had thought of this, though there was little to be done about it. If they could breach the lower levels, find the orb, and dispatch the Suman guards, perhaps they could break out through the door at the back passage's end. That might at least gain them something . . . and again perhaps most of the guards would be drawn into the keep in a search.

"First we retake our weapons, then the orb, and all else . . . we will deal with as needed." He glanced at Osha. "Ready?"

The elf nodded once, and Chane grabbed the door's handle. He let his hunger rise, expanding his senses, and he prepared to rip the handle and, he hoped, the lock bolt out so he could pull the door open.

A shout carried in the passage beyond the door, and he froze.

Then he heard a clang of steel and the clatter of a sword on stone, followed by one rough thud and then another that carried through the floor stones under his feet. After that there was silence outside in the passage.

Chane hesitated and looked to the others. It was obvious that at least Osha and Shade had heard something as well, and the dog's ears flattened. Something clinked outside the door, and then came a scraping of metal near the lock. The door's lock bolt clacked, and Chane shifted left, ready to strike as the door swung inward.

In the narrow space of the open door was a leather mask over a hooded figure's face.

"Wait," it said in Numanese with a rolling thick accent not correct for a Numan.

That person pushed the door wide until it banged carelessly against the wall. Somewhere behind Chane he heard Shade snarl in warning.

Beyond the strange figure in the doorway, at least one guard lay unconscious in a heap upon the passage floor. He could not see the other, but he heard no movement outside. Still ready to strike, he looked their would-be rescuer up and down.

The figure raised a tawny-gloved hand and slid the mask upward into its hood.

Aupsha eyed him in turn. "I have freed Counselor Columsarn, and he has gone to do the same for the duchess. Come with me."

It was all too convenient, and Chane did not move, even when he heard the others in the room step nearer.

Aupsha's forearm was encompassed in a hardened leather bracer. The same type of armor, suitably shaped for a woman, covered her torso. Even her thighs and shins were protected, and everywhere on those pieces of darkly dyed armor were ornately carved swirling patterns that obscured symbols Chane could not quite make out.

"Freed?" Nikolas asked. "My father and Sherie were locked up?"

Aupsha's eyes shifted briefly toward the young sage before returning to Chane.

"The duke has sealed the keep, even to the servants in their rooms," she said. "The counselor was locked in his chamber but not under guard, so I released him first." Her tone grew impatient. "The duke has left, taking his Sumans and some of the keep's guards on horseback. But he is aboard a wagon . . . with a covered load in its rear."

"Back up now," Chane ordered.

Aupsha lingered for a breath before retreating to the outer passage's far side.

Chane slipped out, looked both ways, and found that the second guard was also down. The others came out behind him.

"We cannot delay for your doubts," Aupsha added sharply.

Osha immediately rushed for Wynn's room as Shade dashed to the passage's end and peered down the stairs. Chane remained poised before the tall dark servant, now dressed and armored more strangely, more foreignly, than she herself had always appeared.

"Do you know what's in the wagon?" Wynn asked, stepping in on Chane's right.

"My guess would be the same as yours," Aupsha answered, "and I have little patience left."

Chane was about to push Wynn back and sidestep toward her room when Osha returned and handed off his blades. Chane took them and quickly strapped them on as he kept his eyes on Aupsha.

"Is my staff still there?" Wynn asked.

"Yes," Osha answered.

At Chane's glance, the elf was already stringing his bow, and the strange and narrow canvas bundle was again tied over his back.

"Get your staff," Chane told Wynn. "Nikolas, go with her."

As the two ran off, Shade came trotting back.

"Anyone?" Chane asked, and Shade huffed once for *no*.

Only then did Aupsha look away at Shade with a brief narrowing of her eyes. "I will go below and verify that the artifact has been taken," she said.

"Why would I trust you for that?" Chane challenged.

Aupsha let out a slow breath, as if suppressing distaste. "Whether it is there or not, the duke has tried to lock away everyone who knows him . . . and has fled the keep. That alone is enough reason to stop him from whatever he has been doing."

Chane was half tempted to remove Aupsha here and now, but if the duke had been so mad as to use the orb in some way, the man would not have relinquished it in taking flight. Still, Chane wondered what might happen if he was mistaken. What if Aupsha, who knew the duke much better, had a reason for sending all of them off and out of the way?

"Someone must find the counselor and the compass I left with him," she said. "Only that device has a chance to locate the artifact if it has been removed. You will also need Lady Sherie to manage any remaining guards."

"Wait—where are you going?"

At that, Chane found Wynn at his side again with her staff in hand.

"You and Nikolas get our packs," he told her, and she looked from him to Aupsha. "Please," he added, "we must move quickly and be prepared for anything."

With obvious reluctance, she and Nikolas went off.

Chane barely turned to see Aupsha heading for the passage's back. And before he could go after her . . .

"I come with you . . . to help," Osha called out.

Aupsha halted and turned. Her mask was down over her face once more, and it was impossible to gauge her reaction.

Wynn returned and handed off Chane's packs. It was obvious what Osha intended to do, and she held out a cold-lamp crystal.

"Take it, just to be sure," she told him. "Meet us in the courtyard when you're done . . . and be quick."

Before Osha even nodded, Aupsha had turned away. He took the crystal and followed her.

"Nikolas, Shade, and I will find Jausiff and Lady Sherie," Wynn said to Chane. "You get our wagon ready, but be prepared to clear us a path if the guards won't listen to the duchess."

Chane disliked the idea of them all splitting up this way, but there were too many paths to follow, and Wynn was already headed for the stairs with Shade.

Only Nikolas lingered, eyeing Chane, until Chane stepped off after Wynn.

Osha slipped ahead down the stairs to the passage's rear, and Aupsha said nothing. He did not like having her at his back, but whatever lay below, he intended to see it first, and he brushed Wynn's crystal across his tunic several times to heat up its light.

He would have preferred to remain with Wynn, but he had seen her face upon learning that Aupsha intended to verify the orb's presence or absence beneath the keep. He had seen such an artifact once in his time with her— and Magiere, Léshil, and Chap. He would know another one when he saw it. But when he and the strangely armored woman reached the rear passage with its end door out the north side . . .

Around the corner and down the two steps, the door leading below was wide-open.

He glanced at Aupsha, but the mask made it impossible to read her. This door being open did not bode well, and she slipped into the lead as they descended more stairs beyond the door. Another passage at the bottom led them into a narrow stone chamber with six heavy doors of old wood, three to each side.

Aupsha halted, and Osha had to sidestep to view the chamber. Something more caught his attention immediately.

A body lay crumpled on the floor, though Osha recognized it only by the garb of a Suman guard. The man looked nothing like any guard he had seen, for this one was aged, too old to be in service. The corpse's eyes were half-open, as was his wrinkled mouth, but those eyes were as clouded and pale as his near-white hair.

Aupsha was still frozen in place and looking down when Osha heard the crackling squeak of leather. He followed the sound to her nearer gloved hand, now clenched in a fist.

"You see this before?" he asked.

At first she did not answer, and when she did so, she did not look at him.

"Once. Among my dead . . . a few were not broken but left like this . . . dead or dying."

Osha waited no longer and ran from one door to the next. All were locked except the second one on the right. The only things he found in that small, dark room were a plain old table and a strange iron stand. The latter had a waist-high round hoop at the top, in place of any surface on which to set anything. When he left that room, Aupsha had not moved.

"Nothing here," Osha said. "Other doors locked."

Aupsha stared down at the body a moment longer and then turned back toward the passage out. "It does not matter. The artifact would have been guarded, always. It is gone."

"We find it," Osha said, quickly following. "We take it back."

Again he slipped ahead to light the way, anxious to protect Wynn now that they knew the orb had been taken—or at least moved. He slowed as they reached the stairs and listened for anything above. No sound echoed to his ears as he crept up the stairs and through the opened door. He closed his hand over the crystal as he peered around the archway's side.

There was no one in the back passage along the way they had come. He heard no sounds except the sea outside below the keep—and then a snap of cloth.

A sharp movement of air, like a brief breeze, tossed Osha's hair. He looked back and then spun fully around. Wide-eyed, as he looked down the stairs, he opened his fist to release the crystal's light.

Osha saw no one, even in the lower passage.

Aupsha was gone.

* * *

Chane reached the keep's main hall at a run and raced on to the front doors. He halted to crack them open only a little.

He saw no one near the stable or the other, smaller structure on the courtyard's left, but the rented wagon was still outside. To the right were the barracks and what might be another small storage building, and straight ahead two keep guards in gray tabards huddled together before the gate and peered out through its lattice ironwork. Another one atop the wall to the gate's left faced the other way, looking down the road. That one held a heavy crossbow.

Chane had no difficulty in hearing them.

"Where could he have gone?" the shortest man on the ground called up to the one atop the wall. "And why did he take Lieutenant Martelle?"

Sharpening his sight, Chane recognized the man on the ground as Captain Holland.

The man on the wall did not even turn around as he answered. "Don't know. He just ordered the lieutenant to gather a few others, and they headed off with the duke and those Sumans. Good riddance on the latter!"

"How long ago?" Holland called back up.

"Not long," the guard above answered. "Going by the wagon's lantern, they turned off below and headed inland instead of along the coastal road. But they had no provisions that I saw, not for what little bulk was in the wagon. And no instructions from the duke. He just ordered us to open the gate."

Chane grew uncertain. Preparing their own wagon would not be so easy if the captain and his men were confused by the duke's taking men out in the middle of the night. If Chane headed for the stable, he might be detained and questioned. Such an event could be better handled if the duchess was here to at least try to clear the way.

Lost in thought, he did not hear the fast footfalls until they grew close.

Chane turned and reached for his sword. Osha came at him at a run through the main hall, but he was alone.

"Where is Aupsha?" Chane whispered.

Osha shook his head. "The way below not locked. We found no orb. We return to back passage . . . near door to outside . . ." He shook his head again.

It did not make sense to Chane. "Why would she break us out, accept our help, and then vanish?"

Osha shook his head once more.

Chane turned back to peer through the cracked-open door. The situation was even more uncertain now, for it seemed they had two choices: risk going for the wagon and team without attracting attention or wait for Wynn to arrive with the duchess.

The former seemed an unlikely success, so he held his place a little longer.

Wynn trotted with Shade behind Nikolas toward Jausiff's study, for that was where Nikolas suggested that his father would return once Sherie had been freed. The young sage, with his slightly longer legs, shot out ahead and reached the door first.

"Father?" Nikolas called, banging on the door. "Are you in there?"

When no one answered, he tried the handle and found it locked.

"Where else might they be?" Wynn asked.

"I don't know," Nikolas answered. "Maybe Sherie's chambers."

Before Wynn could say more, he strode back down the passage toward the stairs. Wynn trotted after, followed by Shade, and halfway there they heard voices carrying down the stairs.

Jausiff and Lady Sherie stepped down into the passage.

"Father," Nikolas breathed in relief, and perhaps his first instinct had been right.

"Nikolas?" Sherie said, hurrying toward them. Her gaze shifted to Wynn and then Shade. "You are free."

"Aupsha let us out," Wynn answered. She quickly told them everything that had happened that she knew so far, and then focused on Jausiff. "Aupsha wants you to get her device to track the artifact's direction."

"One moment," Jausiff said, unlocking his chamber with one key on a heavy ring. "I haven't seen a single guard wherever I went in the keep. All I know is that Karl left with his Suman contingent. You say Aupsha went to the lower level?"

"Yes. Osha went with her to verify that the artifact had been taken."

Jausiff hurried to his desk and this time pulled out a tiny brass key on a string around his neck. He unlocked the chest behind his desk table and began pulling out various things and setting them aside in meticulous stacks.

Wishing he would hurry, Wynn bit down on her impatience. He finally straightened up, turned about, and set a small case of thick, stiff leather on the desk. When he undid the lashings and opened it, there was the piece of ruddy metal to which he referred as a "compass."

Shade pushed in close at Wynn's side before the desk, and her ears pricked up. But Wynn barely glanced at the dog as she waited for Jausiff to do . . . something.

Jausiff stretched out his arm, his hand open and palm up with the slightly curved piece of an orb key resting in it. Wynn was so fixed upon the object that she was startled as the old sage whispered something.

Jausiff's eyes were on the "compass," and when Wynn looked down, for an instant she thought she saw the ruddy metal quiver, or perhaps move or rotate just barely. The master sage closed his grip on it.

He stepped around the desk, with the device held out in his upturned fist. He kept turning slightly left and right as he walked all the way into the outer passage. Wynn rushed in behind him as everyone else present followed.

Jausiff went all the way down the passage to the stairs leading to below. He turned rightward once, and there was a scowl of confusion on his old face. The aging sage quickly turned to face up the passage again toward the keep's rear.

Jausiff halted in only three more steps, and his hand holding the piece of an orb key dropped to dangle at his side.

"The artifact is no longer inside the keep," he said.

Wynn turned on Sherie. "My lady, that artifact is dangerous. It's what has been causing changes here in your brother, as well as in the surrounding land. Chane is trying to ready our wagon even now, but we need you to get us out of here past any remaining keep guards."

Sherie appeared stricken, troubled, and doubtful as she looked from Wynn to the keep's counselor. It was obvious that she had difficulty understanding anything that had happened here—that her own brother had ordered her locked into her room.

"Why would he leave?" she demanded. "Why take this object away from here after all he has done to hide it and whatever he has been doing with it?"

"I don't know," Wynn answered honestly. "But if you want to help him—and stop all of this—you must get us through the front gates."

At that the duchess turned halfway and looked to Nikolas right behind her. Perhaps she wondered what he had to do with all of this, though he wouldn't have much to tell. It seemed to take effort for Nikolas to even meet Sherie's eyes, and when he finally did so, he simply nodded to her.

"This way," the duchess commanded, walking forward to take the lead.

Chane, thinking that he—and Osha—should take a chance and head for the stable, began to doubt his choice to wait.

"Chane?"

At that whisper, both he and Osha turned to find Wynn and Shade hurrying toward them, along with Nikolas, the elder sage, and the duchess in the lead.

"Why aren't you out there?" Wynn asked. "Are the horses harnessed?"

Chane shook his head. "The guards outside are agitated by what has happened. I thought it best to wait for Lady Sherie."

"Where is Aupsha?" Jausiff asked, pushing in closer.

"Gone," Osha answered.

"Gone?" the elderly sage repeated in shock.

"Step aside," the duchess ordered, advancing immediately.

Chane did so. She passed him without slowing and pulled open one of the front doors. She did not pause as she strode out in the courtyard and straight toward the gates.

"Get to the horses," Wynn urged as she passed him in following the duchess. "Osha, go and help him."

Neither of them hesitated as the others followed Wynn.

Chane quick-stepped with Osha on his heels as they aimed straight for the wagon. When they reached it, Osha jumped up before the bench, and, as Chane was about to go into the stable for the horses, he paused, looking up at the elf.

"If the duchess cannot convince the guards, can you put down the one atop the wall before we near the gate?" Chane asked.

Osha finished untying the reins from the brake lever and straightened. At his simple shrug, his strung bow dropped off his shoulder, and he caught it without even looking.

"Not one," he answered. "All three."

Chane, not interested in the elf's bravado, rolled his eyes as he turned at a trot for the stable doors.

Wynn stayed close behind Nikolas as they followed Sherie, and Shade remained at her right, while Jausiff came along a little wide on her left.

"How does your device work?" she asked.

He glanced sidelong at her and then held up his hand, still gripping the small metal object.

"Simply hold it once it is active, as now," he answered. "It produces a . . . a pull in a general direction."

Wynn couldn't hold back one more question. "Was Aupsha the one who carried your messages to Calm Seatt?"

"This is hardly the time—"

"Did she?" Wynn insisted, for there might not be another time.

"Yes," he admitted. "She possesses certain . . . abilities and was able to escape the keep. No one knew she was gone, because she and I were believed to be locked away in a self-imposed quarantine."

Wynn glanced ahead. Sherie had almost reached Captain Holland, who stood waiting, his troubled gaze on only her.

"Did Aupsha have the device with her?" Wynn rushed to ask.

"Certainly," Jausiff answered. "How else would I have it now?"

Wynn ignored that, for this all told her something more, at a guess. The key piece, the device . . . the "compass" was the only way anyone could have tracked the orb hidden away with the Stonewalkers. Both messenger and would-be thief *were* one and the same somehow, though this didn't explain how Aupsha had traveled from Calm Seatt to the dwarven underworld in one night.

She must have been so confused, probably thinking the orb of Spirit had been moved to Dhredze Seatt on the peninsula. Only when a blank wall of rough stone had stopped her had she fled back here, realizing the orb she was after was still in the keep.

And yet she now knew where another orb lay hidden. Worse than this, that bit of severed, ruddy metal in Jausiff's hand left Wynn wondering.

Could any key be used to track any of the orbs? And, again, how had the orb of Spirit been located among Aupsha's people and then stolen?

"Captain Holland, open the gates," the duchess ordered.

All of Wynn's fearful speculations ended—and then shifted—when the captain didn't move.

"My lady," he said. "Do you know where the duke has gone?"

"My brother has run off with what is left of the treasury," Sherie returned. "There isn't even enough left to pay the guards or servants. I am in charge while my brother is absent, so why are you questioning me?"

Wynn wondered whether this was a ruse, or if the duke had also stolen money from the keep.

"The treasury?" Holland asked, incredulous. "Do you wish me to go after him?"

"No. I'm sending others instead."

The duchess said nothing more and stood there staring at him.

The captain, a hardened soldier probably bent to the breaking point with all that had happened in the past day and night, merely stared back a moment longer. But it seemed he would still obey the duchess, for he looked to the other guard nearby and nodded. The two of them began sliding the heavy iron bolts out to separate the gates.

Wynn kept silent until she heard rolling wheels and clopping horses behind her. Chane and Osha had the wagon in motion.

"Give me the device," Wynn whispered to Jausiff.

He glanced down in surprise. "No. I am coming with you."

"So am I," Nikolas added.

"You can't, either of you," Wynn countered. "Neither can Lady Sherie . . . not for an assault on the duke! If this fails, someone will have to speak for us, so none of you can be involved."

Before anyone could argue further, Wynn held out her hand to Jausiff.

The master sage scowled and slowly held out the device. "Do not lose hold of it," he warned, "for once it has been activated, it must remain in contact with your skin, or it will cease to function until reactivated."

That didn't sit well with Wynn. There might come a moment when she would have to let go of it, if events took an even worse turn. As Jausiff placed the ruddy metal in her hand, she closed her fingers around it.

"I'm coming," Nikolas then argued again. "Karl is my friend, and I'm going to help him. He'll listen to me before any of you."

Wynn shook her head. "Whatever the duke has been doing with that artifact, he isn't the man you knew anymore. Look after your father and the duchess, and leave Karl to us. Do not leave the keep until you hear from me."

Nikolas, almost looking at Sherie, barely turned his head and didn't say another word.

Wynn knew he would stay, and judging by the silence behind her, she knew the wagon was close. She turned to find Chane up on the bench with his long dwarven-made sword unsheathed beside him. Osha stood in the back with his bow in hand and the quiver of black-feathered arrows rising above his right shoulder. Wynn was thankful that a show of force was unnecessary as she scrambled into the back with Osha, and Shade loped out ahead through the open gates.

Chane was about to flick the reins.

"Bring my brother back," the duchess said, looking right at him.

No matter the role he had played in this place as bodyguard to Wynn, perhaps she recognized another noble when she saw one and tried to appeal to his honor.

He would make no promises.

Chane snapped the reins, and both horses broke into a trot, heading out the gates and down the slope along the road. He looked ahead through the dark for Shade, as the dog would never go far from Wynn.

They were barely out of sight of the keep when Wynn made a change.

"Osha, take the reins and drive," she said. "Chane, back here with me."

"Why?" Chane asked.

"Just do it!"

Osha climbed over the bench, and Chane handed off the reins to join Wynn. He found her awkwardly removing the sheath from her staff while still holding the strange piece of ruddy metal. Once the sheath was off, and the staff's long crystal was exposed, she began digging one-handed through his pack and pulling things out at random.

"What are you doing?" he rasped. "What good will your staff be against—"

"Look at this," she said, holding out the piece of metal. "It's part of an orb key or handle."

Chane looked up from her hand. He was not certain what this meant, but he did not care for it.

"Aupsha's people had a key for the orb stolen from them. They cut it into pieces so it could never be used with the orb . . . but they did something else to it . . . somehow." And she looked up at him. "It's activated now, and so long as someone holds it, this piece of key can be used to point the general way to an orb . . . and not just the one the duke has. I know this because Aupsha was the one who broke into the Stonewalkers' realm in tracking the wrong orb."

Chane was momentarily stunned. Before he could form a question, Wynn turned back to his pack and pulled out his gloves, mask, and glasses.

"When you found the orb of Earth in Bäalâle," she went on, "Sau'ilahk had gotten ahead of you. You found that the orb was still there, but you didn't find a key handle. When Magiere returned from the Wastes, she had a key to match the orb she found there, yet the orb in Bäalâle had none. We couldn't figure out why Sau'ilahk left the orb of Earth, but perhaps it wasn't the orb he really wanted. Maybe he took the key instead . . . and maybe he knew how to make it work in another way."

Chane did not like what she was hinting at. "No . . . Neither I nor Shade have sensed an undead in this place."

"Maybe he's kept enough distance. Maybe you couldn't sense something through the keep's stone . . . or down below it. But who else could have taught Karl how to tamper with an orb . . . or might have a key to open one?"

Chane wanted to dismiss all of this, but he could not. He had not bargained for carrying Wynn into another confrontation with the wraith. Perhaps she was wrong.

Wynn put everything else she had pulled out back into his pack until all that remained in her lap were his gloves, mask, and scarf, and the original pair of dark-lensed glasses that had been made with her sun-crystal staff.

"Get these on and pull up your hood . . . and be ready," she said.

Chane sighed, a habit left over from life. He did as she asked, for once he was completely covered, Wynn could freely ignite the sun crystal as necessary, and he could withstand its arcane light for a short while.

The possibility that she might need to use the sun-crystal staff stripped away all comfort in being prepared. Then something more occurred to him.

"If Shade senses an undead, she will . . . go berserk. She might try to attack alone and drive it off before it senses you. That is what I would do in her place."

Somewhere out in the dark Sau'ilahk could be with, trailing, or awaiting Duke Beáumie.

Wynn leaned forward. "Osha, faster!"

Chane pulled his gloves on and reached for the mask.

CHAPTER NINETEEN

Sau'ilahk sat on a wagon bench while Guardsman Comeau drove the team of horses down the inland road. The coastal wind blew relentlessly at his back and made him wish he had thought to bring a cloak. What a strange thought that was after centuries of never *feeling* any physical sensation.

A heavy oil lantern rested between himself and Comeau and provided some light. Under the bench, behind his feet, was a small locked chest filled with gold sovereigns of Witeny—the Beáumie family treasury. And around his neck hung the orb key he had stolen from a forgotten dwarven seatt and learned to use to find the orb.

Three Suman guards, including Hazh'thüm, rode in the wagon's back, where the orb was stowed in a small trunk beneath a tarp. The other three jogged behind the wagon, followed by four mounted keep guards, including Lieutenant Martelle.

Those last four, along with Comeau, believed they accompanied their duke, Karl Beáumie.

Sau'ilahk had purposefully chosen to turn inland and take the long way around through the duchy to the nearest port. There would be less chance of encountering anyone presumptuous enough to question the "duke" traveling by night with a contingent.

The magnitude of what Sau'ilahk had accomplished slowly began to sink in.

He possessed flesh again, which would soon need proper care, as well as the mending of any effects inflicted upon it by the orb. The extent of his success so far was almost overwhelming. Still, a few doubts and worries nagged at him.

For one, he had left Wynn Hygeorht alive.

That choice galled him, though he had seen no way to kill her before leaving. With his new body, he could not slip through the keep's stone to take her life in the night, even if he had ordered her isolated from her companions. Nor, as the duke, could he simply have her executed, for others present would question such an act and likely speak of it later to others. The guild would hear of her death eventually, and for now he needed to remain an inconsequential noble in a nation that had abandoned its monarchy.

He was also uncomfortably uncertain about how much of his previous nature remained at his command now that he had taken living flesh. He had not considered this carefully enough in his maddened desire. Besides his ability to feed upon the living, how much else could he still do?

And last but foremost, what of Beloved?

Sau'ilahk no longer needed to slip into dormancy each dawn, only to suffer dark restlessness in the coils of his god until the next dusk—or so he assumed. Against all unknowns, he could accept other losses in exchange for that. Oh, yes, he would still serve his god, but only for his own return to power.

Looking down, he studied the unmarred left hand inside its black glove. As of yet, he had not wanted to examine the other deformed one too closely, though he would find a way to mend it soon enough. As the wagon rolled along, his thoughts turned to other things.

Using his teeth, he removed the glove from his left hand and rubbed his fingertips together. The hand was perfect, slender but strong. After a sidelong glance at Guardsman Comeau, attentively managing the wagon's horses, Sau'ilahk reached down and flattened that hand upon the side of the bench.

There was one thing he could test now, in the dark, when no one would see.

Applying his will, as he had once needed in order to make his hand solid, he pressed against the bench's side. Almost instantly he felt his fingers and palm sink as if pressing through mud instead of wood. Pressure soon mounted. He felt wood press around his flesh and begin to crush it.

Sau'ilahk jerked his hand from the bench.

"Something wrong, my lord?" Comeau asked.

Sau'ilahk saw only puzzlement in the young guard's face. "No, merely a sliver from the old wood. I will tend it later."

Comeau nodded, turning his attention back to the reins.

Sau'ilahk cradled that one perfect hand in his lap. It was enough to know he could still alter himself, though inversely from what he had once required when taking phyiscal action as only a spirit. Perhaps when sated on more life, he might come and go as he once had, unlimited by physical barriers. As with other things, learning more of what had changed would have to wait.

His thoughts turned to more immediate matters.

He knew very little of this land and nation, only that Witeny was a politically ambiguous place, maintaining its noble lines as part of its heritage but not as a governing class. All decisions of state were handled by a national council, which was reputed to be as corrupt as any aristocracy. He had no intention of remaining a minor lord in a remote duchy and collecting a pittance of taxes from the coastal villages under his stewardship. He intended to return to his native land, and for that he needed true wealth.

Whatever coin he had taken from the keep was hardly enough, but his title as a duke was something with which to work; titles could still open ways closed to commoners. Perhaps he could claim unrest in his province and seek advice and aid from those of Karl Beáumie's station or above. That would be a start.

The wagon lurched and jumped under him, and he gripped the bench's edge.

"Sorry, my lord," Comeau quickly offered. "I can't see all the little holes in the dark."

Sau'ilahk offered no rebuke, as he continued pondering more important matters. Then something dark caught in the corner of his sight.

It was almost as if he had glimpsed himself—his former nature as a black spirit. He turned his head too quickly and too far, straining his neck as the wind at his back blew hard across his face. Slapping the hair from his eyes, he looked more carefully.

Something rushed through the night among the north-side trees along the road. Before he could utter a warning, a dark figure in a cloak and hood shot out toward the left horse before the wagon.

The animal lurched, threw up its head, and screamed.

The figure veered off, rushing back into the trees, as the horse began to fall.

"Whoa!" Guardsman Comeau called, heaving on the reins.

The wooden shaft in the falling horse's harness snapped as the horse collapsed against its companion, and the wagon's left front wheel struck the first struggling beast. The horse on the right was trapped by its harness as it went down.

Sau'ilahk's eyes widened when the wagon lurched upward, nearly throwing him into the back. As the wagon toppled sideways, he jumped.

Inertia threw him toward the trees to the left, and by pure chance he missed any of their trunks in the dark. When he hit the earth, his feet gave way, and he tumbled out of control. Shock numbed his mind at the pain of being battered and whipped by bushes and leaves as low branches snapped under his wild fall.

Sau'ilahk rolled to stop on his stomach with cold, damp mulch against the side of his face and some in his mouth. He was too stunned at first to move, and then pain came back.

Was he injured, broken, harmed in any way? This could not be happening to him after waiting so very long to have flesh again.

Hearing the noise and shouts of men, he carefully pushed himself up and turned on one knee.

A fire burned at the front of the overturned wagon resting on its left side.

At least one of the downed horses was screaming. The lantern had broken and its oil ignited, and flames threatened to reach the wagon's bench. Two of his men tried unsuccessfully to free a third one pinned under the wagon's side. Something dark, likely blood, leaked from the side of the man's mouth.

Guardsman Comeau stumbled toward the wagon's front and shielded his face from the flames as he tried to reach the horses. Amid confusion, the four keep guards dropped from their horses to follow the other three Sumans.

Looking about in shock, Sau'ilahk saw that the orb's trunk had toppled to the roadside and was exposed from beneath the tarp still dangling from the wagon's upturned side. One keep guard ran by, ignoring the chest as he tried to pull the tarp free and tamp down the flames.

Sau'ilahk struggled up, but not to run in and help. He turned all ways as he looked among the trees. The person who had caused all of this was still out there in the dark.

"Grab the bottom!"

Sau'ilahk turned back as Lieutenant Martelle was directing the others in trying to tilt the wagon to free the pinned Suman.

"Lift on the count of three," Martelle shouted.

At the count, two of Sau'ilahk's men and another keep guard heaved but to no avail.

Sau'ilahk had no interest in this, and he hurried toward the orb's trunk. Then he spotted Hazh'thüm with two more Suman guards at the wagon's rear.

"Retrieve and guard the trunk," he ordered in Sumanese. "Then find the treasury as well."

With a sharp nod, Hazh'thüm waved to his men and pointed toward the trunk. They both ran in, grabbing for its end handles. As the second man touched it, dust or a sudden mist appeared to blow in around him upon the wind.

The cloaked figure took shape before Sau'ilahk's eyes.

The figure rammed a shimmering blade through the Suman guard's yellow silk tabard, and the man dropped his end of the orb's trunk and fell across it. Sau'ilahk stood frozen at the sight of the tall, slender, masked figure with a now-darkened blade in its hand.

Hazh'thüm shouted something that made Sau'ilahk blink and look away for an instant. When he looked back . . .

The other Suman had dropped his end of the trunk and reached for his sword's hilt. The cloaked figure lunged in. The blade had barely sunk into the man's chest when the cloaked one vanished in a whirl of dust swept away by the wind.

The second Suman guard toppled before Hazh'thüm arrived. No blade protruded from the man's chest, though his yellow tabard began to darken. Blood soaked through and spread in a circle as his back hit the road. He lay still and silent, and his eyes remained open.

Hazh'thüm spun about, looking in all directions.

Two Suman guards were dead. A third was still pinned under the wagon and dying. Oil on the roadside still burned brightly. And Sau'ilahk shook off his shock and looked everywhere for any sign of the one who appeared to have blown away on the wind. Then he realized the wind no longer came straight in from the west.

It now came a bit more from the north. He and his contingent were on the road's north side. As he stepped fully out of the trees, he peered southeast across the road and ignored the groans of the man still pinned under the wagon.

Three of his Sumans were functional and would obey unto death—for greater fear of him. He was uncertain how far the keep guards would obey their duke after what they had just seen.

"Hazh'thüm!" he barked. "Take your men and drag the trunk and treasury chest into the trees behind me." He turned on Lieutenant Martelle. "Take your men and search the south-side woods more to the east. That has to be where this assassin went. Work your way west against the wind to flush out the assailant."

Only then did any of them notice the sudden silence. The horses had gone quiet, and the pinned Suman lay still and slack with his eyes open and unblinking. Lieutenant Martelle, his expression unreadable, glanced at the man.

Without a word, he led his own men around the wagon's back.

Guardsman Comeau began to follow, but Sau'ilahk stopped him.

"I have another need for you."

The forest to both sides blurred past as the wagon raced along the road, and Wynn clung to the sidewall with one hand. With her staff lying beside her, she kept her free hand clenched around Jausiff's—Aupsha's—device made from an orb key.

On one knee, Chane gripped the wagon's opposite wall. Every bit of him except for his eyes was now covered, and the glasses hung around his neck on a leather cord.

Wynn could barely make out Shade loping out ahead as Osha drove the wagon's horses too hard. It wasn't a safe speed, but she didn't tell him to slow down.

Then, without warning, Osha leaned back sharply on the bench and pulled hard on the reins.

Wynn threw her free arm over the wagon's sidewall to hang on.

"What is happening?" Chane called, his rasp muffled through the mask.

"Shade stopped," Osha answered.

Once the wagon shuddered to a halt, Wynn grabbed her staff with her free hand and rose to see. Perhaps twenty yards ahead, Shade stood poised in the middle of the road.

Wynn jumped out the back and ran ahead to crouch as she touched Shade's shoulder.

"What is it?" she whispered.

—Shouts . . . men—

Wynn didn't hear anything, but she did spot a flickering light as from a small fire far down the road. At rushed footfalls behind her, she looked back.

Both Chane and Osha closed on her.

"I can hear and see it," Chane said.

—Wagon . . . fall—

Wynn turned back to Shade. "The wagon has overturned?"

Shade huffed once for *yes*.

Wynn held out the device. At first it did nothing, but when she swung her hand left and right, she felt the device try to twist back each time, as if it was out of balance or invisibly longer and heavier on whichever side it wished to turn. It was in full balance only when she pointed straight down the road.

"It's here . . . the orb," she whispered.

Osha stepped up on Shade's far side and peered down the road. Perhaps he could see and hear nearly as well as Chane.

"Shade says the wagon has overturned," she added. "They're delayed, and that means we have a chance to catch them unaware."

"Osha," Chane rasped, "if I come at them from the north side, and you from the south with Shade, we might take out enough before they spot us that the others will surrender . . . or at least I might get to the orb and run."

"That is ridiculous!" Wynn argued. "From my count, the duke has eleven men with him. You'll need me to—"

"You are staying here," Chane cut in.

"Don't even start!" Wynn shot back, and when Shade looked up, she added, "Not you, either!"

Shade still growled, obviously agreeing with Chane, and likely Osha, too, though he remained silent.

Wynn knew she had to put all of them in their place. Shade claimed to have sensed a Fay in the keep, but under the best circumstances, she would do almost anything to keep Wynn from being alone out of the wild. That was where the Fay preferred to appear, out of anyone else's sight.

"Listen," she began again. "You need a distraction, and I—"

Shade suddenly dashed a few strides down the road. She halted, her whole body stiff with her ears fully upright. Wynn didn't even have time to follow or ask anything, for Shade whirled and charged back, snarling. Wynn retreated two steps in reflex.

Osha rushed in and held out his bow to block Shade. "What she do?"

Wynn held out her hand, trying to halt the dog, and then she stiffened at one memory-word in her mind.

—Undead!—

Shade looked to Chane, and Wynn couldn't help but do so. Chane was staring down the road and turned only his eyes to her.

"She senses something more, yes?" he asked.

Wynn hesitated before she answered. "She says there's an undead out there."

"Undead?" Chane repeated.

"Is it Sau'ilahk?" Wynn asked, turning to Shade. "Is it the wraith?"

A moment passed before . . . *—Different—*

"Undead?" Osha repeated as well.

He had not heard—nor would he have understood—the earlier exchange between herself and Chane in the wagon's back. Chane appeared somewhat stunned, or as much as she could tell from his posture and eyes. Perhaps he had donned all the gear without really considering how someone could have located the orb of Spirit hidden among Aupsha's sect.

"What do you mean, 'different'?" Wynn asked Shade. "Like Chane?"

—No . . . Different—

"What is wrong?" Chane demanded.

Wynn shook her head. "I think Shade doesn't know . . . or isn't sure, whatever it is. Only that it's some kind of undead, perhaps one she has never sensed before."

Chane stepped straight at her. "Enough! Shade, take Wynn back to the keep now."

Wynn backed away, almost ramming into Osha, and held out the staff like a spear. "I'm not going anywhere!" she warned.

Chane halted barely beyond the staff's crystal.

"What happen?" Osha asked, looking among everyone before fixing on Wynn. "What new danger to you?"

With a grimace, Wynn rapidly explained a little about Sau'ilahk, the wraith who had tracked her over the past year, and his possible presence here.

"But that's not what Shade senses," she added. "Even if he or some other undead is out there, I have the only weapon that will work against any undead. They cannot get to me, so long as I can use the sun crystal."

Still watching her, Chane let out a breathy hiss.

"We do this my way," she said. "The orb means more than any overprotective nonsense from any of you! Chane, take the north side, as you said, but Osha goes with you."

Both of them tensed.

"Not another word!" she warned. "Take a position where you can see the wagon and whoever is there and then try to spot the orb. It will probably be covered or in a container, and you both know the rough size of one. Shade and I will cut through the south-side trees. If Sau'ilahk—or any undead—tries to come for me, Shade will know and I'll ignite the staff. If not, once Shade and I close on the wagon from the south, I'll ignite the staff anyway."

She paused, waiting for her words to sink in—or for any more futile arguments.

"If Sau'ilahk isn't here or doesn't attack," she continued, "igniting the staff will cause chaos, maybe momentarily blinding some guards. Osha, do not look for me or to the south, as only Chane has protection for his eyes. Once the staff ignites, Chane goes for the orb. Osha, you keep the remaining guards off of him. Once you two have it, get out of there and don't look back. Shade and I will meet you at our wagon."

For a few breaths no one spoke, and she finally asked, "Agreed?"

It wasn't really a question.

Wynn knew this was the best they could do with this unexpected opportunity. Each of her companions had reasons for not trusting the others, even though Shade and Chane had learned to work together. All of them, including Osha, had reasons for staying close to her, and those reasons were now getting in her way.

Wynn noticed that Osha didn't have the bundled sword on his back this time. He must have left it in the back of the wagon.

Chane was still glowering, but his gaze finally shifted. "Shade, one more thing."

He reached over to remove his left glove, exposing the ring of nothing on his left middle finger. This arcane object shielded his nature as an undead from anyone or anything with the capability of sensing him—such as Shade. Obviously he was giving the dog fair warning, for he pulled the ring off.

"I want all my senses unimpeded," he explained, "and I do not care who or what senses me. If there is an undead out there, my presence may draw it out."

Wynn wasn't certain she liked that. Shade grumbled only once, for by now she'd become accustomed to suddenly sensing Chane's true nature when he removed the ring.

Chane tucked the ring into his coin pouch and dropped that inside his shirt. As he slipped his left glove back on, he looked directly at Shade.

"Howl at the first hint of an undead anywhere near you."

Shade's jowl twitched with an indignant growl at that unneeded reminder.

Osha didn't look happy at any of these arrangements, but he didn't argue, either.

Wynn ignored all of them; the only thing that mattered was the orb. "And don't kill the duke unless you have to," she added. "Take him alive."

With his hand on the man's chest, Sau'ilahk held Guardsman Comeau pinned against a tree. Comeau's flesh aged and his hair turned ashen as his life drained away. Sau'ilahk stepped back, fully sated, and Comeau's withered form crumpled in the night forest.

Sau'ilahk ignored Hazh'thüm and the other two Suman guards watching fearfully out among the trees. He tilted his head and listened for the keep guards somewhere off in the forest on the road's south side.

Would mere keep guards, likely no more than country peasants with a little training, be able to catch an assassin who seemingly moved on the wind? Should he attempt to create a servitor to search as well? What specific but simple instructions could he give such an elemental construct to find what the guards might not?

Nothing he pondered justified wasting his bolstered energies, and only mundane solutions remained. Of the wagon's two horses, one was now dead, and the other was tangled and hobbled beyond use. But the mounts of the keep's guards were still sound.

"Hazh'thüm," he called, walking off toward the orb's trunk. "Gather the saddled horses and bring them here."

He did not even have to look, for he heard his servant guards rushing through the trees behind him. Perhaps they wondered whether killing him was even possible now. They knew only what he had once been . . . an untouchable being of death who commanded them.

A simple but effective plan was the only recourse. He would tie the orb's trunk and the treasury chest to one horse and then take another mount for himself. That left only two mounts, and obviously one was for Hazh'thüm. The fourth he would leave behind as a tease for the other two Sumans to use together, if they survived in covering his escape.

A noble of Witeny appearing before others of his rank but without adequate guards would only add credence to a tale of insurrection.

Wynn crept behind Shade through the south-side trees, as the dog had much better vision at night. Shade understood the plan as well as anyone and always remained just within sight of the road.

"This is about the orb," Wynn whispered, "not me. You remember that."

Shade didn't answer.

Gripping the staff was difficult for Wynn while still holding on to Jausiff's device. But she wasn't about to lose contact with it, for fear it might go dormant. If something went wrong, she might still need the device to track the orb.

Shade suddenly stalled, and Wynn bumped into the dog's haunches and stumbled. Hesitant to speak, she reached down and touched Shade's back.

—Men . . . walking . . . in the trees—

From what little Wynn could see, she and Shade were only halfway to a position directly across from the wagon. It was vital that they get into position in time to blind the guards for the orb's retrieval. She hoped Chane and Osha were already set.

Wynn closed her fingers in Shade's fur to push the dog onward.

The snap of a branch carried through the trees.

She quickly dropped low, and her eyes followed as Shade's head swung. The dog backed up into her.

—Ahead . . . to . . . right—

Wynn peeked over Shade but saw nothing in the dark forest. Then she heard twigs and leaves crackling damply underfoot. Between the low branches of one tree and the thickly barked trunk of another, she spotted a lighter shape moving.

A keep guard in a gray tabard came forward in halting steps as he looked about. A moment later another appeared farther off to the left and halfway to the road.

Wynn wondered what they were doing out here. Had she given herself away somehow?

"Distract them," Wynn whispered. "Draw them away from me."

—No— . . . —Not . . . leave you—

Wynn yanked on Shade's tail. All Shade did was swing her head around, bare her teeth, and refuse to move.

"All right!" Wynn whispered. "Get us around them . . . without being seen!"

And if that failed, well, she would have to use the staff sooner than planned.

With a huff of agreement, Shade veered away from the road and deeper into the forest.

Chane made good time, and Osha had no trouble keeping up. It did not take long before they spotted the overturned wagon by a fire burning near it. As they crept closer, Chane heard a horse whinny. He ducked low behind some brush among the trees when he spotted the tall Suman with the close beard leading four saddled horses between the wagon's near side and the tree line.

Two other Sumans and Duke Beáumie stood waiting.

"Down at . . . feet," Osha whispered behind him.

Chane rose a little and saw a small trunk and an even smaller chest at the duke's feet.

As the Sumans struggled to get the horses close, Chane looked about for any keep guards. He saw none, and this bothered him, for there should have been five. Where were they? Moments passed as the Sumans stood talking lowly among themselves, and one produced a rope.

Chane gripped the dark glasses dangling against his chest. Wynn should be in position by now, but nothing happened. He remained waiting, and the only sound that took him by surprise was when Osha pulled an arrow and fitted it to his bow.

Talk among the Suman guards ended abruptly. Two of them lifted the trunk and managed to settle it atop a horse's saddle. The third began uncoiling a rope and preparing to tie the trunk down.

Chane grew instantly edgy. Between the trunk's size and that of the smaller chest, only the former was big enough to hold an orb, and it was heavy enough, judging by the way it was handled. One of the Suman guards let go of his end and turned, though he cowered strangely before the duke as he retrieved the smaller chest.

There was no time left for Wynn's plan.

Chane glanced over his shoulder at Osha. "We cannot wait. We must—"

Osha rose suddenly. Drawing his bowstring, he fired.

Wynn had gained only a short distance deeper into the forest when Shade halted and backed into her knees. The wind rustled too many branches, and it was two breaths before she heard what had stalled Shade. With booted steps ahead, another keep guard came into sight between the trees to the south.

Wynn ducked back behind the low branches of a fir tree as Shade retreated to join her. How many guards were out here—and why?

"Anything?" the man called softly, and his voice sounded familiar.

"No, sir," another answered, even closer off to Wynn's left.

There were at least three of them now, and they were spread out. With no way to tell whether more were out here, Wynn realized that sneaking past this many wasn't going to work.

—Chane . . . waiting—

Wynn almost uttered a frustrated retort. Yes, Chane had to be in place by now and was likely wondering when she would act. She had to do something—something desperate—and she crouched to whisper in Shade's ear.

"When I say, charge the closer guard to the left. You're dark enough that he may not see you at first. Snarl and growl all you want but do not howl. The first guard's shouts should draw the other two. Once they come running, I'll be right behind and flash the crystal once. That should blind them for an instant, and hopefully Chane and Osha will act while we run for the wagon."

Shade growled low, but not a word popped into Wynn's head. Wynn hoped a short flash wouldn't panic Chane into thinking she was under attack. If she and Shade could hold these guards here for a moment, it might be enough for Chane and Osha to do as she expected.

Wynn knew she couldn't risk using her glasses with their near-black lenses. While holding the device and the staff, she wouldn't have a chance to pull them off before she had to run. In her thoughts she replayed the Sumanese phrases that Domin il'Sänke had taught her to ignite the staff's crystal.

From Spirit to Fire . . . for the Light of Life.

"Go," she whispered.

Shade ducked rightward around the tree and then veered left to weave around behind the underbrush. Wynn slipped the other way around the broad fir to hide from the guard ahead and the one deeper in the trees on the right.

All she heard at first was the infrequent soft rustling of brush in Shade's passage.

"What's that?" called the guard nearest the road. "Stay there, whoever—"

A snarl and clack of jaws was followed by a scream.

Wynn shuddered as shouts rose in the dark. She heard the other guards tearing through the brush toward the growls. She waited until the first of the footfalls was directly inland and east of her. She was already shouting in Sumanese as she rushed out.

"Mên Rúhk el-När . . . mênajil il'Núr'u mên'Hkâ'ät!"

With the last word, Wynn clenched her eyes shut.

The burst of light from the staff's crystal was still sharp through her eyelids. Light quickly faded, and she opened her eyes and ran for the last place she'd heard Shade. And there was Shade, facing away toward a downed guard, who rolled on the ground with his hands over his face.

Even as Wynn closed from behind, Shade didn't move. About to urge the dog to run on, Wynn saw Shade's hackles on end and her ears flattened.

Shade snarled, and Wynn followed the line of the dog's muzzle.

A dozen paces ahead, someone else stood among the trees.

The shadowy figure held one forearm before the hood of its long cloak as if shielding its face. Even before that arm lowered, Wynn thought there was something strange about it. Why was the bracer on its forearm so darkly colored instead of shimmering like steel?

The arm lowered to chin level and exposed a masked face.

Wynn tensed at the sight of Aupsha in her way. The mask and the cloak's hood made it too hard to see the woman's eyes.

Then someone shouted, "Over there!"

Wynn glanced toward the sound of the voice, and when she looked back ahead, in place of Aupsha's dark masked and cloaked form was a fading apparition. It vanished like dust—or sand—blown away on the wind.

All Wynn heard was the wind and the shouts of approaching guards as she leaned close to Shade.

"Run!" she whispered.

* * *

Sau'ilahk grew anxious even in certainty that he had made the right choices. All four horses stood before him, and two of his Sumans had lifted the trunk as Hazh'thüm prepared to tie it down.

The guard on the horse's near side suddenly squealed.

A black-feathered arrow appeared to sprout from his right haunch.

Sau'ilahk flinched in a back step.

The man released his end of the orb's trunk, and the trunk fell before the guard on the horse's far side could get a better grip. Hazh'thüm drew his sword and ducked behind the horse and out of sight. The guard in pain spun wildly, crying out again and grabbing at the arrow in his buttock, and the orb's trunk hit the ground and rolled down the roadside's slant.

Sau'ilahk rushed the other way.

He slipped behind the low branches of a roadside pine tree and carefully inched out to peer into the woods. He tried to trace the arrow's trajectory from what he remembered of its angle when it struck, but he could not be certain and saw nothing among the trees.

A flash of light erupted in the forest to the south.

Sau'ilahk spun about. The overturned wagon blocked his view across the road, and the light had already faded, but it *had* come from somewhere in the south-side trees.

What had caused it? And who had fired that arrow out of the forest now behind him?

Backing farther around the pine, he inched along to look around the wagon's front and the downed horses.

A cloaked figure rushed at him around the pine's inland side, but all he saw in that instant was a mask inside a hood.

Chane bit down in anger as Osha's arrow hit home, for he had not been ready. He pulled his glasses up into place, drew both swords, and charged through the forest as the struck guard cried out again. Even with Chane's sight widened by hunger, it was hard for him to see through the glasses.

A burst of light came as he passed directly south of the wagon.

Chane barely flinched in reflex, for the flash had already died out. It had not come from close enough to the road's south side. But he had agreed that, no matter what, he would use that distraction to get to the orb, and Shade had not howled in warning.

Chane stalled for an instant this time, for he felt something.

That tiny sudden emptiness made the beast within him stir and rumble. Had this been what Shade had sensed from far up the road? It did not feel like any undead he had ever been near. He angled right and rushed out upon the roadside inland from the wagon.

There was Duke Beáumie, and the duke saw him in turn.

One Suman guard—the one with the close-cut beard—came running, and Chane charged with a sword in each hand.

Sau'ilahk spun away, stumbling and slapping through the pine's branches. How had that windblown assailant gotten around him to attack from behind? Sword in hand, Hazh'thüm came rushing past him along the wagon.

"Kill him if you must!" Sau'ilahk shouted. "Pin him if you can."

If possible, he wanted to know who this lurker was before taking his life, and why and how that one kept appearing suddenly on the wind.

As Hazh'thüm continued his charge, Sau'ilahk paused to follow with his eyes.

The attacker did not look like the one who had earlier killed two of his men.

This one was cloaked and masked but taller than the first and broader shouldered. Instead of a curved Suman dagger, he wielded two straight-bladed swords, one long and one short. With almost a lack of effort, he swung with the shortsword first.

The blade collided with Hazh'thüm's first strike and blocked it. Instantly the assailant brought the longer blade up and across. Hazh'thüm tried to slip his curved sword's hilt up to catch the second strike on his own blade. The masked one rammed his shorter blade forward along Hazh'thüm's sword with a screech of steel.

The shortsword's tip bit into Hazh'thüm's abdomen. The longer one came across high and struck his neck. His head was gone in a spatter of blood.

Sau'ilahk spotted the head only when it struck the wagon's upturned bench and then tumbled to the ground before . . . Hazh'thüm's body dropped, and the curved sword fell out of his limp hand. Sau'ilahk did not take his eyes off the newcomer.

The masked figure stalked toward him. Sau'ilahk retreated farther. Only then did he truly see inside the attacker's hood.

Black-lensed glasses covered the eyeholes of a leather mask.

Sau'ilahk stalled in shock at the sight of Chane Andraso.

Wildly he looked around, but he had only two Sumans left—and only one of them was able-bodied. That one was running toward the trunk, and the wounded one dove out of sight behind the broken wagon.

Sau'ilahk needed to act.

He thrust out both hands and envisioned nested shapes, sigils, and symbols in his mind's eye.

CHAPTER TWENTY

Chane took in everything as one Suman ran toward the trunk—but he lost sight of the guard Osha had wounded. There were four saddled horses; a small chest lay beside one of them, and the slightly larger trunk had rolled off the roadside. The running Suman skidded to a stop behind the trunk with his sword drawn as the duke backed up to the right of the man.

But where were the keep guards?

Chane felt that same tiny emptiness in his gut.

The beast within him lunged to the end of its bonds as he stalled longer in staring at Karl Beáumie. What he felt now was impossible. His senses told him the duke was a living man; he could smell this. Even if he had still worn the ring of nothing, he would have sensed an undead this close, if not sooner. Then he spotted the ruddy *thôrhk*—an orb key—around the duke's neck.

"Step away from that trunk, both of you!" he rasped.

Instead the duke thrust both hands outward as his mouth began to work without a sound.

Nothing learned so far suggested the man had arcane skills. Then those silent utterances became whispers.

"Osha!" Chane rasped as loudly as he could. "His hand!"

* * *

Osha reached over his shoulder as Chane charged and felt for an arrow without a thread ridge above its feathers—one without a white metal tip. He pulled and fit it to the bowstring in one movement as he shifted laterally from tree to tree for a better line of sight. And he listened for any sound in the forest.

Too few guards of any kind were in sight, compared to the reported number that had left with the duke. One Suman stood over the trunk while another partially hid behind one of the saddled horses, but Osha saw not a single keep guard. Suddenly the Suman that he had hit with the first arrow came back into view—from a position crouched behind the upturned wagon—and this one reached for his sword.

Osha's next arrow hit the thigh of the man's same leg.

The Suman screamed out as he collapsed.

Hoping this might keep the other one near the trunk where he was, Osha drew another normal-tipped arrow as he shifted again.

He heard steel clash against steel just once and, when his sight line cleared again, he spotted Chane through the trees. Too much had changed in that instant, and a headless Suman lay on the ground.

Duke Beáumie faced away from Osha, and his empty hands were outstretched toward Chane, perhaps in fear and trying to hold off the undead.

Osha took aim at the armed Suman standing over the trunk.

"Osha!" Chane rasped. "His hand!"

Osha hesitated, quickly checking everything. Did that mean the duke or the Suman guard?

Then the duke's head turned.

It took an instant before his gaze fixed. There was intent—not fear—in his eyes, and he twisted around with his hands outstretched toward Osha.

Osha's aim shifted as the air between the duke's hands began to warp. Before he could loose the arrow, fire erupted at the duke's feet and then raced out through the trees straight at Osha.

Osha held his place as he released the bowstring.

* * *

Sau'ilahk spotted the elven archer out between the trees and immediately turned his conjuration on that new target. Flames erupted at his feet and raced into the forest.

His right hand lurched violently aside, and he cried out in sudden pain.

Shock chilled him at the sight of an arrow's shaft through his malformed hand . . . and then he heard Chane coming.

Whirling back the other way, he saw his last able guard attempt to engage Chane . . . and actually block Chane's first swing. The fight would likely last only a few moments at best.

Sau'ilahk reflexively reached for the duke's sword on his hip, but he possessed no skill with such a weapon, and his hand was wounded, still impaled with an arrow. He was injured and outnumbered, and his body was not yet immortal. He doubted he could lift or drag the trunk with only his left hand.

The key he had once used to find an orb was still around his neck. He could use it again if need be.

With a hard swing, Chane sliced through the guard's chest, and the man went down.

Sau'ilahk ran into the forest.

The instant the arrow left the bow, Osha threw himself aside. In his roll, he heard low branches and fallen leaves crackling as a heat struck his back. He came to his feet, still scrambling away before he turned.

All that was left of the racing line of fire were sizzling sounds, smoke, and bushes burning here and there. His first instinct as an'Cróan was to stomp out every last flame before the forest caught fire. Instead he drew another arrow and looked back along the fire's path.

He spotted neither the duke nor Chane nor anyone through the smoke-hazed darkness.

Shock vanished at how the duke, a mere man, could send fire out of nothing into trees.

Osha fitted another normal steel-tipped arrow to his bow's string and held it in place with the first finger of his bow hand as he ran for the road by the shortest route.

"Chane!" he shouted.

As he broke through onto the roadside a dozen paces west of the wagon, he did not have a chance to look for the undead.

The black majay-hì—and then Wynn—burst out of the forest on the road's south side at a run. Osha veered toward them and then skidded to a stop as Captain Martelle came out on their heels.

Another guard came right behind the captain, and both men had swords in hand.

Wynn ran on for the overturned wagon, but Shade wheeled when she reached the road's center.

Osha would never let anyone harm Wynn, or a majay-hì, but he hesitated at shooting men who were deceived in their duty.

He aimed and fired in front of the captain.

When the arrow struck the road, the captain stumbled in trying to halt, and the guard following behind collided into him. Both lost their balance and struggled to keep their feet.

Osha had already fitted another arrow and drawn it back, but he would not fire unless he had to. As he was about to warn them off, a swirl of dust passed him and rushed down the road.

A shape took form within it, and Osha stalled longer.

Dust in the darkness faded and a slender, cloaked figure clubbed the keep guard at a run. The guard collapsed as the figure halted two steps beyond him and turned.

Osha barely made out a mask obscuring the face within the cloak's hood, but he did not mistake it for Chane.

Aupsha lunged before the captain could spin around—or Osha could take a clean shot.

She clubbed the captain with the heavy, dirt-coated branch in her hand. The blow struck the side of his head, and he went down and still in a blink. Shouts rose in the trees beyond the road's far side.

Expecting more guards, Osha glanced away in less than a blink, and when he looked back . . .

Aupsha was gone.

He had no more time to ponder the way the masked woman had appeared. He ran for where Wynn had likely run behind the upturned wagon.

Wynn never slowed, knowing Shade would harry the guards long enough. She rounded the downed horses and ran behind the upturned wagon. Most of the flames from a fallen lantern were dying out, but . . .

A headless body in a yellow tabard stalled her. Another body in yellow lay not far beyond the first.

Chane stood between one Suman still alive on the ground and a trunk toppled on its side. The Suman leaned up against the wagon's vertical bed just beyond another dead guard pinned under the wagon. He cowered away from the point of Chane's longsword. A black-feathered arrow protruded from his thigh . . . and another from his haunch.

Chane's head turned, and he pulled his glasses down upon spotting her. Only his eyes showed a little through the holes in his leather mask. She heard someone coming behind her and turned, ready to flash the staff's crystal.

It was only Osha, and he stopped behind the downed horses, spinning around as he drew and aimed his bow back toward the open road.

"Shade!" he shouted.

The dog appeared within a breath and raced in at Wynn's side.

Wynn had no idea what had happened here, but any relief that they'd all survived was short. The duke was nowhere to be seen, and she hurried to Chane.

He didn't even look down and merely grabbed her forearm to pull her away from the wounded Suman as he tilted his head once toward the trunk.

"Open it quickly," he said. "See that it contains the orb."

"Wait," Wynn countered. "Where is the duke?"

Shade started clawing at the trunk, and Osha soon came to help her. Wynn looked back and up to Chane, for he still hadn't answered.

"Where's the duke?" she repeated.

"Run into trees," Osha answered instead, but Wynn still waited on Chane.

He brushed back his hood, stripped off his mask, and stuffed it into his belt. As he took a step toward the forest, she shifted Jausiff's device to her other hand, holding it and the staff as she grabbed his arm with her free hand.

"Osha is correct," Chane said. "But . . . perhaps so was Shade . . . somehow."

Wynn didn't know what that meant, but she let go of him and looked warily in all directions.

"Sau'ilahk is here?" she asked quietly.

There was a long pause. "No."

She looked up and found Chane, with his longer dwarven sword in hand, still watching the trees.

"I sensed—felt—something," he said almost absently. "I could smell the duke, and he was alive . . . but . . ." His narrowed eyes shifted toward Shade.

"Did the duke have an orb key?" Wynn asked.

Finally Chane looked down at her. "Yes. You stay with Shade and Osha and—"

As Chane's gaze shifted again, Wynn followed it.

Both Shade and Osha had backed off from the opened trunk. There inside of it was the dark form of a globe and a spike, as if carved from one piece of stone.

"Get it to our wagon and guard it!" Chane rasped.

He took off into the forest before Wynn could make him explain the strange things he had said. Osha rose, bow in one hand with another arrow fitted to its slack string, and he stared after Chane.

"We have the orb, so the duke is no longer needed," he said in Elvish. "Why did Chane go after him?"

Wynn ignored this and looked down at Shade. If the duke knew how to manipulate an orb with a key, had he also learned—from the wraith or on his own—how to use a key to track an orb?

"Go!" she told Shade. "Help Chane get that orb key, no matter what."

Shade hesitated, but perhaps she knew enough to value what was at stake. Leaving Wynn and Osha alone with the orb, she bolted off after Chane.

"Martelle and that other guard could awaken any moment," she told Osha. "There are more keep guards out there . . . and Aupsha. We need to move now."

Osha crouched and grabbed one end handle of the trunk, then waited for her to do likewise as he eyed the one Suman left alive. Wynn didn't turn to look at that man, who'd been watching and listening.

How much of what had been said had that one understood? What else, if anything, might he know to connect to what he'd heard? Her thoughts turned darker than she would have ever imagined.

That guard should not be left alive.

One living horse tangled in the wagon's harness kicked and whinnied.

Wynn turned, looking at it lying half across its dead companion. It kicked again uselessly into the air with one forehoof. There was no time to worry about such a thing while trying to safeguard an artifact—a potential weapon—sought by the Ancient Enemy's minions.

And yet . . . too many innocents always ended up suffering in her wake.

"Osha, give me your dagger."

As he held it out, she hesitated and looked down at Jausiff's device, which she still gripped along with her staff. She had the orb, but she was reluctant to let go of the slightly curved central piece of another orb key. It would go dormant when she did so, and she did not know how to reactivate it. It could be of so much use in finding the final orb, but she certainly couldn't hold on to it endlessly until then.

Tucking the device inside her robe, Wynn let go of it after another brief hesitation. She took the dagger from Osha, but then stalled in eyeing that one Suman now warily watching her.

"Bârtva'na!" Osha whispered in an'Cróan—*Do not.*

Wynn didn't look at him and went off to cut the horse free.

Chane ran through the trees with his senses fully widened. He paused every thirty strides to listen, but he did not hear any movement ahead. Then he heard something coming behind him, and ducked behind a bramble.

When he heard earth tearing under claws, he rose and stepped into the open even before Shade raced out around a moss-laden oak. At least she had not howled in her hunt, though perhaps she did not sense what she had on the road. However, he was not pleased that only Osha remained to guard Wynn.

This provided all the more reason to find the duke as quickly as possible.

Shade did not slow and raced straight by Chane.

He stared after her before he realized she might track their quarry better than he could. He took off after her and exerted himself to keep up—to keep Shade's tail in sight. Not that he needed to do so, for he would have heard her from a distance by the way she tore through the brush. Perhaps so would the duke.

Shade suddenly swerved.

When Chane caught up to where he had last seen her, she was gone. The whole forest was silent as he peered around the fringe of a clearing. His gaze finally locked on a dim form in the darkness who was watching him from the clearing's far side.

The duke must have realized that running was pointless.

The arrow was gone from his right hand. Perhaps he had snapped and pulled it out midflight, but that gloved hand looked wrong more than wounded. Its black leather bulged, as if the hand had swollen too much, and the ends of the glove's fingers were split open.

Chane did not see bloodied fingertips. Dark talons protruded in their place.

The duke suddenly raised his other hand outward as his mouth began to work.

Chane was too far away to hear clearly. He charged into the clearing to close the distance before the duke could unleash another line of racing fire. For an instant he almost remembered seeing that effect once before.

Violent wind slammed in all around Chane and almost twisted him off his feet.

Leaves and debris from the ground swirled up around him and blinded him as he stumbled. Almost instantly, painful droplets of water whirled in to pelt him harder and harder until he felt their sting too much. Everywhere he tried to look, he ended up shielding his eyes and face as those droplets began turning into wind-driven hail.

He no longer saw, smelled, or heard anything in the wind's roar except the crackle of branches around the clearing's edge. He whipped his longsword all around and tried to draw the older short one as he fought to regain a sense of direction. Even when he tried to run blindly, the pelting and hammering maelstrom still engulfed him.

Either the duke was trying to gain time to flee or to hobble him in order to . . .

Chane kept slashing with his sword as he turned every way to keep from being assaulted from behind. Amid panic, something else came to him.

This spell or . . . whatever . . . was too much for a mere dabbler such as himself. He had even heard of a thaumaturge who could manipulate the atmosphere in this way. Without many years of training, the duke could not have the knowledge and skill for this arcane effect—and less so for a spell rather than a ritual or using an object made through artificing.

Chane picked one direction and tried to run in a straight line. He had to reach the cover of the trees. He stretched out both swords ahead of himself in the hope that one might hit something to warn him before he did so.

The wind turned to a roar in his ears.

His face and hands began to burn as pelting hail turned to bits of ice. Hunger rose to eat the pain, and the beast within him began wailing in fear as well as in fury . . . until Chane thought he *heard* that sound with his own ears.

The wind suddenly died. Though his ears still rang with its roar, he heard branches and leaves rattle under a sudden rain of hail and ice chips falling to the ground. Then came a familiar wail—no, a howl—all around him.

And then a scream . . . and then a snarl . . . and the tearing of cloth.

Chane spun toward those sounds as wild hunger made the night too bright in his eyes.

A huge black dog—wolf—tumbled toward the clearing's center. It righted onto all fours and charged back toward a man dressed in black who was scrambling up to his feet.

Chane barely recognized Shade. Amid hunger fueled by panic and rage, he knew only that she went at his target, his enemy . . . his prey in the moment. His lips curled back from extended fangs, and he charged.

Sau'ilahk called upon his reserves, bolstering his flesh. The sensation was like nothing he had felt before, as if his sinews heated within and his bones grew dense. He willed the lives he had consumed to spread through the duke's body . . . his new body.

The dog had taken him by surprise. Gouges atop his right shoulder from her teeth still burned, and Shade came again, leaping for his face as her jaws widened.

Sau'ilahk lashed out with his deformed hand.

His talons struck along her neck as her jaws snapped closed on his forearm. The pain was nothing to him as he slashed, tossing her aside as if she weighed a fraction of what truly she did. She hit the clearing's earth to his right and yelped as she rolled. On instinct he grabbed the hilt of the sheathed sword on his hip.

There was no pain anymore in his arrow-wounded hand.

Sau'ilahk had been the highest of Beloved's priests, not a warrior. But he did not need to be so to sever the head of a beaten dog. He drew the blade and took one step, and then he saw Chane Andraso coming. He barely raised his sword up at the first strike of Chane's longsword.

At the impact of the steel, he wrenched his own sword aside and let his bolstered strength add extra force.

To his shock, Chane whipped a shorter sword across and down on both of their longer, entangled blades.

Sau'ilahk's sword was torn from his hand.

In the same instant teeth clamped hard around his right calf.

He struck down as he closed his empty sword hand, and his fist connected with an audible crack against the dog's head. He kicked her away, and she made no sound as she tumbled off.

Sau'ilahk saw Chane's gaze flick toward the dog as his broken voice rasped something. He used the instant of distraction and grabbed both of Chane's wrists. Squeezing his grips tight, he summoned the last reserves he had left.

Chane's eyes widened as his face wrinkled in pain. Even his lips spread wide around a mouth full of fangs and teeth . . . like the dog's. Both swords dropped from his hands, and Sau'ilahk twisted, trying to snap Chane's wrists.

Chane's hands closed on Sau'ilahk's own forearms and locked their holds together.

Sau'ilahk was sick of dealing with Wynn Hygeorht's minions. He would make one of them falter.

"I will take back all that is mine," he whispered at Chane, "and then take your little sage from you—finally!"

Some small part of Chane quieted inside. He stalled for an instant as his mind cleared.

Those words meant something . . . that brought memories and fear.

Fire had raced in a controlled line into the forest toward Osha. Chane had seen that before in the underworld of the Stonewalkers, when he, Wynn, and Shade had sought out clues to any remaining orbs' locations.

An orb had been found in a lost dwarven seatt of ancient times. And again he and Wynn, along with Shade and Ore-Locks, had been seeking it out. But the key to that orb was missing when he and Ore-Locks had gone for it.

Both times Sau'ilahk had been there.

Chane's gaze locked on the *thôrhk*—the handle, the orb key—around the duke's neck. . . . *And take your little sage from you . . .*

Karl Beáumie knew Chane only as a hired guard, but those words implied something else. Shade had sensed an undead, as Chane had, but like no other that either of them had faced.

The only one he faced here and now was the duke.

Chane looked into Karl Beáumie's manic eyes, and what he thought then was impossible.

The duke suddenly wrenched and pulled down on his right linked grip as he shoved hard on the left one.

Chane spun around the duke and lost his footing.

The force was too immense for a living man, and Chane did not regain his stance quickly enough. The duke drove him backward toward the trees at the clearing's edge.

Wynn laid her staff aside to cut free the one living horse harnessed to the wagon. As it thrashed up, she grabbed her staff and quickly backed away. All four of its legs appeared sound, though its left shoulder had a deep slash, among other cuts and mud smears, and blood from its dead companion was spattered across its body. It would have to fend for itself and, she hoped, find its way back to the keep.

Wynn turned back. Wind pulled at the hood of her robe as she faced into it.

There was Osha, with his bow in hand and an arrow held fitted to its string, standing halfway between her and the orb's trunk. For one moment she had thought to kill the last Suman guard for secrecy's sake. Osha had somehow known and stopped her.

He had changed much because of what had been done to him. In the time Wynn had spent in his world, he had seemed kinder and more moral—even for an anmaglâhk—than anyone she had ever known. That hadn't changed, not completely, and, knowing that the wounded Suman was still watching, she glanced toward the orb's chest.

She wondered if Osha's choice had been wise. Perhaps it would cause a problem in what might come, though she didn't question it now.

Osha suddenly spun the other way and drew the arrow back as he aimed toward . . .

Air swirled with dust, or maybe grains like sand, and the wounded Suman choked and covered his face with an arm as it passed.

Wynn dropped Osha's dagger and gripped her staff with both hands as a figure formed out of dust in the night.

"Do not move!" Osha ordered.

Aupsha stood there, cloaked and masked, and glanced once toward the freed horse. She then looked at only Wynn and ignored Osha entirely.

"The artifact belongs with my people," she said.

Wynn hesitated—not at those words but rather at what she had just seen. Aupsha appeared to come and go at will, and yet she hadn't gone straight after the orb. Was she here to explain herself, to try to take it through reason?

"No," Wynn answered. "I know as much about the . . . artifacts . . . as you and yours, perhaps more. I, and those with me, have successfully found and hidden three of them. Your people cannot safeguard even one anymore. It would be found—again."

Perhaps she said too much, though the woman had already heard about the orb of Earth, another "artifact." Wynn simply needed to make an impression and avoid more bloodshed. Aupsha might be an opponent in the moment, but she and hers were not enemies as yet.

"You *think* you know more?" Aupsha asked with spite. "Then you know the artifact must not—cannot—be destroyed. And it must not be used again."

Wynn faltered at this hint of new information. She had contemplated whether any of the orbs could be destroyed, but why "must not," and what did that mean?

"My people guarded it for an age," Aupsha continued, "from the time of our honored—and sacred—forebearer, who stole it at the cost of his life. We will guard it again and forever."

A reply caught in Wynn's throat. The mention of anything—or anyone—known from the war or the time of the Forgotten History tempted the sage in Wynn with many questions. But any delay would only give Aupsha a chance to act.

What mattered most—first—was taking control of that orb, and yet . . .

"What are your people called?" Wynn blurted out.

Even through that mask, Wynn heard Aupsha's choked scoff before the answer.

"We do not *call* ourselves anything . . . to be known or sought!"

At a sudden thrashing of brush from the road's far side, Wynn backed up, glancing around the upturned wagon's front. A keep guard with a sword in hand stumbled out of the forest onto the road's southern side. His head was bleeding, and Wynn quickly glanced back at Aupsha.

Had the woman in the mask gone back and attacked the remaining guards? That would explain their absence until now.

Aupsha retreated slowly, and Osha tracked her with his bow as she looked around the wagon's rear. Wynn glanced back to the road.

The newly arrived guard halted at the sight of Captain Martelle and one of his comrades lying in the road. His gaze lifted to Wynn, and then his head turned sharply toward the wagon's far end; he had likely spotted Aupsha.

The guard's features twisted in anger.

Out of the corner of Wynn's eye, she saw Aupsha move.

"Osha!" she shouted.

Then all she saw was Osha's arrow fly, striking nothing but air, for Aupsha was too fast. Osha took off for the wagon's rear, as Wynn sped around the other end and startled the injured horse.

"No!" she shouted, thrusting out the staff's crystal, but it was too late to ignite it.

Aupsha reached the guard as his sword came around. She blocked the strike with a curved dagger, its blade flattened along her forearm. In the same instant, she struck into his chest with her other hand and her momentum. He went down.

"Aupsha, don't!" Wynn shouted as Osha came out on the road beyond the wagon's far end. "They've been tricked, only following false orders."

Wynn saw Osha draw back his next arrow.

Aupsha turned, running west up the road and into the wind, and Osha did not fire as she passed him in her escape. Her form suddenly came apart like dust and sand, and she vanished, blown away by the breeze.

Osha turned back and bolted around his end of the wagon, and Wynn quickly did the same. She barely reached the roadside to peer behind the upturned wagon.

Aupsha was there, gripping one end of the orb's trunk as Osha reappeared beyond her. Wynn didn't have a chance to even raise her staff.

As she had on the road, Aupsha vanished like dust, along with the trunk . . . and the orb.

Wynn cried out in anguish and turned every way until reason took hold. Aupsha had to have come from inland along the road at first. And this time she wasn't just moving unseen among the trees. She was moving on the wind, and that would limit where she could go.

Hearing a groan, Wynn looked back to see Captain Martelle attempting to push himself up with one arm. Osha raced toward her behind the wagon, and Wynn faced him.

"She's moving on—"

"Wind, yes," he finished.

He scrambled up the wagon's wheels before Wynn said more, and he stood on the upper wagon wall as he looked inland along the road.

Pulling the arrow out of his bow without looking, he slipped its steel head back into the quiver over his shoulder. When his hand came back down, Wynn thought he'd pulled out the same again. But the one he now held had a thicker white metal tip.

"She would have an easier time on the road in the dark," she said, this time in Elvish.

"I need more light!" he shouted.

Wynn ran up the roadside to behind the wagon so as not to blind him. She grabbed the glasses dangling around her neck and held them over her eyes as she raised the staff's crystal high.

"Mên Rúhk el-När . . . mênajil il'Núr'u mên'Hkâ'ät!"

A blinding glare ignited behind Osha and lit up everything. Though he had his back to it, the intensity made him squint. His eyes quickly adjusted, and he spotted the whipping dark cloak down the road.

Aupsha had gained too much distance for him to catch up at a run, though she was not running while carrying the heavy trunk. That was good. Perhaps in riding the wind she could not go far with such a burden, and it now slowed her even more.

Osha needed every advantage possible, as he dared not miss, and he drew back a black-feathered arrow with its diamond-shaped Chein'âs point.

His gaze dropped from Aupsha's swinging cloak to the clearer target of her right thigh. He did not aim along the arrow's shaft, as only a beginner would do. He kept his eyes on his chosen target point, let his body adjust the bow's angle by his intention, and then released the string.

Aupsha's cry carried up the road as she fell, and the trunk tumbled from her grasp.

Sau'ilahk drove Chane toward the closest fir tree. Lower branches snapped and shattered as he rammed the maddening undead against the tree's trunk.

Chane's eyes rolled up as bark cracked and shattered under his impact. But Sau'ilahk lost sight of his victim as branches snapped back in around him and needles cascaded down from the shuddering tree.

Feeling Chane's grip on his left wrist falter, Sau'ilahk immediately wrenched his taloned hand free and drew it back. He could not kill an undead with mere claws, but he could slash out Chane's eyes. Once blinded, the tall undead would flounder, and Sau'ilahk could take Chane's head with the duke's sword. And Wynn, in watching for her protector's return, would see only the duke command his own guards to seize her.

And if the guards were not there, she would die even more quickly.

Burning pain suddenly shot through Sau'ilahk's forearm. Teeth pierced his skin, and he screamed more in shock and anger than in pain.

The dog's touch did not burn him as it once had in his spiritual form.

Sau'ilahk had to let go of Chane as Shade wrenched on his arm, and this time he cried out as his skin tore. He closed his left hand in a fist.

Branches still blocked clear sight, but he did not have to see to strike.

At the loud crack of his fist's impact, skin on his other arm tore again. But the jaws came off, and he thrashed out of the branches to find the dog on the ground.

Her eyes were barely open where she lay slack-jawed and motionless.

One of Wynn's precious protectors was dead. There was one more to finish before he could find her.

A hissing rasp rose out of the tree behind him. Sau'ilahk had begun to turn when a heavy weight slammed into his back and drove him face-first to the earth.

Panic and pain more than hunger fed Chane's fury as he fell atop the duke. He had heard Shade attack, and then the duke's grips had torn away one after the other. He had heard the deafening crack of a fist and then nothing more from Shade.

Trying to get free, the duke bucked wildly beneath him. With one hand

Chane slammed the duke's face back into the earth as he fought to keep the man pinned. Chane could feel the damage to his ribs along his back. He could not hold the duke down and still reach one of his swords. Fright and fury brought back all that happened.

The line of fire in the forest . . . the strange, tiny emptiness he had felt . . . Shade halting, poised in the road upon first spotting the overturned wagon . . .

It all nagged him again with what was not possible and yet had to be.

There was no duke anymore; the only thing that could have caused all of this was the wraith.

Somehow, Sau'ilahk had taken a man's flesh.

The wraith had maimed Nikolas, murdered and fed upon young sages, and now killed Shade—and it kept coming for Wynn.

Panic and pain died. Hunger took their place. The beast inside consumed Chane whole, and the night grew brilliant in his eyes.

He snarled his fingers into the duke's—Sau'ilahk's—hair and wrenched his prey's head aside. Diving down hard, he sank his teeth into the exposed side of the neck and throat. Blood welled and leaked from his mouth as his prey went into a frenzy. Chane clamped down until his teeth hit bone.

No euphoria came this time as life filled him. He drank until the thrashing beneath him grew weak. He kept on and on until he heard a beating heart begin to slow.

Chane tore his teeth out before that heart stopped.

He wanted that black spirit to know—*feel*—its last moment. After a thousand years or more, it would die in horror, knowing that it had failed and would never touch Wynn.

The beast within Chane settled into sated contentment.

But there was no such contentment for him as he stared at Shade's still form. Why did he feel such sorrow, such loss, over one born as a natural enemy to his kind? They had tolerated each other only for Wynn's sake.

Slow, shallow wheezing reached Chane's hunger-sharpened ears. He barely noticed it at first beneath the breeze in the forest. Then it caught and rolled, as if the next breath came before the last one could finish—two different, barely audible breaths overlapping each other.

Chane looked down at the torn mess of Sau'ilahk's throat and then back at Shade. Without thinking, he clamped his hand over the duke's mouth and smothered any further breaths until the duke's heart stopped.

Still he heard a weak, slow set of halting breaths.

Chane lunged from his crouch and cleared the distance to drop on all fours beside Shade's limp form. It was painfully long before he heard another shallow breath from her.

Osha jumped from atop the wagon and ran up the road before Wynn could even call to him. The light behind him winked out: she had likely let the staff's crystal fade. It did not matter—he knew exactly where he would find Aupsha lying hobbled.

He kept his eyes on that spot in the dark and drew another arrow with a Chein'âs head as he ran, until he actually saw and closed on her.

Aupsha lay curled on her side and clutching the shaft of the arrow deep in the back of her thigh. She watched him from within her leather mask, and he heard pained panting. Beyond and to the right of her lay the trunk, toppled over on its front.

Osha's relief came at that sight, for the orb that Wynn sought was safe. Almost looking at Aupsha again, he took a step.

A handful of mucky dirt and pebbles struck his face and chest.

He retreated instinctively, swiping the back of his hand across his face. His sight cleared as Aupsha came out of a roll and grabbed one handle of the trunk. He drew back the next arrow, and then she and the trunk came apart.

Aupsha and the trunk blew away in the dark—and the orb was gone again.

Osha stood wide-eyed for an instant. He rushed along the road, keeping the breeze directly against his back, and he followed where it pushed him slightly toward the northern side.

He was not beaten yet. He would not be beaten at all.

From what he had seen when she had first taken the trunk, she could not go far with it.

Osha halted shy of the roadside trees and raised the bow outward while drawing back the arrow set in its string. He waited, feeling for the piece of white metal beneath the bow handle's leather wrap to grow warm and begin to pull in his grip.

He waited for the handle to track the Chein'âs arrowhead embedded in Aupsha's thigh. The bow handle did not move in his hand.

Osha panicked.

On his way to Wynn's homeland, every time he lost an arrow during practice and then sought it out, he had felt the bow try to turn in his grip and lead him when he went astray. Why did it not do so now? He calmed himself and began listening, just as the tainted greimasg'äh had taught him.

Brot'ân'duivé had been merciless, forcing Osha to find every movement of air along any path an arrow could fly. What could not be seen of the air's movement often left something to be heard in its passing. There were also sounds that distinguished anything not caused by even the slightest breeze.

It was dark now without Wynn's light. In his thoughts he noted the position of every form he knew only by the way the air's movement changed its sound.

He heard underbrush rustle softly, and not from the wind.

The bow's handle tried to torque that way in his grip. He let it turn him as he dashed off the road, and only a few steps into the trees a glint ahead caught his eye. He ran for it only to look down upon a black-feathered arrow lying upon the forest floor. Its white metal head was obscured with blood; this sight filled him with alarm and two thoughts.

The bow handle could not track an arrow while the thief rode the wind.

Aupsha had pulled it out, and now he had no way to find the orb in her possession.

He snatched up the arrow and held it in his grip upon the bow, and he turned, aiming the other notched arrow among the trees. His panic only grew at having failed Wynn, and he had left her alone, unguarded, in trying to do as she had asked.

Osha went still and listened again.

Either of the guards left unconscious upon the road might soon recover, and there was still one keep guard unaccounted for. More troubling, the one remaining Suman, though wounded twice, remained near her. Osha was torn between continuing here or running back to Wynn.

But she placed the orb's retrieval above all else, including herself.

Leaves rustled in the forest as a branch crackled.

At that sound not made by the air, Osha took off through the trees.

He traversed across the wind until it blew straight at him, always keeping his eyes fixed toward the position of that sound. When he found a clear line of sight, he halted, raised and drew his bow, and turned slightly as he peered through the forest.

It was a dangerous place to stop, but if she tried to come on the wind, she would have to appear right in front of him . . . or behind him.

A dark shape passed behind one far tree trunk.

"Stop!" he ordered in Numanese.

The form halted as it hobbled beyond the tree's other side while it dragged the trunk. Its hooded head turned toward him. He could not see the masked face inside the hood and did not need to.

"Drop trunk," he shouted. "Step way."

"You think . . . you do what is right," she called back, her words broken by labored pants. "It belongs with . . . my people! You cannot keep it safe . . . more than we can."

"Drop!" he commanded again, inching forward, blindly feeling each step before weighting a foot.

He did not want to kill. He had never done so, even after being given his place among the Anmaglâhk. He had seen enough death since then or knew of too many who had died suddenly in the night after Brot'ân'duivé and Most Aged Father declared war among the caste.

Osha did not have to kill to stop Aupsha, but he would not let her take to the wind again. His gaze dropped along the black shadow-filled split of her cloak to her unwounded thigh. She could not see his face—his eyes—inside his own hood any more than he could see hers.

Aupsha threw herself backward.

Osha almost released the arrow but stopped himself as she vanished from his sight behind that far tree. He lowered the bow as he rushed leftward, and then heard her shift the other way in her stumbling. At his next reverse she countered again, keeping the tree between them.

She was listening as he would for any move that he made.

He planted himself in silence. He now needed distance for what he must do.

There was one further thing he had learned of his "gifts" from the Burning Ones. This he had not shared with anyone, even the blood-soaked greimasg'äh.

Osha raised his bow and drew back the arrow with a white metal head . . . just as he had one late morning on the way to Wynn's homeland.

One morning in the Broken Lands, he had stayed out too long in practice. As he had aimed at a far oak's knot on his final shot of that day, the air grew still, and he let loose. In the same instant, Brot'ân'duivé shouted for his return. The distraction caused a flinch, and his aim shifted.

Even as the arrow left the bow, Osha knew it would miss the oak on the right side. He cursed under his breath and swung the bow out of his way to watch the arrow's flight.

And the arrow neared the oak in an instant. . . .

Osha heard Aupsha struggling away beyond the far tree, and he let fly through the dark just to the left of the tree's trunk. In less than a breath, as the arrow passed the trunk, he shifted his hand—and the bow's hand—directly in line with the tree.

It was not just the bow's white metal handle that answered to the call of a like arrowhead.

Both were one and answered to each other.

That late morning alone in the woods, as the greimasg'äh had called out, the arrow missed the oak on the left instead of on the right . . . when he had shifted the bow out of his line of sight.

Out in the dark, the arrow's flight turned slightly as if nudged by a sudden breeze.

It vanished beyond and behind the tree, and Osha took off at a run before Aupsha even shrieked.

He only hoped—wished—the wound was not mortal as he rounded that far tree. And he saw nothing but the small trunk containing the orb rolling and crackling through low weeds down a slope to his feet.

Osha left the trunk where it lay and ran on, fitting the already-bloodstained arrow to his bow's string. Atop the rise, he halted to listen. The only sounds he heard were those caused by the wind in the forest. He lowered the bow to his side and held its arrow against the string with his left hand.

Even if Aupsha had slipped away upon the breeze, she would be too far downwind to quickly double back for the trunk. She had been wounded again, though he did not know how badly or where. He could track her again by the second arrow carried with her once—if—she reappeared.

Osha hurried downslope for the trunk—and the bow twisted in his grip.

He halted, looking down it, for he had not raised the bow up to seek out an arrow.

One step below the rise's crest lay the arrow he had guided around the tree. Its white metal head was obscured with blood, as was two-fingers' width of its shaft. He snatched it up as he ran and slid downslope, for there was no time left to wonder where Aupsha had gone now.

Osha slung his bow over his shoulder as he slid both arrows back into his quiver. He grabbed the trunk containing the orb and stalled for an instant at its weight. Then he went running through the forest for the road. Often glancing behind himself, he hurried back for Wynn.

No one, especially a cloaked and masked shadow, reappeared among the trees.

Osha had the orb. He had not failed Wynn.

* * *

Chane ran with Shade in his arms, and she did not stir even once at being jostled so roughly. Her breaths were still slow and shallow. The blow might have done more damage than he could sense or see.

Back in the clearing, he had hesitated only long enough to grab the blood-smeared orb key off the duke's—Sau'ilahk's—shredded neck. He then quickly hung it around his own neck and retrieved his swords before he had gathered up Shade.

Amid his flight, shocks of pain shot through Chane's back into his chest as he began to wonder . . . to fear. . . .

Had the death of the duke's body truly taken Sau'ilahk with it? Had the wraith been trapped and killed by that as well? And, worse, how much should he tell Wynn?

She—they—had one too many times believed Sau'ilahk to be finished off. How could he tell her what he had realized in the final moment as he had faced the duke, and then share his own uncertainty? What was crueler, to know or not, and either way be left in doubt?

Unable to even shout at Shade to awaken, Chane looked down on her. He let hunger come again to eat his pain and charged faster through the trees than a living man could have with such burdens. His anger grew at the knowledge that even Wynn—or anyone within reach—might be unable to do anything for Shade.

Wynn anxiously watched for Osha's return, for he had been gone far too long. She was about to go after him when Captain Martelle climbed to his feet.

Looking around, the captain appeared beyond confused. There were two other guards on the ground. One of them wasn't moving, but the other began to stir as the last of the keep guards stumbled from the trees with a large knot on his forehead. That one stopped and stared at the others as Martelle continued turning slowly, looking everywhere.

Karl Beáumie was nowhere to be seen.

Wynn was lost for what to do. If she ran after Osha, what would happen if Chane and Shade returned to face the guards? She looked into the northern trees, but even if they were returning, it was too dark to see anything in there.

Someone snatched the staff out of Wynn's hand.

She turned in surprised anger and looked up into the bleary and equally angry eyes of Captain Martelle. He now held her staff in one hand and a sword in the other.

"Where is the duke?" he demanded.

Wynn hesitated again, trying to think of a believable lie. "He ran off . . . after . . . after some of the Sumans turned on him. My swordsman went after him."

For the moment, trying to take her staff back would be foolish, even if Martelle believed her. She could hardly blame him, since she'd used the staff to blind him and his men. Grabbing the staff in a sudden lunge to ignite a flash might not work this time.

Martelle's angry expression turned confused as well, and he didn't make another threatening move. After all, she was a sage, and Aupsha was the one who had actually attacked his men, though they wouldn't recognize the servant woman the way she was attired now.

All that became pointless as the captain stepped around her and headed for the wagon's front end and the dead horse. Wynn clenched her jaw as she followed. What would he think when he saw the dead bodies of the Sumans that lay beyond the overturned wagon?

The horse she'd freed had rushed off but remained in sight down the road. The captain halted before he fully rounded the dead one, and Wynn knew what stalled him.

A headless body lay there, likely Chane's first opponent.

She circled wide so as not to startle the captain, but by the look on his face, he wasn't remotely troubled by the deaths of the duke's foreign guards. Perhaps he understood that something was terribly wrong with his duke and this was all part of it, but Wynn grew worried over something more. She stopped herself from spinning frantically to search and perhaps prodding the captain to act rashly.

The one wounded but still-living Suman was gone from behind the wagon.

Wynn swallowed hard, half wishing she hadn't let Osha stop her.

Martelle stepped along the wagon's back, but Wynn again looked down the road—and still there was no sign of Osha. She considered whether to tell the captain what was truly happening here. When she glanced back, he had paused, taking in all that he saw. He finally stopped studying the carnage and almost turned.

The captain looked out into the trees but farther inland than where Chane had gone. Wynn wasn't certain what Martelle saw. His features hardened, and his breaths grew heavy, sharp, and audible. He took off into the trees at a rush, and Wynn hurried after him.

It was so dark that she wasn't certain what he was doing. When he stopped ahead of her by one tree and stood there looking down, she reached into her robe, pulled out a cold-lamp crystal, and swiped it along her robe.

Wynn stepped wide around the captain as the crystal ignited in a soft glow. The captain didn't even look up.

Beyond his feet lay the body of another keep guard.

The man's hair was so grayed that it looked nearly white under the crystal's dim light. He had shriveled and aged beyond recognition of who he was . . . had been.

Wynn knew what this meant. Her breaths quickened until she began to shake as she looked everywhere through the trees.

Sau'ilahk was here somewhere.

"Did you see what happened to him?" Martelle asked.

Wynn spun on him. "Give me the staff now!"

The anger in Martelle's face increased, as if bits and pieces of all that had happened to him came back. He faced her and didn't even glance at the staff.

"Where's the archer, the Lhoin'na?" he asked.

"Give me that staff, or we're all dead! It's the only thing that can stop who did this."

The captain leaned the staff farther out of reach and raised the point of his sword into her way. Then she heard footsteps behind her and looked back. Another guard stepped around the wagon's front and the dead horse as he looked from her to his captain.

Wynn turned and bolted out of either's reach for the nearest open way between the trees. A loud thud from somewhere on the road carried in the night.

"Not move! Stay!" someone shouted.

Wynn knew that broken Numanese before she even halted and turned.

Osha stood some twenty paces inland, in the middle of the road. He had one arrow drawn back as he aimed at the guard and the captain near Wynn. Another arrow was gripped in his hand holding the bow.

And at his feet was the orb's trunk.

Wynn didn't have time for relief. Osha suddenly swung the bow and pointed it up the road past the overturned wagon.

"Stay! Quiet!" he shouted, likely at the other guards still out there.

Wynn barely heard the captain shift a slow step behind her. She didn't turn as fast as Osha did, and she followed the line of his aim back to Martelle watching her and him. And then she flinched back another step.

A sword's tip appeared from behind the captain and dropped lightly on his left shoulder.

"Do not move!" a voice rasped. "I do not wish to harm you."

Chane stepped out of the shadows behind Captain Martelle; the tip of his long dwarven sword still rested on the captain's shoulder. Wynn sagged in relief for an instant and then hurried in to jerk her staff out of the captain's grip. Up close, she stalled at the sight of Chane.

He wasn't wearing his cloak, and his hair was wet. A dark smear showed on one side of his jaw, as if something had been wiped away in careless haste.

And a *thôrhk*—an orb key—of ruddy metal hung around his neck.

About to ask, Wynn looked him straight in the eyes. Chane shook his head once and quickly looked away, leaving her at a loss. Obviously he didn't want her saying anything as yet, but where was Shade?

Chane looked over her head toward the wagon's front. His eyes narrowed as his features hardened, and his gaze remained fixed as his head jerked once toward the wagon. Wynn backed away from the captain before she turned to see the one guard near the wagon's front retreating slowly.

"Osha?" Chane shouted, though it was only a strained rasp.

"Have them all!" Osha shouted back.

He swung the bow slightly as he tracked the retreating guard, and Wynn quickly threw the lit cold-lamp crystal out to give him more light. It bounced to a stop a few yards from the trunk.

"Please join your men," Chane said as he nudged the captain to follow the one guard. "We have no intention of harming any of you. You need only listen to what I will tell you."

Wynn glanced at the orb key still around Chane's neck, though he kept his eyes on the captain.

Wynn and her companions had not only recovered an orb but its key as well this time. They had all survived, but . . .

Wynn grabbed Chane's arm as he passed, but he wouldn't look down at her.

"Back the way I came," he whispered. "A short way into the trees. She is . . . injured. Hurry . . . and I will come for both of you."

Wynn swallowed so hard that it hurt. She didn't even question her safety in knowing Sau'ilahk could be near, and she took off into the dark forest.

"Shade!" she shouted, trying to get out her spare cold-lamp crystal as she ran.

She heard nothing but her own clumsy footfalls and her own fast breaths. She didn't get the other crystal out until she spotted a dark heap in the open between three tall trees.

Wynn recklessly dropped the staff and fell to her knees as she swiped the crystal twice across her thigh. All but Shade's head was covered with

Chane's damp cloak, and the tip of her tongue hung from between her front teeth.

"Shade?" Wynn whispered, leaning close.

The dog didn't even twitch, though her eyes appeared open in the barest slits.

Wynn carefully peeled away the cloak. A careful touch revealed that blood was still wet in Shade's neck fur and along one foreleg, but there wasn't much, not enough to leave her in this state. Wynn carefully felt everywhere, though she feared causing more injury. Her fingers lightly passed over the back of Shade's head.

Her fingers stained red, and her breath caught.

"Please open your eyes. . . . Look at me. . . . Say something."

Not one memory-word came to Wynn.

Her bloodstained fingers trembled in hovering less than a finger's length above Shade's body. Her sight warped and blurred as the tears began to fall.

"Don't you leave me, sister," she whispered. "Not like this."

Almost holding her breath as she watched Shade, Wynn still sat there in the dark. Even when Chane and Osha came, she couldn't move.

Chane quickly rounded her and crouched on Shade's far side, and still Wynn watched only Shade.

"We must leave," he whispered. "I have given the keep guards the treasury chest and as much of a story as I could concerning the duke taking flight. We need to go before they question anything and turn back."

Chane lifted Shade, and Osha had to pull Wynn to her feet.

In a forest clearing, a corpse lying facedown in the wet dirt twitched in the predawn.

Sau'ilahk opened his eyes but saw—heard—nothing at first. Everything was so quiet—too quiet—now that all of the wind had died. He lay still, not even blinking, as he tried to understand where he was. Then he remembered

Chane Andraso and the black majay-hì. At that he panicked and tried to lift his head, but it barely rolled over the wet earth.

The sound of that movement was all he heard. Not a footfall, a paw's claws upon the ground, or even a breath.

Sau'ilahk grew frantic. Why could he not even hear his own breaths?

And he remembered . . . dying . . . after Chane tore out half his throat and then suffocated him with one hand.

Sau'ilahk sucked in air and choked on blood congealed in his throat. He struggled to push himself up and put a hand to his neck. He felt the mess of his own flesh, and his hand came away coated in a sticky black-red mess.

Shock numbed his mind, and when he could actually think again, there was something missing . . . something he had not felt in that one touch to himself.

The *thôrhk*—the orb key—was gone.

And he could feel no heartbeat within his chest.

Sau'ilahk.

At the hissing whisper from Beloved, his god, Sau'ilahk tried to scream and only choked.

You have what you always desired . . . a body immortal and immune to death. Does this not please you?

And the only way he could answer was within his own thoughts. *No! Not flesh like I was . . . not undead still. What have you done—allowed to happen?*

You blame me?

Sau'ilahk faltered. Beloved had not led Chane Andraso here, had not instigated the fight that led to this. Still, had his god somehow known? Once again Beloved had deceived him, tricked him with a half-truth as fulfillment of a promise from a thousand years ago.

Something more occurred to him. . . .

He had lost both the orb and the key to which Beloved had guided him.

It is of no matter. That orb . . . that anchor of Existence . . . served its first purpose and will serve again where it now travels. It shall serve, as you will, until I am free at last.

Sau'ilahk went colder inside than the chill of his dead flesh.

He—his desire, his anguish—had been nothing more than a tactic for some purpose known only to his god. He was left with a corpse, not as a body but as a prison.

Be content . . . servant.

This time the hiss carried a threat, like the scales of a great serpent grinding grains of sand in the dark place of dreams where it slept.

Sau'ilahk felt a faint, uncomfortable tingle on his skin.

Light grew over the forest to the east, and he waited for it to turn him to ash . . . and he waited. To see a dawn after a thousand years would have once been a joy. To face it now would at least be freedom from the cruelty of his Beloved.

Sau'ilahk watched as the sun did rise, and he began to moan and sob. But the dead could not weep, for a corpse could not shed tears.

CHAPTER TWENTY-ONE

Magiere leaned over the rail of the *Djinn* and anxiously looked out at the enormous, seething port of il'Dha'ab Najuum. She didn't care how large or daunting it was. All that mattered was getting herself and her companions off this floating coffin of a ship.

The only other stop they'd made along the way was at a small place the name of which she couldn't pronounce. It had been little more than a coastal trading post south of the desert's southern reaches with no docks or piers. The ship had anchored well offshore, and only the captain and one of the crew took to a skiff that came out to retrieve them.

That one crewman had eyed her a bit long as they left. Stranger than that, the captain came back alone. Magiere hadn't cared and still didn't. She could easily imagine that none of the crew would stick to this vessel longer than necessary.

The air had grown continually warmer and then hotter during the journey south. Once they were on land again, they'd have to rethink their clothing and perhaps purchase lighter attire—and yet more coin would be used up. If not for that last part, she might have been relieved to think on simple things after the strain of a long, questionable voyage.

Every day, she'd felt a constant threat aimed toward someone she loved or cared for as Leesil had struggled to keep them fed without being caught. She couldn't help but feel a little grateful that Brot'an had a hand in that as well.

Now it was over, and it wouldn't be long until they disembarked. For once nobody had to coax Wayfarer into packing and coming out of hiding.

The girl stood on Leesil's other side at the rail, with Chap between her and Brot'an. They were all unwashed to the point of their hair looking dull, and everyone had lost weight, but they'd survived.

Wayfarer and Chap seemed to have come to terms with the girl's catching his rising memories at a touch. Brot'an still knew nothing about it, and Leesil thought it might even be useful instead of the dog's jabbering in their heads with memory-words. Wayfarer might be able to take Wynn's place in helping Chap clarify what he needed to say.

Magiere wasn't so certain about that. There had to be more to how a quarter-blood girl, cast out by her ancestors, could catch memories from a majay-hì. But there were too many other things to face as she studied the girl.

As the ship neared another noisy city and seemingly endless port filled with humanity, Wayfarer's expression blanched. Even to Magiere, the place looked so . . . foreign . . . compared to anything she'd seen in her travels.

Some structures deeper into the city still peaked high above the waterfront buildings. Some had to be huge, at a guess, for they also appeared to be set farther—and farther—into the immense capital of the Suman Empire. Every structure within closer sight was for the most part golden tan sandstone, aside from heat-grayed timbers and planks.

"What's first?" Magiere asked.

"I know exactly what," Leesil provided. "Find a decent inn, a bath, and a meal!"

Magiere eyed the tangled mix of vessels moored at the huge and long piers, and humans, mostly dark skinned, mingling in chaotic masses shifting along the waterfront.

"Does anyone speak Sumanese?" Wayfarer asked very quietly.

The answer was obvious: not one of them.

Magiere knew from times in other ports that it was likely some people here would speak other languages—hopefully ones that she or her companions understood at least a little.

"A place to stay first," she confirmed. "We'll take the day for ourselves. Tomorrow we search out this Domin il'Sänke that Wynn wanted us to find."

Leesil had earlier suggested they set out straight for the Suman branch of the Guild of Sagecraft, but after all that had happened at Wynn's branch, Magiere thought otherwise.

Dealing with the Numan sages hadn't been anything like what she'd expected when they had returned to their old friend the little sage. Magiere didn't care for even the chance of the same in a culture they knew nothing about. Better to have a place of their own, perhaps not even mentioned, when they went seeking "hospitality" from an unknown Suman sage, and a domin at that. The upper ranks of Wynn's branch had been the least friendly of all.

Leesil had eventually relented on all this, and Brot'an had agreed, though the old assassin likely had his own reasons to keep their chosen place unknown unless necessary.

Now Brot'an turned from the rail to look about the deck, and Magiere already knew whom he sought.

"Saeed," he called out.

The young man was helping to ready the ship for docking. He was the only one on board whom Magiere trusted a little. He left his pile of rope to come closer.

"What is it?" Saeed asked.

"We need an inn with someone who speaks Numanese," Brot'an said.

Saeed nodded once. "There is a place close to port called . . . well, perhaps you might say 'The Whistling Wasp.' In my tongue it is al'D'abbú Asuvära." He spoke the last words slowly, but Magiere wasn't sure she could ever repeat them as he went on. "The owner is at least as honest as I." He smiled a little more. "And he speaks Numanese as well as myself."

Saeed stepped in at the rail beside Brot'an and pointed into the nearing port as he gave directions.

While grateful, Magiere wondered again what someone like Saeed was doing on this ship with a captain and crew slightly above pirates, slavers, and slaves alike. When the *Djinn* finally docked and the ramp was lowered, the head of all rodents aboard appeared near the prow.

Captain Amjad glowered at his passengers, but Magiere could swear she saw something of a smile before he turned away. Was he simply looking forward to selling his cargo?

"Oh, dead deities, finally!" Leesil said, not really noticing the captain.

He hefted his pack and hoisted their travel chest as he headed toward the ramp.

Wayfarer stalled, casting a final look at Saeed. As with previous goodbyes, she didn't say a word. Perhaps she didn't know what to say, though, as Magiere watched, the girl nodded slowly to Saeed, and he returned the same with another smile.

Chap nosed Wayfarer along, and when they all reached the ramp's bottom and the pier, Magiere ushered the girl directly in front of herself. Chap trotted up to join Wayfarer, who slipped the makeshift leash around his neck for their usual deception. Brot'an stepped in at Magiere's side as his large amber eyes shifted in looking everywhere. And Leesil led the way.

The hot, dry air was soon laced with spice, mixing with the odors of sea brine and sweaty people. It was as if one mass of smells was being used to mask the other, and Magiere wondered how strong the scents might become inside the city's narrow ways.

Most of the dusky-skinned and dark-haired people in the crowds wore light, loose-fitting cloth shifts or equally loose leggings or pants. Wraps upon their heads were done up in all sorts of short or tall, thick or thin mounds. Some herded goats or carried square baskets of chickens and other birds she couldn't name. Many people spoke to one another, but Magiere couldn't follow a word being said, though at a guess it sounded as though not all of them spoke the same tongue.

She began perspiring into the shirt beneath her hauberk. Out ahead, Leesil tugged at his collar with his free hand.

"We're going to need some other clothes," he muttered.

Magiere saw no trees or plant life anywhere, only an endless stretch of light-toned buildings. The travelers stepped off the pier's landward end and onto the walkway along the shore.

"Do you know where to go?" she asked Brot'an.

"Yes, Saeed was clear. For now, we walk a few streets inland."

Their small group had gone only a few steps when Leesil halted. Even from behind, Magiere saw him tense and look slowly around. She grew instantly wary, following his gaze. What she saw she didn't like.

Beneath a wind-scarred sandstone arch, like some gate into the city between two buildings, about a dozen men stood watching her and the others intently. Each of them was dressed the same, in tan pants tucked inside tall boots, dark brown tabards over cream shirts, and red scarves tied around their heads. All wore curved swords in ornate sheaths tucked into heavy fabric waist wraps and peaked steel helmets polished to perfection.

Leesil's head turned again as he looked, likely for any option of retreat, back the way they had come. Magiere did the same.

Up the pier, before the *Djinn*'s ramp, Captain Amjad watched them as he appeared to be talking to three more of the uniformed men. There was one sailor with him as well, and Magiere thought it might be the one who hadn't returned from that small trading station.

"Left now, and out of sight," Leesil whispered.

The armed men up the pier were already advancing. As Magiere turned back, she spotted the ones ahead clearing the archway . . . and then clusters of more to the left and right, pushing through the crowds.

She reached for her sword as she looked for the best position to protect Wayfarer, and something more made her panic sharpen.

Someone was missing, though he couldn't have slipped around her.

Brot'an had vanished.

Wynn knelt beside Shade, who still lay silently on a small, rickety bed at the inn in Oléron. It had taken the previous night, the following day, and until well past dusk before they reached the small port where they'd first hired the team and wagon. Osha and Chane had traded off in driving during their onward rush—in which Chane had lain dormant during the day under a cover of canvas in the wagon's back. Osha stopped them only briefly during the past day to rest the horses.

And even now Shade hadn't regained consciousness.

"Please, wake up," Wynn whispered far too many times to count.

She took a soaked rag from a bowl of freshwater she'd gotten from the innkeeper. Again she tried to squeeze a bit of water into Shade's mouth. If Shade didn't revive soon to drink or eat . . .

Wynn shuddered and pushed aside the rest of that thought.

Along the journey she'd forced Chane to tell her everything that had happened—including everything he hadn't planned to tell her. She still wondered how the wraith could have taken Karl Beáumie's body. At that, she glanced at the trunk sitting beyond Shade's bed in the room's rear corner.

Everything Wynn learned of the orbs only made their true purpose more uncertain and the need to hide them forever that much greater. But hiding one wasn't so easy.

Once they'd gained room at the inn, Osha and Chane had started arguing about how and where to hide the orb of Spirit. Perhaps their bickering was aggravated in part by frustration, for none of them knew how to help Shade. Wynn had carefully cleaned Shade up as much as possible and then used the last of any healing salve she still possessed to tend the minor and more visible wounds. The dog never even flinched in pain.

Of course Chane wanted to turn over the additional orb to Ore-Locks and the Stonewalkers. Osha vehemently countered that Aupsha had already discovered that there was an "artifact" hidden in the dwarven underworld. Even when Chane pointed out that Aupsha couldn't get anywhere near that orb, Osha remained unconvinced—and so was Wynn. Their incessant arguing finally drove her to push them both out of the room, and they'd left in silence.

Wynn again tried to squeeze a little water between Shade's jaws, but most of it ran out to soak the bedding. She collapsed on the bed's edge and stared at Shade until she finally closed her eyes and reached out blindly to slip her fingers in Shade's neck fur.

So many had been hurt or lost along her way; yet losing someone dear wasn't something she'd been prepared to face. And not Shade—never Shade—and not so slowly and cruelly.

And nothing was finished yet.

Magiere, Leesil, and Chap—and Brot'an and Leanâlhâm—were searching for the last orb. If they found it on their own, would that even be the end? Worse, Wynn now had a device made from an orb key that might make finding the last orb easier.

But it was now dormant . . . useless . . . and she couldn't go back to the keep to speak with Jausiff.

There was no telling what had happened there after the keep guards returned. Chane seemed certain that Nikolas was safe with the duchess and his father until the young sage found his own way back to the guild. Even then there would be questions from his—and Wynn's—superiors.

And what of Aupsha? Where had she gone? There was too much risk of her coming after the device and the orb if Wynn tried to go back.

Even returning to Calm Seatt and the guild was now a severe risk. Eventually the duke's body would be found. If by chance she arrived before word of all that had happened, sooner or later her superiors would hear of the death of a nobleman in an allied nation. Then there was more of her "meddling," all under of the guise of a sage in the wrong order, in critical affairs and secrets of a war to come. Without any proof of what had really happened concerning the orb and Sau'ilahk—without revealing the orb itself—what could she possibly say in her own defense?

The last time she'd gone afoul of her superiors would pale by comparison. The best of outcomes would end with her being cast out once and for all. Even Premin Hawes, if she were still at the Numan branch, wouldn't be able to circumvent that. And more likely Wynn would end up in a cell under the rule of the city guard, if High Premin Sykion had her way. More and more it seemed that perhaps turning the orb over to Ore-Locks was the only option to keep it safe . . . before Wynn faced anything else.

She shouldn't have wept anymore, but she did, clenching her fingers in Shade's fur.

—Remember—

Wynn flinched. She didn't want to think about one more orb to hide . . . one more to find. All she wanted was for Shade to come back to her.

—Remember . . . device—

Wynn flinched again, blinking the tears out of her eyes. She barely lifted her head, wondering . . . what? One long breath with an awful smell ran warmly over her face.

Wynn slapped the tears off her cheeks and stared into half-opened crystal-blue eyes . . . and they blinked once.

She almost lunged in as Shade groaned, the first real sound the dog had made since her injuries.

—Remember . . . whispers—

"Don't!" Wynn exhaled, quickly putting her hand over Shade's eyes, and then she added more softly, "Don't talk; don't move. Just . . . just rest."

Shade tried weakly to move her head. Wynn was caught between stopping this and fearing she'd caused more harm to an unknown wound. One of Shade's eyes peeked around her fingers to gain a line of sight. More memory-words rose in Wynn's mind.

—Remember . . . device . . . whispers . . . Jausiff—

Wynn tried to understand. Shade was obviously struggling to tell her something important, though she shouldn't be straining herself this way.

The only thing that came to mind that matched up with those isolated words . . .

Wynn thought back on the moment in Jausiff's chambers when the elderly master sage had first displayed the device. He had whispered something over it, and she tried to remember anything more. Whatever he had said had been too soft for her to hear as he'd stood there behind his desk and . . .

Suddenly the whole memory shifted dizzily in Wynn's head. Her perspective changed, dropping low until she just barely saw over the desk. That angle of view blurred into and over her own as the one moment began again from its start.

The whispers suddenly magnified, more distinct, until she heard the old sage's words. That second memory overlying the first vanished suddenly and left Wynn's head spinning. As she clamped a hand over her mouth, she was thankful that she hadn't even eaten yet this night.

"Don't . . . do that again . . . please," she barely got out.

Shade's eyes were already closed again, and Wynn leaned in quickly in returned fright.

The dog snorted once in half sleep, and Wynn relaxed a little in quick, shaky breaths, as she hoped such effort hadn't harmed Shade any further. But Shade had heard the words Jausiff had spoken and, between the two memories, somehow made them clear to Wynn.

The only problem was that she didn't understand one word that she had heard.

She sat there, waiting and listening to Shade's even breaths, and then finally reached inside her robe. She took out the center third of the orb key and stared at it. What she'd heard sounded something like Sumanese, but it wasn't any dialect she recognized.

How old were those words? Likely they were from a lost time, when Aupsha's ancestors had first cut up an orb key so that it couldn't be used on an orb, but the pieces were still functional for something else. A part of Wynn already doubted too much, but she quickly repeated those exact sounds as Shade had heard them.

She closed her hand on the device and waited, for there was an orb already in the room—and nothing happened. She lifted the device and swung her arm in an arc, toward and away from the orb's chest—and again nothing.

Wynn sagged where she knelt, closing her eyes.

Of course it didn't work like some children's fairy tale of strange words that could cause miraculous things to happen. Even when she'd learned key phrases to ignite the staff's sun crystal, it wasn't words that mattered.

It was the *meaning* that sparked her intention to make the sun crystal respond.

Wynn scrambled on all fours to her pack, then ripped out and tossed aside its contents until she found quill, ink, and journal. Using the symbols of the Begaine Syllabary, she quickly scrawled those words as best she could without knowing them. That was all she could do for now, but simply possessing the unknown phrase changed everything.

She needed someone like herself, who understood all that was at stake. She had to find someone who also knew of orbs, of a war to come, of the dangers of simple fragments of knowledge . . . and of dead languages from another land. That wasn't even Premin Hawes.

Wynn rose to her feet, quietly stepped close to Shade, and whispered, "I'll be back right away. Don't move."

With that she hurried out to find Chane or Osha, for all of their plans had changed.

Osha returned down the road into Oléron. As in any stop made on the way to that little coastal town, he—or Chane—had always gone back along the road to watch and listen for any sign that they were followed. Tonight he had heard nothing as he stood listening to the wind for what it could tell him . . . and for any other sound it did not cause.

Osha walked softly through the dark past the stable and on toward the inn where he had left Wynn.

A majay-hì—a sacred one—had fallen in battle against an undead. For that, he felt shamed in his relief that Wynn had not been harmed, though Shade was so different from her own kind, or at least from what he knew of them.

How different and dark was this world outside of his people's lands. Perhaps no darker than what he had left behind, but all the more confusing, for he did not understand it.

An undead and a majay-hì, enemies by their natures, fought side by side. And they did so because of a precious little human woman and her purpose.

Osha knew little of the undead: he had seen them only once before, when he had gone with her, Magiere, Léshil, and the sacred one called Chap to search for an artifact in some frigid peaks. If he had known then what that would lead to, would he have stopped it if he could have?

No . . . not if it had meant never knowing Wynn.

Even in the brightest light of day, darkness was not always seen until it revealed itself. He was well aware that she had considered killing that one Suman guard . . . the one whom he had wounded twice and left helpless.

Darkness had taken part of Wynn, just as it had taken him. She did not see it as he did within himself. One could not fight an enemy if one did not know it was there. He had learned at least that much in his time among the Anmaglâhk. And knowing was worth even more than seeing.

In seeking Wynn Hygeorht, Osha had traversed half the world, only to find someone else.

Where was the woman he loved?

He had to find her and bring her back. For the present there seemed to be little hope of this, but he had learned to be patient, to watch . . . and to listen.

He arrived at the inn's front to find that the undead was not there.

Claiming concern that the keep might have a shoreside dock below the cliff, Chane had gone his own way to the docks. A boat might be used to reach the port by sea instead of by the road. It was a short walk from the landing to the inn, and he should have returned to the inn first.

Osha went for the inn's door but stalled. He could do less than even Wynn could in helping Shade. That frustration, the helplessness, had led to his arguing with her undead companion. It only made her desperation, and his, that much worse.

So he stood in the dark outside the inn. He heard the footfalls even before he spotted Chane's approach.

"Anything?" the undead asked.

"No," he answered. "You?"

Chane shook his head once and stared at the inn's front door. "Have you gone in? Is there any change with Shade?"

Osha eyed Chane, who in turn did not look at him. "No. Not go in. Wynn not come out."

"So . . . we have a truce between us . . . for her?"

The sudden question almost made Osha snap a denial. This was a strange world; perhaps he would have to be strange as well for now.

"Yes," he answered, "for her purpose, we have truce, but not for—"

The inn's door swung open, and there she was. Wynn started slightly at the sight of both of them. Osha had no chance to finish, though his faltering with Numanese might have been less clear in attempting to say . . . *but not for Wynn herself.*

"Shade?" he asked quickly, cutting in before Chane could speak.

Wynn swallowed once. "Better, I think. She . . . she awoke briefly to speak with me. I don't know yet how bad it is or . . . how much. . . . She needs more time and care."

And, of all the stranger things, Osha heard the tall undead heave a sigh that sounded like relief.

"All right," Chane said. "Can she be moved to a ship, perhaps tomorrow? We need to leave here as soon as possible and head north directly to—"

"No, we're not going to Dhredze Seatt and Ore-Locks," Wynn cut in. "We're heading south."

No one said a word for a moment, and then Osha noticed something in Wynn's hand.

She held that strangely discolored bit of metal she had used to track the orb and the duke.

"What are you talking about?" Chane demanded.

Wynn turned on him in an instant. In the argument that followed, Osha could not keep up with what was said. All he caught was what seemed to be a name he thought he had heard once before, though he was not certain.

"This is madness!" Chane finally rasped so harshly that it had to have hurt his throat. "You cannot trust him. Even any truth he utters is only a trick for his own means."

"I know that now!" Wynn returned. "But he's the only one left that I can approach about how to activate *this* again." And she thrust the piece of an orb key into Chane's face. "This is the quickest way to find the last orb. Even with another orb still in our hands, that's why we have to go south now."

"And to Magiere—and Leesil and Chap—as well?" Chane shot back.

Wynn looked away and said nothing. Osha could see that was an answer unto itself.

"I am going to look in on Shade," Chane rasped at her.

He jerked the door open and slammed it shut after he entered.

And still stranger, in only now understanding what their argument was about, Osha found himself in agreement with the undead—concerning the orb, at least. He was finally alone with Wynn once more.

Osha held back the hundred or more questions concerning what had changed her so much. All he could ask was . . .

"Who is this . . . Il-san-kay?"

EPILOGUE

Domin Ghassan il'Sänke was shoved roughly through the doors of the great domed chamber atop the imperial castle at the center of il'Dha'ab Najuum. At present that wide, round space—at least half a stone's throw across—was empty.

The four imperial guards in their golden raiment retreated outside and, when they shut the huge doors tight, a double boom echoed around him.

Ghassan looked about the mosaic floor. Its polished shapes of colored marble were arranged in a looping, coiling pattern centering upon a single one-step dais three yards in diameter. All of the great chamber was awash with tinted sunlight filtering through a like mosaic of glass panes in the dome above. There was only one other exit: the far doors, of purest ivory slats, with sweeping golden handles as long as his forearms. Beyond those doors would be even more imperial guards than on the route by which he had been brought here.

This was not a place that anyone wished to visit.

Aside from serving as a location where dignitaries met in negotiation with the emperor, it was a place of judgment under the heavens. He was to be judged before the emperor, perhaps for treason—or something worse.

He no longer wore the midnight blue robe of Metaology, for he had been in hiding. His short, dark brown hair with the barest flecks of silver was in disarray: strands dangled to his thick eyebrows above piercing eyes separated by a straight but prominent nose. His borrowed clothing of a plain head wrap, a dusky linen shirt, and dark pants over soft leather boots was little more than that of a wanderer.

When he had been found—however he had been ferreted out—he had not struggled to escape, though he could have. His life might end here in this highest of places, but this was where he needed to be. Among those who might come here, there was one he hoped for . . . as the far doors began to open.

Ghassan il'Sänke dropped to one knee and lowered his head and eyes, but not enough to keep from watching those who entered. First came more guards, a dozen at a count, and then the "sovereign" advisors, but only three of the seven always in residence in the imperial palace.

All were either first daughters or second and third sons of the seven kings of the empire. Calling them advisors was proper, for they were the emissaries of their fathers. They were also hostages to keep the royal houses obedient to the imperial throne. But Ghassan took no notice of which were present as another trio entered under the protection of four more imperial guards.

High Premin Aweli-Jama of the guild's Suman branch was dressed in gray as premin of Cathology. He was flanked by Premin Wôl'ya and Domin il'Bänash, both robed in midnight blue. That the head of Ghassan's branch had chosen two metaologers to accompany him showed fear of the one to be judged.

Conjury was preferred among Suman metaologers, versus the preference for thaumaturgy in the Numan branch . . . and both Wôl'ya and il'Bänash were highly skilled.

Ghassan was versed in conjury as well as the forbidden third magic, resurrected in secret by his sect more than two hundred years ago. And it was feared and reviled throughout the known world.

Suspicion of sorcery was certainly part of why he had been brought here. The presence of the metaologers also suggested to Ghassan that judgment might have already been passed upon him.

The next to enter caused him to stiffen in wariness.

Imperial Counselor Wihid al a'Yamin, personal advisor to the emperor, was in his late seventies, but his eyes—and awareness—were still as sharp as a hawk's. Unlike many who graced the royal court, he always dressed simply, in tan pantaloons and a cream shirt beneath a sleeveless dark brown robe. By his age, his hair must be white, but he always covered it with a red headwrap, echoing colors worn by the guards—as if he fancied himself to be a warrior or wished to give that impression, although he had never served in the military. His face was lined, and he was stooped with age, appearing frail, but Ghassan was not fooled by this. Counselor a'Yamin was one of the most powerful men in the empire.

Ghassan carefully maintained his composure and gave no notice to the rest of the retinue, but the last to enter shocked him. It was not Emperor Kanal'am.

Prince Ounyal'am, firstborn heir of the imperial throne, watched only Ghassan il'Sänke as he alone stepped up onto the dais and stood at its center.

He was small for his people and darker toned in hair and skin than most, and, at thirty-eight years, he had yet to take even a first wife. This was fodder for gossip in an empire mindful of heirs and with kingdoms always vying for the closest tie to the imperial throne over generations. But even the emperor had not sired his first "legitimate" heir, Ounyal'am, until he was fifty-seven, and Kanal'am was now older than most of his recorded predecessors.

Ghassan bowed his head and lowered his eyes.

"How do you account for the unexplained deaths and disappearances within your order?" the prince demanded.

"I cannot, Imperial Highness . . . as yet," Ghassan answered. "But I assure you that I . . . we . . . will uncover the truth."

It was a careful half lie. He could account for such deaths—or most of them—and he dared to raise his eyes a little.

The prince still watched him and briefly flipped his right fingers upward without raising that hand.

Ghassan, tall for his people, rose to his feet but remained silent as he waited upon the prince.

"Untrue, great one!" Aweli-Jama suddenly challenged.

The high premin took two steps closer to the dais's right side and bowed his head to the prince. But his next words were for Ghassan.

"You know more . . . a good deal more!"

As head of Cathology in the Suman branch, Aweli-Jama was elderly, though not too much so. He was reminiscent of a lean and wizened "vizier" pulled from ancient folktales that predated unification and the birth of the empire.

Ghassan remained composed, looking only to the prince. "If I may beg a question, my prince, about the emperor?"

Prince Ounyal'am eyed him coldly. "My father is . . . tired . . . and has left this matter to my discretion. Now, is your high premin correct? What is this I hear of a hidden sect among the metaologers, including you . . . Domin? Is it true that all involved but you are dead?"

Ghassan's composure began to fracture from within, though he kept his expression and posture relaxed and poised. Who else had been speaking to the prince—or worse, the emperor?

Aweli-Jama would never openly admit to a loss of control inside his guild branch. Although the high premin and all of the premin council had had no knowledge of the sect, let alone its purpose, Aweli-Jama was responsible for all in his branch. He would bear much blame for what had happened, whether he had known or not.

Ghassan would not expose the worst—the unknown part of a nightmare his brethren had faced in their end.

An undead, as invisible as a thought, had escaped them and its captivity. It had killed all of his sect but him, or so it was thought. He had been away when this had happened, and now a monster of a past age was loose among the people . . . *within* the people.

Ghassan quietly scanned the chamber and all of those present.

The "specter," for lack of any better term, could not survive daylight without a living host, but so many days and nights had passed since its escape. Deaths in the night throughout the city attested to its survival, but who among the people was not who he or she appeared to be?

It could be anyone while hiding in flesh during daylight.

It could be in this very highest of chambers throughout the land.

The prince let out a heavy sigh, pulling Ghassan's attention.

"Your premin has demanded a list of your sect's members," the prince went on, "those dead and those who might have fled into hiding, like yourself. Yet you remain silent on this. It is a matter of time before an account of those who cannot be found would comprise such a list. Why do you not shorten the effort?"

Ghassan's tension grew. The answer was why he would not speak—because not all of his brethren might be dead. Of the bodies he had found and left in their hidden sanctuary, upon returning from tracking Wynn Hygeorht into a lost dwarven seatt . . .

One was missing.

"I am waiting for your answer, Domin," the prince added sharply.

As of yet, Counselor a'Yamin had not spoken, but he listened attentively to every word.

Ghassan tried to calculate a reply to the prince . . . even as he called up symbols, signs, and sigils in his mind's eye and surrounded them with glowing geometric shapes.

The great doors behind him slammed open.

Before he dared to look back, still holding the patterns shaped in his thoughts, he saw the prince's eyes widen under a brow creasing in annoyance. It was impudent for anyone to interrupt a specially convened audience of judgment.

When Ghassan dared to look, he was at loss for what he saw.

A contingent of city guards flanked by imperial ones marched through the wide main doors flung open. The lead pair, with swords drawn, dragged in two manacled and gagged prisoners, a man and woman. Of the two, it was the woman who had her arms spread wide and chained to a steel bar spreading out from below her shoulders. A steel cage followed, rolled in after them, and contained a snarling silver-gray wolf too large for its kind. And lastly came a young girl with wide, frightened eyes, and, though she was gagged, her hands were tied in front. She was nearly lifted off her feet as the guards holding her upper arms propelled her in.

But the caged animal caught Ghassan's attention most of all.

Along with its open growls and stiffened hackles, it glowered at everyone in the chamber. What fixated Ghassan most of all were its narrowed eyes. Above its wrinkled jowls and exposed teeth, those eyes sparked like gems . . . like pale sapphires.

"What is the meaning of this?" Domin Aweli-Jama demanded. "The imperial prince is in private counsel with the guild!"

The contingent never slowed. From among them, one broad-shouldered man wearing the gold sash of the imperial guard quickly bowed once and hurried up to kneel before the dais. The prince stepped forward, though he barely lowered his head as he listened.

Ghassan was close enough to hear pieces of the guard's rapid whispers.

"Marauders . . . murdered . . . one Captain Samara . . . his crew of the *Bashair*."

Imperial Prince Ounyal'am sighed once through his nose, as if he had been interrupted by something he could not ignore. Giving Ghassan no notice for the moment, he straightened in studying the prisoners, and Ghassan carefully turned his head enough to follow the prince's gaze.

In addition to the city and imperial guards, there were two Lhoin'na—a man and woman—standing back near the open doors. He had rarely seen any with such bright blond hair. Their attire was unremarkable, but both carried swords that he recognized by their hilts.

They were Shé'ith, guardians of the Lhoin'na's territory, but they were not at all dressed like such. This pair looked more like wanderers, and their clothing did not appear cut properly for them.

A disgusting man with a protruding belly and greasy hair pushed between them into sight.

Still on one knee, the guard before the prince spun around. "My imperial highness, these two of the Shé'ith have been tracking the offenders since they left Drist, and this captain"—he gestured to the foul-looking man—"assisted them in arranging capture." The guard spun back, bowing his head. "Forgive the intrusion, I beg you, but since this involved official guardians of another nation, I felt obligated to bring this to your attention."

The prince said nothing and only lowered his eyes slightly, perhaps in looking at the man and woman tossed to the floor in their bondage.

Ghassan thought he saw the prince's eyes widen slightly, but before he could turn and follow that gaze . . .

"Lock them away," said Counselor a'Yamin quietly, "and turn them over to my jurisdiction." His voice was as clear as his eyes.

"The counselor is correct. Lock them away, Imperial One!" Aweli-Jama begged. "They may be more dangerous than mere murderers and marauders. Please. . . . Lock them away!"

Ghassan disliked his high premin, but he had never seen Aweli-Jama turn so quickly emotional and with such urgency. Did he know something more about these prisoners . . . or did he simply wish to turn attention upon a guild branch tainted with conspiracy somewhere else?

"Forgive me, my sovereign."

At the corpulent captain's interruption, Ghassan glanced back.

"For the risk and cost, but not for doing my duty," the captain went on, "would there be some . . . reward?"

Ghassan's mouth soured at such greed. The prince could be far more generous with the people than his father had been, but he did not like impudent attempts at obligation. Then Ghassan noticed Aweli-Jama still stared at the prisoners in almost open fear, and Ghassan finally gave his full attention to those prisoners.

One was male, obviously Lhoin'na, though the structure of his face—his ears—was not quite right. Half-breeds were nearly unheard of, and this one was darker skinned than most of his kind, as were the two Shé'ith, now that Ghassan considered on this.

He looked to the woman bound with the steel bar.

She was beautiful in a barbarous way, though clearly in need of a bath, as was her companion. She was as pale as he was darkly tanned—perhaps too pale—and her black hair glimmered with strands of dark red under the light of the glass dome.

There was something familiar about her, though Ghassan was certain he had never seen her before. And when he looked again to the wolf in the cage and met its crystal-blue glare, something sparked in his thoughts.

No, he had never seen this group, but he had read of them.

Ghassan had done his best to memorize every critical passage from Wynn Hygeorht's journals, which he had been able to gain access to during his stay at the Numan branch. In particular he had focused most on anything concerning her travels on the eastern continent. The recognition of these three brought him no peace or comfort as his gaze returned to the pale, black-haired woman.

There were other unwritten things he knew.

There were words written only in thoughts, recorded in ensorcelled memories among his sect, to keep them from prying eyes.

And yet the pawn in the war to come had been moved into the open too soon . . . and captured.

A dhampir crouched in bondage before the imperial prince.

Ghassan barely suppressed panic as he looked to Prince Ounyal'am. The prince only stared at the woman whom Ghassan recognized from Wynn's journals as the one named Magiere. He quickly finished the last of his spell.

Have you snuck into my thoughts yet again . . . Domin? Do you see what has happened?

And now that he had, Ghassan lowered his gaze before his focus might be noticed by others.

Yes, my prince.

True to Ghassan's mentoring, the prince never revealed anything in his expression.

Then flee now . . . before I am forced to take your life.

Domin Ghassan il'Sänke did not reply in word or thought. The next forms and signs and sigils filled his sight as he looked down upon the mosaic floor and thrust against it with his whole will. He shot upward, quickly covering his head.

The impact shattered the glass dome amid shouts and screams from the imperial court.

Ghassan's wits dulled as the bright blue heavens grew suddenly dim before his eyes.